Harmonica Blues

Elly,

Thank you for being my friend. You have always believed in me and my dreams. You will always hold a special place in my heart.

Love Always

Annetta

"16

Harmonica Blues

FINDING LIGHT IN THE
DARKEST PLACES

Lucille Summers

Library of Congress Control Number: 2015919212
ISBN: Hardcover   978-1-5144-2773-6
                 Softcover   978-1-5144-2774-3
                 eBook   978-1-5144-2775-0

Print information available on the last page.

Rev. date: 12/21/2015

To order additional copies of this book, contact:
Xlibris
1-888-795-4274
www.Xlibris.com
Orders@Xlibris.com
711259

Dedication

I would like to thank my mother and father for giving me life.

Thanks to my girls, Samantha and Brigette
for giving me a reason to hope.

Thank you to my biggest fan, my husband
Walter, for always believing in me.

Thank you to my brother Alven for standing
together against the storms of life.

Thank you LeVada, for being the mother I
needed throughout my difficult journey.

Thank you to all my friends and family, you know who you
are, who listened to me for years about writing this book.

Thank you God for keeping your promise.

Introduction

A Dark Night

August 9:10pm – Diary entry

"Tonight I feel discouraged. I feel like my goals and dreams are so far out of reach. I feel like no matter how hard I try to stay hopeful, confident, patient and faithful, I only end up feeling like I do at this very moment, sad, lost and hopeless.

If I'm to be all, I have ever wanted to be. Then why has it taken my entire life and I still haven't reached my dreams? I honestly don't know how long I can hold on to them. Should I accept defeat and let them go?

Maybe the reality is they are just dreams. Dreams and desires that are impossible to reach now.

God, help me to move these mountains of doubt. My faith is larger than the mustard seed. I thought.

I surrender. I need your power to show me what to do. I'm afraid if nothing happens soon, I will let go of all hope. Help me to hold on to my dreams. You gave me these desires. Help me to manifest them."

Thank you, and Amen

Chapter 1

It was about three o'clock in the afternoon on a sunny day in September. The weather in New York City was gorgeous. The streets were crazy and crowded as usual, and there was construction on almost every block. The traffic was bumper to bumper; honking cars and taxis and the sounds of sirens were in the background of all the madness.

I felt calmer since this time I didn't have to take a taxi. Instead I was to be securely tucked inside a midnight-black Mercedes Benz stretch limo. My eyes lit up as I made my way through the busy LaGuardia Airport and noticed my driver holding a sign—or should I say some kind of electronic tablet—that read "Welcome, Ms. Alexandra Knight" in a fancy chalkboard cursive font and in my favorite color, pink. *Super fabulous,* I thought. It was a bit cheesy but exactly how I pictured this moment would be.

The driver bowed as I approached him and then introduced himself as Adam. Adam was tall and dressed in a tailored navy suit with a crisp white shirt and tie. He was very handsome and clean-shaven with dark hair and bright blue eyes. His smile was pleasant, and I felt like I was in good hands. He immediately grabbed my bags and put them in the back, and then he opened the door for me. I stepped inside the limo and was amazed at how beautiful it was. It even had a large vase of long-stemmed red roses with a card that read "Welcome to New York City, Ms. Knight. We hope you enjoy your stay." It was signed by the mayor and his wife. There was smooth jazz music playing softly in the background and small bottles of Perrier chilling on ice on the table next to the roses. Everyone knew how much I loved Perrier.

It wasn't my first time in New York City. My first visit was when my best friend turned fifty. She invited me to go with her to celebrate her birthday. We had so much fun. I now visited annually in honor of her. As Adam tried to navigate through the hectic New York City traffic, I took a moment to look away from my cell phone, and my eyes caught a glimpse of an area my friend had raved about on our first adventure together in the big city. I remembered how excited she was and how I was trying to calm her down, because I didn't want anyone to notice how vulnerable we were as first-time visitors. I guess I had watched too many movies and heard one too many news reports about the crime in New York City. She didn't care; she was way too excited to listen to my reasoning. I chuckled at the memory of my dear friend. She was always fearless.

Her name was Star Louise Hensley. She said her parents named her that because she was lucky to be alive. They said she was their lucky Star. Louise was her grandmother's name on her dad's side, and she died just days before Star was born. Funny how that works because they said she had the spark of her grandmother Louise. Apparently Louise was quite the character.

Star and I met when my mom and dad had relocated to a small town outside of Atlanta, Georgia. My dad was an engineer for a company that was downsizing and laying off employees unless they accepted jobs at other locations. Dad was an awesome man and provider. He would do anything it took to provide for our family. We never wanted for anything.

My parents are happily married and have been for more than fifty years. I have a large family; I'm one of eight children. I never saw my parents struggle. My mom stayed home and raised us while my dad worked. We were middle class and well respected in our community. My mom and dad knew everyone, and everyone knew us.

All my siblings attended private school, including me, except the year I met Star. It was my first time attending a public school. When we were old enough to attend high school, our parents gave us a choice to either continue private school or go to a public school. Of course, I chose public school. Star and I met our freshman year. Star always reminded me how fortunate I was, but I never really understood why she'd say that until now. I see things much differently now than I did back then.

Adam pulled up to the Times Center, located in the heart of New York City near Times Square, just a couple blocks from where Star and I stayed during our last visit. I loved this center. It was exactly what Star would've pictured. Adam opened my door, and a woman in a dress-suit that looked like something Michelle Obama would wear greeted me. It was elegant and classy, yet it said, "I'm in charge, so pay attention to me."

She held out her hand and introduced herself as Beth Jacobs. "We've spoken many times before. I'm your event coordinator. I will monitor your visit and whereabouts until your departure. Come this way—I have several people waiting for you. We must get started to stay on schedule. I hope you slept on the plane because this is the city that never sleeps, and I doubt if you'll get any the next few days."

Ms. Jacobs was walking fast in her stylish Vince Camuto shoes, one of my favorite designers. I quickly trailed behind, trying to keep up. As she was walking and talking, she asked how my flight was, and she wanted to know if I got the mayor's greeting card. I assured her everything was fine, and yes, I did receive the mayor's welcome.

We entered the doors of the Times Center, and I was blown away by how amazing this place looked. It was the perfect venue. We walked down halls and around corners, taking an elevator to another level. We entered a beautiful room where my production crew greeted me.

"Ms. Knight, welcome! Let me introduce you to Jessie—he's your hair and makeup artist—and Scotty—he's in charge of your fabulous wardrobe for the next few days. Lawrence has your script; he'll be going over it with you soon. This is Marissa. She's the reporter here representing one of New York Cities top magazines; to whom you agreed to give an exclusive interview. I believe this is the first time you've spoken to one of our journalists. Am I correct?"   "Yes, you are."

Marissa extended her hand, and we shook like equal peers. Ms. Jacobs continued to introduce me to everyone. "This is Bobby, our stage manager; he'll assist you with dress rehearsal, which is scheduled for six o'clock. And that's Pam—she'll be your personal assistant. If you need anything, just let her know. She'll be able to assist you with all your needs.

"I hope you had time to eat lunch before you came," Ms. Jacobs continued, "because it will be late before you have a chance to get a decent meal. After your performance, an honorary reception will follow. There will be plenty to eat there, but I doubt you'll have time to enjoy the spread. Most likely you'll be too busy mingling with your fans, sponsors, investors, and the press. No worries though. We have a slower day planned for you tomorrow. You're scheduled to meet with some school-age kids from Queens. They're on a field trip to the 9/11 memorial. You'll be giving them a short speech outside the south tower fountain. Then you'll be having brunch with the mayor and his wife, and later that evening they plan to give you the key to the city at a ceremony in Times Square. You'll have a little me time after the ceremony—a couple hours before the gala that starts at eight o'clock—so enjoy it.

Oh, and by the way, we've spoken several times via e-mail and phone, but now that I have the honor of meeting you in person, I want to say I'm happy to be of service to you and your mission, Ms. Knight. I am a big fan. It is my pleasure to assist you over the next couple days. Welcome back to New York City! We hope your stay is more than magical. We want this year's visit to be one you never forget. Let me know if you need anything or have any questions about the next few days. Again, if you need anything, you have my direct number."

My head was spinning. So many things were going on, and everyone was smiling, acting like they were so happy to see me, shaking my hand, and being accommodating. Adam, my limo driver, told me he would take my luggage to the New York Palace, where I'd be staying. Before he departed he asked if I had everything I needed. I asked him to leave my Louis Vuitton extra-large tote bag. I traveled a lot and kept everything I needed in that bag—gum, walking slippers, lotion, Excedrin, protein bars. You name it—it was my go-to bag when I needed something no one else could provide. He gladly picked it out of the luggage and sat it next to my purse on the table next to a large, red plush sofa.

"Thank you very much for taking care of my bags," I said.

"My pleasure, Ms. Knight," Adam responded as he bowed once again and tipped the top of his hat like they do in the movies. I wanted someone to pinch me at that moment, but instead I chuckled softly inside, thinking how much Star would have gotten a kick out of all this.

My personal assistant, Pam, escorted me to my dressing room. Inside the room was so much food. There were fancy, heavy hors d'oeuvres and a wet bar with a personal bartender waiting patiently for any request. The room was large, not the typical dressing room I'd seen on TV, and had art deco paintings everywhere. It had a modern flair and was clean but edgy. It had an ambiance to it that was whole and complete. I can't exactly explain it, but something about the room made me feel confident, safe, and secure. I noticed fresh, colorful flowers everywhere. I happened to walk by a beautiful arrangement and noticed it was from my mom. The attached card read, "Good luck, Ally. I always knew you could do this."

I felt a tear drop from my eye, almost so fast I couldn't stop it. It was a very emotional moment for me; I just wished Star were here to share this special moment together. If it weren't for her, I wouldn't have been here.

Pam escorted me to my makeup chair so Jessie could do his magic. He and Scotty chitchatted about what he had in mind so Scotty could pick out some outfits that would complement the look Jessi was going for. Once they finished their many uh-huhs, they bumped fists, and Scotty politely excused himself, telling me he'd be back later for my fittings.

Pam asked if she could get me a glass of champagne, and I gladly accepted. The bartender was happy to pour the first of many drinks, for the night was still young. Pam also took it upon herself to put together a small plate of hors d'oeuvres. It was as if she had studied my likes. She selected the same foods I would have. She added imported cheeses, stuffed mushrooms, some smoked salmon, and a few shrimp with cocktail sauce. It was light and perfect finger food to keep me from feeling too hungry before the reception later tonight. She also put a small bottle of Perrier on the makeup station in case I needed it. Perfect!

Everyone was patiently doing their jobs, and Marissa was waiting until everyone had me settled enough to conduct her interview, since this was the only time my agent was able to squeeze in an interview during this visit. I didn't mind. I was used to talking with food in my mouth. People love talking at socials and dinner parties, and lord knows I had my share of those the past few years.

Pam got Marissa a chair to sit next to me, kind of at an angle. It was close enough for us to hear each other but with enough distance to allow Jessie to do his thing. Marissa's presence didn't bother anyone; they all seemed to be accustomed to it.

Marissa started out by thanking me for taking the time, for allowing her to interview me, and for giving her magazine an exclusive story. She said she was honored to finally meet the one and only Ms. Alexandra Knight and that she was excited about my visit back to the Big Apple. She said to let her know when I needed a break because she wanted to cover as much as she could to get the full story. She thanked me one more time and promised to compile her notes at the end of the interview, hoping to give me the best cover story the magazine had ever had. I responded by saying I appreciated her enthusiasm and would do my best to answer her questions thoroughly.

Marissa began by asking me what I remembered most about my best friend, Star. I remembered so many things. I remembered the first time she trusted me with her secrets. Star didn't grow up like I did. She didn't have loving parents, and she didn't grow up with the light of a loving and caring family. Her life was full of darkness.

Star and I were two peas in a pod. When you saw her, you saw me. We spent every moment we had outside of family and school with each other. We would hang out a lot at my house, sitting on the front porch and talking for hours. She enjoyed coming to my house and seeing the type of family she'd always wanted. My mom and dad loved Star. They thought she was a bit rough around the edges, but they knew she meant well, so they never judged her, and she respected them for that. They treated Star like she was their daughter. When I met Star, we were like sisters. She would always tell me how blessed I was for having both parents still married and in love, with eight kids and owning a big, beautiful home. She said she'd never met anyone who had parents like mine, or a family that was so close and everyone loved one another. Star talked about her life and all that she remembered while she was growing up. Star told me everything about her life ...

"I remember not remembering most of my life, and what I do remember, Ally, I wish I could forget.

"I remember the first time I heard the sound of a harmonica; my father was playing it in our living room, alongside of one of his brothers who played guitar and a couple of his friends. He sang and played the harmonica a lot when I was growing up. When my father played the harmonica, he was my hero. It was the only time I saw him as a loving father. Listening to the unique sound of what he called his G Baby, named after his favorite key, which he played it in. I remember how the harmonica always soothed me on the inside. I loved its edgy bluesy sound. I connected spiritually with the vibrations of its melody. It was as if it had a hidden soul inside those wooden keys. The sound was like an old soul, a spiritual message just for me. I always felt my soul was connected to whatever or whoever was speaking too me through the rhythm of those notes. It made me feel safe. I'd always felt it was a sign, a symbol of hope, a message of love and peace. It somehow made me feel that I was older and destined for more than the life I was living. Life would someday be different. I would somehow overcome the hurt, pain, and suffering I felt every day. Someday I would be free. Someday I would feel loved.

"I remember growing up feeling very sad and alone. I remember never seeing my mother smile. I remember never smiling myself. I remember how much my mother hated me. Once, she threw me up against a heat radiator and knocked me unconscious. She thought she killed me, and in a panic, she called my dad. He rushed home from work to see about me. By the time he arrived, my eyes were open, but I couldn't talk. He said I had a huge knot on the back of my skull. He cried. He asked my mom why she did it, and she said because I wouldn't stop crying and she couldn't take it anymore. The swelling didn't go down for weeks. Dad said I was different after that. He said I had fear in my eyes all the time. My mom was a young mother. She had a short temper and no patience. I believe, from that day on, that angels were watching over me, this is why I survived.

"My mom was so mean. I'm not sure why; she was just ornery like that. She would pinch me and hit me upside my head a lot when I was a toddler. She'd shake me real hard until I felt like my brains were exploding. Once she spanked me so hard with these switches tied together like twines, and afterward, I was paralyzed with fear anytime I heard the sound of her voice. When I started forming words, I couldn't talk well. I stuttered a lot and would get my letters mixed up. I couldn't say dog; I would say gog. This would make my mom very angry, but I couldn't help it. She'd hit me in the back of my head each time I said it wrong. I was convinced she never wanted me.

"I hated having been born," Star continued. "I wanted to believe God wouldn't allow me to be born only to live like this forever. My heart ached for what love was and what it really felt like. I knew this wasn't how it was supposed to feel. I knew God's love had to be much better than this feeling of hopelessness.

"I worried my mother would die by the hands of an angry man. Or she would have a heart attack and die right in front of me. I never did understand why I even cared what happened to her. But I did.

I remember living with this fear every day and how that fear of the unknown controlled me. Every day, I'd wake up fearing this was the last day I would ever see my mother alive. I never really understood why I allowed this fear to consume me. I mean, in my heart of hearts, I wished her dead a million times. So why did I bother to care?

"I suffered from severe insomnia as a young child. I was terrified of falling asleep, due to the overwhelming anticipation of my father entering my bedroom to molest me night after night. It never failed. Soon after I'd fall asleep, I was awakened by the touch of his hands caressing my innocent body. He touched me in places he shouldn't have and did things to me that a father should never do to his daughter. I never quite understood why this was happening to me, but what did I know was that I was a hopeless child born into a life of two very confused parents. Lucky Star? Well, lucky I never felt, and stars shine bright in the sky, and my light never shined. *What light?* I thought. *Why would someone torture me with a name like Star? Especially when all I see is darkness around me?* My parents were messed up. One loved me too much the wrong way, and the other made it clear she didn't love me at all.

"I loved my little brother, Dallas, more than I loved my mom, my dad, even myself. I thought Dallas was the safest one among the four of us. When I say safe, I mean his innocence kept him safe. I felt that he deserved a better life, even though I was the one who was cursed.

"I always felt different and alone. I was always frightened, scared, and ashamed. I felt like something was wrong with me all the time. I felt paranoid like someone or something was out to get me. I felt someone or something wanted to hurt me. I felt something evil was surrounding me. I felt like I would never escape this life.

"I remember the beatings I got regularly from my mother for no reason at all. She was harsh. She had a lot of rage inside her. She was miserable and irritated all the time. She was sneaky and mysterious yet my mom had a creative, artistic, talented, smart side to her. She painted, did pottery, sketched beautiful portraits of nature and animals. She was very talented. She was the unknown artist no one recognized, not even herself. Dallas and I hardly had time to enjoy that side of her. Despite her negative characteristics, our mom was a remarkable woman. If only she had realized it, maybe things would be much different.

"I remember feeling lonely all the time. I felt like my life was a burden on my mom and a curse with my father, even though my father said he loved me so much every night when he crawled into bed with me. I believed him.

"I remember Mom locking me in dark closets for hours. I'd yell and scream for her to let me out, and she never did. I would cry myself to sleep in the darkness and wake up from the light when the door finally opened, wondering just how long I'd been in there. I grew a hate for my mom I thought I could never overcome. She never treated Dallas the way she treated me, and I always wondered why we were treated so different.

"I had severe nosebleeds regularly. It reminded me of something out of a demonic horror movie. They were so heavy that I would soak a large bath towel with my blood in seconds. You would have thought I needed a blood transfusion afterward. I'd never heard of these things happening to other kids, so I was even more convinced something was wrong with me. *I'm different, I'm cursed, I'm weird, and I'm always going to be miserable.* The doctors never found out what caused my nosebleeds. It's still a mystery.

"I dreaded the times my mom would leave the house and take Dallas with her because I knew it was only a matter of minutes before my dad would enter the room, sit down beside me, and lure me in front of the television. He would put in a dirty video with naked people doing some of the same things he did to me in the middle of the night. He would make me look at dirty magazines in hopes of teaching me how to please him better. He told me we were not stars in the movie but in real life. I remember the severe pain I suffered for years and not being able to cry out for help or tell anyone, because it was a secret. Even then, in my innocence, he was still to me the best dad ever. I knew he loved me, and I was his special little girl."

Star paused her story a minute as the sun began going down. My mom brought us some blankets to keep us warm and cleared the paper plates and cups off the small wicker table that sat in between our chairs on the porch. Mom had served us sloppy joes and homemade french fries an hour ago for dinner. As I listened to Star tell her story, I couldn't imagine any of it being true. With a little guilt, I thought to myself, *She's got to be making all this up.* It just seemed so unreal; I couldn't imagine a life so loveless and cold. Mom made sure we were fine and said we'd need to wrap up soon so she could drive Star home before it got too late. I said okay, and Star nodded her head in agreement. She smiled at my mom and thanked her for her gracious hospitality. "Thank you, Momma Doris," she said.

Star then continued, "Once I remember sitting in class trying to concentrate while listening to my teacher Mrs. Stanley. I was in junior high school. It had been a typical morning of fighting with my mom before school. I took her usual abusive words of wisdom with me each day: 'You're not better than me! Who do you think you are? You're nothing! Stop looking at me like that!' I was miserably going over the argument over and over in my head. Couldn't concentrate in class, as usual. Next thing I knew, I was being lifted off the cement floor. I had fainted once again. I heard loud laughter from all of my cruel classmates and Mrs. Stanley calling the nurse's station for help, running around in shock, trying to calm the class down, not knowing what to do for me in her panic.

"Fainting was another curse I had to live with. My fainting spells were just as bad as my nosebleeds. No one knew why I would suddenly lose consciousness and just faint. One minute I was fine, and the next I would get dizzy and black out.

"One summer afternoon, Mom sent Dallas and me to the neighborhood store to pick up a loaf of bread. We rode our bikes. We didn't have bike locks back then, so one of us had to stand outside the store while the other went inside to get the items. Well it was my turn to watch the bikes, so Dallas went in the store to get the loaf of bread. When he returned, he found me passed out on the sidewalk with both bikes on top of my limp body; they had fallen with me when I fainted.

"Dallas was scared. Dallas kept screaming my name. 'Star, Star, wake up, wake up, Star!' Dallas was shaking me and crying because he thought I was dead. I could hear him, but I couldn't speak or respond. It was like I was aware but not aware. Then I suddenly felt alone. I think Dallas had to leave me lying there while he went back inside the store to ask the clerk if he could use the phone to call home so he could tell our parents what had happened. Dallas later told me dad was there in a flash. When I opened my eyes, after what felt like forever in a dream state, I was in my father's arms. The look of fear on my dad's face was frightening. It was as if he felt it was his fault, and he was worried.

"Dad told Dallas to go home on my bike. He assured him that he would handle things from there, and he said to tell my mom that he was going to take me to the hospital. We didn't own a vehicle back then; my dad put me on the crossbars of Dallas's bike, and my weak body laid against his. He propped me up and rode me all the way across town to the nearest hospital. I remember feeling safe with my dad as I watched the sun go down and the streetlights glare and guide the ride. My dad was my hero.

"My parents were very concerned about my fainting spells. Losing consciousness wasn't a laughing matter, and the doctors had no idea why it was happening.

"When I was thirteen years old, I was excited about cashing my first real paycheck. I was working as a summer school teacher's aide. I had gone to the bank and was standing in line, and suddenly my body felt warm, my legs felt weak, and my head felt dizzy. Then everything turned black.

"Next thing I remember, my uncle Danny, Mom's older brother, was standing over me in a medical clinic that was next door to the bank. When I was coming to, I became frightened when I realized I was no longer at the bank as I last remembered. I was now staring up into my uncle's eyes. He told me everything was going to be all right and not to worry. I remember thinking to myself, *Dang! I must have been out for a very long time, to wake up in a strange place and see Uncle Danny sitting next to me.*

"Uncle Danny checked all my vital signs, as he was an emergency medical technician and worked for one of the local ambulance services. He gave me a big, comforting hug and asked if I could stand up. I said yes and tried to stand up. My legs quickly gave out again, and I fell into his arms. He caught my weak body and carried me to his car and took me to his home. He told me on the drive to his house that they had called him because they couldn't get in touch with my mom, as he was the next of kin listed.

"I loved Uncle Danny so much for rescuing me. He gave me some pink liquid medicine, some water, and then he made me lay down on his couch to rest. He covered me with a blanket, and I went to sleep. I remember feeling safer and more loved than I'd ever felt in my entire life.

"I loved school and hated school all at the same time. School provided a temporary escape from the horrible abuse I suffered at home.

I hated school because I was bullied every day. We were poor, and I had to wear the same outfit to school sometimes three days in a row.

I only had two changes of clothes most of the time. We had no soap to bathe or soap powder to wash our clothes. We had no deodorant, no toothpaste, and even no toilet paper. I remember using newspaper many times to wipe myself. It felt degrading attending school and knowing kids could smell me, and they teased me all the time. I felt so ashamed.

"I used to go to school after washing in the sink with just hot water, and bathing with my hands, because there were no towels or washcloths. The few we did have were so dirty that they stunk worse than I did. We never had the luxury of a washer and dryer in our home, nor did we have money to go to the Laundromat on a regular basis. If we were lucky, we'd launder our clothes once a month.

"I would go days without eating. School lunches would sometimes be the only meal I had the entire day. We moved so many times that I was always the new person, and no one ever welcomed the new kid. I was always teased and bullied. Kids were cruel. They would form a circle around me so that I couldn't escape and start chanting. 'Na-na-na-na! You stink, na-na-na-na, you stink.' They sang this over and over again. The sad truth about it was I did stink. I knew I stank, and there was nothing I could do about it. My clothes stunk, my body stunk, my breath stunk, and my hair stunk. It was true; I was the stinky kid.

"In school, I was always considered weird because I was very withdrawn. I was shy, and I didn't make friends easily. I always felt alone in my misery. I felt people could see my secrets, and if they got to know me, and I didn't want those secrets to be revealed. I was afraid I'd get in trouble if anyone found out about me and my dad and the dysfunctional relationship me and my mom had.

"I had attended more than thirteen schools by the time I graduated from high school. My freshman year I attended three different schools in three different states. I used to think this was normal, until I got older and people kept asking me if I was a military brat. I didn't know exactly what that meant at the time but later realized it wasn't normal to move around as much as we did. I honestly knew no other life, so I thought everyone lived this way.

"I wanted to die every day. I had no self-esteem and wondered what would ever become of me. *Would I ever live long enough to escape this misery? How long does the sadness last? Should I just kill myself now and get it over with?* It hurt so bad, I just wanted to die. It was hard, the thought of ever being able to see beyond the moment or even another day. The days were so long, and the pain was so bad. I hated the thought of waking up to the same old life each day; this made me feel even more hopeless.

"One morning I was having the usual power struggle of verbal abuse with my mom before school. She would always have something negative to say, to purposely tear me down. She would yell at me to do this or to do that. She would tell me that I would never amount to anything, not to look at her that way while she's talking to me, and if I didn't stop, she would slap the taste out of my mouth.

"She'd say, 'You are not better than me, so don't even think that you are! You have no idea how hard it is raising two children on your own without help! If it were you, you couldn't do it any better! I should have killed you when I had the chance! You must think you're something, but let me tell you, you are not! Now get out of my face and go to school and don't you say another word!'

"This was actually a better day than most. I mean, keeping more secrets—that was easy. She just needed her drugs to calm her down and mellow out, I thought. She was just stressed out from having to raise Dallas and me all by herself. Dad never helped out; he was a deadbeat. At least this is what she told us, and from the results, we never questioned it.

"I was so close to freedom once, yet I begged to stay a prisoner for fear that Dallas and I would be separated by a broken system trying to save us.

"That same morning after arriving at school, my first-hour class was one of my favorites. It was my interior design class. My teacher, Mrs. Calhoun, was passing out our papers from the last test we had taken. My teacher was tall and slim, with reddish brown hair. She was very elegant. I admired her. Mrs. Calhoun was firm with the students yet warm and understanding.

"I felt overwhelmed this morning, just tired of having to deal with my mom and her issues. I was tired of her depleting me by sucking what little life I had left. I was contemplating suicide for the hundredth time. I was so sick of my mom's crap and abuse that I just wanted to end it for real this time. I hated the world I was born in, I hated both my parents, and I hated the thought of living another day in this cursed, evil world of mine. All I could think about was how miserable my life was.

"When Mrs. Calhoun handed me my test, I looked at it; it was an A+. I suddenly broke down and started crying out of control. She had no idea why I would be crying with such a good grade. She asked if I was okay. I said yes and apologized for disrupting the class with my out-of-control emotions. She asked me to excuse myself from the classroom and go outside in the hall until I could get myself together.

"After a while, she excused herself from the classroom to come check on me. I was crying harder and couldn't talk. She was very concerned and didn't know what to do, so she walked me down the hallway to the counselor's office, hoping I would open up to one of them and they would be able to better assist me. I could tell she was very concerned.

"I ended up speaking to a counselor by the name of Mrs. Turner. Mrs. Turner was a black woman with a caramel-colored complexion and big, bushy, shoulder-length hair. She was very well dressed and seemed sharp and smart. However, her demeanor made me feel uncomfortable. I immediately got the feeling she thought she was better than her current position and felt this job was beneath her, especially having to waste her valuable time listening to another troubled teen. She looked down rolling her insincere eyes across her face with disgust. She gave me the impression she was tired of seeing adolescents of my type and had long given up on trying to help hopeless kids like me. Her entire body language was rude and I could tell she wasn't concerned about me, or my problems. As I watched her, I could almost hear her saying, 'Hurry this up; I have better things to do with my time than to try and save your worthless life.'

"I found it odd that I had never really noticed her even working here before now. I don't know if I didn't want to cooperate with her because she was a woman or because she was black, or if it was because of that old cliché of black folk growing up with our parents telling us over and over never to discuss our personal business with strangers, no matter who they are.

"Meanwhile, this very intelligent, highly educated, stuck-up counselor tried to calm me down by using all the professional techniques she learned in college. I refused to cooperate. I shut down like a CIA agent held in capture against my will by the enemy. Mrs. Calhoun was so concerned with me that after the bell rang to dismiss first-period class, she hurried back down to the administrative offices, knocked on Mrs. Turner's door, and politely interrupted our session. Mrs. Turner welcomed the interruption, not more than I did. Mrs. Calhoun asked if she could speak with me for a moment. It was obvious she wasn't getting anywhere. I think I hurt her uppity feelings. Oh well …

"Mrs. Calhoun looked at me with sadness and concern in her eyes as if, to say, 'I know something is seriously wrong with you, and I wish I knew what it was. I wish I knew what to say to get you to open up and talk to me because I care about you more than you know.' I could feel her true concern. However, I had held this misery in for sixteen years, and I refused to release it any other way than by taking these secrets with me to my grave as soon as I could get enough courage to make sure I got it right the first time. I didn't want to wake up in the hospital with my mom looking down at me, angry for messing that up too.

"By now, Dallas had heard that I was in the main office crying my eyes out, and he asked his second-period teacher if he could be excused from his class to come check on me.

"Up until now, I was the rock in his eyes. I was the strong one and had never broken down through all the abuse by our mother, until now. Dallas never knew about the sexual abuse. I'd never told him because I wanted to protect him from the pain and suffering of knowing too much. There was a lot he didn't know or understand. I sheltered him from a lot of truths about our dysfunctional family.

"When Dallas heard I was crying, he was very concerned. He knew it had to be something seriously wrong, because I refused to cry over spilt milk. I remember crying harder than I had ever cried before—at least in front of people. I cried all the time at night in my bed. I was so torn and confused. I just couldn't stop. I was miserable. I didn't know if I was crying because I was finally ready to end my life, and I knew these would be my last tears, or because there would be no more tears after today.

"When Dallas found me, I looked at him, and I started crying even harder, and then he started crying with me. He didn't know what else to do; it hurt him to see his big sister who always wiped his tears away and who had always been there for him to keep him strong during our abuse at home, finally break down out of control, especially in public. This was forbidden. But I just couldn't stop. I was in so much pain. Words couldn't explain it; my tears were my only communication.

"Mrs. Calhoun was talking to Mrs. Turner. They were whispering. Then Mrs. Calhoun asked if Dallas and I would go with her and take a ride. She wanted to talk to me outside of the school and see if she could find out what was wrong. For some odd reason, I trusted her. I agreed it would be okay for us to leave with her. I looked at Dallas and reassured him it was okay. While we were riding in the car, she told us that she had a close friend who was a very nice man she wanted to introduce me to. She explained how she thought he would be able to help me. She said he helped kids like me all the time, and she knew he would be able to get me to talk. She told me not to be afraid and that I could tell him anything. He would keep it confidential, and I could trust him.

"We pulled up at a clinic that looked like a miniature hospital. We walked right by the reception desk as if they knew we were coming, and they gave us no hassles about the usual procedure of checking in and waiting to be seen. We walked right into this man's office. He greeted us as if he was Santa Claus. He was smiling and very friendly. He was short with a medium build. He had light brown hair, with a slight receding hairline, and was wearing a fun-colored bowtie with a crisp white shirt, the sleeves rolled up. He seemed thrilled to meet us, somewhat honored. Weird right? Yeah, I thought so too.

"He called each one of us by name as if we'd known him our whole lives. He hugged Mrs. Calhoun as she excused herself from the room, telling us she would return soon. No worries, we were in good hands. She had to go back to school and finish teaching her morning classes. She was in between classes when she left; her second hour was her time to do lesson plans. She assured us that we were in the best of hands and asked us to trust her, and she kept repeating that everything would be fine—she promised. She said no one would ever know we were gone and that she would take care of everything by excusing us from our classes until we returned.

"First thing the nice gentleman did was made sure Dallas and I were comfortable. Then he introduced himself. He said, 'Hello again. I'm Mr. Calhoun, your teacher's husband.' We both suddenly felt very special. I was like, 'Wow, you're Mrs. Calhoun's husband?' He said, 'Yes I am.' He then explained to us that he was a clinical psychologist and that he helped people in all types of situations.

"He explained to us the types of situations he's helped other people with. He gave a few examples, hoping one of them would connect with what I might have been going through. He started asking general questions about my background and about my home life, like if I had one or two parents in our household. Questions like if our parents were still married or divorced. He asked how much I knew about my parents.

"Then Mr. Calhoun asked Dallas politely to leave the room so he could talk to me alone. He wanted to know what triggered my unusual crying episode. He called in his assistant to escort Dallas out of his office, and she attended to his every need. They wanted him to feel safe and to make sure he was not afraid.

"After Dallas left the room, Mr. Calhoun asked me to explain to him what a normal everyday situation would be like at our house. So I did, in great detail. He asked me to tell him how I felt about my mom, and I did. He asked how I felt about my dad, and I told him. He asked how I felt about Dallas, and I told him. He asked me if my dad had ever done things to me that made me feel uncomfortable. I told him yes, but he was my dad, and I couldn't stop him. He asked me the same question about my mom. I told him the only issue I had with my mom other than her verbal and physical abuse was that she didn't realize how much I loved her, and I just wanted her to know that I loved her more than she knew. He asked me why I lit up when I talked about Dallas and why he was the only one I loved more than I loved myself.

"I explained I'd always loved Dallas more than myself. Who would love someone like me? My mom didn't love me, and my dad sure didn't love me, but my little brother, I knew he loved me, and I loved him back! Dallas's love was pure, genuine, and unconditional. He loved me, and I knew it. I wanted to protect Dallas and his love for me. I cherished our relationship. It was the best part of my life. Dallas was not just my little brother; he was my best friend.

"By the time I finished telling Mr. Calhoun everything, the look on his face was frightening and a bit disturbed. He was no longer smiling and didn't have that warm, inviting look on his face. He asked how I felt after telling him everything. I told him I felt relieved. I had never told anyone about what my childhood was like or what I dealt with on a regular basis. He told me he could tell I was relieved because I had stopped crying. I hadn't noticed. He thanked me for trusting him. He asked his assistant to allow Dallas to return to the room. He never even asked Dallas a single question.

"He explained to us that what we were dealing with was called parental abuse. He told us that it was serious enough to call child protective services and have us removed from our home immediately. When I heard him say this, I lost it! I started screaming, 'No! I can't leave my mom! She's sick, and she needs me! No! I won't leave her!'

"Mr. Calhoun was shocked at my response. I was also shocked. He saw the fear in my reaction and heard the sincerity in my voice. I absolutely refused to leave my mom, even if she was abusive. He knew how serious I felt about my obligation to take care of her because she was sick, and even though she had issues, I felt I was strong enough to deal with them. She needed me, and we were all she had left. I would not allow Mr. Calhoun or anyone to take us from our mom. I was convinced this would only make things worse, not better.

"Mr. Calhoun couldn't believe my reaction. To hear me refuse the chance to finally, safely escape emotional, mental, physical abuse and neglect? In spite of all the pain and suffering I was going through, I knew my mom's days were numbered. Her heart condition was serious, and she could die any moment. I didn't want her to die alone or with guilt of being a bad mother. I was willing to continue dealing with the abuse. I just never wanted to leave her, not like this. Yes, it was hard, and yes, I was miserable, and yes, I'd rather die than to see her suffer. I knew I could deal with it more than my mom could. If they took us away from her, her heart would stop for sure. I knew things were hard, but Dallas and I were her lifeline.

"Mr. Calhoun just stood in silence, in disbelief. I begged him not to call the cops or child protective services on my mother. I pleaded with him. I asked him to pretend this conversation never happened. I told him if he called anyone, I would deny everything. I would tell them he made it all up and that it was all lies.

"Dallas looked at me and agreed. He no more wanted out than I did. This was still our mom, and we felt obligated to take care of her. Regardless of how bad it hurt us, she was our mother. If we made it that far, we could make it further until were old enough to be on our own, and then we could watch her suffer and die on her own, without the guilt of exposing her for the type of mother she really was. There was no way I could live with that hanging over my head. Secrets are secrets for a reason; they are to be kept secrets. No one tells the family secrets, no matter what.

"Shortly after our session, Mrs. Calhoun returned. She spoke to her husband briefly while Dallas and I sat in the waiting room. When we left the clinic, Mrs. Calhoun took us to their home. It was beautiful; we had never seen a home as big as this home—the kind of home I could only imagine living in someday, only in my dreams. I admired everything. It looked like a house I'd seen on TV, on a show called the *Rich and Famous*.

"We sat around her large kitchen island on these high stools with backs. In awe, we watched her prepare lunch for us. She knew we had an emotional morning. I was exhausted. She was very polite and continued to go out of her way to make us feel comfortable and relaxed before returning to school. This was the first time in my life I knew what an omelet was and saw anyone make one from scratch. It was so good! Dallas and I ate those omelets like they were our first and last meal. I'm sure we looked like those hungry third world children on the commercials. It was obvious we didn't get to eat like this often, or I should say ever.

"As I sat there eating my food, I thought to myself, *I have the coolest teacher ever. Mrs. Calhoun really went out of her way to help me. I feel like I let her down. No one can ever know how this feels, the obligation to live in misery.* Why was I was determined to see this through at whatever cost? What was I thinking? *I'm just a child, and a child should stay in a child's place; they should be seen and not heard. At least that's what Mom always told me. Therefore, I am being a good child because I am being obedient.*

"I honestly felt it would be worse to legally be taken from my mom. I felt like that was taking the easy way out. Even the thought of suicide felt better than that option.

"I knew the best decision was to keep my mom from having to deal with the legal system and facing the embarrassing scrutiny of our family knowing the truth about her and our messed-up lives. I knew I made the right decision. I already knew I was much stronger than she was, and I was willing to endure the abuse a little longer. I would turn eighteen in two years; hopefully it would go by fast. I was determined to take care of my mom until death do us part.

"Mrs. Calhoun never brought the subject up again. She kept her promise and kept our secret. I will never forget what she and her husband did for us. It kept me from committing suicide. I decided I wanted to live after that, because they showed me that I do have choices. Kids can tell on their parents and get out of abusive situations. There are people out there who will listen, believe them, and help them.

"They showed me that it isn't a bad thing to open up to a professional—well, back then they called them shrinks. Mr. Calhoun told Dallas and me that they had not heard of an abusive situation as bad as ours in years. He said we deserved a much better life, with better parents who would love, cherish, and protect us like parents are supposed to.

"I believe Dallas would have followed my lead, no matter which decision I made. I keep convincing myself that I did the right thing. All I know is that I followed my heart. I knew no matter how evil my mom was and how bad she treated me, I loved her for being my mother. I loved her enough not to leave her.

"I remember going home that day and walking into the same situation I had only hours before walked out of as I listened to my mom nagging for no reason. But for some tiny reason it felt different. I felt that it was my choice to put up with my mom's ignorance, and if I really wanted to end it, I could with just one phone call. I know it may sound a bit harsh, but just knowing this deep down inside my soul gave me a glimpse of hope."

My mom came out to say it was time to take Star home, and she gathered up our blankets she had given us to stay warm under the cool night lights. I rode in the car with my mom, as Star only lived less than a mile away but too far for two young girls to walk at night. When we pulled up to her house, Star hopped out the car and said, "Thanks, Momma Doris." Then she said, "See you tomorrow, Ally. I had a great time."

I said, "Me too. See you tomorrow."

Marissa's mouth was wide open, and her eyes were in shock. She said, "Oh my gosh! That is so sad. Star actually had a way out of her miserable, abusive life and chose to stay with her mom in spite of everything? Wow. I wonder why. Sounds like she really had a rough childhood. My goodness. How in the world did you guys remain friends for so long? And how did you feel about the type of life she was living? Especially having to leave her every day in that environment? This had to be heartbreaking for you, knowing how awful her home life was."

I said, "I really didn't know how to feel. Star seemed fine most of the time. So I really didn't think it was all that bad. Star would tell me these stories with love in her heart. She never showed anger and regret. She never wanted or asked for sympathy. Star was just happy to finally be able to share her situation with someone she could trust. She was always telling me how lucky I was for having wonderful parents who really loved each other and having a strong, large, loving family. She said she had always wanted the life I was fortunate to have.

"My mom and I are so close. I couldn't ever imagine not getting along with my mother or my father. I had a hard time wrapping my mind around her life. I'd never met anyone like her."

Marissa asked, "Was Star sad when you guys hung out together?"

I said, "No, she wasn't. Star was full of light and love. She was fun and was always happy and always made me laugh. I enjoyed being around her. She helped me break out of my shy shell. She was good for my self-esteem and the dearest friend anyone could ever have. There was something about Star. If you met her, you would have never known she lived in such darkness, because the light of her attitude always outshined her pain."

Chapter 2

Jessie was now moving to my makeup. He asked me if I liked my hair. I said, "It looks beautiful. I love the extensions; they look so natural and blend with my natural hair so well. I absolutely love it! Thanks."

Jessie was glad to hear how much I liked his work. He then said, "Ms. Knight?"

I said, "Please call me Ally."

He said, "Okay, Ally. I am amazed by your friend Star. She seemed like a very strong little girl. I know we all have a story to tell, but hers is so sad. I mean, who would want to be abused by both parents? I mean, poor thing, she never had a chance."

I said, "Yeah, I know, Jessie. I'm very fortunate to have two loving parents. I could never imagine walking in Star's shoes."

He apologized for interrupting Marissa's interview. She said no worries that we needed to take a short break anyway. "I'm sure Ally would like to get up and stretch her legs, go to the powder room, and nibble on more of this nice spread they have laid out for her. It's enough to feed an army!" she said.

I started laughing. "Yeah, it is a lot. Help yourselves, everyone. There's no way I'd be able to eat all this food. I don't want it to go to waste." Jessie, Scotty, and Lawrence didn't hesitate; they were all over that food.

Pam, my personal assistant, directed me to the powder room. She asked if I needed anything else. She was on the phone with Beth, who had called to check up on things to be sure everything was going smoothly. Pam assured her I was in good hands, everyone was taking good care of me, and we were making good time. We were on track, and she would let her know when we started dress rehearsal.

Marissa even decided to relax a little and nibble on some goodies with the crew. I liked Marissa. She was easy to talk to. She was patient, and the questions weren't hard to answer. I didn't feel like she was judging Star, and I hoped she edited the story to make sure Star shined like the star she was, because this isn't a sad story. Star's story is of hope, not defeat.

The break was much needed, especially after flying all morning and feeling like I had no break until now. I enjoyed the crew Beth put together to take care of me. They were all down to earth and easy to get along with. I would always remember that special moment, feeling like a movie star. Everyone was laughing and talking amongst themselves, as if no one was really at work. I enjoyed that. We had a lot to do, and this was just the beginning. *So far, so good*, I thought.

Jessie called me back over to his chair in front of the mirror and started applying my makeup. He said, "I know it will be hard to talk to Marissa with me all in your face, but I know she's not going to stop interviewing you, so we'll just work around it. Is that cool with you, Ally?"

I laughed and said, "Sure. We'll make it work. Thanks for understanding."

Marissa pulled her chair a little closer, turned her small recorder back on, and asked more questions. She mentioned how she remembered reading in another article how Star hated her birthdays. I said, "Yeah, she hated her birthdays for sure. She said she never got what she wanted, and something bad would happen every year for as long as she could remember. She hated them for sure. When Star and I were adults, she called me one day after she found a letter from her mother behind a picture of her mother in an old picture frame. She had forgotten she had put it there. It was a letter her mother had written to her on her seventeenth birthday." I remembered that letter ...

May 15

To my dearest daughter,

Well, it's been seventeen years since you first made your grand entry into this confused world of ours. Wow, what a day. For a while, I wasn't at all sure my little girl was going to make it.

Thanking God for each and every day for the beautiful blessing he sent to me. You've made me very proud of you and proud to be able to say I'm your mother.

From a little apple-head crybaby, you've developed into a gracious and lovely young lady.

With your talents, ambition, and courage, you can accomplish anything. You have filled my life and heart with so much joy and happiness (I'm glad I kept ya, "smile").

Being seventeen brings you to adulthood in the next year. One year, and you won't be my baby anymore. You've come a long way, baby, and that's no joke.

Hopefully I've been able to give you the fundamental ingredients necessary to approach this word of conflict and turmoil. But regardless of what your future may bring, always remember: nobody loves you like your mother loves you. Always and no matter when, where, or why, you can always turn to your mother.

As a mother, I can say you're confident, capable, and terribly stubborn, as a typical Taurus would be.

I'm so happy you came into my life seventeen years ago. You and your brother have made my life so complete with your love. On this day, I want you to know that I love you and trust you with all my heart.

You're still the sweet and innocent loud-mouth child I fell in love with on May 15, 1954. Because you are my firstborn, you will always have a special place in my heart.

Through the years, we've had tears, joys, and pains, but because of my children and with your strength, we've carried on.

I am so proud to be your mother; my heart is bursting with joy, and best of God's blessings to you for the years to come

Happy birthday to my special baby,
Your Mother

Ten Years Earlier

May 15

Today is my birthday, and I am seven years old. Mom, Dad, and Dallas and I now live in a tiny, little town located in Arkansas. My dad used to live here when he was a boy. Our apartment is located on the second level of a four-unit building. I hate climbing the stairs, because my legs are so short.

I noticed there was a serious discussion going on between my parents. It was so serious I think they may have forgotten today is my birthday. Of course being the optimistic little girl I am, I just figured they were waiting until I got home from school to celebrate.

In my bliss of birthday haven, as I was getting ready for school, I heard my parents' voices start to escalate, and the atmosphere became a bit more tense. Not that I wasn't used to these heated arguments, it's just today seemed to be different than most.

When I was eating a bowl of cereal, I noticed the milk was spoiled. I dare not interrupt my parents to let them know. Instead, I choked it down for fear of getting in trouble for complaining about something so trivial, like a good little girl should. We were taught to never waste food. I thought I would puke as I gagged on each spoonful, and the tension between my parents continued to escalate.

After breakfast, I finished getting dressed for school. I heard bits and pieces of their argument. Mom would say, "Now, honey, did you touch that girl or not?" Dad answered, "Of course not. She's lying. I never did anything to that girl." My parents went back and forth, and the argument soon turned into a physical encounter. My dad hit my mom in the face to get her to shut up. It didn't work. It never does, and she continued to yell even louder. I couldn't quite figure out what girl they were talking about. I used to think my mother loved the physical abuse, as much as I felt she provoked my dad, especially knowing he would hit her. I know it sounds sick, but that was the way things are in my home.

Their relationship has been like this for as long as I can remember. I've always wondered why they hate each other so much. I continued listening, trying to ignore them as I walked out the door for school. I was hurt they forgot my birthday. They didn't even say happy birthday to me this morning. Oh well, I was too excited and felt special today. I was sure by the time I got home from school, they would remember, and we would celebrate my birthday.

Today, I felt pretty even though I never really thought I was a pretty girl. I prayed every night that God would turn this ugly duckling into a beautiful swan some day. This was one of my fairy-tale dreams. I hate my birthdays. I'm never sure if I should celebrate another year living or mourn the day I was born. Deep down inside, I am happy to be a year older. Each year, I feel a sense of silent joy. I feel someone whispering in my ear every year, and I look forward to hearing that special voice. It says, "Happy birthday, Star Louise. Grandma loves you." It always makes me feel safe and special. I know it's Grandma Louise. She is watching over me. I know she is. Even though I've never met her, I know she's always with me.

I've never really felt as pretty as I've pretended. However, I'm a pro at covering up the truth; therefore, I feel there is no harm in feeling and dreaming of a better life than this one. I just think of Cinderella, and I feel that some day my prince charming will find me and rescue me from my wicked parents. In the meantime, I'm only seven; I have a long time to wait for that.

I was wearing a pink dress and a pair of black patent-leather shoes, a bit scuffed, but they'd do. My mom got them from the Goodwill store. I took out my braids, which I had put in all by myself the night before, so that I could pick out my hair into this huge Afro, one of my favorite looks. My mom hates my Afro because she says it's considered too grown-up and I could be considered a fast girl, another word for loose. This isn't allowed in our culture, especially if you are a good girl. However, she was too busy arguing and fighting with my dad to notice I left the house with my hair down. It made me feel pretty, and that was all that mattered.

Off to school I walked, only two blocks away. This is one of the smallest towns I've ever lived in. It has a Kmart, a movie theater, a park, a small corner grocery store, and only one public school, grades kindergarten to twelve. Every kid goes to the same school from start to finish. My dad went to this same school when he was my age. It has no city buses, only a few cabs. Heck, you can walk out of the city limits just by crossing a gravel road. Dallas and I think that's the neatest thing, so we cross over to the other side of the road as often as we can.

It makes us feel somewhat rebellious. I still don't understand how and why we actually ended up here. One night I went to bed, and the next morning I woke up, and Mom and Dad had our entire lives packed in a U-Haul, and we were on our way to another new life. Just like that, no questions asked.

When I got to school, I was happy. I love my second-grade teacher. She reminds me of Marilyn Monroe. She has bleach-blonde hair, with long, silky, loose curls toward the end. She is medium height, not slender but average weight. She has a full figure, with hips, but she's not fat. Ms. Hunt was wearing a three-piece suit. She paired it with a polyester blouse with a beautiful colorful design, which brought out her natural tan suit just right. Ms. Hunt is my favorite teacher; she has a warm heart but doesn't take any crap from anyone, not even me. She is especially hard on me. I must have challenged her a time or two, because I seem to always be first in line for a paddling when the class gets in trouble.

I started daydreaming in class to clear my mind from all the chaos that surrounded me when I was at home. Right when I was just about to get married to Michael Jackson, I heard Ms. Hunt talking about people touching you on your private parts and how this is not right, and if someone you know touches you there, you need to tell someone. I instantly started paying attention to her instructions, as I had no idea what she really meant, but it sounded like a lesson I didn't want to miss. I was confused at why someone needed to be told and why this was a bad thing. As she continued, I wondered why this would be bad if we are playing a game. Everyone plays the secret game. Right?

Then I started thinking about my parents' conversation this morning and tried hard to connect the dots, as I like trying to figure things out. I think they were talking about my friend who lives across the street. I play with her a lot. Our parents swap babysitting privileges. I go over to her house after school until my parents pick me up, or she comes over to our house until her parents pick her up.

Mom kept asking dad if he had touched her. I wonder if she means if dad plays the secret touching game with her like he plays with me. I have no idea why this would be so bad or why this would upset my mom, but listening to how Ms. Hunt explained this to the class, it must not be a good thing to do. Ms. Hunt continued to stress if a stranger touches you on your private parts, you should tell someone you trust. This is a bad thing. Well, my dad isn't a stranger, and he play-touches me all the time, so it can't be wrong. But if she feels someone should know, who better to tell than my mom? Right?

When I got home from school, Mom was so sad. She had been crying. She looked distraught. She had no idea I had even come in the house. I went up to her, thinking that I could help her and me at the same time with the good news about dad. I looked at her and said, "Mom … Dad play-touches me too." Mom looked at me with this odd look on her face and asked me to repeat what I'd just said. "What did you say?" I excitedly repeated my good news. I said again, "Dad play-touches me too, just like he does with my friend. Isn't that who you guys were talking about this morning?"

Wham! Next thing I knew, I was lifting my tiny body off the floor. My mom slapped me so hard my knees buckled, and I fell to the floor. As I was picking myself up from our filthy tile kitchen floor, I was shocked and started crying hysterically, screaming, "Mom! Mom!" I was scared, I was stunned, and it was painful. I have no idea why my mother just slapped the crap out of me. She started calling me all kinds of names, hitting me harder and harder, screaming louder and louder. "You nasty little girl, you slut, you whore, you liar, how dare you lie on your father like that? What is the matter with you? You want attention on your birthday this bad that you would tell such stories to get it? Huh? Huh? I better not ever hear you say that about your father again! Do you hear me! Do you! Now go to your room!" I ran as fast as I could from my angry mother.

I am hurt and scared. I am bruised more emotionally than physically and very confused. She hit me so hard, my face is swollen, and my mouth is split open. I can still taste my blood. I have no clue what just happened or why. All I feel is that I had once again done something wrong, and this was the worst birthday ever.

Mom sent me to my bedroom, and this is where I've spent the rest of my birthday. I wonder what all those mean loud words meant. Liar, I understand, but I didn't lie. Whore—I don't know what that means. Slut couldn't have been anything nice either. Bad, nasty girl sounds the worst of them all. I know it's bad because I've heard my dad say some of those same words to my mom. I feel alone, sad, and can't believe this is happening on my birthday. I mean what is really going on? Seriously, can someone please explain to me why this is happening? Isn't today supposed to be a special day? Where is my cake and ice cream? Where are my presents? No one sang 'Happy Birthday' to me. Where is the love? Doesn't anyone know I exist?

One word in particular stuck in my head for many years to come. Liar. I will never forget my mom actually thought I had lied to her. I know right from wrong; at least I thought I did. I'd been taught to never lie about anything. If you lie, you will go to hell. Grandma Maria had always told me that. She said hell is a very bad place, and I never wanted to go there, and lying was the guaranteed route to hell. I was terrified of the thought of ever ending up there.

I did not lie about my daddy play-touching me. I guess someone else had accused him of it as well. That day was the start of the birthday curse.

Later that night after finally being released from my bedroom, my dad was still not home. I later learned that he was going to be away for a while. All I knew then was my mom was so sad, she cried all the time, and she never looked at me the same. I always felt she blamed me for whatever was going on between her and my dad. It was all my fault. She hated me. I'm sorry I hurt her. I loved her so much, and I still loved my dad too.

Six Years Later

May 15

Today I am a teenager. We were awakened by this pounding on the door. Bam! Bam! Bam! "Open the door, Lil Bit. I love you. I'm sorry. I promise I will never hurt you again. Please let me in! I know you're in there. I checked with the front desk. You should have changed your name. I knew I'd find you. You can't run or hide from me." Bam! Bam! Bam!

I was frightened. My body froze, and the tears falling from my eyes blurred my vision. My heart was beating out of my chest. We had been found once again. No place was safe. *We will never be free from him until he kills her*, I thought.

Lil Bit is my mom's new pet name by the new maniac lover in her life. Mr. Bruce is what I call him. Mr. Bruce is six foot five, light skinned, good-looking, and a smooth talker. He is intelligent and has a cunning personality and a temper that would scare the socks off you. This was hard to do, knowing my family. I come from a family of seven aunts, and it isn't easy to frighten any of them, as they are some pretty tough girls who can hold their own. Mr. Bruce was once a professional football player, but early in his career he suffered a knee injury and never fully recovered. I could blame his crazy temper on that, but that would make things too easy, so I won't.

I have no idea how my mom or Dallas felt about this entire mess carrying on outside our motel door, but I was horrified. I was scared and angry at the same time, wondering if my mom was going to be weak as usual and give into his demands. She made us live in this stupid motel for the past week, in hiding, right before the most important birthday of my life. I mean really, turning thirteen is like getting married. This is an important day for me. Surely Mom wouldn't let this crazy, no-good creep in our room so we can watch him beat the living daylights out of her again.

Mom was sitting on the other bed, frightened and confused. Dallas and I were sitting quietly on the second bed in the room, furthest from the door. I could see Mr. Bruce's demands were wearing her down. She tried to ignore him at first, but she knew just how crazy he was, so she finally screamed for him to go away and leave us alone. This ignited a fuse in the psychopath, as this made him beat on the door even harder. He yelled louder and louder until my mother finally opened the door. My mom of course was pleading and begging him not to beat the crap out of her, at least not today, because today was my birthday. She knew how sensitive I was about my birthdays.

She pleaded with fear. Her bruised body and blackened left eye were still trying to heal from just days before, which had caused us to flee and landed us in this motel in the first place. At least now we could afford a motel room. Before, we'd be homeless on the streets, wondering where we would go, especially when the shelters were full. Once after Mr. Bruce beat her, we ran through a dark alley. I had no shoes on, and we walked the cold, dark streets with nowhere to go. A nice woman noticed and asked to help us. Of course my mom, with embarrassment, said, "No thank you, we're fine." It was obvious that a black woman beaten with a swollen face and ripped clothes, walking down a dark street at after midnight, with two small children and one with no shoes, was not really all right. The nice lady insisted we go home with her. She fed us and gave us warm, cozy shelter for the night. I will never forget how safe I felt in a stranger's home. She was so nice. She fed us and provided us with a warm bed to sleep that night. We never saw her again after that night. Mom didn't take too well to folks helping us, but she surrendered that night, and I was glad she did. I needed to feel safe.

Mr. Bruce was looking crazy and deranged, his normal everyday appearance. He stared at me, then at Dallas, and then at my mom. He told my mom to leave with him, as they needed to talk. My mom looked at Dallas and me with fear and shame. She put her head down and then left with him. I'm sure she thought she was doing the right thing, to assure me my birthday wouldn't be like all the others. She promised to return soon and said we would make the best of my special day later. I knew we had until midnight, just like Cinderella. It was only three in the afternoon. As I watched her leave, all I could think about was this might be the last time I would see my mom alive. I thought to myself, *Happy birthday to me. Some things never change.*

Dallas, as usual, is all I have. We have become each other's rock during these terrible times. Mr. Bruce is a mean man. He breaks furniture, yells, and hits my mother almost every day and night. I remember, before my mom left our father, he would only beat her during the weary hours of the night, when he thought we were asleep. He hardly ever touched her during the daylight hours. But not Mr. Bruce. He beats our mom morning, noon, and night. He has no time preference. He is so mean. He beats my mother in front of us all the time, and he doesn't care. He loves an audience. He is so scary. He dares anyone or anything to try and stop him. He is crazy for real, and he hurts my mom bad, very bad.

My mom has a serious heart condition. She was born with it. I never quite understood the severity of her condition as a child, but I knew she could die at any minute, and everyone was always so careful around her, and the entire family worried about her all the time. I learned it could have been corrected at an early age, but Mom said Grandma Maria was very religious and didn't trust the doctors with anything as serious as open-heart surgery. She felt that God and prayer could heal anything, and doctors and surgery were not the answer. I think Grandma Maria was afraid my mom wouldn't survive the surgery. Back then, technology wasn't like it is now. Grandma Maria was a nurse, and she didn't trust the medical doctors. My mom was the first born out of nine children, seven girls and two boys. My mom has suffered with this condition all her life. As a little girl, she couldn't participate in gym or do any physical activities other children were allowed to do. She was isolated and treated differently because of her condition. She missed out on a lot of normal childhood fun because everyone always thought she would die any moment. She was even told she could never have children because she would die going through childbirth.

Mr. Bruce is very aware of her condition. However, crazy man could care less. He has no sympathy for her. He is convinced mom made up her illness as her mercy cry so he won't hit her so hard or beat her so bad. He continues to use her like she is his personal punching bag. He is a sick man; he somehow finds pleasure in her pain. He towers over my mom. He weighs at least 270 pounds, all solid muscle. My mom is this tiny, petite 115-pound woman, only four foot nine.

The rumor in the family is Mr. Bruce first dated one of my mom's sisters before he became sweet on her. After living through another family secret and the shame of Mom being the center of another bad family rumor, I realized my mom had nothing to be proud of. If the rumor is true, she definitely ended up with the short end of the stick.

Let me tell you how Dallas and I first met Mr. Bruce. Mom abandoned Dallas and me for almost three months. One summer afternoon, she dropped us off at Grandma Maria's for what was originally supposed to be an overnight stay. Almost three months later, she shows up in this seventies van with a new man. It was pathetic. They were both wearing Dashikis, looking like they just came back from Woodstock, bodies reeking from the smell of marijuana. When they pulled up, they were happy-go-lucky, as if she'd just dropped us off. They wanted to show us the van. When they opened the back doors, we saw what looked like a small living area, all retro with a mattress on the floor. It looked as if they lived in this van permanently.

Dallas and I were forced to accept being deserted by our mom who suddenly shows up with no remorse and at the same time makes us accept her new relationship. We had no idea who this man was and why she pretended to be so happy and free with him. She started telling us about their travels and immediately pulled out pictures. She didn't care about what Dallas and I had to endure listening to, the family gossip and rumors of how much of a whore our no-good mom was the past few months.

She left us with Grandma Maria with no money, no food, no change of clothes, and no word if she was dead or alive. No phone calls, not even a letter. Grandma Maria had no way of contacting her if anything happened to one of us. My mom had really abandoned us, and during that time, we felt helpless, ashamed, embarrassed, confused, and most of all unwanted. Our family was hard on us. They'd already treated us like outsiders. They've never treated us like the rest of the kids. It's like my mom is the black sheep in the family, so they treat us like they treat her. All this didn't matter now, because she had returned, and off we were in just a few hours. She loaded me and Dallas in the back of the van like cargo, and off we went to who knows where.

I see my mother with five stitches over her left eye, two cracked ribs, and black and blue bruises all over her once beautiful petite body. This relationship didn't turn out to be as glamorous as Mr. Bruce wooed her into believing it would be.

After we watched our battered, helpless mom leave with him once again, not knowing if we'd ever see her again, Dallas and I left the room and went on a walk. He knew I found solitude in parks and how much I enjoyed listening to nature and walking around in the beauty of God's creation. I love the peace of parks—the nature of tall trees, the sound of creeks and streams of water flowing, soaking up the sun, and breathing in the air. It always comforts my spirit and my soul. No one appreciates Mother Nature more than I do. Being one with nature, I feel safe. It is the only time I feel peace and hope.

Dallas and I love going on long walks together. We explore every inch of grass, paths, ponds, whatever there is to enjoy. There was a beautiful park next door to the motel. It was large, and we had never been to this park before. Dallas wanted to make my birthday special, so he convinced me, without having to twist my arm too hard, to take a walk and explore. The park was beautiful and amazing. We walked across a brook of running water; it was very peaceful. One of my favorite things to do is to make a wish and watch the reflection of my hopes fade away into fairyland. I believe all bodies of water are real wishing wells. Dallas reached in his pocket and pulled out a penny. He handed it to me and said, "Happy birthday, Star. Make your wish." I sat on the edge of the bank for a minute, embracing the sound of water as it flowed over the rocks in the tiny brook. I was thinking of the perfect birthday, how special it would be. How memorable it would be, and how loving it would be. Then I wished for it to come true someday as I tossed the penny into the water.

I looked at Dallas and hoped that someday we would have better lives and that we wouldn't have to live in fear another day. I prayed for the safety of our mom and hoped she wouldn't die today. I also prayed that someday I would have a birthday that would not be cursed. I thanked God and was glad I at least had my little brother, Dallas, and promised I would take care of him and always keep him safe.

We grow closer with every trail, even more when our mother lets us down at times like this—when she neglects our needs, which she does often, especially when a man is involved. We have a hard time understanding it all.

One Year Later

May 15

Unfortunately, Mom is still with crazy man Mr. Bruce. I have no idea why she's stayed with him. I can't figure out why she hasn't left him yet. The abuse has gotten worse. I mean this man is so treacherous he started beating her in restaurants, in the middle of traffic in the car while driving home at stoplights, in front of her coworkers, neighbors, her fellow classmates, and professors at the local university she is attending, seeking her bachelor's degree. Mr. Bruce is the craziest man I have ever met in my life. Fear is one reason I'm sure my mom has stayed. She is scared to death of him. He will surely kill her one day. I just know it. It is only a matter of time.

Anyway, today is my fourteenth birthday, and so far, it is going better than last year's. So many things have happened, so many things. We now live up north. Uncle Danny and Aunt Krissy live here. I love our new city. It is colder in the winters than any place I have ever lived, but the summers are my favorite. It is beautiful in the summer. The air is fresh, tall trees have dark green leaves, and the streets are filled with busy traffic. Lakes almost everywhere you go, and beaches of soft sand with clear, blue water. And the parks are peaceful and monumental to me. I now have plenty of safe places to escape the madness.

The phone rang. It was my dad. Mom and Dad divorced when I was eleven years old. He never forgets our birthdays though. Whenever we've had a phone, he's called. I picked up the phone, and my dad said, "Happy birthday, Star."

I said proudly, "Thank you, Dad." He asked how I was doing, and I said I was fine. He asked what I was going to do on my special day, and I said I had no special plans. I have learned to not expect anything special on birthdays; it is just another day. The birthday curse was yet to be broken, so why bother to make plans?

Then he had asked me the weirdest question. I couldn't quite figure out why he would ask me such a thing. He said, "Your mom tells me that you got your period."

I said, "Yes, I did, exactly thirty days ago."

He said, "Well, are you on the pill? You know you're supposed to be visiting this summer."

The phone dropped from my hand. My mom saw me drop the receiver and ran over to pick it up, wondering what the heck my dad had just said and why I was just standing there in shock, staring into space. I could faintly hear my dad calling me from the receiver, "Star, Star, can you hear me? What happened? Hello? Hello!"

Suddenly, it all came back to me, just as clear as day, everything, every waking moment of sleepless nights. All the poking and scratching at my innocence, all the Vaseline, and my small mouth being forced to open wider and wider against my will, to stretch over and suck this ugly part of his body in between his legs that smelled awful as he would force my head down further, as I gagged, choked, and cried and begged him not to make me do it, but he would never let me stop. All the nights he made me watch him and Mom do it so that I could understand how he really wanted me to do it with him. The many times he'd set the scene just right. I knew exactly when to sneak out of my bed and tiptoe down the hallway to get to my parents' bedroom. He kept their bedroom door cracked open just right, purposely, so I could peek in the very spot we had rehearsed just hours before. Many times, I knew my mother could feel me outside her bedroom door, listening and watching. I listened to the same moaning and groaning I had heard in the movies Dad used to make me watch with him. I watched and thought, *Who in the world would want to do something that hurts so bad?* It looked painful and no fun at all. I had no idea why it was so important to my dad to teach me how to do this awful act.

Once, I swore my mom's eyes had met mine, between the crack of the door. I was so scared she would get up and yell at me and that I was in big trouble. I stepped back, frightened, just waiting for the wrath, but seconds later, nothing had happened. I continued to follow my dad's orders and crept back to the cracked-open door. I realized that if she did see me, she pretended she didn't, and I did the same.

I knew deep down in my heart that Mom always knew the truth, but she never wanted to admit it herself, so we all continued to live in denial. Our family secret remained safe.

After Mom and Dad divorced, I was no longer the innocent little girl that didn't understand how wrong this was. I had grown old enough to know what was happening. I hated my dad for doing it to me. It made me feel different and wrong. It made me feel ugly, and I felt evil, and I knew God would never forgive me, now that I knew the truth. Even though I knew it was wrong, it was hard if I was alone with my dad to not allow him to touch me. It was weird; I felt paralyzed and helpless. It controlled me; I felt like he had a spell on me. I felt trapped. I realized he stole my innocence, something I would never get back. What would people think of me if they found out? I felt ashamed, embarrassed, and very sad. I started to withdraw from people. I had no one to talk to about this.

Mom continued to live in denial, and she never wanted to discuss the problem. She ignored all the signs of physical abuse. I'm sure I had all the signs of an abused kid. I knew Mom knew. But once again, this was how things were.

I'm getting older, and I'm a young woman now and no longer a naïve little girl.

After I dropped the phone, I realized all the long walks in the park didn't quite erase the bad memories I'd hoped they would. Nor did it stop the nightmares I continued to have night after night, expecting the boogieman to sneak into my bedroom, wake me up, and violate me until the weary hours of the morning. When my dad asked if I was on the pill, he opened wounds I thought I had successfully buried and covered up. Unfortunately, it was still very real. He still violated me when Dallas and I visited him on summer breaks. Now he wanted me to get on the pill so he wouldn't get me pregnant. Seriously?

The only way I've known how to cope with my dad's abuse is to convince myself it was all a dream, and it really never happened, but at that moment, I was reawakened. The nightmare was real, and I began to hate him, more and more, for messing up my life. He was the reason why my mom treated me like I was nothing and blamed me. She could have stopped the madness years ago, when she knew I was telling the truth. However, she chose, for some reason I will never understand, not to protect me.

I never got back on the phone. I knew from that moment on I was alone once again, and I could never tell anyone how it all makes me feel. I can't talk about what's happening to me; no one would believe me anyway. They have all conveniently convinced themselves that I am a liar so that they can pacify their own misery without having to be held accountable for mine. Getting older just makes me have to live with my demons longer, and it's starting to hurt worse. I feel weak, hopeless, scared, ashamed, embarrassed, ugly, and nasty. I don't want to live another day with this shame.

The room was filled with silence for a moment. Then there was a small sigh, and Marissa said, "Wow, poor Star. I can't imagine her life. It is just so sad. Was Star suicidal when you guys were friends?"

I said, "Yes and no. Star was starting to show signs of sadness and felt lonely most of the time, even with me. I could tell the relationship with her mom was taking a toll on her loving spirit and she was sad a lot, but I didn't know much about suicide, we were just kids. I was only fifteen. In some of her lowest moments, I worried about her. Wasn't much I could do, but I know I wouldn't have ever wanted her to do anything to hurt herself. She never talked to me about suicide, other than saying she had thoughts of dying young. She never thought she would live past her teens. Other than this, Star was just always so positive. Always."

Marissa said, "Star got a break when she was younger, right? I remember reading somewhere Star's mom owned her own business once. Can you tell me about that?"

I said, "Oh yes! Star said when she was fourteen, her mom and Mr. Bruce opened their own business, and it was very successful. Star calls that time of her life going from rags to riches. She said she identified with Cinderella."

Chapter 3

Star and I would go to her favorite place, and she would tell me stories about her life. We would ride our bikes to the local park across town and lay a small blanket under a tree for shade and sip on our pop and eat sunflower seeds. Star loved sunflower seeds. She'd been eating them since she was seven years old. She said her mom used to spank her for sneaking into her bag of sunflower seeds when she left it out on the kitchen counter. As we cracked the shells inside our mouths and spit them out just to get to the tiny little seeds inside, Star talked about the time when she moved from Atlanta to Wisconsin.

"Ally, one of my favorites parks was in Madison, Wisconsin. My mom and Mr. Bruce moved us there in the late sixties. I loved how large this park was. It was one of my favorite places to escape, and I always felt safe there. During the summers, the park district offered free lunches for low-income families. We also could participate in the summer and after-school programs. I loved these programs. They had summer counselors who encouraged children who were poverty stricken like Dallas and me. They gave children like us hope. Dallas as usual was very understanding about the long hours I made him spend at the park with me. He had to stay because I was the oldest and watched over him, and I couldn't let him out of my sight. I never wanted to go home and would stay for hours, just sitting and watching Dallas play with his friends and eating my sunflower seeds.

"One day I noticed this squirrel hanging around, checking out the empty shells I'd spit out. I watched as it searched through my shells for any leftover seeds. One day I decided to share my seeds with the squirrel, and it would crack the shells open right along with me. Another day, I built up enough courage to place a few seeds in the palm of my hand,

and it hopped close enough to pick the sunflower seeds right out of my hand. I was amazed. I thought I was so special. I felt so in touch with animals and the earth. This was the only way I could explain such a thing. The squirrel and I would eat our sunflower seeds together while I looked into its tiny little eyes and spoke. I was convinced my furry friend knew exactly what I was saying. One day I showed up at our favorite spot and waited hours for my little friend, and he never showed up. I felt sad and alone again. I kept coming back day after day, hoping he would show up, but he never did. I remember feeling like I had lost my best friend. I missed my furry companion.

"I spent a lot of time at libraries. Public libraries were our free babysitter. My mom couldn't afford childcare, so we were instructed to go the library every day after school. Dallas and I were given strict orders to always follow the rules of the library so that the staff wouldn't catch on to our scam, and to take full advantage of its resources. We did exactly that. I loved reading. It was the best way for me to escape into the many worlds of make-believe. I would connect with an author and read all their books.

I read all the Agatha Christie's series, lots of science-fiction novels, *Nancy Drew* and the *Hardy Boys* series, and the *Wizard of Oz* series. My curiosity wanted to know everything there was to know about every story I read. If it had a continuation, I was hooked. I read Alfred Hitchcock's series and anything having to do with vampires and westerns. Then I graduated to romance novels. I was a dreamer, and romance novels were like fairy tales. They made me feel there was hope for love, even though I knew it could never come true in my life. It felt good dreaming about it. I always felt there had to be something good and remarkable in the universe that would someday make room for me and allow me to experience a little piece of happiness. I didn't ask for much. I just wanted whatever I could get. I believed in the Cinderella story. I always believed it was possible to go from rags to riches.

"A poor little ugly girl trapped in a world of misery and wanting someone to notice me, I desperately wanted to be rescued from my evil mother. I saw nothing wrong with dreaming of a prince charming. I'd get all choked up inside just thinking about the possibility of being loved and wanted in that way.

"We really struggled horribly financially after my mom and dad divorced. We were always hungry. Dallas and I would have to find ways to eat other than the most dependable meal of the day, which was our school lunch. We never knew what to expect for dinner, because if Mom was dating, she always had this thing about making sure her men ate well, and if there was any food left, Dallas and I could eat afterward. We were treated like dogs; we got the leftover scraps.

"Mom always put her men's needs before ours. I guess this was her way of making them feel loved, special, superior, and important. I never quite understood it, because none of them were worth putting before her children. That's just the way things were. Over the years, Dallas and I learned to be creative. When Dallas and I walked back and forth from the library, we would hunt for food. We scoped out people's backyards for gardens. If we saw a garden, we would sneak into their backyards and steal tomatoes, rhubarb, radishes, lettuce, whatever we could find. We weren't picky. Food was food, bugs included. We just looked at it as extra protein.

"We spotted apple, peach, and plum trees. Even crabapple trees weren't off-limits. We ate blueberries, raspberries, strawberries, and lots of blackberries. I loved any berry. They were my favorite. We climbed over hundreds of fences, broke into backyard gates, climbed many trees, and would literally clean them out. I bet these people probably thought they had rabbits or something destroying their gardens, and it was just two little starving siblings trying to survive.

"This was our only means of survival. We'd learned after our parents divorced that if we wanted to live, we had to do whatever was necessary to survive. Our mom took care of herself and whatever man she was dating. We always knew where her loyalty was if she had to choose.

"When we moved to Madison, we had no place to live, so we lived in the love van for what felt like eternity. Uncle Danny lived here. Eventually, we stayed with him and Aunt Krissy a couple weeks. They had just gotten married, and Mom wasn't allowed to bring Mr. Bruce with us. He continued to sleep in the love van. Mr. Bruce and Mom were both working odd jobs here and there. They finally saved up enough money to get us a place to call home. Our place was an apartment-type dwelling called a duplex. We lived on the upper level, and our neighbors lived on the bottom.

"Mom enrolled Dallas and me into our new elementary school. This school was awesome, because no one failed or was held back due to learning abilities. Every child was special and unique and received individual, personal attention. The school was split up in three sections, A, B, and C. The sections were based on how we receive information intellectually. Before registering and attending classes, each student took an assessment test. How you scored on the test would determine what section you would most be successful in as a student. Every student still had lunch and recess together, and the sections didn't segregate us, not like most would think. As kids, each section still treated the other sections the same. The school was also set up like high school. We changed classes and teachers every hour. We were the first pilot kids to attend this unique school. I loved going here; it is so far the best school I've attended.

"Mr. Bruce loved the finer things in life. He never wanted to be poor. His perseverance and my mother's determination is how they were able to open their own cleaning service. They started out small. They would clean dorm rooms during the off-season and small local businesses and restaurants. Mr. Bruce was a smooth talker, and it helped he was very handsome and charming. He was very persuasive and influential. He wasn't a lazy man at all. He believed if you worked hard, it would someday pay off, and he was right. It finally did.

"The name of the business was Cha-Ching Enterprises. I couldn't believe we were actually business owners. Mom and Mr. Bruce had a plan and executed the American dream of owning their own business. Cha-Ching Enterprises was a success. In spite of the crazy love-hate relationship, they were the dynamic duo when it came to the business. They were perfect partners.

"Mr. Bruce may have been the worst boyfriend my mom ever brought home, but he was the smartest, hardest-working, most intelligent individual I had ever known. Once Cha-Ching Enterprises was born, he was determined to raise it to its maturity. The first paid employees were Dallas and I of course. We worked for free in the beginning. We had to get up every morning at two and go to stores, restaurants, and office buildings and help clean. We did exactly what we were told without hesitation, even on school nights. We were still scared to death of Mr. Bruce. He had started threatening and hitting now, because once we made the mistake of trying to be brave and got in between Mom and Mr. Bruce as he was pulling back to give her another blow to the head. This pissed him off so bad that he came after us and started hitting, threatening us if we got in his way. We were terrified of him hurting us, but when it came to Mom, we took our chances.

"The business was booming, and Mr. Bruce started paying us thirty-five dollars a week. Dallas and I thought we were rich. Mr. Bruce told us if we found any money while we were cleaning that we could keep it. We found so much money that we started looking forward to waking up early mornings to go to work.

"One of our favorite places to find money was at this Italian restaurant. We would find hundreds and fifty-dollar bills tucked between the creases in the seats of each booth. We thought a lot of rich people must eat here to find this type of cash lost in and under seats. The owners were so nice they told Mr. Bruce and Mom that we could help ourselves to anything we wanted in their industrial-size kitchen as long as we cleaned up after ourselves.

"This was music to our hungry ears. Dallas and I ate whatever we could get our hands on. It had by far become one of our favorite places to clean. Word had spread of how good Cha-Ching Enterprises was, and it quickly grew from a small family crew of four to over a dozen paid employees. We had so many contracts and not enough bodies to keep up with the work. Mom and Mr. Bruce had no choice but to employ people to help keep the business growing.

"They had contracts with Zale's jewelry stores and another all-time favorite, Toys 'R' Us. We thought we had died and gone to heaven. I used to run up and down the aisles and play with all the toys that weren't packaged up. It was magical. We had finally arrived. There was still one thing missing. Success came with a price, a price I wasn't so sure was worth the phony image it hid behind.

"The business was stable and successful. We moved to a nicer part of town. It was very sophisticated and clean, with large homes, the kind of houses like those we used to steal food from a little more than a year ago. Our new home was located an upper-middle class neighborhood. Mr. Bruce knew how to communicate and talk to people. He spoke how white folks would call proper. We were the only blacks in the neighborhood. White people accepted us and gave us no problems because they loved Mr. Bruce. His charm made them feel comfortable, and he had them eating right out of the palm of his hands.

We had a beautiful, two-story brick home. We bought all new furniture. It was all top of the line, all the best brand names like Ethan

Allen. We had never lived like this before. It was like a dream come true. Mom bought her first brand-new car. We all had new clothes and shoes, and Dallas and I had our own bedrooms for the first time. We were rich! We actually had a lot of money. Mr. Bruce was so talented that he custom-built my mom's bedroom furniture. He couldn't find one at the store that fit his special taste, so he decided to build it himself. That could've been another business; he was very good at it. It looked like it came from a high-end store. It was the nicest bedroom set I had ever seen. He was so proud. He knew it was awesome, and my mom was happy. She felt special because no one had one like it.

"For the first time in years, we actually had a real life. We were normal, like other people. I had my own room with a record player, TV, clock radio, stuffed animals, and every toy I had ever dreamed of having. I had clean sheets, real pillows, hardwood floors, a closet full of clothes, teenage jewelry, games, everything a child could ever want and more. Dallas had everything too, and our friends envied our new lifestyle. We owned our own business, and our family was known in the community for having its act together, and it felt good. People noticed us. They spoke to us and respected us.

"Dallas and I got to do things that were fun. We learned how to swim at the local YMCA. Mom and Mr. Bruce would take us to museums and historical places in and out of state. We traveled to national parks and amusement parks and beach sites and lakes to picnic and fish. Mom and Mr. Bruce mingled with some people who had more than us, and we were their guests on big boats that looked like houses. We went to fancy dinner parties with other families with larger homes that looked like mansions. I dreamed that we would someday be just like them.

"Once we went camping in Canada, in a real log cabin. It was just like in the movies. It was way cool. We rented a boat and fished on Lake Erie. We had so much money; we didn't feel the financial strain we used to feel when Mom was a single parent. We loved to live and lived to love, not having to worry about the little things anymore.

"We went to the movies every Saturday and went out to eat every Sunday. We shopped a lot. Dallas and I were allowed to catch the bus uptown and downtown to buy stuff on our wish lists. Our money would burn holes in our anxious little pockets. We had so many choices and didn't quite know what to do with all that money.

"Our weekly allowance had gone from thirty-five dollars a week to eighty, and sometimes we got one-hundred-dollar bills. We had more money in our pockets than we could spend. This kind of money given to teenagers made us feel like we were millionaires. For the first time in our lives, we didn't want what we couldn't have, and we didn't need what we couldn't get. I never wanted it to end. We had prestige. We were the coolest family on the block.

"Whenever we went out to eat, it was at the finest restaurants, most of them owned by our clients, and therefore we were treated like royalty. When we entered these places, people would pay attention to the nice-looking, well-dressed black family. Whatever we wanted, it was at our beck and call. Most of the time, we wouldn't even get billed.

"We ate well. Mr. Bruce loved teaching us about a culture of people who have money. He wanted us to learn the difference between soul food and gourmet food. We ate food like jumbo shrimp, lobster tail, crab legs, raw oysters, prime rib, salmon, and filet mignon. Mr. Bruce soaked up the celebrity treatment, and it fed his already overinflated ego.

"It didn't take long to adapt to this style of living. It felt so good. I'd forgotten just how poor we once were. I felt like this was how I was meant to live. It all came so naturally to me. I couldn't get enough of the great food and the shopping. I was hooked for life. I had learned to appreciate having nice things and living well.

"Cha-Ching Enterprises had become had become a part of the city. People knew us. The city started to bus poor kids to the rich schools and rich kids to poor schools to mix up the segregated communities. Mom and Mr. Bruce didn't approve of the school Dallas and I ended up having to attend, so they used their influence to convince the school district to let us attend the elite school. They were upset that we finally had a chance to attend a rich school and they wanted to bus us to the poor school. They decided we would catch the metro all the way across town, every morning, to attend the better school. They wanted us to experience the best schools. We had never been to nice schools that only rich kids attended. I was a freshman in high school, and Dallas was attending middle school.

The two schools we attended were separated by a football field. This worked out great, because if either one of us needed the other, we were only a field away. We loved being that close. Having our schools right next to each other meant we could catch the same buses back and forth to school. We loved it. We loved feeling extra special because our parents refused to give in o the new bussing system. This allowed us to be even more independent than we already were.

Mom was attending the local university, trying to earn her bachelor's degree. Mr. Bruce was a very jealous man and didn't like Mom doing anything outside of the business, especially since he couldn't keep his eye on her. The more independent Mom would try to become, the worse he would beat her. Mom hid most of her bruises by wearing long sleeves and pants, even on hot summer days. She would never go out in public until her visible wounds like a blackened eye or a busted lip would heal so that no one would notice. She wore sunglasses a lot when she had to go out during these moments.

"One evening, Mr. Bruce returned home without her, and I was scared he had killed her and didn't tell us. He was acting weirder than usual, and he was nervous. He couldn't sit still. He kept pacing the floor. We were afraid to ask him where Mom was. He was that intimidating. We feared what his answer might be. Hours passed before our mom finally came home. It was after midnight. Mr. Bruce had retired to their bedroom and fallen asleep. We heard a strange vehicle pull up outside our home. Dallas, and I ran to the front door and opened it, we watched our mom get out of a cab all bandaged up. She could hardly walk and had this terrifying look on her face of shock and confusion. I will never forget the sadness I saw in her eyes, of fear and shame. That's when she told us what happened.

"Mr. Bruce had gotten so angry with her and told her to get out of the van, and when she refused, he managed to open her side of the passenger door and push her out. She said he didn't slow down, and sped off and left her to die." For the life of me, I couldn't understand why she just wouldn't leave Mr. Bruce. Cha-Ching Enterprises was registered in her name. *We can leave him, and we'll be fine,* I thought. If it were only that easy.

"I had no idea how long she would be able to survive these vicious attacks. I'm sure my mom must have felt the same fear. I think one of the reasons she stayed was because we had money now and a very successful business, and we were supposed to be happy. She didn't want to take this away from us. She was afraid of Mr. Bruce. She had tried to leave several times before, and he'd find us, and when she returned, things would continue to get worse. We all lived in fear every day.

"I hated living like that. From the outside, things looked great, but behind closed doors, our life was a living hell. I remember trying to run away once. I got frightened and returned home after it got dark because I felt no one had even noticed I was gone. I had always wondered if I had stayed out a few hours longer or maybe even slept in the park overnight, would they have tried to find me? Now, I would never know. That evening everyone was in their individual worlds as I watched them all around me and no one cared enough to ask where I had been?" I hated living this way, and I wanted out. I wanted to escape forever. I decided I'd rather starve than live like this one more day; it was the worst life ever.

"One day I had the courage to beg my mom to please leave Mr. Bruce. I was sure he was going to kill her and I would have to witness her death. I knew this would destroy me, and I couldn't live with the guilt if she died. She would always get upset if I dared to share any of my childlike wisdom with her. It had always been this way. Ever since I told her what Daddy had done, she would purposely ignore me, as if I wasn't even talking to her. I tried to explain to her that I was convinced Mr. Bruce would kill her if she didn't leave. I was so terrified of this happening that I couldn't sleep at night. The fear and anxiety kept me up every night, listening to her cry and scream and yell for him to stop beating her. The more she cried, the longer he'd beat her. Mr. Bruce was the devil; he had no soul.

"His eyes were bloodshot red. His temper was out of control, and he walked around the house with rage and pitiful pride. He had this sinister smile on his face as if nothing was wrong. He was pure evil. Now that Mom was attending classes, trying to do something more with her life, he used that as an excuse to accuse her of cheating on him.

"One day, out of nowhere, like all the other times, things would be going fine, and next thing we'd hear something break, and that was all she wrote. However, this time was a bit different. Mr. Bruce was angrier than usual. He went around the house breaking everything made of glass he could find. He destroyed our glass coffee table, the matching end tables, our glass dining table, and even the glass doors to the new stereo system. He was really pissed. Then he went after my mom with vengeance and rage like never before. My mom actually ran for the first time. She was scared. He ran after her, which made Dallas and I run after him.

"He started beating her like never before. He grabbed our mom and threw her across the room. We saw her fragile body fly in midair, right in front of us, like some ragdoll. She landed against the wall, and he continued taking out his anger on her. He hit my mom so hard that blood was flying everywhere. Dallas and I were trying to stop him. We jumped on his back and started hitting him as hard as we could, begging him to leave her alone. He stood up like the Hulk, with us still hanging on his back, and slung us across the room and kept on beating her.

"She was scared to death. She looked at us as if she wished we were strong enough to protect her from the beast, but we weren't. She was in and out of consciousness, and each time she was unresponsive, we'd scream and beg her to open her eyes. Mr. Bruce was so angry we tried to save her that he turned around and chased us out of the house. He was hitting us as we ran as fast as we could to get away from him. He chased us out the backdoor, and he was still behind us, when we had nowhere else to go but to jump the wooden fence. We were terrified. I remember hurting my arm really bad when I jumped that eight-foot fence; I was terrified he was going to kill all of us.

"Dallas and I came back from around the fence and quietly snuck back in the house so we could try again to save our mom. I was able to get to the phone on the kitchen wall and picked it up to dial 911. Mr. Bruce must have sensed my next move. Before I could finish dialing the numbers, he yanked the phone out of my hand and off the wall, and then he hit me across my face with the phone and I fell to the floor. He told me he'd kill me if I ever tried that again. Dallas was frozen in shock. He couldn't move. He just couldn't move. Tears were falling from his face. I couldn't save him.

"Mom had managed to regain consciousness enough to try to get up and run for her life, but Mr. Bruce saw her out of the corner of his eye and ran after her. She ran downstairs to the basement. I'm not sure where she thought she'd go from there, unless she was looking for somewhere to hide. He caught up with her and decided he was going to kill her for sure this time. I could feel it. This time was different. His rage was different, his anger was different, and the look in his eyes was different.

"He was beating on her so bad, and we couldn't stop him. He kept throwing her limp, weak, battered body up against the concrete walls in the basement, and she'd look at us with this hopeless cry and apologetic look of sadness. It was like she was sorry we had to watch her die this way. We felt helpless; all we could do was sit there and beg Mr. Bruce to stop and leave our mom alone.

"Mr. Bruce got even more upset that we were watching and crying and screaming for him to stop. He couldn't take our cries any longer, and he stopped beating our mother and turned around again and ran after us. He chased us back up the stairs and threatened that if we came back down he would do the same thing to us. We believed him. We were terrified. We wanted to run for help but didn't want to leave our mom.

"One minute we heard our mom crying and fighting for her life, and the next it was complete silence. The silence lasted way too long. Next we heard Mr. Bruce running up the stairs. We quickly ran and hid in the guest room closet. We knew he was coming to finish us off too. We heard him rumbling through some things, and then he ran out of the house, got into his car, and sped off.

"I will never forget that moment. I realized I may not have had the best mom in the world, but she was still the only mother I had, and I needed her, and I didn't want her to die, not like this. I remember finally having enough nerve to walk down the stairs to confirm she was dead. I told Dallas to stay upstairs. I got to the bottom of the stair, there was blood spattered everywhere. I knew it wasn't Mr. Bruce's. He didn't have a scratch on him, and I knew it was my mom's blood. I saw her lifeless body curled up like a frightened infant, and it was a horrible sight.

"I couldn't tell if she was breathing. Her face looked like someone had smashed it in with a baseball bat. I yelled upstairs for Dallas to go get Uncle Danny, who lived a couple miles down the street. I told him to hurry. 'Run as fast as you can.' Dallas did as he was instructed, as I heard him run out the front door. By now, I realized she was breathing but still unconscious. I held my mom's limp body in my arms, lying on the cold cement basement floor. I was crying and yelling at her to please open her eyes, begging her to respond. It took what seemed like forever, but she finally opened the one eye that wasn't as swollen as the other. She looked at me with her right eye and immediately started wept from relief that she had once again survived. I think a part of her wished she hadn't. But what would have happened to Dallas and me if she had died?

"It was hard getting her to her feet. I yelled at her to get up. 'We have to leave now! Come on, Mom! Get up! I have to get you out of here! Now! Right now!' I kept yelling and crying. Mom kept saying, 'But what about our lives, our money, our home, and the business?' I said, 'What about your life? That's all that matters right now, Mom! Your life! We don't care about the rest. Let's go!'

"I used all my strength to encourage her to help me move her wounded body up the stairs and out of this house before Mr. Bruce came back. He always came back. I held my mother's limp, fragile body against mine as we slowly made our way to safety. I remember thinking, as I was helping my mom, that it took almost losing her life to finally get her to walk away from what we and others thought was the good life. A life, even with financial stability, wasn't any better than when we had nothing. My mom was a battered woman living in fear and was afraid to leave. It was the best life she had ever provided Dallas and me, and she was willing to die to keep from having to take this so-called wonderful life away from us.

"Uncle Danny arrived in a matter of minutes with Dallas in the car. He helped his sister into his vehicle and took us to his home. We felt safe. Uncle Danny and Aunt Krissy owned their home, and Aunt Krissy had just given birth to their first son, just a few months ago. Uncle Danny was so angry at what Mr. Bruce had done to his sister that he wanted to kill him. But Mom and Aunt Krissy begged him not too. They didn't want Uncle Danny to go to jail and leave his new family. We didn't stay at Uncle Danny's house long. He gave Mom enough money for us to catch the train to our next destination. We never returned to our home. Uncle Danny thought it would be best to leave everything behind. Therefore, mom left everything. When we boarded the train, we had nothing more than the clothes on our backs, we left everything behind and never looked back."

Chapter 4

Jessie finished my makeup, and it was flawless. I felt beautiful. I couldn't wait to see what Scotty had picked out for me to wear. Right then, Scotty rolled in the wardrobe cart. My eyes lit up like a Christmas tree, as the items on the cart were fabulous! Scotty said, "Ms. Knight, I hope you like your selections. I hope they are your taste and you're satisfied."

I said, "Scotty, you really know your stuff. You have a talent for this job. I'm impressed! These selections are fabulous! Now the question is, what do I pick first?" Scotty suggested I try them all on and then go from there. I agreed. Marissa turned off her recorder and waited patiently as I enjoyed my fittings and modeled my fancy wardrobe. We were all a bit tipsy by now, and the night was moving along just fine, still on schedule.

"Dress rehearsal is coming up next. Bobby will be here in about an hour to scoop you up and take you down to the auditorium. In the meantime, pick out your wardrobe for tonight and then for the reception afterward, and, then for brunch and the key ceremony, and the gown for the gala tomorrow night. Lot's of choices, so let's get going," said Scotty.

Marissa sat down with the rest of the crew while Scotty assisted me in and out of the outfits. Jesse didn't want my hair or makeup ruined, so they pampered me like the Princess of Wales .

As I was getting in and out of several casual and formal outfits, I remembered the time Star moved from Madison back to Georgia. Her grandpa lived there now. She said he moved to Georgia shortly after he and Star's grandma Maria divorced. That's when I met Star. She had moved there and enrolled in the same high school I attended after leaving private school. I asked her what school she transferred from because I hadn't seen her around town before then. She said, "I've gone to twelve different schools before this, and I'm only fifteen years old. This would be lucky number thirteen. I'm starting all over once again." She said she hated starting all over. It seemed that that was all she'd done her entire life. She said she hated being the new kid on the block. It was horrible having to try to make new friends over and over again, only to leave them and start all over again. Having to learn new surroundings, adapting to new circumstances, and hoping this time things would be better than the last. It sucked. I told Star I would be her friend if she liked, and the rest is history.

Star was originally from Chicago. She said she loved the big city. I've never been to Chicago. My parents lived in a small town in Illinois before relocating down south. I was too young to remember. Star mentioned her mom's family was always full of drama and how she purposely stayed as far away from home as possible.

"Mom hated staying so close to her family. There was always some kind of drama going on, and she didn't like being around it. None of her sisters ever seemed to get along, and Grandma Maria and Grandpa Ralph were always having major relationship issues—even more after they divorced. It was always a mess and very emotional and stressful to be around, even for us children. I loved when Mom took us home. I loved Chicago. But Mom always had a hard time going home and having to deal with so much negativity. She was the oldest, and she felt overwhelmed trying to keep the peace between everyone. It was exhausting for her.

"Mom had a new boyfriend already. His name was Maxwell, but we called him Max for short. I guess they met sometime between her leaving Mr. Bruce and us moving around. I honestly couldn't tell you how she met Max. For all I know, Max could have been the real reason Mr. Bruce was so jealous. Maybe there was another guy in the picture the entire time. Who really knows? Mr. Bruce was always obsessed with my mom and was heartbroken that she finally left him. He found out she had another man and went ballistic. Mr. Bruce wanted to be the only man in my mom's life, even if she didn't want him. Mr. Bruce was a stalker. He always found Mom when he wanted to terrorize her.

"One day, Mom didn't come home from her temporary job at her normal time. Dallas and I started to worry. We thought maybe she was with Max—until Max showed up at our house looking for her. Then we were even more concerned. Rumor around town was someone had spotted Mr. Bruce. We assumed he had kidnapped our mom. Max had heard about the last episode between Mom and Mr. Bruce and was determined to be a hero and go rescue her from the Big Bad Wolf. Max was trying to help us find her. I was afraid Mr. Bruce had come back to get his revenge. He would rather kill her than see her move on with another man.

"We couldn't find her anywhere. I remember thinking we were surely going to find her dead body laying in the woods somewhere. Mom was missing for hours. Then she showed up at the house with a neck brace around her neck. She had been to the hospital. Mr. Bruce had taken her to a motel so they could talk privately, and of course, like old times, he lost his temper and started beating her. She said she started screaming for help as loud as she could. Mr. Bruce started strangling her to keep her from yelling for help. She said she couldn't breathe, and he kept squeezing harder and harder, and at that moment she knew it was over. She said she realized he was not going to let go and his rage was out of control. She said he was looking straight into her eyes and saw her fear, and he would squeeze her neck even harder. She knew he was there to finish her off for sure this time.

"She said a small voice spoke to her and told her to stop fighting. She suddenly stopped breathing and lay there limp on the bed. Mr. Bruce panicked and ran out of the room. Mom said she stayed still minutes after in fear. When she realized Mr. Bruce wasn't coming back and she was safe, she took a deep breath and started gasping for air. She was terrified that after all this time, this man still wanted to bring harm to her. She used the room phone to call 911. An ambulance came and took her to the hospital. Mom had pretended to be dead, she said, because she knew he wouldn't have stopped otherwise. She never pressed charges against him. After that, we never saw Mr. Bruce again.

"Our new place was nasty; it was infested with mice and roaches. It reminded me of when we used to live with Grandma Maria. Her house was always infested with rodents. She had mice, rats, and roaches everywhere. It was unfortunate we lived like this, but it was home, and we had a roof over our heads, and at this time, that was all that mattered.

"We hadn't lived here long before we received a call in the middle of the night. I answered the phone; it was Aunt Krissy. She sounded very serious when she asked to speak to my mom. I went to get Mom, and when she got on the phone, she suddenly started screaming and crying and saying yelling, "No, no, no! This can't be!" She melted down to the ground, sobbing out of control. When she got off the phone, she told me Uncle Danny had died. He had a massive heart attack in his sleep right next to Aunt Krissy, who was pregnant with their second child. She was due to deliver any day. Aunt Krissy was a registered nurse. She tried to save him but couldn't. She blamed herself.

"Uncle Danny was the kindest man I had ever known. He and my mom were very close, just like Dallas and me. He was the oldest boy and mom was the oldest girl out of the nine. This news broke my mom's heart. She took Uncle Danny's death very hard. Dallas and I were not allowed to attend the funeral, because Mom couldn't afford to fly us back to Madison, and we didn't own a car. Aunt Krissy gave birth to their second son two days before the funeral. I felt so sad for my new little cousin. He would never get to see his father. It was a very sad time for our family.

"Max was tall, over six feet like Mr. Bruce was. He was a darker complexion. He had a deep voice, kind of raspy and sexy. He was nice at first; they all seem that way at first. Until one evening, they started arguing, and he picked up an ashtray and threatened to bust my mom upside her mouth if she didn't shut up. Well that was the beginning of another abusive relationship. Max wasn't as mean as Mr. Bruce, but he was just as strong and scary. They all were to me, because mom was so fragile. These men are so weak. Why do men hit women? I really couldn't quite wrap my mind around it. How can you hurt someone you say you love? Is this love? I was confused about relationships. I had no idea what was a good relationship or a bad one. All I knew was what I'd seen and lived. I knew nothing else.

"Max was the first man, other than seeing my father's hunting rifles, who I knew owned a gun. I guess he was the type of man who felt he needed one. He was a bit rough around the edges and seemed to be more streetwise than most men Mom had dated. He had a drag to his words just like a southerner. People teased us because they said we talked proper like white folk. I never understood what that meant exactly, because I spoke English like most people. Maybe our Chi-Town language was different than southern charm talk.

"One early morning, while loosing another night's sleep, trying to stay up and listen to the madness in case I needed to call the police, I heard these clicking noises and didn't know what they were. I tiptoed closer to my mother's bedroom door and saw Max holding a pistol to my mom's head, threatening to shoot her. My mom was scared; she was shaking and crying with fear in silence so she wouldn't wake up her children. She followed all his pathetic instructions while he put a fear in her and gaining total control. I hated all her boyfriends. None of them were good to her. They were all sorry, good-for-nothing men.

"It didn't matter what I thought about any of her lovers. Mom continued putting their needs before ours. I hated her for doing this, because they didn't deserve it, and they shouldn't have come first because we were here before they were, and we are her children. Why would she choose them over us? I never quite understood that. They come and go, but Dallas and I are always here to help her pick up the scattered pieces of her many failed relationships.

"We weren't doing well financially. Mom struggled to keep food on the table. She had always been into smoking marijuana, drinking, and taking pills. They were very tiny pills. I overheard her telling someone they were called Microdots. I had no clue what those were, but they made her happy, and I guess that was all that mattered. Anything to keep her mellow, I was all for it. Mom had become mean over the years. She yelled more and spanked us more and was just always out of control when she didn't have her drugs.

"One hot, humid evening, Dallas and I walked to the gas station where mom and Max both worked. We were hungry and wanted to ask what we were going to eat that night. It was a long walk, and we were happy to finally see them and ask what we were having for dinner. Mom gave us some money and sent us to McDonald's a couple blocks down the street to get Max a Big Mac value meal. She didn't give us enough money to buy us anything and told us to bring her back the change. We were very obedient kids; we did as we were told, even when we disagreed. When we returned with Max's meal, we watched him eat it in front of us, and we were so hungry that our stomachs were hurting from hunger pains. We asked our mom if she was going to buy us anything to eat, and she said no and ordered us to go back home. We couldn't believe our ears.

"We couldn't believe she would do this to us. We were not babies anymore; we needed to eat. We needed more than the thirty-three cents she used to leave on the kitchen table for us to go to the local store and buy a can of SpaghettiOs to split between the two of us. That was how we survived when we were in elementary school. We were growing teens, and it had been days that we'd gone without eating dinner, surviving off of our free school lunches.

"Dallas and I walked back home, sobbing in disbelief. We were hurt and confused. We couldn't believe that after all we'd been through with our mom, nothing had changed. We were so upset and angry with our mom. We hated her. What kind of mom doesn't feed her own children? We hated Max even more. What kind of man would be with a woman and let her children starve? When we returned home, I held Dallas in my arms and we cried together and I promised him I would take care of him, and I said that we had to stick together. I told him it wouldn't always be this way. Things would get better. Deep down I don't think I believed my own words, but at the time, it was all I had.

"Mom's health was getting worse. She was in and out of the hospital a lot. One day she walked to grandpa Ralph's house to get money to buy food or drugs. Most times, I didn't know, because she was never out of drugs, but we were always staring into an empty refrigerator.

"I always worried about my mom's health, and I got worried it was taking her longer than usual to return home. I decided to walk the same route I thought she had taken in hopes of meeting her on her way back, in case she needed my help with something. I just had a feeling something wasn't quite right. I'd just turned the corner, and I saw my mom walking toward me. She smiled and waved at me. I waved back. We were about a block away from each other, and suddenly she collapsed. I panicked and ran as fast as I could to her aide. She was not breathing. I started CPR immediately. I had learned how to do this years ago when I volunteered to be a candy striper at a nursing home. It was one of the requirements necessary to volunteer at the nursing home. As I was administering CPR, Mom started convulsing, having seizures. This frightened me, but I knew this was a good sign, because at least I knew she wasn't dead. I held her head up so she wouldn't bite or swallow her tongue, and I put her delicate body against mine until she stopped shaking. She was still unconscious. I tried to drag her out of the street, but I realized dead weight was heavier than my small body could handle.

"I had to do something fast, so I told Mom to hold on. I had to go and get help. I kissed her on her forehead and told her I'd be right back. I told her I loved her. I started running as fast as I could to the nearest house and banged on the door for someone to please help me and to call an ambulance. An older lady with the look of confusion and fear on her face hesitated as she cracked her door just enough to see who was causing this ruckus. She saw tears streaming down my face. I was speechless and kept pointing to my mother's body lying in the street. I begged her to call for help. She said she would, and I ran back to my mom and stayed with her until the ambulance arrived. I prayed to God to save her. I pleaded with him not to let her die. I told him I needed her and how much I loved her. I told him I couldn't live without her. I asked God to please save my mom.

"When the ambulance arrived, they immediately put her into the back of the wagon and asked me if I wanted to ride with my mom. I told them I couldn't because my little brother Dallas was home alone, and I had to make sure he was taken care of. I assured them I would find a way to get to the hospital as soon as I could. I told them to take care of my mom. They promised they would. I kissed her once again and ran home to get Dallas.

"My mom had her first open-heart surgery, and even then I was too young to understand it all. I remember going to the hospital to see her afterward and how much better she looked, and I could tell she felt much better. I was so happy she was alive. I really couldn't imagine life without her. The thought of losing my mom terrified me.

"Unfortunately, Max was still in the picture. He cheated on my mom right in front of us. He would take Dallas and I over to his mistress's house and tell us not to say anything to our mom. We kept his dirty little secret because he would bribe us with money and take us roller-skating every Saturday night. Back then, that was our new thing to do. We loved roller-skating. Mom found out about the other woman, and Max made it difficult for Mom when she wanted out of the relationship. He flat-out refused to leave. He'd go back and forth from our house to his mistress's house. It had all gotten to be a bit much, not just for Mom but all the children involved. Max had kids with this other woman, and we had become close to them, and we were all confused at this love triangle our parents had brought us into.

"One day Max lost his temper like never before. He was beating on my mom so bad it brought back those horrible memories of when Mr. Bruce used to hurt Mom. I was feeling helpless and afraid to get involved for fear of getting hurt. I grabbed Dallas and we ran out of the house as fast as we could to get help. We ran to my grandpa's Ralph's house, figuring we would tell someone who could save Mom for real this time. I was sure her dad wouldn't want a man beating on her like that, especially with her heart condition.

"When we got to grandpa's Ralph's house, I was crying and shaking so bad I could barely get out what was going on. He told us not to worry and to stay at his house and that he would take care of it. We felt safe. We did as we were told. We waited and waited and waited, for what seemed like eternity. When Grandpa Ralph returned, Mom was with him. She didn't say much to us. I was sure she was glad her dad came to her rescue. She said, "Come on. Let's go home." We obeyed as usual and didn't say a word. We were glad to see Mom was okay. We never knew exactly what happened that evening, but we didn't hear or see Max again for a long time.

"Mom was single once again. She hated being alone. I never knew what was worse—her having a man to put his needs before ours, or not having one. When she didn't have a man around, she would take out all her anger and frustrations on us. She seemed meaner when she was alone. She had nothing to focus on but us, and she didn't like that much. It made her worry more, and it made her face the reality of having to be more responsible for our well-being. It made me feel like we were burdens. Like she didn't want us.

Dallas is a freshman now. It was fun being together once again. We were popular in high school. Dallas was into sports, and I was a cheerleader. We had friends and had grown to love living in Georgia. This was by far the longest place we'd ever lived, and I never wanted to leave. I had my first real boyfriend when I was sixteen. I broke up with him because his mother was an alcoholic, and I felt his pain, feeling obligated and responsible for her. He had to be there for her, and at that time, I needed someone to be there for me. His obligation to his mom reminded me too much of my life, one I was trying to escape. I couldn't deal with his and mine at the same time. So I broke up with him.

"My mom was the coolest mom on the block because young guys were always attracted to her laughter. She had the best personality and was fun to be around. She would smoke marijuana with the young men. She supervised them in the summer youth work program. These young guys would come visit after work. They would hang out at our house, drink alcoholic beverages, and play cards with my mom. As long as they weren't trying to flirt with me, everything was peachy king.

"I always felt my mom was a little jealous of me. I know it sounds strange, but I felt it came from her denial that my father chose me over her. She'd always treated me different than she treated Dallas. She didn't need to admit the truth, because her actions toward me always let me know she knew the truth. She knew Daddy molested me. She just didn't want to face it.

"I didn't like my mom doing drugs. I was embarrassed these guys were so smitten by her charm and that she was just so cool in their eyes. I had promised myself I would never do drugs or drink, because I didn't want to be like my mom.

"We had gotten to know these guys well, and Dallas loved them. This was the first time men had actually been around him who loved our mom and didn't want to harm her. They would hear about the horror stories of Mom's past boyfriends and would tell Dallas that he didn't have to ever worry about her, because as long as they were around, nothing like that would ever happen to her again. That made him feel safe, and he admired and looked up to these guys.

"To my surprise, as I was trying to stay out of Mom's limelight, a young man named Ethan only had eyes for me. He had a soft laughter and a smile bigger than life, especially when he looked my way. I'd blush a little but not too hard, because this guy was too old for me, and I was still in high school. I also knew there was no way Mom would ever let me date one of these guys.

"Next thing I knew, this guy Ethan was following me around in his car when Ally and I would walk around the neighborhood minding my own business. He was always trying to get my attention. Ally thought it was adorable and at times I found it embarrassing, but it was also flattering. I'd never really been pursued, so I thought it was exciting, and it made me feel special.

"After I wouldn't pay him any attention, I think he asked my mom if it would be okay if he started a courtship with me. To my surprise,

Mom said it would be fine as long as I was okay with it. Well, I was because I knew he liked me. I hadn't felt this excited since I'd made the cheerleading team.

"I had a new boyfriend. He was twenty years old. He was nice and sweet to me. He was perfect. My girlfriends envied our relationship. He spoiled me rotten. He would come by early each morning to pick me up from the bus stop, to keep me from having to ride the bus with my friends to school. He opened doors for me. He would surprise me by waiting for me when I got out of school to drive me home. Everyone noticed. One day, he let me drive his car. He taught me how to drive. He took me to get my driver's license. A year later than most kids, because when I turned sixteen mom didn't have a car. Ethan treated me like a woman, and I felt special. I was excited when he would come and took me out on dates. I could tell Mom wasn't so happy about me being happy. It bothered her somewhat.

"Ethan would take me out to dinner, to the movies. We spent a lot of time at parks, just chilling. One of the local parks had become our favorite places to hangout. All our friends hung out there. It was the thing to do, the place to be in those days. He introduced me to marijuana. Of course I said I'd never touch the stuff, but he was very influential and said it was no harm, so I tried it. The first time, I thought I'd lost my mind. But after a few more times, I quickly learned what all the fuss was about. I was hooked. He'd also introduced me to alcohol. I drank beer and wine for the first time. I learned to enjoy it all to fit into his world.

"One day, I didn't feel to well and made an appointment to see my doctor. I found out I had an STD. I was like, 'What is that?' My doctor explained an STD was a sexually transmitted disease. How naïve I was. I said, 'You can only get this by having sex?' My doctor said, 'Yes, unprotected sex between more than two or more people.' I never knew exactly what protected sex meant; this was the first anyone had ever explained that to me. My understanding is, someone else had to have this disease, I've just been diagnosed with and it has passed onto me through sex. My doctor wrote me a prescription and gave me directions on how to treat it. He also told me in order to completely get rid of it, I would have to talk to my sexual partner and let him know so he could get treated as well. He explained how important this was to keep us from transferring it back and forth to one another. I sat there in total shock. I still couldn't quite grasp what my doctor was saying. I had never in my life had any kind of nasty disease. Even when my daddy used to play with me, I had serious pain, but never did I have a disease. I suddenly became furious. I realized at that moment Ethan had to be involved with someone else. There is no other way I could've gotten this STD. I never had a reason not to trust him until now.

"Oh, and did I mention it was Valentine's Day? I had a romantic date planned with Ethan later. He was taking me out for a romantic dinner. Well, these plans are cancelled, now, and so is our relationship, and I couldn't wait to tell him face-to-face!

"His house wasn't far from the doctor's office. I thought I'd pay him a visit. He should be home from work now. When I got there, I noticed his car wasn't in the driveway. He hadn't made it home yet. I couldn't help thinking, *He's probably over at his other woman's house, taking care of her, so he can spend time with me this evening.* His mother let me in. I wasn't sure how I felt about her just yet. She was a bit strange. Couldn't quite put my finger on why I felt this way about her, but I didn't feel she cared for me much either.

"I went upstairs where his room was. I was anxious and started looking around. I noticed this huge Valentine's card on his dresser. I picked it up and read it. It was signed *I love you* and had a female's name. *This was just the proof I needed, I thought.* The love of my life really was cheating on me. I felt betrayed. All I could think about was all the times Ethan said he loved me and how wonderful it felt to be loved. I was crazy in love with Ethan. I knew without a doubt we would marry some day.

"I tried not to cry, but the reality had set in. Right then, he walked through the door and snatched the card out of my hand and accused me of snooping through his things. Nothing about why the card was in his room in the first place or why was I even there. I tried to explain what the doctor had told me and that the card validated there was indeed someone else. He was busted.

"He was so upset his perfect world had come to an end. He wasn't quite sure how to handle being backed into a corner like this. I was waiting for him to come clean and tell the truth. I mean, he had told me so many lies up until now that if he told the truth, he risked losing everything. So instead he hauled off and slapped me! Right dead in my face! In that moment of shock, I looked at him with disbelief, with my hand holding my face, I turned and ran downstairs as fast as I could, out the back door of his mother's house, and kept running until I got home.

"I was devastated. When I got home, I couldn't do anything but run upstairs to my room, slammed the door, and cry the rest of the night. He kept trying to call me, but I wouldn't pick up the phone. My mom was upset that I wouldn't take his calls, and I wouldn't tell her why. I told her we broke up and I never wanted to see Ethan again. Dallas was sad. He loved Ethan. He was cool with him. He had found a new buddy. Dallas admired Ethan, and I hated him. I hated myself for trusting him. I hated the fact that even after all of this, I knew I still loved him.

"It didn't take long before he wore me down with apologies, flowers, candy, the whole nine yards. He was determined to get me back and make it all up to me. When I finally gave into his charm, he promised he would never hit me again and that he was sorry. He explained to me that he was no longer seeing that other woman. He said she was obsessed with him and wouldn't leave him alone. He said he tried breaking up with her after we started dating, and she tried to commit suicide. He said he continued having sex with her out of pity, and that was how he must have given me the STD. He admits it wasn't the best way to handle the situation, but didn't know what else to do. He assured me it was over between them. He loved me and only me, and he said that if he lost me, he wouldn't know what to do. He wanted to be with me forever and I believed him. I wanted to believe him. I loved Ethan.

"He sent a dozen roses to my high school on my eighteenth birthday. I was in love. I was still by far the coolest senior with the older boyfriend. All my friends signed my yearbook with several comments about my new love, wishing Ethan and I the best of luck in the future and writing comments about us getting married. Their wasn't a single person in the class of 1972 that didn't know I was all his. I was so excited about graduating from high school so we could start our lives together.

"I didn't have any real plans after graduating other than being a stewardess. I wanted to find a career where I could escape from everything and everyone and travel the world like I always wanted. This was a sure way I would have the opportunity to do this and get still get paid.

"College wasn't an option. I always felt dumb and really struggled in high school. I know most of it was because my home life was so stressful and I had low self-esteem and no support from my mom. She never discussed college with me or even encouraged me to go. I knew we were poor and had no money, and I knew college was expensive. I did my research on this stewardess school in Hawaii and planned to fill out an application to attend soon after I graduated. I'd asked my mom for a set of luggage for graduation so I could buy my one-way ticket out of this dump. I started wondering if it was really what I wanted now that I was in love.

"Ethan still lived at home with his mom. He had a good job, his own car, and he was smart, intelligent, not to mention very handsome. He had dreams, goals, and ambition. I knew he was going places, and I wanted to go with him. I knew without a doubt I was in the right place, and I felt a real happiness for the first time in my life. I knew I was ready for this new life.

"The happier I was, the nastier Mom got. She hated seeing me happy. She purposely made my life a living hell, as if I hadn't already gone through enough. I felt like she was trying to break me. Her abusive words had become unbearable. I started spending as much time away from home as possibly could. It was just so ridiculous. We argued all the time about stupid stuff. She was always in my face, confronting me about things that didn't matter. I'd wash the dishes, clean the house, and do my homework and any other chores before I left the house. I'd still do everything she expected me to do, but it just wasn't good enough.

"One day I just couldn't take it anymore. Ethan came to pick me up and take me away for our solitude and moments of peace and harmony. We originally planned to go to a party. I had begged my mom the week before to grant me permission. I wasn't allowed to go to parties, because she thought I wasn't old enough, even though I was now eighteen. She treated me like I was still too young to do things other kids were enjoying. But this time she finally gave in and said I could go as long as I was home by midnight, and I promised I would be.

"When Ethan picked me up I was more upset with my mom's rage than usual. I was just sick of the fights, the yelling and the screaming matches. I was tired of her loneliness and her misery and her taking it out on me every day. I just wanted to be happy. I was fed up with being sad all the time. Ethan asked if I wanted go to a hotel instead of the party. We had started going to hotels regularly to make love and just talk and be alone. We never had privacy with both of us still living with our parents. We had became more than lovers. We had developed a special friendship. I gladly accepted his invitation and let him know that we had to be back by midnight or Mom would be even more upset. He agreed to have me back home on time.

"When we got to the hotel, we didn't make love this time. We talked, and he held me, and I fell asleep in his arms. I was safe, and I felt happy. Ethan must have fallen asleep too, because when I woke up, it was 2:00 a.m., and I panicked. I knew I was in big trouble. How was I ever going to explain this to my mom? Ethan hurried to get me home, and the entire time he drove across town, all I could think was if she would believe me. This was the first time I'd ever done anything like this. There were plenty of times I never wanted to come home, but this wasn't one of them. This really looked bad. I mean, we really hadn't been getting along at all, and this was just the excuse she needed to really let me have it. I was not looking forward to facing her wrath.

"Ethan pulled up in front of my house. It was a dreary kind of darkness that morning. He opened the passenger car door to let me out and kissed me goodbye. I watched his car drive off. At that moment, my heart started beating fast, and before I could get in the house, my mom came outside and started yelling at me at the top of her lungs. She was furious! She'd gone to the party, but I wasn't there. I was shocked she cared enough to look for me. This was a first. It really wasn't looking good for me right about now. Now, we were both screaming at one another.

"By the time I made my way inside the house, I had noticed my clothes, and personal items scattered everywhere. I was like, 'Are you serious? With all the crap I put up with being your daughter, how you never protected me from dad, and how you abused me mentally, physically, and emotionally, my entire life? How you always treated Dallas like he was the golden child and me like I was the problem child, and you still think I'm the worst child you ever gave birth to?' Yes, I said these things to her. I was just as upset as she was but for different reasons.

"She told me I lied about Daddy touching me and that he never did. I'd do anything to get some attention. I said, 'You can stand here and look me in the face now after all these years and still not protect me? You're still accusing me of lying?' I told her she knew I was being molested, and she just didn't want to do the right thing. I told her she pimped me out to my father so she could do what she wanted. It made it easier for her to do her sneaking around.

"I suddenly had flashbacks of when we lived in Arkansas and mom would take Dallas and me to the park to play. A couple of times I noticed she met a guy there, and they would kiss and hug while we played on the swings. Mom thought I was too young to know what was going on. I watched how happy this guy made her. I'd never seen her smile like that with Daddy. I didn't understand the entire scope of these secret meetings, but as I got older, it made more sense. She was clearly having an affair. The same guy would show up in the most unusual places over the years. She finally introduced him during one of his mysterious visits. It was in between one of our many transitions of running from abusers and trying to rebuild our lives. I never learned the history behind their love affair, other than maybe the timing was never right. I really don't know. Mom never talked about her past. I honestly knew nothing about my mom. One thing I did know was she really loved this guy, more than I think she loved any other man.

"I snapped back into reality when Dallas came running down the stairs, yelling at me to get out. He was following Mom's lead. She was yelling at me to get out of her house and to never come back! I was so angry, that all I could do was cry. I ran upstairs to my room, only to find the rest of my things already thrown in a large box sitting in the center of the floor. All of my belongings broken and my poems, I had written over the years torn and shredded into pieces. I wasn't sure how I felt or what to think. I couldn't believe this was happening.

"I started grabbing whatever else I could while Mom continued cutting me down with her harsh words, singing the same old song: 'I knew I should have dropped you from that window when I had the chance. You think you're something, don't you? But you're not. You'll see you're nothing. You'll see you can't do any better than me. You always thought you were special, but you're not. You'll see, just wait; you won't amount to nothing, because you are not better than me. Hurry up and get your stuff and get the hell out of my house and don't you ever come back!'

"I'll never forget, at that moment, all I could think was, *This is what she's wanted the entire time. She couldn't wait for me to slip up so she would have an excuse to finally be rid of me for good.* I mean, really now, all those years I was loyal to her. All those times I could have left, and

I didn't. All those times I could have reported my dad for molesting me and didn't because all I could think about was how it would have devastated her, the family shame and embarrassment. I wanted her to do it. I wanted her to admit the truth and say enough is enough, let's put this no-good child molester in jail. I wanted her to come to me and say, 'I believe you, and I'm sorry I let him hurt you,' but she never did. All she did was allow him to continue molesting me into my teenage years. I know in my heart she knew I wasn't lying about what he was doing to me, but it was easier for her to blame me for lying than to blame herself for letting him do these things to me, because she wasn't strong enough to stop him.

"My mom always used her words to build others up while she tore me down. She was the master at this. I was angry. I just kept thinking, *After all these years, this is the thanks I get. This is how she rewards me for protecting the family by keeping our dirty little secrets safe. All the abuse I suffered by her. All the sleepless nights I stayed up on standby, outside her bedroom door, making sure her men wouldn't kill her. I honestly don't think she has any idea how horrible my life has been trying to protect her all these years.* I did it because I loved my mom. Regardless of how bad she mistreated me, I still loved her.

"Dallas has no idea how manipulative Mom can be. She has brainwashed him, and he has no clue she set this whole thing up. This was her plan all along. She never wanted me anyway. I felt sorry for him. But then I thought, *Why? He actually has it made. He was always treated better, so he'll be fine. I don't have to worry about his safety any longer. I have to save myself. Dallas is no longer my responsibility. Mom either.*

"I struggled, dragging the box filled with what was left of my belongings down the stairs and out the front door. By now Mom and I were really going at it hard. We were both yelling and saying things we could never take back. I had told her I hated her and "don't worry—I won't come back." I told her she never had to worry about me ever again because I was tired of putting up with her crap. She slammed the door in my face one last time. I stood outside in the dark for a moment to gather my thoughts. *What just happened?* I looked down the street wondering where I would go. I had no idea, but I knew I had to get away from here.

"I started dragging the box down the center of the street. It was easier than going over the bumps on the sidewalk. The neighborhood was still asleep. No one was awake. No house lights were on yet, only dimmed streetlights shining. It was a few more hours until sunrise. I kept thinking how sad this entire situation was. *I can't believe I make one mistake, and Mom couldn't find it in her heart to give me a second chance.* There was no room for forgiveness, no room for understanding, no room for compassion, and most of all no room for love. *For eighteen years, I've taken on more than a child should ever have to endure. Yet, this is how it ends. At this moment, I wonder if it was worth it. What could've I have done different? I didn't expect this.*

"Just as I couldn't drag the box one more inch, I saw headlights coming down the street. The car was moving slowly. To my wonderful surprise, it was Ethan. He said he was worried and came back to see if everything was okay. I melted in his arms, and more tears flowed from my eyes, with no words, just pain. He put the box in the back seat it was too large to fit in the trunk and drove us back to the hotel since we originally had the room until noon. He never quite understood why the relationship with my mom was so horrible. I honestly never had a clear answer to that question.

"I never felt close to her. Ever since I was a baby, we had distance. Mom was really hard on me. She treated me bad most of the time. I wanted her to love me, and I did everything I could to please her and earn her love, but it was never enough. I was emotionally drained dealing with her issues. I knew as a child it was just too much. *Maybe this is for the best,* I thought. *I am no longer her problem, and she is no longer mine.*"

Chapter 5

Once again, there was an uncomfortable silence that hovered in the room. I felt I needed to break the silence and said, "Hey, you guys, you can't make this shit up." And everyone started to laugh. I joined them and said, "All you can do is laugh sometimes, because Star's life was no joke. She struggled most of her life trying to find peace and love. She was one of the nicest people you would ever want to meet. She was always laughing and smiling and positive about everything. She loved life. She just felt she was dealt a bad hand for a very long time. She never felt lucky and never believed in luck. She always told me things happen for a reason, good or bad. It's just the way the universe operates. There is no getting around it. She got kind of deep on me in our older years."

Pam said, "Ms. Knight, you look like you're ready to go to the prom in that gown. It is absolutely beautiful on you. You should wear that one to the gala. You look like Cinderella in that gown."

Marissa asked, "Did Star go to the prom?"

It's prom night, and I have no date. Ethan was too old to be my prom date. He knew how bad I wanted to go, but I couldn't because it was for seniors and juniors only. To make up for me missing my senior prom, he bought me a pretty white dress for graduation. I looked forward to wearing it and feeling pretty on graduation day.

We now live with his mother, and she wasn't too thrilled to have me staying here. I actually didn't know who was worse, my mom or his. Ethan's mom was a bitter old woman. She had five boys and no girls. It was almost like she resented having all boys. She said she always wanted a girl. I never felt comfortable living with his mom. Ethan's older brother Luke lived at home with his mom his entire adult life. Luke had some health problems and was like a little kid that never grew up. He lived like a hermit. He never left the house. He was very nice, and we developed a bit of a confidante relationship. Luke was easy to talk to, but was a little mysterious like his mom. Agnes, Ethan's mom, was strange in a frightening kind of way. My spirit never felt safe around her. Instinct never lies.

Graduation was less than two weeks away. I was excited. The last couple weeks of school were difficult. I was attending school away from home. I was trying to concentrate on finishing so I could start my new life. I still had hopes of attending stewardess school but realized it wasn't an option, especially when I was filling out the application and saw they had a height requirement of five foot five, and I was only five foot tall. I thought, *How unfair. A height restriction? Really? Now what do I do?* That's all I really wanted. I dreamed of traveling the world. I knew something was better out there in this world, and I was determined to find it. I wanted to go places I'd only seen on TV.

Ethan did all he could to comfort me. I hadn't spoken to my mom since that awful night. She was mad at me, and I was still mad at her. Dallas didn't try to contact me either. I saw him in school, and he would ignore me and act like I wasn't even there. I couldn't believe how he was treating me. I knew he was under the witch's spell. Mom was no joke, and he knew better. If he'd acted like he missed me or was concerned about me, he knew she would sense it, and he'd be in big trouble. All I wanted to know is if they even cared I was graduating from high school in spite of our differences.

Graduation day arrived, and I was not feeling very happy. It was bittersweet. All I had was Ethan—no family support. I thought for sure, regardless of everything that happened between Mom and me, that she would at least swallow her pride long enough to attend my high school graduation. I mean at least through all the madness, I managed to get out of high school without getting pregnant. Teenage pregnancy was on the rise, and it was a battle for mothers just to get their young girls out of high school with no kids. I thought this would make her proud. But I guess not.

I was all dressed up in my new white dress. I had on my matching silk-like, solid white cap and gown. I watched all the other students hug and kiss their loved ones before we departed behind stage, where we took our places before we walked across the stage. I remember feeling lonelier than I'd ever felt. I even missed the madness. At least when I was a part of it, I was a part of something. It felt better than being a part of nothing, and right now I had nothing.

I kept thinking at any minute I'd see Mom and Dallas waving at me from the crowd. I had high hopes all the way, from the time my name was called, and when I walked across that lonely stage with no one yelling and screaming my name. Nothing like all the other kids who had family and friends breaking all the rules of silence, by screaming their names, clapping and whistling as loud as they could. Instead, I sat down and watched all the other students receive their diplomas. I waited a long time, thinking the list of names would never end.

As I sat there, I still had hope. I knew mom and Dallas had plenty of time to get into position and find me outside in the hallway after graduation was over. *Once they find me, they'll give me hugs and congratulate me then. They were just running late—that's all. They're here, I'm sure of it.* The ceremony was finally over, and all the students were with their families taking pictures and celebrating their achievements with their loved ones. I saw girls getting roses, sons getting handshakes and hugs from their proud parents.

I searched and searched for Mom and Dallas. I wanted to be sure I stayed put periodically, long enough for them to find me in case they were looking for me as well. I didn't want us to keep missing each other. After a while, I turned, and there he was, the only support I had. Ethan was standing there, smiling from ear to ear, proud to be there and share this special moment with me. He was holding a dozen red roses. He gave me a hug and whispered, "I love you" in my ear. I embraced the moment for what it was worth. He was all I had. As he drove me back to his mother's house, the car was silent, as I was at a loss for words. I was sad. I felt sick to my stomach. I couldn't breathe. I was miserable. When he pulled into the driveway, I didn't want to go inside the house. I told him I needed some air, and I needed to be alone. He hesitated to leave me alone, but he could tell there was nothing he could say or do, to feel the void of me missing my mom and my brother as he watched me walk away.

I walked down the sidewalk in darkness as my white cap and gown lit my path. I cried. I asked God, "How did I end up here? After everything you put me through, after everything I endured. Why am I still alone? Why, God? Why?" I honestly had no answer to my question and was hoping God would have one for me. The sky was clear and full of stars. I wanted to wish upon them, but I had nothing to hope for. All I could think about was, *How could my family do this to me? Was I really that bad of a daughter? Why am I not worthy of my mother's forgiveness?* I walked to my house to see if anyone was home. It would be the first time I'd been home since my mom kicked me out a few weeks ago. I needed to see them. I needed my family. When I got there, no lights were on. No one was home. I wondered where Mom and Dallas could be. I really needed them right now. Did they forget I graduated tonight?

I decided to walk to Ally's house. I knew her family would be celebrating her graduation, and I was hoping they would allow me to be a part of their unconditional love. I needed that right about now. I envied Ally and her family bond. It was genuine. Her family was close; they all supported and loved one another—unlike our family. Mom's sisters never got along. They backstabbed one another all the time. I'd never known a time in my life when all of them actually got along at the same time.

That's probably where my mom inherited so much of her bitterness. I couldn't imagine growing up in a large family where no one got along. That's just sad, but not Ally's family. They really loved one another through thick and thin, just the way love should be. No one was perfect, but the love they had for one another was flawless. Someday, I wanted to know what that love felt like. I needed it now more than ever. I walked until I made it to her house. Cars were lined up outside, the lights were on, music was playing in the background, and I saw shadow figures of people everywhere. It was a full house. I was afraid to ring the doorbell. I felt a bit embarrassed. I gathered up enough courage to ring the bell anyway.

Her handsome older brother answered the door. I'd always thought he was so good-looking. When I walked in their house, I saw Ally surrounded by family and love. She saw me and ran over and gave me the biggest hug. She knew my situation and was glad to see me. Her family invited me to celebrate her graduation and mine as if I was their daughter too. I felt loved and accepted. They were close, so I knew she had told them what happened between my mom and me. I could tell by the pity they all had on their faces when they looked at me. I didn't care. I was okay with it. I just wanted to be somewhere I felt love.

They started including me in all the family portraits. They didn't make me feel like an intruder at all. They loved me and didn't judge my situation or me. I was glad I found myself there at that moment. Their doorbell was ringing a lot that evening. Ally had a huge family. More of them were stopping by to congratulate her. She deserved it. I was happy for her more than me.

The doorbell rang again, and to my surprise, mom and Dallas walked through the door. I didn't think mom knew where Ally lived. I was sure Dallas showed her how to get here. He probably had something to do with her being here as well. It was an uncomfortable moment, as my mom didn't crack a smile. She was still determined not to show any signs of emotion. Dallas was happy to see me. He ran over to me and gave me the biggest hug. I could tell he missed me. I missed him so much more.

Ally and her family continued taking pictures and celebrating as they welcomed my mom and brother into their home. Ally introduced my mom to her parents. My mom sat there watching all the love her family had and didn't have much to say to me. I think she was proud, but she was tight-lipped about expressing it. She and Dallas stayed about ten minutes, and then she told me she had to leave. She told me to take care of myself. I told her I would, and I watched her and Dallas leave. I didn't stay too long after they left, because my emotions had gotten the best of me. I was glad to see my family. It meant a lot to me. I knew my road would be long and hard, especially without their support. I realized at that moment I had become an adult.

Mom and Dallas moved back to Chicago shortly after I graduated. Word in the family was I'd run off with this older guy and had become this fast and promiscuous girl. Grandma Maria was upset. She sent me letters begging me not to ruin my life with this man. She said I was living in sin, and God didn't want me living this way. I loved Grandma Maria and took everything she said seriously and tried to be as obedient as possible. I knew Grandma Maria had my best interests at heart. She just had some crazy ways of going about showing it. She meant well though, and deep down inside, I knew she was right.

This wasn't how I'd planned it. I had no plan other than becoming a stewardess. I never thought about what I'd do if that didn't work out. I knew I couldn't go to college because I barely graduated from high school. My grade-point average was so low I honestly wondered how I skated by with a high school diploma. I didn't feel I had earned it at all.

There were times I wondered if something was wrong with me. I felt I did not comprehend information like the other kids did. Things would just come easily for my peers, and I always seemed to struggle more. I was awesome in art and design classes, sewing, and cooking classes. But, anything else, like algebra, literature, or biology, even English, I always struggled. At this point, it doesn't matter, college was never an option.

Where do I go from here? I hated living with Ethan and his mother, Agnes. He had another brother who lived with them. His name was Dennis. I had to get out of his mother's house. I was miserable living here. Grandpa Ralph had a girlfriend named Ms. Mabel. She and I had gotten to know each other quite well. Her and my grandpa Ralph had a son; I used to babysit him when they went out on dates. I asked her if I could stay with her for a while until I could get on my feet. She said yes but under one condition. I had to attend church every Sunday and bible study on Wednesdays. I was fine with that. My mom didn't like church; she thought people who attended church were all hypocrites. Mom grew up with a strong Christian foundation, and Grandma Maria was very strict. Mom loved God but didn't show it in the way grandma Maria had raised her. I could relate a bit to my mom's resentments toward the whole church thing. As a young child growing up in such dysfunction, I questioned my faith as well as others around me all the time. Nevertheless, I attended church as expected. I enjoyed church and felt safe and secure there.

In the evenings, I worked as a waitress at an ice-cream parlor. I enjoyed being nice to people and getting awesome tips. I felt independent. I also worked at a local bank as a teller during the day. I'd had this job since my senior year of high school. I attended school in the mornings and worked a few hours in the afternoons at the bank; it was my part-time senior work program job. I caught the bus everywhere I needed to go. Ethan needed his car to get back and forth to work. He commuted. His job was about thirty miles outside the city limits. Our relationship grew more serious, and we started to talk about marriage and someday having children.

Ms. Mabel wanted me to start giving her money to stay with her, and I was upset because that wasn't the original agreement, and I had not only attended church on Sundays and Wednesday as agreed, I also kept her house clean and watched her son so she could spend time alone with my grandpa. The amount of money she was asking me to contribute cut deep into my savings. I was already helping out with groceries and some other minor bills, but she wanted even more. I felt if I gave more, I would never be able to move out of her house. I'd done everything she'd asked me to do, but she had an attitude and changed her mind and started expecting much more from me. Don't get me wrong; I was grateful Ms. Mabel allowed me to stay with her, but I felt she should keep her word and not change the rules or make up new ones to suit her needs. I was respectful and appreciated the shelter she was providing me. I did this in addition to working two jobs.

However, unfortunately, this was not enough. I knew I couldn't go back to Ethan's mother's house. No way I could deal with evil Agnes again. I found myself once again in desperate times and had to figure out what to do and where to go. Ethan's father George, decided to help me out and graciously cosigned for me to get an apartment on the west side of town. George lived in the same town and was raising the youngest son of the five boys. He was a nice man. I didn't understand the story of why he and Agnes divorced and how he ended up with the youngest boy. Their entire story was very weird and full of lots of missing pieces.

I loved my first real place. It was clean and modern. The apartment was located in a nice area of town and right on the bus line. It was perfect! I was grateful for Ethan's father's generosity. Ethan felt he could move in with me since his dad helped me get the apartment. He was glad to get away from Agnes. Their relationship was a bit odd. I never quite understood why.

Shortly after we moved into our new place, Ethan lost his job, due to an injury on the job. He got into a workman's compensation battle with his employer after his injury, and they let him go. I was the only one bringing in any income, and it was hard for him to find another job. His car was repossessed shortly after, and being unemployed was really hard on his ego. He felt like a failure. To make things worse, we found out I was pregnant. I was shocked to hear the news of a baby growing inside me. I struggled, with my choices to keep it or not. I didn't want to be pregnant. It wasn't a good time, and wasn't planned. I guess I skipped a pill or two accidently, with my crazy schedule trying to keep up with two jobs. Ethan wasn't sure if he was ready either, and we both discussed me aborting the baby.

I made an appointment at the women's clinic and met with a counselor to discuss my options. Ethan's mother found out about the pregnancy and cast some kind of weird spell on me. This was the biggest issue I had with Agnes. She was really into spells and potions, and black magic. I think that's what they call it. She was heavily into witchcraft. She practiced it daily. Once she insisted Ethan and I drive her all the way from Georgia to this tiny town in Indiana close to the Michigan border to visit some voodoo shop where she could stock up on her supplies. The place had all kinds of special candles, powders, oils, magic kits, ritual tools, spell recipes, crystals, special herbs and spices—you name it, they had it. I had no idea places like this even existed. I had questioned Agnes's faith in God after learning more about her beliefs. Her unusual practices really bothered me.

I'd always felt my faith in God was all I needed and that those who participated in such practices did not put all their trust in God. I also thought this was sinful. I believed in prayer and positive-energy healing and meditation, but this was some weird stuff. I didn't agree with her practices at all. Her witchcraft would be the thorn in our relationship.

Before my abortion appointment, Agnes had said three snakes would cross my path and I would have difficulties with the pregnancy. I blew it off as another one of her crazy comments and tried to ignore her as usual. But she had a presence about her that was so eerie it was almost impossible not to be a bit frightened by her unusual warnings.

A few days had passed, and I had forgotten about the spell. I was walking to the abortion clinic to speak with a counselor about aborting the baby. There wasn't a sidewalk on my side of the street, so I had to walk on a worn grass path. I was thinking about what the counselor would say, and if she would try to talk me out of aborting the baby or if she would let me schedule the appointment to have the baby aborted immediately. Suddenly I was startled by something slithering across the path. I think it was a snake. I hated snakes. I was scared to death of them. I continued walking toward the clinic, which wasn't far away, and I noticed another snake crossing my path. I started to panic by now and was afraid because I really didn't have many options of getting off the path. Traffic was too busy to walk in the street. Right after seeing the second snake, I thought of Agnes and her wicked spell. Then the third snake crossed my path, and I almost stepped on it. *"Yikes!"*

I thought, *Seriously? Don't worry about that dumb spell. Nothing's going to happen.* I made it to the clinic, and my counseling session went well. They agreed to allow me to schedule an appointment to abort the baby on Monday. It was Thursday, so I had just three more days. I think they do that on purpose to give you time to think about it more, in case you change your mind. I didn't want to change my mind because I wasn't ready to be a mom. We were struggling financially, and I wanted us to be able to provide more for a child, and right now we couldn't.

I remembered how hard it was for my mom raising Dallas and I. I could barely take care of myself. I knew a child deserved better, and I wanted more for me before I could provide for a child. Ethan decided to join the marines since he was unable to find employment, and we were preparing for his deployment to boot camp. The plan was for him to complete boot camp and become a marine, as the recruiters ensured us this would give him and us a better future.

We were excited, and the hope of having a better life someday was worth us being apart for a few months. It was Saturday, and Ethan and I had returned from the arcade down the street. This was the cheapest entertainment we had outside of watching TV at home in the evenings. The arcade only cost a quarter to play the games. My two favorites games were Pac Man and Galaga.

I had this unusual pain that evening. It was so unbearable I could barely breathe. I had no idea what it was, but it hurt worse than any pain I'd ever experienced. It felt like something wanted to come out of my body and was trying to rip me apart. The pain got more and more intense by the hour. The pain had me curled up in a ball so tight I thought I was going to die.

I noticed the pain was coming from my abdomen and somewhere inside my lower pelvic area. All I wanted to do was get on the toilet and scream. Ethan was frightened. We had no car. He couldn't drive me to the emergency room. We didn't have a phone, and he couldn't call an ambulance. He suddenly ran out of our apartment to get help. He left to see if he could get a family member to come take me to the hospital.

I sat on the toilet in excruciating pain, praying for the pain to stop. I started bleeding heavily. I knew this wasn't a good sign. It felt like my insides were literally ripping apart. Next thing, I felt a ball of thick mush release from my lower body into the toilet. I suddenly felt no more pain after that, just mild cramping. I removed myself to turn around and see what was in the pool of blood. I saw a tiny little fetus, and I realized my baby was dead. I'd lost it. I started crying, for reasons I wasn't quite sure. It was surprisingly emotional. *Do I flush it?* I thought. *Why am I crying? I didn't want it anyway, right?*

Ethan returned with his father's car. I showed him our baby floating in the toilet. We said a prayer for whom we thought might have been our unborn son, and flushed him down the toilet together. Ethan took me to the emergency room. I was still having some pain and bleeding. I was examined and needed to have surgery to remove the afterbirth that was still inside me. After surgery, I was in the hospital two more days for an additional observation. When I returned home, I had nightmares about what Ethan's mom had said to me about the snakes. It kept playing over and over in my head, and I would wake up in a cold sweat. I couldn't stop thinking about how evil Agnes had put a spell on me. What if Ethan and I wanted the baby?

The doctors said I couldn't have sex for at least six weeks. I would have a normal period again in about a month or so. I was given instructions to relax a couple days and not go back to work for at least a week. I was instructed to get plenty of rest. Ethan and I thanked God for this painful blessing. We knew we weren't ready to become parents, and losing the baby just confirmed it for us. This was our chance to do it right and get our acts together so we could be better parents in the future. I also saved us a couple hundred dollars not having to pay for the abortion.

Five weeks passed, and it was time for Ethan to leave for boot camp. Losing a child, even though we didn't want it, was emotional for us. It brought us closer as a couple. We were having a hard time preparing for our temporary separation. However, we knew we wanted a better future, and this was a sure way for us to have one. I followed the doctor's instructions, and we were not intimate until the night before Ethan departed. We made love, and it was beautiful.

I was alone again and trying my hardest to stay on top of the bills. Ethan promised to send money as soon as he completed boot camp and received his first military check. Until then, I was struggling to make ends meet. Ethan's father checked on me from time to time and gave me a little cash here and there. He also bought groceries and delivered them so I would have something to eat. Two of Ethan's brothers, Dennis, and Paul, who's the third son, would also stop by from time to time to check on me, to make sure I was safe and didn't need anything. I was grateful for their support. Ethan's mom, Agnes, and I barely spoke; I didn't like her, and I'm sure she didn't care for me much either. She never stopped by, and I accepted those boundaries.

With all the worry of how I was going to maintain my lifestyle for the next few months, I'd completely forgotten I hadn't had a period yet. I recalled my doctor saying not to worry if it didn't come right away, because sometimes after a miscarriage, our bodies take time to recuperate and get back on track. However, I thought I surely should have had one by now.

I made an appointment to make sure nothing had gone wrong during the minor surgery I had. The doctor gave me a complete check-up and said things were fine, my body was healing well, but he took a urine sample as precaution. He came back and told me my urine test came back positive and that I was pregnant. I was in disbelief. I told him there was no way I could be pregnant because I'd never had a period and hadn't even had sex in months. He looked at me and said, "Well, I'm sorry to be the one to confirm such unexpected news, but you are definitely pregnant." I was at least six weeks pregnant, and I was in shock. I couldn't believe this was happening again. *What in the world went wrong?* I wondered. *How could this be?*

While I was riding the city bus back home, I calculated when this could have happened, and it hit me—it had to have happened that one time Ethan and I made love before his departure. I felt confused. I had no idea you could get pregnant having sex one time, and I had no idea you could get pregnant without ever having a period. I hadn't had a period in almost three months. How naive was I? There was nothing I could do to change it.

I had no idea how I was going to break this unexpected news to Ethan. I wasn't mad, just surprised, because all the plans we'd made didn't include another mouth to feed. I had no thoughts of aborting this child. Never even crossed my mind this time. I wanted this baby and felt this happened for a reason. I actually felt some kind of happiness. I felt ready, and I really wanted this baby. *What changed in the last few weeks? I don't know exactly.*

I anxiously checked the mailbox, which I did each day hoping to hear from my man in uniform, and in the mix of the past-due notices from bill collectors, there was my first letter from Ethan. I must have read it a hundred times. He said he loved me and missed me so much. I missed him too. I couldn't wait to tell him the news about us expecting again. This was not in the plans, but we would figure it out. We always did.

A couple weeks later, I came home from work and found a piece of paper taped on the front door. It was an eviction notice. The apartment complex was giving me a thirty-day notice to catch up on my rent or leave. I was more than a month behind on the rent and had no idea how I was going to catch up. I had lost my job at the bank, because my drawer kept coming up short, and they thought I was stealing the money. I'm not a thief. I tried hard to balance my drawers every evening, but for some odd reason, I kept coming up short.

I cried when I received the eviction notice. I thought this was not the time for this to be happening. I didn't make as much money waiting tables as I did at the bank. I'd been looking for other employment but wasn't having any luck. This was a difficult time to find jobs. I was hungry and was looking in the fridge to see what I could prepare for dinner when I heard a soft knock at the door. I wondered who it might be, because I was in no mood to deal with any of Ethan's family today. I knew they meant well, but it was not a good day.

I opened the door and saw this guy standing there with a huge smile on his face. He was almost bald and a little stockier than I'd remembered. He had a camouflage duffle bag over his shoulder. It was the father of my child! Ethan was home! He grabbed me and picked me up and gave me a hug so big; I never wanted him to let me go! I was happier to see Ethan more than I think he was to see me. I wasn't expecting him to be home; he still had several more weeks left of boot camp. Ethan explained how awful it was and how being in the Marines wasn't for him. He said one guy had even committed suicide, and he couldn't deal with the emotional and physical stress the training was causing him. He received a dishonorable discharge because he admitted he smoked marijuana. He apologized for letting me down and promised he would do all he could to provide a better life for us. I told him I was pregnant, and he shouted for joy! It made his day! He was happy to be home and excited that he had another chance to become a father. He was determined to do all he could to be the best dad for our baby.

Once Ethan returned home, it was still difficult for him to find a job. Thirty days had come and gone, and we had to move back with

Agnes. I was pregnant and miserable. I hated living with her. Her home was wicked. It felt evil. I never felt comfortable. I felt frightened. Agnes chanted around the house all the time. She always had this strange look on her face I didn't trust her. It felt like I was always under a spell. It was awful. The bad energy was like living in an evil haunted house.

I never felt she supported the relationship I had with her son. But now that I was pregnant again with her grandchild and once again had nowhere else to go, therefore, she tolerated me like I tolerated her.

I just didn't want her to harm my unborn child again. Ethan finally managed to land a job driving school buses part-time, and a few months later we saved up enough money to move out of Agnes's house. We moved into a tiny apartment in a high-crime neighborhood, on the second floor. I remember the stairs being so steep you couldn't see the steps in front of you as you walked down. It was dangerous going up and down those steep the bigger I grew each month.   One day I was walking home caring groceries and noticed a sharp pain between my legs. I panicked because I knew for sure something was wrong with the baby. By the time I got home, I was bleeding. I sat down and put my feet up to relax and waited for Ethan to get off work. I didn't want to alarm him. Shortly after he arrived home, we went to the emergency room, and they immediately admitted me. I was in the hospital three days on bed rest and under observation. I remember how frightened I was. I really wanted this baby more than ever and was concerned something was seriously wrong. The heartbeat was fine, but they had no idea why I was bleeding. The doctor released me and told me not to carry heavy items. His theory was I overexerted myself. I followed my doctor's orders and took it easy.

Ethan and I started arguing more than usual. I couldn't figure out if it was due to all the stress of our financial struggles or the stress of becoming parents, or maybe we just weren't meant to be together. I knew one thing for sure. I was sick and tired of arguing. The arguments got worse and worse, and one day it happened. He hit me again! I thought at that moment, *You got to be kidding me. You hit a pregnant woman? How dare you!* I was so angry. I started packing my things, with nowhere to go, but I knew I was getting away from him. Anyone who would hit a pregnant woman had some serious issues, and I didn't want to be with anyone who would harm my child and me. I refused to raise a child in an abusive environment. I was having flashbacks from when

I was growing up, and it wasn't pretty. All I could think was, *I'm not doing better than my mom right now*, and it felt awful.

I was torn, confused, and angry. Ethan had broken his promise to me. My hormones were out of control, and his stress level was higher than normal, trying to provide for us on a part-time job. We were both scared and had no one to turn to but each other, and we were probably too stubborn to admit we just didn't have all the answers.

At this point, I didn't care why we were arguing all the time. When he hit me again, that changed everything, and I was leaving this abusive relationship. I was getting out now! I refused to end up like my mother. This wasn't what I signed up for, and I was determined to breach this contract.

Ethan immediately started apologizing and begging me not to leave. He kept asking where I would go. Who would take me in this time? He knew I honestly had nowhere else to go. Once again, he was right, and he talked me into staying. Emotionally, I just couldn't deal with anything other than having a healthy baby. Two weeks later, we were married.

Chapter 6

"Wow, what a life," said Scotty. "Star's going to be a mother now," he said.
Jesse said, "Yeah, and so young. She's only eighteen years old."
Pam said, "Girls had babies younger than eighteen in the early 1900s."
Marissa said, "They sure did."
I said, "Yeah, we had just graduated from high school, and I had gone to college, so I wasn't with Star when she was going through this stage of her life. I knew things were tough for her, but I honestly had no idea Ethan was abusive. She never told anyone. They say battered women protect their abusers without even realizing that's what they're doing. They keep the secret because they are embarrassed and ashamed and scared. It's a slow process before getting to that stage. I hear it takes seven times for a battered woman to try to leave her abuser before she's successful. That's if they're lucky, because most of them don't care about protective orders and break them all the time. It's so sad. When I was a young girl, I never saw any violence in my home, so I could never relate to the hardships Star went through. I was completely naïve about her lifestyle. Completely naïve."
I had the perfect outfit for the dress rehearsal. It was a satin, sunshine-yellow sheath dress with a tasteful, small scoop cut out back above the lower bra strap. It was very classy and fit me in all the right places. It had short sleeves that fit tightly on my shoulders so the scoop in the back didn't reveal much skin. Scotty topped it off with a pair of Christian Louboutin yellow, patent leather, closed-toe pointed shoes with a flirty flare design. "This is very sharp," I said. "I love it! Scotty, who designed this dress?"
He said, "An upcoming new designer named West Avery, a good friend of mine who just relocated here from London. Out of all the

dresses on the rack, he'll be thrilled the famous Ms. Alexandra Knight picked one of his masterpieces. He'll be at the show and the reception this evening, so I'll introduce you to him."

"I look forward to meeting him. I feel very professional and elegant in this dress. I believe we picked out the entire wardrobe for all the events. Right, Scotty?" Scotty agreed as he was separating the pieces we didn't pick from those we did. Along with it was the gorgeous gown everyone agreed I should wear to the gala tomorrow night. The mayor and his wife were putting on this fundraising event for Star's foundation. This would be my first gala, and I was the guest of honor. I was a little nervous. So far everyone had been amazing, so I hoped my luck didn't run out before the weekend was over. I must say I did enjoy representing my friend Star. That was the easy part, but when it came to being Ally, I sometimes had a hard time. *I'm not as exciting as Star. I'm just Ally, a girl that was fortunate enough to know the real Star.*

Bobby entered the room, and the expression on his face was priceless. He was amazed at how awesome Jessie and Scotty had dolled me up. He said I looked amazingly beautiful. I politely said, "Thanks to these two guys," as I pointed toward Jessie and Scotty, blushing with pride from ear to ear. "They are very good at what they do. I need to hire these guys to be with me full-time." Bobby was happy I was happy, and Jessie, Scotty, and Pam were all happy.

"It's show time, folks!" yelled Bobby. "Ms. Knight, let me escort you to the stage." Bobby held out his hand, and he carefully escorted me down the hall and through a few doors to the auditorium.

Once we arrived, my eyes started to tear up a bit, and Jessie started to panic, saying, "No, Ms. Knight, no crying. You're gonna mess up your makeup. Hold up now. Let me pat your tears. It's gonna be okay. We got you. I know it can be overwhelming, but we got you, and you can do this, girl." Pam was giving me a pep talk as well, and Bobby was glad the auditorium had such an effect on me.

He said, "My job is done. I worked on this setting for weeks to make sure it would be to your liking, Ms. Knight. I'm so glad you approve."

I said, "Of course I do. This is more than I could've ever imagined. I know a lot of famous people all over the world have performed in this auditorium. I'm honored to be on the A-list of those who get this opportunity. I'm living Star's dream."

Marissa was following along, speaking into her small tape recorder along the way. She wasn't missing a beat. *I can't wait to see my face on the cover of the magazine. I'm probably going to be famous after this weekend. I might even get that movie deal Star always wanted. It's been a long road getting to this point, and things haven't been easy. Today, it all comes together. The light shines down on Star once again. I feel blessed. Speaking of lights, suddenly that's all I'm seeing,* I thought as I got out of my head and snapped back to reality. Bobby's stage people were talking to him, playing with the lights, showing me where I needed to stand and checking the sound system. They showed me where my water would be in case I needed to take a swig during the performance. *Star loved oldies but goodies music, and I love having one played when I'm introduced to get the crowd going. Star used to talk about her dream of becoming a motivational speaker. She wanted to dance onto the stage while one of her favorite songs was playing. In honor of Star's dream, I now do this. Star was right, it really gets the audience going.* The song I chose was Earth, Wind, and Fire, "Shining Star." *I just need to keep my head held high and save the tears for later so Jessie doesn't get all worked up and having to touch up my make-up again. I do look flawless. Jessie's the real deal. I've never had a makeup artist as good as him, and he does hair; he's super fab.*

Lawrence made sure I understood my queues as we practiced parts of my performance. "We need to make sure sound, lighting, and everything is to your satisfaction, Ms. Knight, before the event starts. Can you go through a short performance for us so the crew can practice their queues with the music, lighting, sound, etc.?"

"Sure. Usually I take a chapter out of Star's book and discuss it and link it into the performance. Marissa and I stopped our interview at Star getting married. Let me pick up from there and talk about that. "This will be a good performance test run."

Lawrence was pleased and agreed. He said, "This way, you won't have to perform the exact same story you plan to tell tonight, but it will still be as effective as if you did." He gave his crew full control over the show and my performance. Bobby and Lawrence sat down in the audience along with Jessie, Pam, Scotty, and Marissa. Adam the driver had returned. I had given him a VIP pass, so he came back to enjoy the festivities. The live show started in less than two hours, so he decided to come early so he wouldn't miss a thing.

I walked behind curtains as the MC came out and took the microphone off the stand. He started saying all these fabulous things about me and why I was there, then he introduced me. The lights and music started playing, and my mock audience clapped and yelled like they were at a rock concert. "Shining Star" was playing as I danced my way out to the center of the stage toward the MC. He handed me the microphone, and we started dancing together a short time before he danced off the stage. Then I gave the queue to end the music. I said hello to my fans and thanked everyone for showing up. I promised to give them a performance of a lifetime as I shared Star's story with them. I told them that by the end, they would love her as much as I did, and their lives would never be the same, as she had a way of impacting and changing how we think about the world we live in. "You'll see what I mean in about an hour. Let me start with chapter 6 of her book. Has everyone read my book?" My mock audience yelled, and some of them held up my book to prove, yes, they had read it. "In this chapter, Star and Ethan get married ..."

We didn't have a wedding and considered going to the justice of peace. We didn't feel worthy of getting married in a church, especially since we were shacking, as Grandma Maria calls it, and with me already pregnant, this was considered a sin. At least this is how I was raised. Our pastor agreed to marry us with two witnesses in our apartment instead. It was simple. I wore my graduation dress and jazzed it up with a new pair of red and white heels. I don't really like red, but the shoes were cute and sexy.

Things were still bad for Ethan and I financially. The car we owned was a piece of crap. Ethan inherited it from an uncle who passed away. It needed a muffler, and the passenger floor was missing. It was very difficult trying to keep my feet from hanging out of the bottom, especially now that I was seven months into the pregnancy and larger than life. Picking my feet up off the floorboard was like riding in a Flintstones car. I didn't enjoy it at all. It needed struts really bad. I literally felt every bump we drove over. I was more miserable in that car than walking on my swollen elephant feet.

Ethan attended all the Lamaze classes. We planned to have our baby in the new natural birthing center. This program had been developed for mothers who preferred natural childbirth and not the traditional assistance of drugs. I chose this option because I wanted to have my babies like women did before they were treated with drugs to reduce the pain. I wanted to experience the complete natural childbirth. I knew I was strong enough to do it this way. I looked forward to it. Each unit was set up like a small apartment. It had a small kitchen, bathroom, living area, and the bedroom where you would give birth if you chose that room. They even provided you with your own midwife. We met with her biweekly so she could track the progress and read the medical reports from my primary doctor. The rooms were warm, relaxing, and private. Each mother had her own private room, and that is where she would stay to get to know her newborn even after delivery, instead of being admitted to a regular hospital room with a curtain divider between patients. I looked forward to giving birth to our child naturally.

I was excited about learning all the breathing techniques. I enjoyed having my husband share this experience with me, especially when I saw other mothers had no support. Some were alone, or with a sister or mom to assist. I felt special having Ethan with me, learning how to assist and help me so he'd be ready when I gave birth to our child.

Ethan's bus route had changed, and he would drive in front of the apartment every day, and I would run downstairs and sit outside on the front steps and wait for him to drive by so I could wave and blow him butterfly kisses. He enjoyed that special moment of our day as much as I did.

One day I was getting ready for our daily greeting, and at the top of the stairs, I proceeded to take my first step and completely missed it. My stomach was so big; I couldn't even see my feet. I found myself falling down the stairs. I wasn't able to grab onto anything to help break my fall or even brace myself hard landing. I was falling so fast, bumping down each step as if I was a bouncing basketball. I will never forget how bad it actually hurt. I was in severe pain when I finally reached the bottom. Of course, like any other time dealing with pain, I didn't cry or even give it a second thought. I mean, pain was a normal part of my life, and I hadn't been allowed to cry about it then, so why bother now.

I picked my badly bruised pregnant body up off the bottom landing and slowly readjusted myself. I didn't feel the baby inside me moving. It was probably a little shaken over the fall. *I'm sure I'll feel it move again soon after it gets over the shock.* I continued outside and sat on the porch, to wait for my love call. Around the corner came the yellow bus. I was so excited. Ethan was right on time. He honked the school bus horn, and I waved and blew my kisses. This was a happy time for us. We were waiting for the baby to arrive any day now. We didn't find out the baby's sex and were anxious to find out if we were having a boy or a girl. We picked out a girl's name and hadn't been able to agree on a boy's name yet but we figured we still had time.

I noticed a few days had passed, and the baby still hadn't moved. I remember talking to it and praying for it to move so that I would know it was okay. I was scared. It never crossed my mind to go to the emergency room or to contact my doctor and inform them about the fall. I was naïve and young and just didn't know any better. I started to panic, and next thing I knew, I felt it move. It didn't move as strongly as it had before my fall, but I felt it move slightly inside me, and that was good enough for me. I was relieved.

I gained more than thirty-five pounds with this pregnancy and was big as a house. It looked like I was carrying twins. I wasn't much of a milk drinker, but I could put away a gallon a day. I was always hungry, and I didn't drink or smoke during my pregnancy. I couldn't wait to deliver so I could get back to my adult routine. I had a craving for BBQ something fierce, and Ethan and I drove to one of our favorite spots for takeout. We then went to our other favorite place park to enjoy our meal. Earlier that day, I felt some sharp pains, but ignored them as being Braxton Hicks. These are false labor pains that feel slightly like contractions, and my doctor explained to me they were normal and not to be alarmed. So of course we continued to talk and enjoy our meal.

Out of nowhere, I had a pain so bad it made me jump up out of my seat and actually scream. It surprised me. It came on strong. Not a good ten minutes later, I felt another, even more intense. I looked at Ethan with a confused look because I had no idea what was going on. We immediately remembered our instructions in Lamaze class and started timing what we thought had to be contractions. We were to go to the hospital if they were less than five minutes apart. I remember the pain hurting worse than they explained in Lamaze class. I was a pretty tough cookie and had a high tolerance for pain. We timed the contractions. They were coming more frequently, and the pain was becoming unbearable. I was speechless. I looked at Ethan with excitement and fear in my eyes. I said, "If this pain gets any worse, I will probably die." He took that as his cue to rush me to the emergency room. We were about to have a baby.

We explained we were signed up for natural childbirth so they wouldn't take us to labor and delivery. We were immediately assigned our special room, and I was upset because my doctor was on vacation, and no one on duty knew anything about me. The baby wasn't due for two more weeks. Nevertheless, it felt like I was not being treated with the care I had expected under the circumstances. The doctor on duty seemed distant and clueless. I didn't like her at all.

By now, the pain had worsened, and I was trying all the techniques I had learned, but they were not working. I was breathing right and positioning myself just right. I even went so far as to do some of the extreme emergency methods I learned, and even they weren't helping. I hated the nurses tugging, poking, and examining me. I just wanted to be left alone. Everyone around me was acting like business as usual and looked at me like I needed to suck it up and calm down. I was unable to get them to realize I felt something wasn't right. I really felt I shouldn't be in this much pain.

I'd been having contractions less than a minute a part for hours. *Surely, I should have delivered this baby by now.* I felt pressure like no other, and yet they kept telling me I wasn't dilated enough. I felt like my insides were tearing apart and that there was no way I couldn't be completely dilated by now. It was awful. Fourteen hours later, my body started to push. The nurses yelled at me to stop pushing, and I told them I couldn't help it; my body just naturally felt the urge to push. They panicked and told me to stop, and I just couldn't control it; my body was ready to deliver no matter what they said.

Suddenly, I reached down because I thought my water had broken, which hadn't happened yet, another mystery to everyone. I was very wet, and when I pulled my hand out from underneath me, it was covered in blood. I immediately went into shock at the sight of all the blood. I started vomiting uncontrollably. The last thing I remember was being prepped for emergency surgery and my doctor looking over at Ethan asking him if he had to choose between me and our baby, if life depended on it, who would he want them to save? I heard him say without hesitation, "My wife of course. We can always have more children." I was rushed away quickly. I had never been more afraid.

I woke up, and there was no baby in my arms. There was sadness surrounding me. I looked up, and Ethan was sitting next to my bed, and we were no longer in the birthing center. I was in a recovery room. I was afraid to hear the bad news. I looked at him as he looked at me. He smiled and gently kissed me on my chapped lips. I looked like I had survived a hurricane. My hair was all off to one side of my head like the wind had blown it in one direction. My face was swollen from the pain I had endured. I was weak and a bit nauseous.

Ethan looked at me and told me he was glad I had lived through it and how he had never been more afraid. He said he went to the hospital chapel immediately after they rolled me away and prayed that God would let me live. He said when the doctors came out to give him the news that I had survived, he was overwhelmed with joy. He said when they told him our baby had also made it, he burst into tears. He said, "Thank you, God."

Ethan said they asked if he would like to see his daughter for only a brief minute, as she was being observed for birth defects and other physical concerns due to the nature of the delivery. He said she was absolutely beautiful. He said he couldn't wait for her to meet the strongest mommy she could ever have. He said he was very proud of me for dealing with all that pain and that he was sorry, he had no idea it was not a normal delivery. He said the doctors explained to him why I was in so much pain.

The doctors explained the placenta was in front of the baby. This was why I couldn't dilate properly. They said the baby was trapped and couldn't come down the birth canal because the placenta was blocking it. The baby went into distress and was suffocating from the internal bleeding they also weren't aware of until I started hemorrhaging. They asked if I had any trauma before going into labor like a bad fall or something. I immediately realized this happened when I fell down the stairs. My insides shifted out of place at that time, and that explained why I didn't feel any movement those few days. I was shocked this could even happen and had no idea how dangerous it was to take a fall during pregnancy. I felt guilty and thought it was my fault my baby had almost died.

It had been hours, and I still hadn't seen my precious daughter. The worry that came over me paralyzed me. I knew something had to be wrong with her. Ethan and I waited in my recovery room, praying she was okay and that they would allow us to see her soon. I wanted to bond with her and was curious about what she looked like. *I'm a mother now.* I almost couldn't believe it.

Right then, in came the nurse with a small portable glass crib and a tiny little baby girl that was crying. The nurse said she had been crying for hours. When she handed her to me, I was filled with joy. I hushed her and spoke to her. I introduced myself to my newborn, and the minute she heard my voice, she settled down as if she was now safe and had no more worries.

The nurse said she just wanted her mommy. She was amazed at how fast she calmed down and said no one was able to comfort her for hours as they ran their tests. All the tests came back fine. I was the proud parent of a healthy baby girl. I felt blessed.

I looked at the most beautiful baby I'd ever seen calmly resting in my arms. I kissed her so many times, I was suffocating her with all the love I had. I loved her so much. I loved her more than I loved my Ethan, my mom, Dallas, even myself. I knew she was a gift from God. I thanked him for trusting me with her life, her future, and her well-being. I was determined not to disappoint her.

I decided to do everything natural and couldn't wait to breastfeed her. I knew she had to be hungry. The nurses were given instructions not to feed her formula, because I planned to breastfeed. It took her a while to latch on, but eventually, her tiny little mouth naturally figured it out, and finally, I bonded completely with my daughter.

Only a mother will fully understand what that moment felt like. I had fallen in love, and it was a love deeper than any love I had felt before now. I remember thinking how innocent she was and how she totally depended on her dad and me to take care of her. I could never imagine her coming to me and telling me someone harmed her and then not protecting her. I would kill for her, and I would die for her. We named her Sophie.

Ethan and I wanted to be good parents. We started going to church regularly. We stopped smoking marijuana and drinking. We were devoted Christians, and we were happy we made those changes in our lives. My mom traveled all the way from Chicago back to Georgia to meet her firstborn granddaughter. She was so proud. It was hard for me to see her that happy holding my daughter in her arms. It was the first time we had seen each other since graduation. As usual, we faked our way through the situation and put our differences aside for Sophie's sake. It was good seeing something so small and innocent make her that happy. She was a proud grandma. She loved Sophie as much as I did, maybe even more. They immediately shared a special bond.

One day we came home, and there was a note posted on our door. Our duplex had been condemned by the city, and we had to move out immediately. Of course we had nowhere to go, and once again we ended up at Agnes's house. Again I was miserable. I hated having our baby in that negative environment. Ethan's bus-driving job wasn't bringing in enough money quickly enough for us to have a down payment on first month's rent and deposit. I felt desperate, so I decided to look for a job. I thought being a nanny would be ideal if I could convince them to allow me to bring my baby to work with me. I contacted a couple that had an ad in the paper. I asked witchy poo (Agnes) to watch Sophie, my daughter, so I could go to the interview.

When I returned from the interview, I found my monster-in-law dowsing my little Sophie in some liquid potion, chanting something, and Sophie was screaming and crying uncontrollably. I was shocked. When I witnessed this, I completely lost it. I'd never cursed at an elder in my life. My mother may have had her issues, but she did teach me to respect my elders. But this time, it was war!

I wouldn't allow anyone to harm my child. Casting spells on my daughter was unacceptable. Agnes had crossed the line. I ran over and snatched my baby out of her wicked arms so fast and started telling her off like I had always wanted to do. I was screaming at her to never ever put her hands on my child again! I told her she was sick and I didn't believe in the crap she practiced and did not want my child to be a part of it.

I called Ethan, on his job, crying so hard he could barely hear why I was so upset. He left work immediately to come see about Sophie and me. He was furious with his mother. Of course he was torn a bit, because he loves his mother, and he has lived with her ways his entire life. This was normal to him. I really had an issue with it. I couldn't accept it. I may have had a dysfunctional family, but this took the cake. We believed in God and only God, not some hocus-pocus bull crap! We had to get out of his mother's house soon. I told Ethan there was no way I could live like that any longer. Ethan was torn between pleasing me and respecting his mother, especially since we lived in her home. It was a very difficult time for us, and it put a huge strain on our young marriage.

A couple days later, I found out I got the nanny job. I was so excited. Now I could make enough money to help us get out of Agnes's house. Ethan got a promotion with the school system as a grounds maintenance worker, making more money. Unfortunately, I was fired from my nanny job a month later. The couple said I wasn't paying attention to details, and I missed the little things they needed done. They felt I was slacking on my responsibilities. They felt my work wasn't up to their expectations. They handed me a severance paycheck and drove Sophie and I back to Agnes's home. I didn't see it coming. I had no idea I was that bad of an employee. I mean, how hard was it to watch two babies and keep a mansion clean? I was embarrassed and ashamed that I had neglected my duties and wasn't able to keep working for this awesome family. They gave me a chance, and I blew it. I was crushed.

Ethan and I loved our new place. We've been here two weeks now. It was in a better neighborhood, and we were finally on a lower level. We even talked about having more children. We didn't want our kids to be that far apart in age, so we decided we would start trying for another after our Sophie turned one. Didn't take long. Four months later, we were expecting again.

Like most couples, we had our good days and our bad ones. It was Easter Sunday, and I was ironing a shirt for Ethan to wear to church when the phone rang. It was Agnes. She told me Ethan's older brother Luke had died. I wasn't quite sure how I would relay this news to Ethan, so I walked over to him slowly and just handed him the phone, so his mother could tell him. It was a sad day for the family. Luke was a diabetic. I didn't quite understand the disease. I knew he didn't do anything but live upstairs in a room next to Ethan's, and he never left the house until once after Sophie was born. He came by our home to see her. I was shocked. He had never left the house before then, but he loved Sophie. He loved her enough to break out of his shell to come visit her. I will never forget that day. All of Sophie's uncles loved her. They spoiled her rotten. The news must have shocked me more than I realized, because I burned Ethan's shirt. I had put the iron facedown on his shirt when I received the call and forgot to take it off until after, I handed Ethan the phone.

I thought our lives were finally starting to move in the right direction, and now this. Things were looking better financially. We were excited about becoming parents again. We were hoping for a boy, so we could have a boy and a girl. We thought that would be picture perfect like in the movies. We didn't want to know the sex of our unborn child, just like before Sophie was born. We wanted to be surprised.

My doctor encouraged me to have a C-section, due to the complications I had during the first delivery. I was totally against it, because I wanted to try to have it naturally again. My doctor felt it would be too risky but agreed to allow me to go into labor and carefully monitor me in case we needed to do an emergency C-section. I was cool with this decision.

Ethan changed after Luke died. He seemed lost, depressed, and distant. He lost his temper more often than usual. He started staying out late and coming home drunk. I was always on edge, not knowing what would set him off next. It frightened me.

I'm seven months pregnant and Sophie will be two years old next month. Ethan came home later than his usual time. My back was killing me, and I had already put Sophie to bed. I had also gone to bed early placing a pillow between my legs, hoping to relieve my painful backpressure. This pregnancy was harder than when I carried Sophie. Ethan came home intoxicated, looking for a fight. He loved to pick fights. He wasn't happy unless he was complaining about something. One minute I was explaining why I was in bed so early, and the next thing I knew, Ethan had grabbed me by my hair and was dragging me to the floor and started bashing my head into our bedroom wall. I was screaming for him to stop. I had one hand on my belly holding my baby, trying to protect him from hitting me in my stomach, and the other on my head, trying to soften the blows. I thought he had totally lost his mind. I thought he was going to kill me. I could barely stay conscious. I felt my strength weakening and Ethan's getting stronger the more I tried to fight back. I could not get him to stop. He frightened Sophie. She had climbed out of her crib to see why her mommy was screaming and crying. When she saw her daddy hurting me, she pleaded with him to stop hurting his mommy. But he didn't hear or see her. With my only free hand, I motioned to her to leave the room, and she ran back to her room crying. I was sad because I couldn't protect her.

Ethan's drunkenness finally set in. He had physically worn himself out, and let me go. He tossed my pregnant body to the side, stood up and just walked away, like nothing happened. I got up as fast as I could and grabbed Sophie out of her crib to get her to stop crying. I was dizzy, my head was bleeding, I couldn't tell from where and my body was badly bruised. I was terrified. I thought for sure he killed our unborn baby. I worried more about Sophie and what she had just witnessed. Once I calmed her down, I put her back in her crib and told her to stay there until I returned. I went to make sure the monster was not coming back to harm me. He was sound asleep in our bed. I called the police on Ethan for the first time. When I opened the door, and they saw my bloody face and my large stomach, one of the cops, said, "Where is he? I am going to give him a taste of his own medicine. Who does this to a pregnant woman?" He was furious. They asked me if I wanted to press charges. I said no, I just wanted to get out and needed them to help me get out so I could feel safe. They took Sophie and me from my home and dropped us off at the local women's shelter.

I lived in a tiny room at the women's shelter located inside the YWCA. I had nowhere else to go. Mom and Dallas were long gone. The YWCA housed battered women, and as a part of the women-in-transition program, each woman had to attend counseling sessions twice a day, one individual session and the other a group session. I was fine with the one-on-one session, but when it came to the group sessions, I felt out of place. The stories these women would tell were more on my mother's level of abuse. I mean, I felt my abuse wasn't nearly as bad as theirs, and this made me feel like I was in the wrong place.

I tried my hardest to cooperate with the program requirements. I found myself feeling embarrassed, ashamed, and in denial. It had been four weeks since we left. Ethan found out where Sophie and I were. The director of the program said he had been trying to contact me. They don't let the abusers talk to the victims. They protect us from them at all cost. All the women were given strict instructions not to contact or speak to our abusers. I was a couple weeks away from giving birth to our second child. I had been in the program long enough to transition into a home for Sophie and me. We were next on the waiting list. I should've been excited, but my emotions got the best of me. I couldn't imagine giving birth to our second child without Ethan. I didn't want to bring a child into this world, living in a battered women's shelter. I was torn and broke the rules and secretly made arrangements for Ethan to meet me so we could talk. The next day, I voluntarily left the program and went home to have my baby with my husband so we could be a family again. Ethan promised to never hit me again, and I believed him.

He knew I would leave him and call the police on him, and I threatened to press charges next time. Ethan said he almost lost his family, and he said that changed his whole look on life and that now he was a changed man. I wanted to believe things would get better and that Ethan loved me enough to change. I wanted marriage, a family, and a better life. One week later, we gave birth to a beautiful healthy baby girl by C-section. We named her Brooklyn.

Everyone thought we were the ideal couple. We had friends and a lot of family gatherings at our home. We entertained a lot. Our place was the hot spot for people to hang out and drink, listen to music, BBQ, play cards, and just have fun. I don't remember a time someone wasn't knocking on our door or we didn't have a visitor or family member over. We were happy for the most part. We enjoyed our lifestyle.

I thought things were getting better, but I noticed Ethan becoming agitated over the smallest things. I walked on egg shells most of the time, trying not to set him off. He really enjoyed being a father. He would help me with anything when it came to the girls. He fed them, gave them baths, changed their diapers. He even did their hair. We did lots of family things like going to the park, the beach, and family picnics. We took them to visit friends and family regularly. We bought child seats for our bicycles so the girls could ride with us. The girls and I attended all Ethan's company softball games. Ethan played on a summer league, and we'd go sit on the bleachers and cheer him on. We were picture perfect on the outside. But behind closed doors, we lived another life entirely.

Ethan started experimenting with other types of drugs. I started doing them right along with him. It was just the way our lives were back then. I'd surrendered to how he wanted our lives to be without a fight. It was my way of trying to keep the peace and him happy. He became more controlling of me and more jealous. I wasn't allowed to work or have friends outside of his friends. He questioned why it would take me so long to run an errand or go to the grocery store. I found myself answering these questions as honestly as I could, trying not to upset him. It was okay for him to do as he pleased. He could hang out with the boys as often as he wanted. He would stay out all night and leave and come as he pleased. If I questioned him, it only opened the door to more physical abuse, so most of the time I kept my mouth shut.

I started using the drugs to numb the pain and misery of my complicated life. I started drinking more heavily and smoking more marijuana. I wasn't proud of where I was in my life, but I couldn't figure out how to change it. I accepted it for what it was worth and lost all hope of ever having anything better than what I had right now. One evening Ethan brought home some cocaine. I wasn't aware he was using like this, but it all made sense when I really thought about it. He insisted I try it. He said it was a good high. I snorted it and didn't know what to expect, and then I realized I was floating mindlessly in ways I had never experienced with smoking marijuana. Drugs had now become our primary entertainment.

Once, Ethan got a hold of some crack cocaine. He even had a pipe. I wasn't that educated about drugs, so I followed suit as usual. I remember wondering what the big deal was because I didn't feel high. Well, to my surprise, almost twenty-four hours later, I had not slept. I realized I had been higher than a kite that entire time. I had no idea what to expect when I smoked crack, and after I experienced it, I decided to leave that stuff alone. It was more potent than I had ever known, and this frightened me enough not to dibble and dabble in crack cocaine ever again. This drug wasn't for me. Nothing frightened me more than not being in control of the high, and smoking crack cocaine made me feel like I was not in control; it controlled me. I didn't mind snorting a little cocaine or lacing it in a joint every now and then. That was cool. It didn't seem as dangerous as crack cocaine.

I could not figure out how Ethan made so much money, more than we had ever had, but we were always broke. He was always complaining about how we never had enough money. I thought we had plenty and would stay positive and encouraging. I knew things would get better someday. At least that's what I wanted.

It was hard to stay positive as Ethan started lying more, and it seemed like he was hiding something from me. I questioned him with my suspicions, but that usually backfired on me and led to a beating or two.

One day, I received a notice from our landlord that we had fallen too far behind on our rent again. I thought this had to be impossible.

How could this be? I was furious. Ethan was not paying the bills like he said he was, and now we were once again faced with eviction. I was devastated and refused to move back and live with his mother. I called my best friend Ally, she was now married and a new mommy. I begged Ally, to let the girls and I stay with her and her husband Corey, just long enough until Ethan found us another place to live. They agreed as long as it didn't take too long. Ally and Corey lived in the heart of Atlanta, right in the thick of things. We stayed in a much smaller city about three hours from Ally. Ethan moved in with his mother, so he could keep his job and save up enough money. We agreed it would be no more than a month, plenty of time to save up first month's rent and deposit again. Ethan got paid once a week, so at least four paychecks would be enough.

When the girls and I moved to the city, it was humbling for me to say the least. I was embarrassed and ashamed, and once again I felt homeless. It just didn't make sense to me. How could this happen again? I remember feeling like we were a burden on Ally and Corey, especially since they were newlyweds and new parents.

I missed Ethan something awful, and so did the girls. They loved their daddy and couldn't understand why he wasn't with us and why we were here. It became clear that Ethan wasn't missing us. He didn't call us or write us or check on us. It was like he had forgotten all about us. Every now and then, he would show up unannounced, showering me with gifts, and then he would leave without spending any quality time with the girls and me. It was somewhat odd.

Ally and Corey were confused. They wondered where he was getting all this extra money to shower me with gifts while we were left homeless with nowhere to go. How could he just dump his family off on them and not make us his priority and find us a place to live? I hated how Ally would look at me with shame and pity. She had known Ethan since we first dated. She had no idea he was the type of guy that would do this to his family. I had no answers. I felt helpless. I totally agreed with Ally. But I had nothing but Ethan's word. I had to trust that he would do the right thing by us and come get us and take his family home soon.

I started questioning Ethan every time I was able to contact him, but he'd come up with one excuse after another. Once he said he was working overtime and trying his hardest to save money to find us a place to live. I believed him because I was in no position not to at this point. Surely he only wanted the best for his family. Right?

Unfortunately the girls and I had worn out our welcome. Ally and Corey wanted their lives back. They were ready for us to leave. I know this was one of the hardest things for Ally to tell me, but I understood. No hard feelings. I contacted Ethan to come get us, and we ended up at Agnes's house once again. This time the house had gone downhill. When the girls and I arrived, she had no running water, and the toilets and showers didn't work. The house was in a condemned condition, not fit for anyone to live. Yet my children and I had nowhere else to go.

I hated Ethan for once again putting us in this predicament. When we got there, he would find reasons to leave us stranded in the house for hours at a time without letting us know where he was or when he'd be back. He never left me the car, so the girls and I couldn't even leave the house. I guess he had better things to do than to spend time with his family. It was like he didn't want us. Like we had become a burden for him. He kept promising he would find us a place to stay soon, and soon to me just wasn't happening soon enough. All I had was his promises, and his promises gave me a glimpse of hope.

"One thing I'd always admired about Star was no matter how bad things got for her, she always found a way to hold onto a small thread of hope. I didn't know how she did it. I don't know that I could be so strong. Her life was challenging, and she never seemed to get a break. I hated having to put her and my nieces out of my home. I loved those girls so much and hated that Ethan would put his family in such a compromising position and just leave them to fend for themselves. Sending Star back to him hurt me a lot. But I had to think of my marriage and my family. We were both married with children. Both young mother's and still friends.

"Thank you for letting me share a chapter of the book with you all tonight. I will be available for the book signing immediately after the show. If you haven't read the book yet, it will be available for purchase. It is a must-read, not because I endorse it, but because Star shares an amazing story of survival—we can all take something from her life and use it to better ourselves. Thank you."

My small audience of working-crew fans rose to their feet and applauded.

Chapter 7

"We have about forty-five minutes before the live show, Ms. Knight. I hope you're not exhausted from the dress rehearsal," said Bobby as he escorted me off the stage back to my room to relax a minute. I assured him I was fine and that I enjoyed telling Star's story. That was why I was here.

Pam and Marissa followed, talking and whispering to themselves about some of the things I had discussed about Star. They mentioned they had read the book and wanted to know if I would sign their copies. I said, "Of course, and you don't have to stand in line. If you have them with you, I can sign them now". They both pulled a copy out of their purses, almost like synchronized swimmers. I laughed. And they did too. I signed each book with a positive quote Star would always say when things got tough. Then I drew a Star as my signature. I would never sign my name, because this was all for Star, not me.

Marissa asked what I would discuss for the live performance. I told her it would most likely be one of Star's biggest challenges. Star had gone through a lot of things, but the relationship she had with her mom was her most difficult. I tried to choose experiences Star had that others would connect with. Star's life was anything but easy. She always said if her story only touches one person, then that would be enough for her. Just one, she would always tell me, just one.

Marissa asked, "Did Ethan ever come through for her and get her out of his mother's house?"

"Oh yeah, Ethan. He was quite the provider. Corey and I loved him. We knew he loved Star and the girls, but something wasn't quite right with his priorities. He never seemed to be able to step up and be the man Star needed him to be. Star had to find ways to help pull them out of every situation Ethan put them in, and it was never easy. Especially with two small mouths to feed, but Star was determined. She would do anything for those girls …"

I knew I had to start working again, and I found a job. I swallowed my pride and allowed Agnes to once again help out with the girls so I could save up enough money to get us out of her house. Ethan had become more distant, and some of the things he was doing made me suspicious. I couldn't quite put my finger on why I was suspicious of actions, but I had my doubts his recent behavior. I tried not to focus too much on him because I had no time to waste on his ignorance. I had to find a place to live so I could raise the girls. Their well-being was my primary concern.

I finally saved up enough money and found us a place to stay once again. Unfortunately it was on the second level. Ever since I fell down the stairs, I didn't like living on the second-floor. Our neighbors below were these two beautiful young girls. One had a daughter with the same nickname as Brooklyn. Brooklyn had so much baby chub we called her Pooh, like Winnie the Pooh. Charlotte was the one with the baby girl, with the same nickname as Brooklyn's. She was so sweet and her daughter Cassidy was the same age as Brooklyn. The neighbor girls were young and loved to party. Charlotte was an only child from a small town outside of Atlanta. Smaller than the town we currently live. The other was Ginger, a California Valley girl. I'd never met anyone from California before. She was beautiful. Unfortunately, they weren't our neighbors for long. I was glad because Ethan had a weakness for Ginger. She flirted with him all the time, and he didn't even try to ignore her advances. I think he encouraged it. His ego was overinflated. Those girls were way out of his league. When they moved out, an older couple with two boys moved in two weeks later. We thought they were cool and got along just fine. Later we found out they were involved in a huge drug ring. One evening, the feds busted down their door and raided their apartment. I had never seen anything like it before. I was terrified. I was scared they were coming after us and held onto the girls and watched the door, afraid that any second they were coming for us too. One of the DEA agents quietly knocked on the door. When I opened it, he quickly put his finger to his lips, saying, "Shh," and assured me we were not in any danger. He closed the door and went back downstairs, and the commotion continued for hours. I thought it would never end. Then suddenly there was complete silence. I'm not sure if they found everything they were looking for, because a couple months later Ethan was cutting the grass noticed several bags of crack scattered throughout the backyard. Ethan thought he had died and gone to drug heaven.

I was working the graveyard shift at a local nursing home. Ethan didn't like other people watching the girls. I had to get a job that would allow him to watch the girls when I was at work. I hated that job. I never had time to spend with my family, and I was tired all the time. I had even started experimenting with caffeine pills, just to stay awake at work during those awful hours. I didn't like the way high doses of caffeine made me feel, but I took them because they helped me stay awake through my shift.

Ethan had left the maintenance job right before we were evicted from our last apartment, before I had to move in with Ally and her family. I was against it, because it was a factory job. I always felt Ethan could do much better. Not that factory jobs aren't good. They pay very well. I just thought Ethan could do a job that required using his intelligence. I always thought he was a very smart man. Ethan had big dreams when we met. That's why I married him; I knew he could accomplish anything he wanted in life. At the same time, the school district had offered him a full-time training opportunity with benefits to become a licensed electrician. They promised him a very nice raise after he completed the training. I thought, *to actually have a licensed trade, have a real title, something you could become an expert at to perform the job.* I was encouraging him to take this opportunity, even though he wouldn't make as much during the training as he would make at the factory. I was thinking long-term; it would be the best choice. However, for some odd reason, he was adamant about taking the factory position instead. It was better pay right away, and he just didn't want to wait. I believed it was the wrong choice, but it didn't matter how I felt. Ethan always did what he wanted.

Sophie started kindergarten, and Brooklyn was growing up to become quite the mommy's girl. She was spoiled rotten and had to have her way, just like her daddy. I enjoyed being a mom and watching the girls grow up. I just wanted them to be happy, and I was glad we were once again trying to move forward with our future.

One day out of the blue Ethan kept bringing up this woman's name. Kelsie this and Kelsie that. I said, "Who the hell is Kelsie?" He said she was a coworker of his. He talked about her more than I cared to listen, and they were becoming closer and closer. When I questioned their relationship, he assured me I was exaggerating, and to prove they were just friends, he finally mentioned she was married. Soon after, Kelsie invited us over to have dinner with her and her husband. Of course I was glad to know she was married, and the dinner was a bit awkward. Ethan was acting so nervous. It was actually pathetic. I watched Kelsie and Ethan's unspoken body language. I've always said a woman should follow her intuition, because it will never be wrong. I was convinced something else had to be going on between them. After the phony dinner date, I continued questioning Ethan, and he continued to deny they were more than friends.

Kelsie started buying the girls gifts for their birthdays, calling Ethan several times a day. She had become more of a part of my children's lives than I was. Once I came home from work, and Brooklyn told me how she spent the entire day with Kelsie and daddy. I started to feel like this woman was trying to replace me as a mom and wife. I was furious! I told Ethan she was not allowed to spend time with our children ever again without my permission. I was not happy about the way this friendship was affecting our marriage. I started finding receipts for gifts, flowers, and jewelry I never received. Once Ethan surprised me with a blue jean jacket I had pointed out at the mall one day when we were window shopping as a family. Next thing I knew, I found a receipt for the jacket, but on the receipt showed he purchased two jackets. Who got the other jacket? Kelsie? I'm not stupid. The more I questioned Ethan, the more he got defensive, and the more he threatened to harm me physically if I wouldn't leave it alone. He hadn't put his hands on me in a long time, and I wasn't trying to give him a reason to do it anytime soon. I just wanted answers.

He started working even longer hours and finding more excuses to pick a fight so he could leave the house more often. Once he didn't show up in time for me to go to work, and when he finally did, he could not have care less that I could lose my job for being late for work. He had become so full of himself. He was an arrogant asshole.

One Friday evening, he called and said he had to work late, and I said okay as usual. By now my suspicions had gotten the better of me, and I decided to call his job back an hour later. I asked to speak with him, and they said he had clocked out over an hour ago and was gone for the evening.

My stomach dropped. I knew he was with her. I started calling hotels all over town. *I was once Kelsie*, I thought. *I know Ethan and his patterns, his moves, his ways, and how he is making her feel special.* The more I thought about how special he was making her feel, the more pissed off I got. I wanted to find him and catch him in his lie. Of course the dummy actually booked a room under his real name. I asked the desk attendant to connect me to the room. Ethan must have thought I was room service or something because he answered. I finally busted him. He couldn't lie his way out of it anymore. He knew I knew he'd been lying to me the entire time. I was so hurt. I lost my mind, saying so many things I can't remember before hanging up. My pain was so unbearable with all the emotions I was experiencing. I just started crying. He cowardly hurried home. I was still crying. I asked him how long he had been sleeping with Kelsie. At first he tried lying and said tonight was the first time. I wasn't falling for that crap. I knew it had been longer. I kept having flashbacks of their sexual suggestions at the dinner table with their clueless spouses looking on. He finally admitted they had been sleeping together since the girls and I lived with Ally and Corey.

"What? Since Atlanta? You've been sleeping with Kelsie for almost two years?" This explained why he was so insistent on taking the job at the factory. Why he didn't want to become and electrician. It also explained his distance when I stayed in Atlanta. The guilt gifts and why he couldn't save money. He was courting his new girlfriend. Everything just started to make sense. The only thing that didn't add up was "why we were in so much financial trouble once again?" Then I found out Kelsie's husband was a big-time drug dealer. She was the one Ethan had been buying drugs from. She was the one who got him started on cocaine. He hadn't told me just how serious his drug usage had become. I found out it was worse than I had imagined. He was an addict.

Kelsie was a plus size woman. She had thin, long, messy jerry curl and wasn't very attractive at all. She had a light complexion. Her complexion may have played a key role in her thinking she was prettier than me. In our culture, dark skinned girls are considered ugly and light skinned girls are prettier.

Ethan made her feel beautiful and even encouraged her to lose weight. I heard she used to be much bigger, and Ethan was there for her when she lost the weight to look better for him. During this time, they became closer, as they also shared and did drugs together. Working together allowed them the convenience of seeing each other every day, and it contributed to their love affair. To my surprise, they had fallen in love.

I wanted to vomit at the thought of this sleaze bucket sleeping with my husband. I was so upset all I could do was pick up the phone and call her house. I was about to give the fake slut a piece of my mind. Instead, her husband answered the phone. I told him his wife had slept with my husband and that he needed to keep a tighter leash on his whore and hung up. The next day, I was still furious. I went to the factory where they both her and Ethan worked. I wanted to kick her ass. All I could think about was how she smiled in my face and was sleeping with my husband the entire time. Of course I made a scene, and they wouldn't let me past the security gates. I made sure everyone in that factory knew what type of slut she was before I left. I wanted to destroy her life like she had destroyed mine.

Ethan didn't get off easy either. I kicked him out of the house. I was done with him. I had put up with so much from him, and this was the thanks I got. The pain was unbearable and I was overwhelmed with shame. I was embarrassed and felt like the biggest fool ever. *How could I love someone who could treat me like this? How could I be so stupid? Why would he mistreat me like this and not care enough about me or love me as much as I loved him?* I really loved Ethan. He was all I had, the father of my children, and I wanted our marriage to work. Ethan left and went to stay with Agnes, of course. A week passed, and I didn't miss him at all. I was still hurt and very angry. I wasn't sure if I ever wanted to see him again. He called so many times I had to stop answering the phone. I needed time to think and figure out what my next step was going to be.

The only family I had after Mom and Dallas moved away was a family I met through Ethan's brother Dennis. He had a girlfriend and her name was Autumn. Autumn and I became friends even though Ethan didn't want me to have friends outside of his. Autumn knew how he was, and she was fierce and refused to allow Ethan to dictate our friendship. She was a strong young lady. She was younger than I was, but she was not afraid to stand up for herself or me. I loved her. She was sweet, and her family was on the crazy side. I'd never met anyone like them. They were opposite of Ally's wholesome family. Autumn's family was a little ghetto, street wise, and rough around the edges. I liked that. The women were all strong, and I really liked being around women who had a voice. It didn't take long. I had become a sister. I now had a godmother. Momma Laverne had taken me under her wing, and I let her. They were all I had outside of Ethan and his family.

I didn't feel I could talk to my mom about this. We still weren't close, and I never talked to her about things I was going through with Ethan. Everyone thought Ethan was the perfect husband and saw no fault in him. This always made it difficult for me to tell people the truth about who he really was. I had kept this secret for so long; I felt no one would believe me anyway. No one had believed me in the past. Why would they believe me now?

Momma Laverne, was old school. Women were more forgiving when their men cheated. I asked her for advice, and she suggested I do the same with Ethan. She said that all men cheat and that he made a mistake. She said I needed to forgive him. She said if I don't give Ethan a second chance, it would mean I gave the other woman an easy win. She got what she wanted by destroying my marriage. I struggled with this advice, as I felt Ethan didn't deserve another chance. I felt like I had given Ethan so many chances. I didn't want to forgive him. I didn't feel he deserved my forgiveness. I valued her advice and caved in and allowed Ethan to return home. Of course he promised not to ever hurt me again. He was nicer, and he tried to be a better father and husband. Unfortunately, I never loved him quite the same after that. He had failed me, and I no longer trusted him.

The intimacy was different between us. We had always had a great sexual relationship, but after that happened, it was never the same. He knew it but couldn't really complain because he knew he was the reason we had such distance in the bedroom. Ethan had done a lot of things to me, but his betrayal hurt worse than any other pain I had gone through with him up to this point. There was nothing normal about my marriage to Ethan, nothing at all.

It was New Years' Eve, and we were spending it with some friends of ours, a new married couple. Ethan met Blake at work and his wife, Mary, when she'd bring Blake's lunch. We really liked this couple. I envied their genuine love for each other, and I could tell their love was real. They invited us to their lovely home. We had dinner and cocktails. We decided to play cards. Spades was one of our favorite card games. Ethan and I were the spade couple champs. We always won. We enjoyed being the winning couple. No one could ever beat us. We started discussing relationships, and Blake asked if I thought Ethan was the best thing that ever happened to me. I remember pausing for a second, as I had to think about it. I said, "I'm not sure, because I've never had anyone else to compare him to." I had been with Ethan since I was seventeen. I honestly couldn't answer that question. I didn't know the answer.

The subject quickly moved on to more intense relationship conversations. I had no idea at the time that Ethan had felt belittled and humiliated in front of our friends. I did notice his demeanor changed. He started cutting me off when I would talk. He'd give me this mean look when Blake and Mary weren't paying attention. We got through the evening and toasted the New Year in with our friends. I enjoyed our couple's night out. It was nice spending time with other married couples. We had never done that before. I hoped we could do it more often.

We walked into our apartment, I paid and dismissed our babysitter, and as the door closed behind her, Ethan was standing right upon me. When I turned around, he slapped the crap out of me. I held my face in shock. I had no idea why he hit me. He started yelling at me, asking me why I said that about him. I told him I didn't know what he was talking about. He brought up the conversation we had about him being the best thing that ever happened to me. I told him I saw nothing wrong with my answer. Well, he did, and he was furious. He started beating me like never before. I tried running from him. He was hurting me, and I was scared. I thought he was going to kill me. I looked into his eyes, and I saw darkness and anger like never before, and it frightened me.

I tried running upstairs, and he caught me by my legs. I was kicking and screaming for him to leave me alone. I was wearing a gorgeous black dress that night. He ripped if off and then my panties, hitting me in my face the entire time as he pinned me down on the steep stairs. I kept screaming for him to stop, and he forced himself on me. He told me he would show me who the best I've ever had was. He'd show me not to ever disrespect him again; he'd show me who the best was. And he did.

My husband raped me. When he was finished, he looked at me and dared me to say something. I didn't. I just lay there on those hard stairs quiet as a mouse and didn't move. He got up off me and left me on the stairs to soak it all in. I couldn't believe I had just been brutally raped and beaten by my own husband. I had never felt more violated in my life. The feeling of helplessness was horrible.

Ethan did what he always did after hurting me. He fell asleep as if nothing happened. All I could think of was getting my girls out of this madness. I called one of my dearest girlfriends, Sylvia. She and I had been close since high school, and she was getting married soon and had asked me to be a bridesmaid. I couldn't think of anyone else, I could call at that hour on New Year's Day. I had no money. Ethan always made sure I was broke. I didn't have any pride in this moment, so I asked her to loan me enough money for the girls and I to catch the first bus out of town. I had finally had enough. This was the last straw. For the first time, I called my mom. I was crying and asked her if the girls and I could come stay with her for a while until I could figure out what to do. She reluctantly said yes. I could tell I would be a burden on her, just from the sound of her voice. I thought for sure that after telling her Ethan raped me she would have some kind of sympathy for me. But she only said yes because of the girls. She felt more sorry for them than me. I didn't have time to worry about her reasoning. I needed to get out now.

I tiptoed around Ethan's drunken body and got the girls dressed. I packed as little as possible as fast as I could, just enough to get us by. I didn't have much time. It was dusk outside, and he would wake up soon. Sylvia was waiting for us outside the apartment. She drove us to the bus station. We caught the first bus out of town, headed for Chicago where mom was staying. Right when the bus was leaving the station, I suddenly saw Ethan chasing the bus. He was yelling for it to stop. I told the bus driver not to stop, to please keep going, and he did. I remember looking back at Ethan and not feeling sorry for him. I felt safe, and I felt brave for finally leaving him for good. *He raped me. He doesn't love me.* I kept telling myself this over and over so I could try to move on.

Mom picked us up from the bus station. She was happier to see her granddaughters than me. I was used to this by now. She could tell I was torn but didn't have much sympathy for my situation or me. If anything, I swear she was gloating a bit. It was like she wanted to say, "I told you so."

A week went by, and it wasn't easy. She had hamsters, and one of them bit Brooklyn so hard on her finger when she reached in to pet it. It drew blood. She was terrified. I endured another week, and then Mom and I were at each other's throats. I never understood why there was so much strife between us. Why was it so hard for us to coexist? Ethan didn't help any. He kept calling at all hours of the day and night. Mom was fed up with being in the middle of our drama.

Mom got upset because I refused to take any of his calls. I was confused at whose side she was on. By the third week, Mom had started making it clear we were disturbing her life, and she wanted it back. She was trying harder to get me to talk to Ethan and to seriously think about taking him back. I told her no, I didn't want to go back. I just needed a little more time to figure things out. I told her I felt safe staying with her.

I begged her to help me. I told her this was the only chance I had to try to do the right thing for the girls. I told her I needed her help. Mom didn't want to hear it. She suggested I call Dallas and ask him if the girls and I could stay with him instead. I called Dallas. He had gotten married. He had a stepson and a baby on the way. His wife, Jeannie and I tolerated each other but weren't the best of friends. I never knew why, but at the end of the day, I really didn't care. Dallas always had to get her permission for everything, and she didn't think it would be a good idea to take in the girls and me. I couldn't believe my ears. My only family had turned their backs on me once again. I had never asked them for anything before now, and I needed them more than ever.

I felt alone once again. I honestly had no one. Who else was I to turn to? I cried myself to sleep that night. I held onto my girls and promised them someday I would make things better. I didn't know how I would do this, but I promised someday I would. I never wanted them to become like me. I wanted them to be strong and courageous women. They deserved better. I was convinced my life was still cursed. I had become my worst nightmare. I had become my mother.

Mom went behind my back and made arrangements for Ethan to come get us.

When I returned home, I was just as forgiving as I'd been in the past. What else was I to do? This was my life, and I had to make the best of it.

During the three weeks I spent with Mom, I lost my job. I had to look for another job, but this time I wanted something that would help me to better my life, something that would make me feel important. I'd never had a problem finding a job. I just never looked for a job that would actually make me feel important.

By now, I'd been a nanny, a short-order cook and a grocery store cashier. I had worked in the deli department at a grocery store. I had worked in nursing homes as a housekeeper and in the public school lunchroom preparing food. I did laundry for the elderly when I was working the graveyard shift, and that was considered a promotion. I'd even worked in a factory, making pizza boxes. I was unable to keep a job because Ethan's jealously got so out of control; he would accuse me of cheating on him. This was always his way of making my life difficult so his would somehow be better. He would refuse to watch the girls when it was time for me to go to work, and I would end up losing my job over attendance issues. This was how he wanted it. This was how he controlled me. I realized I gave him this power. However, I had no idea how to take it back. I felt helpless and weak. My family didn't help. Ethan knew they didn't want anything to do with me, and he used this to his advantage. He convinced me he was all I had, and no one else wanted me anyway. He tore me down with his words, his hands, and with his dominant behavior.

Regardless of my situation, I was determined to do something. I just couldn't sit back and do nothing. Deep down inside, I still wanted more. I still wanted better. I still wanted to try. The stars lined up just right, and I found a good job with a trucking company as a financial aid representative. I saw the advertisement in the want ads of our local newspaper. I was home battling a summer cold when I called the number listed. The person who answered the phone had a soft voice. The female briefly interviewed me over the phone and then asked if I could come in later that afternoon for a face-to-face interview. I said, "Yes, of course I can." I was shocked and excited. Suddenly I was faced with having to quickly find a sitter; this was so unexpected. I was able to get the new neighbors downstairs to watch the girls for me until I returned. I immediately got dressed. I was still not feeling well and wondered how I would pull this off without ruining my chance to get a good job. I had to catch the bus to the suburbs. It was a long way from our home. Everything was happening so fast. I interviewed and thought it went well. The job was something I'd never done before, and I would have to do a training program set up by the company in order to learn the job. Some traveling was involved, which excited me even more.

The nice lady who interviewed me at the truck-driving company said they had been interviewing candidates all week and wanted to make a decision by the end of the day. She gave me the common handshake and said she would be in touch one way or another soon. I made it back home before Ethan got off work. I was amazed at how fast my day had gone by from waking up this morning with a horrible cold and interviewing for the job of a lifetime. I had forgotten I was even sick. I wanted to make a good impression. I wanted this opportunity.

I was trying to explain to Ethan how my day went. I was still very sick and totally exhausted, but I felt good about what I had accomplished today.

All I could think about was how much our lives would change if I got that job, how things would be so much better for us. We would both finally have good jobs. The company had excellent benefits, and they were a huge corporation. They owned the largest semitruck driving-training school in the industry. There was room for growth and opportunity, something I never had in my previous jobs. The thought of actually doing something more corporate felt good. It made me feel special.

I anxiously waited as the clocked ticked. It felt like forever. I waited impatiently for the phone to ring. I wanted this opportunity more than I wanted anything in a long time. Ethan was already showing signs of jealously, and I hadn't even gotten the job. I ignored him this time. I didn't care how he felt. This wasn't about him. It was what I wanted, and I was not going to let him take it from me this time. I knew I would have to hire a sitter if I got the job because he made it clear he wasn't going to support me. What else was new?

It was 4:45 p.m., and the phone rang. I answered it, and it was the truck driving company, offering me the job. I gladly accepted. She said out of all the people they had interviewed, I outshined them all. She said she was very impressed with my people skills and the fact I came to the interview sick and still pushed through and made a good impression. I was very appreciative of the opportunity, and I let her know I would not let her down. She wanted me to start immediately. She set up the corporate training for me to start in a week. I was on a mission to hire a sitter so I could start my new job.

It was late summer in Atlanta. Sophie was about to start first grade, and Brooklyn was starting prekindergarten. It would be more challenging starting a new job at this time because I would have to take the girls to a sitter, and the sitter would have to get them off to school and pick them up, staying with them until I was able to catch the bus to get them and take the bus with them back home. It would be challenging. I knew I couldn't depend on Ethan to help. He had the car, but refused to assist, even though this also would benefit him. I was determined to make it work. I wanted this more than anything, and the sacrifices I had to make would more than be worth it. I started setting goals financially and meeting them. I set goals for work and even impressed myself. The office had no furniture, no supplies when I started. It was a brand-new location. It only had a recruiter and myself. We started from scratch. It made me feel important to be a part of the beginning of a winning company.

My career took off fast. I was traveling and experiencing a life I had once only dreamed of. The perks that came with this position were too good to be true. The recruiter and I had freedom to run the entire office without supervision. Our district manager would come check on us once a month to make sure everything was on track. Other than that, we were free to do our jobs, as we were trained, without having someone watching our every move. Less than six months later, I had made enough money to purchase my first brand-new car. I'll never forget going to the car dealership and filling out the application, with only my name on the documents, and I was approved. It was a red compact-size Ford. No more catching the city bus back and forth to work. I was happier than I had ever been. I was proud of myself, and it felt good.

Ethan was miserable. He had to face his mistress every day at work. Their relationship ended after I found out about the affair. Everyone at his job knew what an asshole he was, and Ethan and Kelsie argued all the time. They just didn't get along like they did before they were exposed. Did I feel sorry for him or her? Nope. I felt they were getting exactly what they deserved. *Karma*, I thought.

I had my own business cards, my own office, and a toll-free number. My family could call long distance and talk to me anytime they wanted.

For the first time in years, my mom was so proud of me. She called regularly, and we would talk for hours. I'd started looking forward to receiving her calls. We always kept things on the surface. We never talked about the past; we just talked about the girls and how fast they were growing and how much they were learning. It was a cold unattached way of communicating with my unpredictable mother. I was okay with it, because it was better than nothing, and I cherished it for whatever it was worth.

I knew Mom wasn't doing well. By now, she had had two strokes and two open-heart surgeries, and the doctors had given her a life expectancy of about five more years. The doctors suggested another open-heart surgery to possibly add a few more years to her fragile body, but Mom was weak, and her will to live wasn't as strong as it had been in the past. She made up her mind that she was not going under the knife again and accepted her fate. She was now living in her fifth year.

Grandma Maria called me at work one day and laid a heavy guilt trip on me about moving back to Chicago to take care of my dying mother. I said, "No, Grandma, I don't want to. Mom doesn't want me there." But Grandma Maria always had a way of making me feel so low, so I eventually did what she asked. I mean, it was my mother—right? It was the right thing to do. Why didn't I feel good about it?

I struggled for weeks after making the decision to move away. I was at the peak of my career. I was happy. I didn't want to mess up this wonderful opportunity. Was I wrong to not want to leave all of that to take care of a mother who had never been there for me when I needed her? Was I wrong to feel that way after she never protected me from my dad or Ethan? She was the reason I was still stuck in this abusive marriage. She gave me to Daddy and then gave me back to Ethan, all for her convenience. Now I was just supposed to give up everything I worked for so that she wouldn't die alone? Grandma Maria had no idea what our lives were like. She was only being the grandma she'd always been, and her first and oldest child was dying. Her son Danny died just ten years earlier. I couldn't imagine how hard it must be for her to face losing another child. I put in my two weeks' notice and moved back to Chicago to take care of my dying mother. It was not an easy decision. I feared I would never have what I gave up for her again. It made me sick to think about. But like a good girl, I obeyed my elders and did as I was told. Ethan gave up nothing as usual. He was glad to have a reason to quit his job. He was miserable and hated seeing me happier than he was anyway. This was perfect timing for him. He didn't hesitate to pack us up and get us as far from Georgia as possible.

We arrived at Grandma Maria's house. We stayed with her because Mom didn't have the room at her place. The only downfall was Grandma Maria lived about forty five minutes outside of Chicago in a modest suburb on the west side, and Mom lived further south. The daily commute back and forth was difficult, not to mention expensive. We had to start completely all over. Jobs were getting harder and harder to find due to the bad economy. I had all this experience and couldn't find a job. Dallas worked at this awesome factory and tried to get Ethan on by putting in a good word for him. Ethan got an interview, and they hired him immediately, but he failed the drug test. Everything continued going downhill after that. I hated Ethan for failing the drug test. I said, "Really? You couldn't stay clean for a couple weeks to get that crap out of your system long enough to pass a drug test?" Dallas had warned him he would have to take one. So he had no excuse. I felt Ethan wasn't a responsible husband or father. He was selfish and stupid. He just didn't care. He had a job and didn't have to do anything to get it, just pass the damn drug test. That was it. Guaranteed income, and he couldn't even do that. This was the most Dallas had done for me since we became adults. I was grateful he put his name on the hook for Ethan, and he failed him. I apologized to Dallas, and he said, "I did what I could. Ethan blew it." I was furious.

We had gone more than two months without any income. I was late on my car payments for the first time, and I was worried about losing my car. We didn't have gas money to keep traveling back and forth from Grandma's house to Mom's house. Dallas lived in the same city as Mom, but he and his wife were expecting a baby in a few weeks, and of course we weren't allowed to stay there. Mom didn't want us staying at her house either. She just didn't want us around. Even though she knew I left everything to take care of her. It was a complicated situation. It was not turning out the way I had hoped.

Things got so bad that Ethan decided to catch the train back to Georgia. He felt his opportunity for employment would be better back home. He said he would send us money to help out. In the meantime, we were on the waiting list for section 8 housing, but this would take up to a year before our names would come up. I was miserable. I had nothing. I felt I had made the biggest mistake of my life. I would never get back what I left behind. I desperately called my boss at the truck-driving school and asked for my job back, but she said they had just filled the position, and the girl was scheduled for training. She apologized, and I asked if there were any other opportunities, and she said with my skill set, not at that time.

One afternoon, the girls and I were visiting Mom, and we were hungry. It was a bad situation I thought I'd never put myself in again. No job, no money, no place to live, and trying to take care of someone who didn't want me around. Grandma Maria didn't have much to offer but her home. The entire family had lived with her off and on throughout the years. I was grateful Grandma Maria let my family move in with her, but she didn't have the income to feed four more people. Reality quickly set in, and I was starting to regret my decision once again.

Mom knew why I was there, but she continued on with her life as if nothing had changed. She kept telling me she didn't want me there and that I shouldn't have listened to my grandma, because she was fine and nothing was going to happen to her anyway—everyone was just paranoid. She felt I had invaded her privacy. The really hard pill to swallow was she still didn't want anything to do with me. I felt like that neglected little girl all over again, looking for my mommy's approval, yearning for my mommy's love. I was determined to see this through no matter how bad her actions and words cut through my aching heart. This was our only chance to fix this—whatever it was.

Mom was frying chicken, and the girls and I hadn't had a decent meal in days. I was approved for temporary food stamps but hadn't received them yet. I had less than ten dollars to my name. I could barely afford a bag of potato chips for the girls to snack on. I hated not being able to feed my children. Ethan was staying with his mom and hadn't found a job yet. Mom's chicken smelled so good. I couldn't wait to give the girls a couple pieces, because I knew they were hungry. It was hard living with others, not knowing what you are allowed to eat and when. Especially when you couldn't buy your own food.

When the chicken was done, it sat on my mom's stove for hours. She hadn't even offered us any. I finally asked her if the girls and I could have a piece or two, and she said no. She was expecting some guy to stop by, and she had cooked the chicken for him. I couldn't believe what I was hearing. I said, "Are you freaking kidding me?" She was dead serious. She didn't give it a second thought, and I was furious. I asked her if she would watch Sophie and Brooklyn so I could run down to the corner store to get them something to eat. She said she would. She totally saw nothing wrong with this. I think I really needed time to calm down, and I didn't want the girls to see me upset with my mom.

When I drove to the store, I wished I were anywhere but here. I started crying; it hurt to feel this pain again after all these years. I didn't want the girls to know how worried I was. I knew I had to get myself together before I returned. I had no idea how I was going to make it beyond today. I honestly didn't know what the girls and I would do and how long we could live this way.

When I returned, I noticed the girls had been left alone without supervision. I asked them where their grandma Lilly was. They pointed to the bathroom door, which was off the kitchen. I figured she would be out shortly. I waited several minutes, and she never came out. I was worried that something had happened to her. I approached the door and gently knocked. She didn't answer, and I became worried. I was frozen at the thought that something bad had happened to her. Then I heard giggles on the other side of the door. Someone else was in there with her. I knocked again, and Mom slowly cracked the door opened. White clouds of thick smoke came rushing out. I couldn't see anyone at first, but after I fanned away the smoke, I saw a woman I didn't recognize holding a crack pipe, and she passed it to my mom. I couldn't believe my eyes. I think they were both stoned.

I knew Mom smoked a lot of marijuana, but crack cocaine? I was in disbelief. Then when I actually thought about her putting my children in harm's way for a fix, I lost it. I went off. I started yelling at her, telling her I couldn't believe what she was doing. I told her she was wrong to be smoking crack on her deathbed, and how dare she smoke while watching her grandchildren. I was so upset I couldn't breathe. It was like the life had been sucked out of me. Things had suddenly gone from bad to worse in just a matter of seconds.

Mom started laughing. She was confused. My words didn't register at all. It was like she didn't even care. I looked at her and felt pity. I was done. I wanted nothing more to do with her. I told my mom I was through with her. I finally had enough. I was ashamed and felt sadness for her life on a level I had never felt before. I was convinced my mother wanted to die. She didn't want to live. Everything she was doing was self-destructive, and she just didn't care anymore. I was angry with myself for trying to care about her one more time. I'd given up everything to try to do the right thing by her, and this was the result.

I grabbed my girls and told my mom the next time I saw her she would probably be lying in a coffin. At the rate Mom was going, she would kill herself before she could die naturally. I cried all the way to Dallas's house. I told him what happened, and he took up for her as usual. They always stuck together and had each other's backs. Mom could never do anything wrong in his eyes. He always made excuses for her. I wondered at that moment why I even put myself through it. Did I really think these last moments of my mom's life would be any different? Honestly, in my naïve, childlike mind, I actually thought it would. I really thought when a person faces death they change for the better. They forgive when they have the chance, they apologize for the things they couldn't change, and they cherish the moments they can. Well, you know what? I was wrong.

Chapter 8

I was standing behind stage. Bobby told me I had a sold-out crowd. He said the audience was hyped and ready to hear Star's story. He said the energy in the auditorium was so powerful, he had never felt this type of vibe before. He said he was just as pumped and excited. The MC was on stage reciting my boring bio, and as I listened, I looked up to the sky and said a small prayer. I first thanked God for this moment and asked him to continue to use me to touch others and give them hope by lighting their path when all they see is darkness. I said, *If I touch one soul tonight, my mission has been accomplished. It only takes one soul at a time, as Star would say. Give me the strength and courage to bring Star's story to life. Thank you, thank you, thank you. Amen.*

The auditorium was packed with people who were eager to hear about hope, something we all need at least once in our lifetime.

I started to explain how much Star loved her mom but how difficult it was to love her with all the pain that surrounded them. Star wasn't sure she knew what love felt like, because it was always painful, and her heart ached all the time. She was torn and confused from a tiny toddler all through her adulthood. She wanted so badly to understand, to know what real love felt like.

I packed my car in an angry rage, crying the entire time. I got the girls, and off to Atlanta we went to join Ethan once again at Agnes's house. Thank God we didn't stay with Agnes long. Ethan had already found a temporary job and saved enough money for us to move after only three weeks. It wasn't in the best part of town. It was actually a high-crime and violent neighborhood; it was considered the ghetto. I tried to see the positive. At least we weren't living with Agnes.

I hadn't spoken to Mom since I stormed out of her house that dreadful afternoon. I worried about her health and her drug addiction. I still couldn't get that moment of seeing her hit that crack pipe out of my mind. My mom was a crack head. I couldn't quite wrap my mind around that reality. *She's forty-four years old and smoking crack. Seriously?*

She knew her time was limited, and she chose to live out her last days on earth like that? The more I thought about it, the angrier I got. It made no sense to me for someone who'd come so far to make choices that would hurt them instead of help them. Was I wrong to expect more from my mother? Was I really being unfair to think at this stage of her precious life, she would want to make better choices? The complexity of it all baffled me.

A week after we moved in, I was with a good friend of mine. She said she needed to talk to me about something very important. Her name was Angie. Angie picked me up while the girls were in school, and we drove to the park. She had a joint and asked if I wanted to smoke it with her. I was like, *Why not? I could use a bit of mellow high right about now with all the crap I've been dealing with the past couple months. My life has been a complete rollercoaster.* We were smoking marijuana, and she said she wanted to tell me about what Ethan did a couple days ago that made her feel uncomfortable. She said she had stopped by to see me, and I wasn't home. Ethan answered the door and let her inside. He told her I was grocery shopping and would be home soon but that I had just left so they had plenty of time. She was confused about what he meant by that. She said he came onto her. He was trying to have sex with her. She said he told her he'd always thought she was cute and had always had a crush on her. She couldn't believe he would even think she would betray me by sleeping with him. She politely turned him down and left. But before she left, he said, "The offer still stands whenever you're ready. I'd really like to show you how good I can make you feel. I'll never tell. It will be our little secret. Star will never know." Angie said again, "No thanks, I would never do that to my friend. Please let Star know I stopped by."

Angie left but was so pissed that she told her husband, Jeffrey. We've all known each other since high school. Jeffrey thought I should know that Ethan would actually ask her friend to have sex with him, let alone asking a married woman to sleep with him. "Ethan had no respect for you or our friendship," said Jeffrey. At first Jeffery wanted to go and punch Ethan out for disrespecting his wife. But Angie said, "No, he's not worth it. Ethan is no good for Star." They both agreed.

Angie wasn't sure I would believe her, and to her surprise I did. Nothing about Ethan surprised me anymore. He was capable of anything. We were halfway through the joint, and I started telling her about what my mom had done. She knew my mom well. She knew Mom and I never got along. Once I was down the street visiting Angie when my mom showed up at her house high and a little drunk. She was angry about something, most likely her boyfriend had hurt her, and she walked a block down to Angie's house and went on a rampage telling me to bring my behind home right then, that I was in big trouble and to get home. She was yelling and screaming. Angie, and her family, had confused looks on their faces as I walked away with my angry mom. Of course I was humiliated, ashamed, and embarrassed. But I followed her home as ordered. I didn't confide in many people back then, but after that episode, I felt I owed Angie an explanation. She felt sorry for me from that day on. Exactly what I didn't want. That's why I never told people about my life. I don't want your pity. I hate that.

Anyway, I was just getting to the part where I returned from the store and Mom was nowhere in sight. Angie said, "My God, where was she?" I told her I had no idea until the girls pointed toward the bathroom door. I said how I told my mom the next time I saw her, she would probably be dead. The very second those words rolled off my tongue, something shocking happened. It was like a strong, heavy presence entered my body. I felt it. It was alive and powerful. It got my attention, as I was suddenly speechless. This spirit entered my body and stayed there for a few seconds. I knew and clearly recognized its presence. It filled my heart with love and empathy. I heard it say, "I'm sorry, and I love you. Good-bye, Star." When I acknowledged it, and it exited my body, I wanted to speak to it, but it left as quickly as it entered. Poof! Gone!

Angie looked at me and kept asking me, "What? What?"

I was motionless and couldn't respond. Then I said, "My mother is dead. She just said good-bye to me. I just felt her take her last breath. She's no longer with us. She's dead."

Angie looked at me like I had just lost my mind. She took the joint out of my hand and said, "You've had way too much, girlfriend. No more wacky wack for you. You're cut off."

I said, "No, Angie, for real, I'm not making this up. My mom, she just passed away. I know it. Her spirit entered my body and spoke to me and then left. I know my mom is dead. I just know it. Take me home! Take me home! I have to confirm this. I know she's dead."

Angie took me home. She was worried and asked to stay with me until I found out for sure. I told her to go home. Her children would be home from school soon, and she needed to be there for them. I assured her I was fine. The house was quiet. We didn't have a phone yet, so there was no way I could confirm my theory by just calling Mom. I couldn't wait to find out. I had to do something, so I walked to our next-door neighbors who were like extended family. Cindy had a baby by Ethan's brother, Dennis. Her daughter Jasmine was my children's first cousin. We were very close. I asked them if I could use their phone to call long distance, because I thought something had happened to my mom. I told them, "I think she's dead." They too looked at me like I was crazy, but they let me use their phone. I dialed Mom's house; the phone rang and rang and rang. I wanted her to pick up the phone and prove me wrong. I kept begging, "Pick up the phone, Mom, please just pick it up." Deep down, I knew she couldn't. I knew it was her spirit that had passed through me. I knew I would never hear my mother's voice again. I knew this without a doubt. I just needed confirmation. Mom never answered the phone.

I walked across the driveway that separated our homes, back to our apartment. I noticed it was time to pick up Brooklyn from preschool. I was trying to do things as normally as possible to help get my mind off of what had happened at the park. It wasn't easy. I had no choice but to wait for Dallas or someone in the family to find a way to contact me.

A couple hours passed, and I was sure I would've received the news about Mom's death by then. Mom and Dallas lived less than a mile from each other. I'd given them both Cindy's number, with her permission of course, in case of a family emergency. I promised Cindy they wouldn't abuse and call unless it was serious. She was okay with that. Ethan had come home from work, and still no word. I was a nervous wreck. I told Ethan what happened at the park, and he never doubted me. Ethan always believed me. Over the years, I had many premonitions. Ethan had learned to listen to them because when I got them, they always came true. None of them were the same, and it wasn't something I controlled. The signs and visions would just appear out of nowhere, and

I would know either something had happened or was about to happen. Ethan and I waited to hear from Dallas.

There was a knock at the door. Ethan answered. It was Cindy, and she said I had a phone call from Dallas. She said he said it was important. She looked at me, as if to say, *I'm sorry.* I ran over to take his call. When I picked up the receiver, I told Dallas, "I already know; Mom is dead." He said, "Yes, Mom died. How did you know?" I told him she came to me to say good-bye. I was too emotional to go into the entire story at that moment. I started to cry. *It's true. Mom is dead. She's gone; this is the end of our battle, our fights, and our troubled relationship.* I thought of the irony of how it all ended. We struggled all my life to have a normal relationship, and now we'd never get the chance to ever make that happen.

It hurt worse than I ever thought it would. I was angry that she died that way. I was angry we never ever saw eye to eye, and this was how it had to end between us. I felt guilty because I didn't call her and apologize for storming out of her house and calling her names. I knew she was dying, but I was so angry with her. I couldn't see past that. I felt she was failing herself, and I just wanted so much more for her. I had longed to have a normal, loving relationship with my mom for so long. I couldn't believe it was now over. I would never get that—ever.

Everything in my life changed that day. I wasn't the same person. I looked at life differently. My mother's death woke something up in me I had never known existed. I learned who I was and who I didn't want to be. I knew what I wanted, and I knew what I didn't want. I dreamed every day of having something better. My mom died alone, and she didn't have to. She battled so many demons, and they took over her life. They stripped her of all hope. She lost the battle. She couldn't fight anymore. She gave up. She was tired, and she felt defeated. She surrendered. She waved the white flag. She was done fighting the battle within herself.

I promised myself from that day forward that I wouldn't give up on my life, my future, my hopes, and my dreams. I refused to follow my mother's footsteps of self-destruction. I knew if I continued down the path I was currently walking, I would be just like my mom, and my girls would suffer just like me. I thought of that a lot, and I knew if I let that happen, I could never forgive myself. *I don't know how, but I have to make sure this never happens.*

I really loved my mother, even when I hated her. I regret the last memories I have of her and our dysfunctional relationship. I realize the most important gift God has given us is the gift of forgiveness. I was given plenty of time to forgive my mother, and I let pride keep me from doing so. If I had to do it all over again, I would tell my mom, "I forgive you. I forgive you for not protecting me from Daddy. I forgive you for abusing me physically, mentally, and emotionally. I forgive you for not believing me and in me. I forgive you for being an addict. I forgive you for wanting what everyone else wants, to be loved. I forgive you for doing the best you could with so little guidance. I forgive you for not knowing who you were other than my mom. Because now that I'm a mom, I know you had a past, just as I do. I forgive myself for not finding out more about who you were. I forgive you for everything, and I love you."

After Mom's funeral, I was at her home cleaning out her belongings. I was hoping during the time we were not speaking she would have taken time to write me a letter. Years ago, Mom used to write me a lot. Right before Sophie was born, she'd write all the time. I looked forward to receiving her letters. I was hoping Mom had written me a letter saying *I'm sorry, and I love you*. I felt I needed this more than anything. Unfortunately, all I found were over a hundred of those tiny little empty plastic bags crack cocaine is sold in. I remember thinking I needed to get rid of the evidence, because I wasn't sure Dallas knew how bad her addiction was. I wanted to protect him from the truth like I did when we were kids. Dallas idolized Mom. Why destroy his innocent memories of her just because I had accepted the cold, hard truth?

I never found a letter. At first I was angry. However, I did find some marijuana. I decided to roll myself a joint and smoke one for Mom. Why not? I lit it and cherished every puff in honor of my mom. I just sat there in complete silence and reminisced about the crazy life we had.

After I returned home, I felt lonely. I struggled with how I was supposed to feel. I was sad she was gone, and I missed her a lot. But I couldn't wrap my mind around what exactly it was I missed. Did I miss having a mom? Did I miss her? If so, what did I miss about her? I struggled to find positive things I missed. I thought of several things I didn't miss. So I suffered from within, and it hurt on a level that words cannot explain. There were days when I felt my mom's presence. I felt she was in the room with me. I felt her touch or smelled the scent of her favorite perfume. I kept dreaming of the day she passed and became more and more grateful for our spiritual connection, for when my mother's spirit entered my body and she said she forgives me and loves me. She was the hero. She knew even in death that forgiveness and love are the two most powerful tools on earth. I felt a love for my mother deeper in her death than I had ever felt when she was living. The guilt I felt for not realizing this sooner haunted me.

After experiencing another ghost encounter, I was moved to a small tin box where my mom kept all her personal belongings. I opened the box, and inside was every letter my mother had written me over the years. I felt a strong urge to read them. In my excitement, like finding a hidden treasure, I sorted each letter out by date. I then opened the first letter and started to read.

February 14

My dearest daughter and son-in-law,

Thanking you for the beautiful Valentine's card. So nice to hear from you. I have not forgotten the dearest thing to my heart. Missing you and loving you go hand in hand. Just may call you for a lunch date about mid-March. Weather's breaking, and I'm getting ants in my pants already. I'll probably be checking out of Chicago soon. Please give Ethan and his family my love. You're still my baby girl, and I am proud of you.

Loving you forever. Dallas also sends his love. Tell Ethan's father he owes me dinner. See you in March.

Loving you both dearly,
Your Mom

April 5

Dear daughter and son-in-law,

I know you're probably angry, but don't be. So very glad you're both in God's hands. Believe it or not, I don't need to worry so much about you anymore. I know he'll take care of my babies when I can't.

Been feeling pretty good lately. Haven't been really sick since February when I had my heart attack.

Dallas wants to come up to visit you this summer. School is out here June 3. He spends almost all of his free time at his Grandma Maria's. She lets him drive her car anytime he wishes. You know, between the two of us, he's spoiled rotten now. He's been to St. Louis, Michigan, Indianapolis, and who knows where else by himself or with his friends. He made the honor roll this semester. He got all As and Bs. I'm so proud of him. He's given up a lot. Received his varsity letter and wrestling pin last week. You should see the clock he made me for Christmas. He's still lazy about cleaning his room. Some things will never change.

Well, how is married life treating you? I'm sure you're still excited and nervous. I'm so proud of all my children. Especially you. Just think, nineteen years ago, I didn't think you'd make it to nine months. You've made your poor old mother very proud of you.

I may be moving back within the next year. Depends on a lot of things. I hate it here. Your grandma is driving me crazy. Men here are still stupid and dense.

Of course I hear from your aunt Krissy quite frequently. Max was here the weekend you called over to Ma's. He really misses seeing you. He talks about you all the time.

Well, I should be getting up that way about the fifteenth of April for sure this time. Your phone must be out of order. I tried several times to call you. Operator says phone's out of order. So I called your grandpa's girlfriend, Ms. Mabel, who you were staying with and left you a message. I hope you got it. I hear you all still attend the same church. Write to me before the fifteenth of April. Dallas wants to come with me. I don't know if I'll be able to afford that. Rates went up last week on trains and bus fares.

Tell Ethan to be good and I'm praying for you and him. Thank goodness your brother only has one more year to go.

Your mother is old and tired of scuffling to make ends meet every day. I can't find no work here at all. No jobs, no money, nobody who really cares about you (excluding my children of course); it makes me very depressed and alone most of the time. I don't have anything to occupy my time anymore. Dallas is never home anymore. He spends every weekend over at Ma's so he can have the car. He goes out somewhere every weekend. He's really grown up. I hate it when kids grow up. They don't really need their parents anymore. So now I'm feeling useless because you and Dallas don't really need me anymore.

But I still love you because you're mine. Sure will be happy when I can find a job. Everything is shut down here. Not having any money gets to me. I'm tired of being poor. But I'm rich when it comes to the love we share as a family. Please don't forget to write soon.

Loving you always,
Mom

May

Dearest daughter and son,

Hoping this letter finds you in good health and better spirit. Sorry about the delay in sending your package, but it was unavoidable. Feeling much better now, but I still have to take things slower. Still looking forward to spending some real time with my family this summer.

Dallas has a job now, starting May 12, 1973. He will be working at McDonalds on the west side of town, so he'll be able to buy most of his own clothes now.

Still waiting for a job to open up so I can go to work doing something. Your grandfather came down this weekend to make sure I was still alive. He doesn't even give good advice anymore, let alone anything else.

Getting ready to make some major changes in my life real soon. Been going to church with some friends for a while now. Getting ready to make that great change for a better today and tomorrow. Been getting plenty of rest and relaxation, so I'm bored stiff.

Sure hope you like these things I've sent. They aren't much, but they were packed with all the love and caring I could hold in my poor little heart.

The dress is handmade. Someday I will be able to send you a store-bought one. But each stitch was sewn with pure love. Just hope it isn't too small for you. Since I don't know your size anymore. I used a size and a pattern.

Write and let me know if it fits. You can get a white blouse to wear under it. Sorry about the sleeves or lack of them. Tell my son-in-law thanks for the Mother's Day gift. I was so happy to hear from my children on Mother's Day.

Your love is worth more than anything money can buy. Please let me know what you're going to need for my baby. I'll be sending you boxes from time to time, so be looking for them.

God loves you, and so do I. Write real soon.
Mom

June

Greeting in the name of our Lord.

Sorry about taking so long in writing. But I believe God is going to bless me with a job soon. I've had two interviews already. Feeling much better and have more energy now than before the heart attack. Don't worry! I'm not overdoing it.

I believe God has given me the extra strength so I don't abuse it. Been too close too many times not to have faith and know who to give my thanks to.

Remember your childhood friend from Franklin Street? Well she asks about you all the time. Said she'd really like to see you.

You know your brother's seventeen now. Thinks he's grown already (like you did). But all adolescents go through those changes. He's really a wonderful young man, as you are a beautiful daughter. I thank God for my children, Ethan included. School's out today (Thursday). Dallas has done exceptional work. He's the pride and joy of all his teachers. They just love him. He has honorable mentions and awards for all his work.

Been hanging out with his friends on the weekends. He goes skating, riding around at night with his buddies. He's becoming quite a young man. We had a good Memorial Day weekend. Max couldn't come down. He had plans. We didn't invite anyone else.

I'm sending this booklet for Ethan to read. Maybe he'll understand all you have to do is ask God and believe. It works, I know. I hope to see you all real soon. As soon as the Lord blesses me with this job.

Should have another package ready soon. I'll either send or bring it. Hope to bring it. Well, so much for all that. You know your uncle Danny also suffered a heart attack. He wasn't so lucky, so I'm really trying to take better care of myself. Knowing I love you all and will see you soon, God willing.

Love,
Mom

June 20

Hello my darling daughter, son, and my baby!

Well I've started taking some data processing classes at the community college this summer. I have an exam tonight at 5:30 (Monday 6/20/73).

So I still have to study before I can mail this letter. How have you been, and when do I get to really meet Ethan's father?

I do not have any classes on Fridays. I was wondering if you and Ethan (or somebody) could pick me up at the train station on Friday morning at 8 a.m. and drop me off on Tuesday morning to catch the train back home. If you can see any way possible of helping me in any of these areas, then I will be able to come up for the Fourth of July.

So please don't take too long in letting me know. I need to know something before June 29.

Please don't let anyone (except Ethan's father) know I intend to come.

Well, I'll wait to hear from you.

November 3

Hello, children,

It's so good to hear from you and to know that things are well. Glad to hear you're all well, and I'm happy you've found a job. More pleased to hear my little Sophie is fine and healthy. Hope her brief stay at the hospital wasn't too painful for you or her.

As I've mentioned, she will receive her first saving's bond when I see you at Thanksgiving. Now hold onto your seat. I have some good news. First, you know, God has always provided a way when there was none. He has blessed me with a part-time job over the X-mas season at Marshall Fields in the gourmet shop. Marshall Fields is one of the most expensive stores in the nation. They have a strict dress code. Only dress shirts and blouses and dress slacks and sweaters. The job is only for the Christmas season but certainly better than no job at all.

Lord knows I am truly thankful. By the time this job is over, I should know something definite about the disability. See how good God has been to me? And to my children.

The weather has been fall-like but warm and pleasant. Yes, I'm taking better care of myself now than ever. I have too much to live for now. My children, my son-in-law, and my grandbaby. Yes, God has truly been good to me. I do intend to return the favor.

No! I haven't heard from your grandmother yet. May go down there this evening (11/03/73) from six to nine.

Please see if you can get an address for Max for me. I need to write him. I've received some information he should have.

Sure glad I got a job. At least I can get away from my crazy family with a legitimate excuse now. Remember my friend Dottie? She calls me three or four times a week and keeps me updated and gives me something to really laugh about. She says for you to behave and don't get so grown up you forget she loves you too. Tell Ethan I love him, and I will see you all real soon.

Kiss Sophie and give Ethan my love. You take care not to overwork yourself. You're a mother and a wife first. I love you all.

Take care and God bless.
Forever!
Mom

December 9

Hello, my children,

Well, believe it or not, something always seems to happen after things are already planned. I'm so glad I've always had that faith. Just bought Dallas a winter jacket for fifty dollars, and then his final bill for his $160 class ring came in the mail. But as usual, Mom will find a way to overcome. It will be tight, but God blessed me with this little piece of a job for a reason. Otherwise I would never be able to get this ring for him. They only hold it for ten days. He doesn't even know it's back, so it will have to be his Christmas present now.

He started to come up this weekend but didn't want to miss school. He's going for a perfect attendance so he can be one of the first ten to receive their diplomas. Since your brother's ring came back sooner than expected, tell your Grandpa Ralph we could use any assistance he would be able to supply.

I still haven't heard anything from him, but I believe somehow the Lord will provide. He knows I won't ask him again. I shouldn't have to beg.

Glad Sophie likes her stuffed rabbit. Tell her Grandma loves her and can't wait to get her picture. I'm sure we won't be going anywhere for Christmas unless we're blessed with transportation. We plan to take the bus to Mom's for New Year's. Well I have to get ready for work now. Yes, I know, and I will take care of myself. I can hear you now. I love you too. Very much. That is reason enough to be extra careful. Since I've answered all your questions.

Give my love to Ethan's family and wish them a very merry Christmas for me. Tell Ms. Agnes to pray for us. Tell Sophie Grandma loves her. Tell Ethan I send him my love. Of course you already know where you stand in my heart. The first heartbeat of every new day is for my children—you, Dallas, Ethan, and of course my little Sophie. That's all the motivation anyone would need to remember to "Be careful and take care of yourself, Mom!" Of course.

Love ya!
Behave and write (stamped envelope enclosed).
Your Mom

P.S. It won't be long now. I feel like I've been held captive in the *Twilight Zone*. Hallelujah!

December 27

My dear children,

Hope you've had a very merry Christmas. Sure was good to hear from you on my birthday. Dallas and I had dinner with the nice elderly people we always talk about.

Well, God has blessed us thus far, and we will be moving out by the time you receive this letter. Your aunt Krissy said she was surprised to hear I was a grandma. Your cousins have grown into beautiful young men. The youngest will be seven years old. Doesn't seem like it's been that long since your uncle Danny died. But time doesn't stand still for any of us.

I'm sleeping better; it is real peaceful sleeping on a queen-size bed all by myself. Whoopee! Dallas is still working on the car; hopefully he'll have it running before New Year's. Otherwise I will not have a way to get to work all next week through January 7.

Still waiting to hear from the disability board, but nothing yet. With or without it, I'm sure we'll survive somehow. Everyone's mesmerized over my beautiful granddaughter. She's the star topic of conversation. And she's all mine.

Sure hope she learns to enjoy her rocking horse, Charlie. Don't let my baby fall off and bust her head or lip. She should be able to salvage it for her children. They thought I was crazy for buying her a horse, but every little girl should have her own horse. Besides, it doesn't eat much or make poo poo mess. So you can't say she can't keep it.

I just want Sophie to know her grandma loves her even though I don't see her as often as I'd wish. Boy, I can't wait till she starts walking and talking. She can spend the summer with Grandma. I can take her to the fair and make big bucks (only a joke).

Well, you'll have to let me know what you get for Christmas. I'm really looking forward to 1974 with lots of anticipation and shouldn't be under too much pressure from now on. Things should begin to flow easier. I feel more excited about this coming year than any before; that by itself is a positive point.

Don't forget about your brother's graduation, not that he lets me. Now that he has his class ring, he thinks he's grown. He only goes to school till 11 a.m. now. So he's looking for a full-time job. We have plenty of room now. So come on down! Well, I have to get dressed for work now. So I will say I love you and give my Sophie a hug and kiss from Grandma, squeeze oh bah-bah, and Ethan.

Write soon. I'm sending stamped envelopes. Your grandma Maria said to call whenever you wish. I told her how we talk every other day almost. She was jealous. She wishes she had that kind of relationship with my sisters and brother. Yep! I guess I'm a pretty darn lucky lady. Thanks, kids!

Loving ya,
Mom

January 5

My children and grandbaby!

Boy! It still feels good to stretch out in the queen-size bed alone. I'm really enjoying my large bed. Well, work's over, and I can settle down and get this house in some kind of order now.

We have four rooms—a kitchen, living room, and two bedrooms, plus a bath (shower massage that comes off the hook, so you can hold it in your hand). Nice large bedrooms and large kitchen.

Well how's Grandma's baby doing? I got to have some more pictures. Let me know what size clothes she wears. I want to buy her a bikini bathing suit for this summer. I may go to church this Sunday. It all depends on how much money I have.

This letter is really directed to my little blessing from heaven, little Sophie, but since she can't read yet, I have to settle for you. I'm glad you didn't think I was crazy sending her Charlie Horse. Everybody else did. Not that I care.

Still haven't received a word from your grandfather. Though I never did. I should be hearing from the disability board any day now. The suspense is killing me (bad joke).

Dallas has to get the brakes fixed on that car, and the plates and title changed. Then you might be surprised by me on a weekend soon. Besides, I want to see how badly you've been mistreating my baby. I'll be glad when she learns to talk so she can tell on you and Ethan.

Don't forget to send me her dress size and shoe size. We're pretty much settled in already with only a few things left to unpack and put away. I thought about having a house-warming party. Except all my real friends live out of town.

Guess what? I'm thinking of fixing another pot of chitterlings this weekend if I don't go to church on Sunday. Might even fix a pie or two. Is your mouth or eyes watering yet?

Well I miss you and my baby and my son-in-law. I will keep the stamps and envelopes coming as long as you continue to write. I love you all. Tell Ethan I said don't work too hard. Make sure you take good care of my Sophie.

Yeah, I know already. I'll take care of myself. What else do I have to do now that I'm no longer working?

Love you,
Mom

February 14

Hello, children,

Well, it seems as though we're finally getting a break in the weather. Don't know if the groundhog has seen his shadow or not, but the ground is thawing.

Sure am happy whenever I can reach into the mailbox and pull out instant happiness in the form of a letter from my children. You know I miss you and my baby. The warmer the weather gets, the more anxious I get to see all of you.

Grandma's baby girl is growing, and I don't even know how big she is, so I can't really buy her anything to wear. But I can buy her a lot of other stuff. Dallas said he'll be glad when she can talk to him. She'll be six months this month, and you have your first anniversary coming up next month. I remember all the important things (sometimes).

Sophie is a very precious baby, and I intend to spoil her rotten. Besides, every little girl needs her own special valentine, so here is my valentine's doll for all of you (it's really for my baby). I've kissed it all over so it's full of love. Has she started trying to stand up yet? When she does, let me know so I can get her some real shoes.

I really need to see my baby. I had to go for another medical exam by the State Disability Board. Still waiting. Now they say in March maybe. There are three houses in the vicinity that are for rent here in our neighborhood. Weekend after next, there is a three-day weekend, no school. Think about all the possibilities. Just think—you'd have a reliable babysitter if nothing else.

Dallas is still working on that car, whenever time and weather permit. Sure would like to see you all before my granddaughter is grown up too much. Ooh Ba Ba must be getting a little raggedy by now. Sophie should be cutting teeth pretty soon since she's eating more solids now. She has to be big by now. I close my eyes and try to envision what she's doing and how much she's grown. Have her ears healed yet?

Well, so much for my little baby. Now for my big babies. How are you and Ethan doing? Just think I can only go as far as across the street. The lady backs her car up across the street, picks me up, and drives back across the street to her house.

These people are always on time. Dallas goes to school with her son. Her old man can cook his butt off. Homemade pizzas, coconut breads, cakes, and anything edible. I've gained three pounds already, and I've only known them a month.

At least Dallas won't be alone while I'm gone to the hospital anymore. He has matured drastically. He's going to be a fine young man someday, just as you've ever wanted for a brother. He misses you and little Sophie so bad. As you know, he is not the most enthusiastic child I have—typical Gemini, as you are a bull Taurus. But I love both very much.

Well, happy Valentine's Day. Kiss my baby Sophie and write soon.

Love ya!
Mom

Chapter 9

I read the last letter, and the audience stood and whistled and applauded louder than I'd ever heard at any of my other events. They went on and on as I stood there and bowed my head, filled with gratitude. I did a curtsey, and the MC came out to help calm the audience down a bit and help escort me off the stage. Suddenly they started chanting, "Ally! Ally! Ally! Ally!" and I just stood there in awe and amazement, wondering, *What did I do to deserve this? I mean, Star should be receiving this praise. I wish she were here to see their response.* It was priceless. Even her mother, Ms. Lilly, must be shining down on me at this moment. I politely said thank you and allowed the MC to escort me backstage. Bobby, the stage manager, walked on stage shortly after and told everyone that a book signing would follow in the conference room located outside to the right of the auditorium. He told them to line up, and they would also be able to get autographs if they wanted. Everyone slowly made their way to the book-signing area. My makeup artist, Jessie, was grinning from ear to ear, waiting for me to sit in his chair so he could freshen me up. It was a welcome, friendly, familiar smile I needed at that moment, especially after looking into the faces of strangers for the past forty-five minutes.

Jessie gave me the biggest hug and said, "Ally, I was so amazed by your composure. You held it together out there, telling Star's story about her mother dying. I was balling my eyes out, and there wasn't a dry eye in the audience. I don't know how you do it. My goodness! What a powerful moment. Star loses her mom, and she's got an abusive husband and two young girls. She has no one. What does she do next?"

I told Jessie I'd let him know later, to just stick around. Marissa was still doing her job, following me like paparazzi, taking notes and stopping and restarting her recorder. I got through all the book signing and autographing, which included photo ops, so I was glad Jessie cleaned me up a bit, or those pictures would have been horrible. Don't want to disappoint the fans.

Pam was making sure everything was staying on time. Next I needed to go back to my dressing room to take a quick shower and then have Jessie redo my makeup and hair for the reception. The outfit Scotty picked out for the reception was a black jumpsuit. This one was so sexy. It had tapered legs, which I love, because I'm short. I don't look good in the palazzo legs that swallow me up and make me look shorter, even with heels. It hugged my small waist just right and had a cutout on the shoulders; this style seemed to be coming back. I love jumpsuits. Jumpsuits make me feel like I can move around more freely without worrying about how I bend or move, trying not to show too much of this or too much of that. It allows me to mingle better. Only negative is when I have to visit the powder room. It's still worth it when I'm mingling with a lot of people. I don't feel so vulnerable.

Scotty said, "West Avery also designed this piece."

"I'm starting to like Mr. Avery more and more. I might need to hire him as my personal designer. This would give him lots of exposure and would be good for his career."

I arrived at the reception on time. There were some very important people there. Beth greeted me at the door and gave me the rundown on how the reception was scheduled. She said they would introduce me, and I would say something short and welcome all my special big investor fans for coming out to support Star's dream, how this wouldn't be possible without their support, blah, blah, blah. Then I would make a toast to the night and start the festivities. Meet and greet and eat, drink and be merry. One of my favorite things to do was socialize. This gets Star's work recognized and keeps me employed. I have a three-drink limit so I don't embarrass myself. I pace them throughout the evening. So I smile, laugh, and meet hundreds of people as my personal assistant, Pam, collects all the business cards and take notes about each person I meet. When this is over, I can study the notes with the names on the cards to etch a connection in my mind so I don't forget if and when I run into these people again. I've learned over the years this is very important. People love when you remember them. It speaks for itself. Especially in this business, when I meet so many people. It lets them know they were important enough or significant enough to remember.

I have to challenge myself when doing this. I sometimes surprise myself when I get a name right.

I knew it would only be a matter of time for those who hadn't read the book yet to start asking more questions about Star. What happened after Star's mom died? As a small group of people gathered around to listen to my response, I said, "Well, if you guys insist we mix business with pleasure, I guess I can share a little more. Star hated where they lived ..."

Once again I'm living in filth. Another apartment infested with rats and roaches. I hoped when I became an adult; I would no longer have to live this way. No matter how much I cleaned, there was no getting rid of them. It was so bad I had to plug the girls' ears with cotton balls each night to keep the roaches from crawling in their ears. Once I went to the bathroom to start the girls a bubble bath, and a huge rat was waiting to greet me. Seriously, not a mouse but a fat rat! I was terrified. It wasn't afraid of me at all; it just sat there, staring at me. I screamed and ran as fast as I could. I was sure it was going to come after me and attack me. Ethan killed it and got rid of the carcass. After that, I was terrified the girls would have the same experience and encounter another one but wouldn't be so lucky. One would bite them and give them rabies. I lived in fear every day.

The crime in the neighborhood was so bad that I swear I looked out the window once and saw a guy standing on the corner, and another guy walked up to him and shot him in the head. Just like that. I was so terrified that I had just witnessed a murder. I closed the curtain as slowly as I could, turned off the lights, and just listened to the sirens go off and prayed for the victim as I tried to keep me and my girls safe. Our apartment sat right on the corner, so there was always a lot of traffic. Bad drug deals, shooting, fighting, prostitution, you name it, it happened on that corner. Of course you saw nothing in those days, for fear of retaliation. People were terrified to speak up. We lived in fear not just for our lives but for our children's as well. No one was safe. Drugs and crime had taken over the neighborhood.

Things between Ethan and me continued to get worse. He started sleeping around on me again. All the signs were there. Cheating had become a sport for him. He was drinking more and doing more drugs. He was really not present, and when he was, I wished he wasn't. He was never happy; he was always angry. The more I tried to save money, the more it would disappear. He smoked and snorted every dollar he earned. He had no control over his addictions. Once he came home filthy drunk and reeking of cheap perfume. He had pink lipstick kisses all over his face. His behavior was getting worse; he didn't even try to hide his actions. He just didn't care anymore. He would sometimes have his wedding ring off and forget to put it back on. His lies became less and less believable.

I was miserable in my marriage. I wanted out and had no idea how to do it. I had put up with his crap for almost ten years, and he had me right where he wanted me. He knew I had nowhere to go, and he was comfortable I would never leave. The more he cheated, the worse his jealous rages toward me got. One time he came home and picked his usual fight, because he was drunk. He backed me up against the wall, threatening to kill me. He kept hitting me and punching holes in the wall around my body, in a rage. I thought, *This man is crazy for sure.* I screamed as loudly as I could for him to stop. After using me as a punching bag, he finally quit. His usual pattern, he passed out like nothing ever happened. Thank goodness I had put the girls to bed, but I was sure they heard the horrible ordeal. I was their age once, and I heard everything. Everything ...

The next day, while I was in hiding until my bruises healed, there was a knock at the front door. It was one of my landlords, a married couple who actually lived next door. Yeah, they lived next door in this large, expensive home, with a pool and everything. I'm sure when they purchased the place thirty years ago, the neighborhood was safe, unlike now. I'm sure they stayed because the house was paid for and they were retired. It was Mrs. Graham. I didn't want to open the door at first because we were behind on our rent, and I knew she was coming over to ask when we planned on paying it. Of course I had no idea and tried to avoid any conversation with her, especially with the way I felt and probably looked. I cracked the door open just a little.

She stood there looking at me with this concerned expression on her face. She said, "Hi, Star. I was wondering if you're okay". That question kind of took me by surprise. I wasn't quite sure why she was asking. She repeated, "Are you okay? I heard a lot of noise coming from your apartment last night and thought I'd stop by to check on you." I told her I was fine. She stared at me with a puzzled look on her face; I could tell she knew I was lying. I think she was actually trying to help me, but of course I was in denial and assured her I was just fine and said she had nothing to worry about. I thanked her for asking and motioned for her to leave. Reluctantly, after pausing a few moments, she finally left.

After she left, I was angry. I actually had an attitude. I thought, *She's got some nerve coming over here, knocking on my door, trying to get all up in my business.* I was pissed. I honestly couldn't see that she really cared about me and the girls.

This is what happens once you lie to yourself and others for so long about actually being a battered wife. You so badly do not want it to be you. So you don't acknowledge or admit it, because when you do, you are now held somewhat accountable for finding a way out. Not that you haven't tried to escape many times before, but each time gets harder and harder to stay away. Fear will keep you there and lead you back; it never fails. It starts to feel like it can never happen so you might as well stop trying.

Now I knew what Mom felt like when she was with Mr. Bruce. God, I missed my mom, more than anything. She would hate that I kept this from her. She would be so disappointed in Ethan for being such an awful husband. She really loved him. She trusted he would take good care of me and the girls. I thought about Mrs. Graham and convinced myself I was not one of those women. She need not be concerned about me. I had everything under control. I thought she needed to mind her own business and worry about cleaning that dirty pool. Looked like it hadn't been cleaned in years.

I didn't work and had nothing to help pass the time. I started drinking earlier in the day. I would drink myself into drunkenness many times. I smoked a lot more marijuana. I was high all the time. I started to get more paranoid when I left the house, because I thought if someone looked at me, they could tell I was stoned out of my mind. This had just become my life, and right then I couldn't imagine anything different. I felt completely hopeless.

One day Ethan decided he wanted to go back to school and earn his associate's degree. He thought it would give him a better opportunity to find a better paying job. Of course I supported anything he wanted to do, especially if it meant we would have a better future. I had never been to college. I never thought I was smart enough. I wanted to try it as well, so I did everything necessary to enroll in the community college with him. This was an exciting moment for us. We were finally doing something to better ourselves.

Classes started, and we coordinated our classes so one of us would always be home with the girls, and the other could attend class. I should have known it was too good to be true. Ethan's classes started before mine, and when it was time for me to attend my first class, he picked a fight, and I never made it. When it was time for me to go again, he never came home to watch the girls for me. Next thing I realized, I had never attended a class and was forced to drop all of my courses. Ethan continued taking his courses and was doing quite well. He was very good at math. I accepted this arrangement. Again, I would have accepted anything as long as it was toward us having a better life.

It was Sophie's birthday, and we were celebrating. She didn't have a party because we couldn't afford to give her one. She had ice cream and a home-baked cake. She had just blown out her candles when we noticed, from the living room window, a young man running outside in our yard, screaming for help. It startled us as we watched him run in fear. Ethan and I noticed he was bleeding from his head. Ethan quickly ran outside to his rescue. I told the girls to stay inside, and I ran after Ethan. I was scared and had no idea what Ethan was thinking. I noticed these guys were chasing this poor kid, purposely taunting and striking him with anything they could find. They kept saying they were teaching him a lesson.

It all happened so fast. One minute Ethan was trying to save this kid, not knowing this was a gang-related incident. These guys were trying to torture and kill this young man. They would've succeeded if Ethan hadn't stepped in and played the hero. The young man was able to flee while the gang turned the beating on Ethan. It was happening so fast, and a large crowd had gathered around. We were only yards away from our home. Ethan tried to defend himself by taking a couple swings at one of the gang members, but none landed. Both Ethan's eyes were so swollen he couldn't see, and the crowd laughed at the sight of him swinging at air, trying to defend himself. They thought it was hilarious. Next thing I knew, Ethan was fighting for his life. They beat him down so bad, right in front of me, and everyone watched and never lifted a finger to save him. No one was brave enough to try to help him, not even me. I was frozen in shock and fear. One of the gang members pulled out his gun and put it to Ethan's head, threatening to shoot him right in front of all of us. It scared the crap out of him, and he pissed on himself. He thought he was going to die. Finally I heard sirens, and the crowd scattered.

It was only my wounded husband and myself. I was so scared it was hard to walk toward him. I thought he was dead. He was beaten so badly that I hardly recognize him. He kept saying, "Come get me before the cops come. Help me up. Help me." No one wanted to be questioned by the cops. People paid with their lives for being a snitch. Even I wouldn't tell what I had seen, for fear of them hurting my children and me. The police arrived as I was walking Ethan back to the house. It was evident we were victims, but when questioned, I kept telling them it all happened so fast I couldn't identity any of them, and all I cared about at that moment was getting my husband to the hospital. They offered to call an ambulance, but we declined.

Ethan was badly beaten and very afraid. I asked Cindy if she would watch the girls so I could take him to the hospital. Sophie's birthday was ruined in a matter of minutes. Ethan tried to be a hero and ended up a victim. That day took something from him, especially with it happening in his hometown. Everyone knew him, and no one stepped in to help him. Everyone just watched him get the crap beat out of him.

My thoughts were all over the place. One was unmerciful. Like, *I may not be able to beat you down like they did, but it sure was bittersweet to see that someone else could.* I know that may be a bit cruel, but oh well, it was how I felt, and I was not that sympathetic. I just hated that it happened like that. If he was depressed before, this only took him further down that hole of hopelessness. He became one of the worse pessimists I'd ever known. I got tired of him feeling sorry for himself and never able to see any good in anything. He complained all the time and continued drowning his sorrows with more drugs and alcohol.

One day I was at the local video store renting movies. The owner and I had become acquainted, and he spoke to me almost every time he was there to check on his employees. This particular day, he asked me if I had a job. I said, "No and I don't want one." He laughed and said, "Well, when you change your mind, I'd love for you to work for my company." I said, "Here at the video store? No thanks." He laughed again and said, "No, my business office. We need a receptionist, and I think you'd be great." I told him I'd think about it. I really never gave it a second thought. It wasn't a good time for me to work. It never was, and I didn't feel like fighting with Ethan, just to have my independence again. He'd find some way to take it from me, like always.

Ethan became even more paranoid and controlling after his incident. It got so bad that if I sat on the porch and watched the girls play outside, he accused me of sleeping with every man that smiled at me in passing and said hello. I didn't even know these guys. Ethan wrecked my brand-new car when he was running an errand. He couldn't take his beat-up Ford Tempo. He had to drive my car. Of course the insurance had laps on it between the move to Chicago to take care of Mom and the move back home. I never had time to renew it due to financial struggles. Not to mention I was still behind on the payments. It was repossessed shortly after. They took it, dents and all.

One afternoon when the girls were in school, Ethan and I went to look for a new car. The Tempo was repossessed weeks after my car was. We needed transportation because Ethan's temp job was outside the city limits, about thirty minutes from the house. He befriended a female coworker of his, who started driving out of her way to come pick him up each morning and drop him off. *Odd*, I thought, *yet typical Ethan*. The hussy lived in the town they worked in, so she was going out of her way to do this. I'm sure she was more than a friend. By now I was numb to Ethan's ways and just dealt with it.

The car dealership was grilling hotdogs for its clients. We'd been there for hours, filling out paperwork and trying to seal the deal, and we hadn't eaten before we left that morning. Those hotdogs smelled so good. One of the salesmen asked us if we would like a hotdog, and I accepted. He fixed it up and gave it to me, and I ate it. It hit the spot just right. Ethan turned down the offer with an attitude. I was confused at why.

When we returned home, Ethan started accusing me of flirting with the salesman that offered me the hotdog. I wasn't flirting with anyone, but he had made up in his mind that I was, and I got another beaten for that. At this point, I was tired of living that way. I loved Ethan so much, and I knew he needed help, and I tried to tell him we needed counseling. I felt that if we separate for a while and he got some help, maybe things would get better between us.

Bad move on my part. This just angered him even more and made him feel more insecure. He threatened to kill me if I ever tried to leave him. I was convinced he would kill me in one of his drunken rages and wake up later only to find my dead body lying in a pool of blood.

The girls were getting older, and I felt I had to stop drinking away my sorrows and smoking marijuana every day. I knew that sooner or later they would realize I was just like my mom, and I never wanted them to know this side of me. So I quit cold turkey. I stopped drinking and doing drugs. This bothered Ethan, because drugs and alcohol were what he used to control me. As long as I was just as messed up as he was, I had no room to complain.

After I quit using drugs, I was able to think more clearly. I was surprised at how easy it was to leave that lifestyle alone. I'd never imagined being strong enough to not do drugs or drink like a fish every day. The clarity I gained was a whole new experience for me. I was actually sober and not paranoid anymore. It actually gave me hope, and I started seeing myself wanting to leave the ghetto and live somewhere else. I started wanting more; I started dreaming again of living in a nicer and safer neighborhood. I started thinking of ways I could make this happen, and I started wanting it more than anything. I prayed to God, asking him to help give me the strength, direction, and guidance I needed to plan my escape from Ethan. I had always wanted more, but this time I was willing to do what it took to get it. I didn't know how or when, but I knew someday, and that was enough to begin with. It all starts with a thought.

I accepted the receptionist job the business owner at the video store had offered me. Best decision I ever made. His office was located downtown, and it was walking distance from our home. I didn't have to worry about catching a bus. I loved my new job. It was perfect for me. I loved being downtown even more. Important people worked downtown, including bankers, corporate people, and business owners. It felt good to surround myself in this type of environment. I would take my lunches and five dollars to my name and go to the local restaurants and dream even bigger dreams. I wanted more.

I walked everywhere downtown. I had to run bank errands every day to make the daily business deposits. He owned a private airline charter service, several homes, and the video store. To my surprise, his wife was Mrs. Turner, the counselor I had spoken to in high school when I was having those problems with Mom. You remember—the one who thought I was wasting her time. What a small world. No wonder she felt she was too good and all high and mighty. This woman was filthy rich, and her husband was highly respected in the community. I was impressed, as this was a black couple, and I had never seen black people with this kind of money. I assisted with payroll and their billing. I couldn't believe the amounts of money that flowed through these businesses. Owning a private airline and planes says enough. I enjoyed being a part of this corporation; it inspired me even more. I started to dream bigger.

One day I was running my usual errands, and I saw a familiar face. It was a very handsome, distinguished-looking man. He always wore a suit and nice shoes. He had a warm and pleasant smile. He would speak to me almost every time I passed by him. I never thought much about it, as I had always had eyes only for Ethan. This day was different. I passed him, and he said hello. I spoke as usual and continued running my errands. I walked back to the office, and as I entered the building where my office was located, I started taking the stairs to the third floor. I felt a presence behind me. I felt someone was following me, and when I looked back, it was the nice-looking man. He had followed me. I was startled and somewhat afraid. He must have seen this in my eyes and body language.

He assured me with a gentle touch that he was sorry he frightened me. He extended his hand and introduced himself. He said, "Hello, my name is Pastor Brown." I politely responded with my name as Mrs. Moore. I'd always been upfront with men and introduced myself as Mrs. Moore so that there was never any misunderstanding. Pastor Brown said he'd seen me around a lot lately and was a bit intrigued about who I was and what I did. I told him I worked in this building and I was a receptionist. I told him I was late getting back, and it was nice to meet him, but I had to go. He gracefully said his good-byes and said he hoped to see me again soon. I nodded uncomfortably, not knowing how to respond, and almost ran up the stairs as fast as I could.

I honestly thought nothing of meeting Pastor Brown but was a bit concerned that he was following me. Day after day, Pastor Brown made it his mission to run into me, no matter where I was. It was like he purposely planned his schedule around bumping into me, as if he just happened to be where I was by coincidence. At first it annoyed me, but after a while, I started expecting to see him and would be disappointed if I hadn't. He had grown on me, and I looked forward to running into him.

Knowing he was a pastor made me feel safe. I didn't feel like it was harmful to say hello. I was certain this was all innocent. Weeks went by, and hellos turned into two- or five-minute conversations, and short conversations turned into lunch dates. I saw no harm in getting to know a pastor; again, I felt safe. I found out Pastor Brown was married and had children. I think he was happy from what I gathered. He never said a negative word about his wife. We talked about politics, education, and just life in general, anything to keep the conversation going. Pastor Brown could tell I wasn't happily married and dug a little deeper into my personal life, as if he was counseling me. I didn't mind, as I'm sure he did this for many members of his church, and I was hoping he had some spiritual wisdom and guidance to offer me.

We had become close, and he started building an attraction for me. At first it felt good having someone like him think someone like me was worth giving a second look at, in spite of my troubled life. He was very encouraging and supportive of my dreams and my goals. He never made me feel like I couldn't reach them. I told him someday I was going to write a book. He said he couldn't wait to read it. He believed in me. Once he kissed me, and to my surprise, I didn't resist. It felt nice and pleasant, warm and safe. I couldn't believe he had done this, but it happened, and we couldn't pretend it didn't. So we accepted it and continued our special friendship.

I didn't want intimacy between us to become a regular part of our friendship. The guilt overwhelmed me. Pastor Brown was a man of the cloth; I knew I had a one-way ticket straight to hell. This had to be the ultimate sin. We were kissing and touching a lot, and I was starting to feel anxiety. I honestly didn't know how Ethan cheated on me so many times. I hated this feeling, and I'd done nothing but kiss another man. It was awful.

Pastor Brown's attraction toward me became more and more aggressive. He couldn't control himself. He kept pressuring me to have sex with him. I kept saying no, we couldn't, because it was wrong, and it would change our friendship, and we would be committing adultery. It just didn't sit well with me. He wanted more, and I was afraid to ever have sex with anyone other than my husband. I fought him off as long as I could.

I'd started playing bingo with Cindy once a week. She and her mom loved playing bingo, and they would ask me to join them from time to time. This was the only thing Ethan allowed me to do outside of work and grocery shopping. He thought if I was with family, he didn't have to worry about another man wanting me. He kept a tight leash. One night, I told him I was playing bingo alone, and he let me. I was surprised he didn't ask why Cindy wasn't going that night. I met Pastor Brown in the parking lot of the bingo hall. He knew we only had a about a three-hour time slot. I got in his car, and he drove us to the nearest park. We talked. I was nervous. He started kissing and fondling me something heavy, and we both got excited, and the next thing I knew, we did it. It happened so fast. I realized I had just committed adultery.

I immediately began to cry. I couldn't believe I allowed this to get out of hand. It didn't feel good, and I couldn't figure out why people engaged in this type of activity, because it was not how they portrayed it in the movies. Pastor Brown felt worse than I did. He had assumed it would be something we both wanted. But he realized he wanted it more than I did and had pressured me until I gave in. He held me in his arms and tried to calm me down, but he knew how difficult it must have been for me. He kept apologizing and said he loved me and he would've never hurt me. He said, "This isn't at all how I thought it would be when we first made love." He said I deserved better than this, and he was sorry he let it happen. He said all he wanted me to know was how much he loved me. Pastor Brown had fallen in love.

He drove me back to the bingo parking lot, and I went back to my miserable life as if nothing had happened. Pastor Brown worried about me, and he checked up on me every day that he could. He was so concerned about how I was handling what happened between us. He was a dear friend, and I valued his friendship regardless of what had happened. He was a good man, and I was a good woman. We are human, and sometimes humans make bad choices. We recognized our weakness for each other, and we talked about it a lot. Our friendship was priceless, and we didn't want anything to change that.

One day after a lunch date, we held hands, and he prayed for our souls that God would forgive us and have mercy on us and forgive us for our sins. It felt good to do this, as I really needed to know God wouldn't be mad at me for committing this sin.

Once Pastor Brown contacted me outside of our usual working schedule. He kept driving by my house, hoping I would notice so he could motion to me that he needed to speak to me. I was nervous Ethan would see him. I knew it had to be quick, so I stepped outside after he circled the corner for about the fifth time, when Ethan wasn't paying attention. Pastor Brown quickly pulled his car over to the curb where I was standing and said it was very important that he speaks to me. I was concerned his wife had found out about us, but he assured me that wasn't it. He said he needed to speak to me in private. I told him I would make up an excuse to go pick up something at the grocery store, and I would meet him there within an hour or so. He nodded and drove away.

My mind kept racing, wondering what could be so important. I had never seen Pastor Brown look so concerned. When I arrived at the store parking lot, he was patiently waiting. I got out of my car and into his. He asked me if I'd been feeling weird or itching. I didn't quite understand what he meant. His eyes looked down toward my private area. It took me a minute to comprehend exactly what he was asking me, and when I realized what he meant, I said, "Now that you bring it up, yes, why?"

He said, "Because we have crabs."

I said, "Crabs? What is that?" I had no idea what crabs were or how you got them. He explained to me how you get them and said I had to have given them to him that night we crossed the line. I felt dirty and nasty, but Pastor Brown was calm and very understanding. He knew I didn't do it to him on purpose. He was more upset that we both probably got them from Ethan. I'm sure he was right. Sadly, if Ethan had crabs, he would never admit it, because it would be more proof that he was still cheating on me. *What a selfish, inconsiderate jerk!* I thought. *Typical Ethan.*

I was pissed. "What do we do now?" I asked. To my surprise, Pastor Brown didn't want to give them to his wife, and he knew we wouldn't be sexually active again, but he wanted to help me get rid of them as well. He had come prepared; he brought some over-the-counter crab treatment. He explained to me how to use it and for how many days to be sure I got rid of them completely. I took the box of liquid treatment home with me and followed the instructions until they were gone.

The entire time I was treating my crabs, I was waiting for my no-good husband to come forward with this news. I noticed he stopped having sex with me, because he must have been afraid he would give me crabs, but it was too late, I already had them. I remember him acting as secretly as I was during that time. I think he was waiting for me to ask him or complain about it, but I never did.

I thought about Pastor Brown and his wife and children. I knew he loved them. I prayed that whatever caused him to stray from his marriage that God would heal his heart and his wife, so they could have a better marriage. I believed all marriages were gifts from God. No one is perfect, and no marriage is perfect. But God's love is, and his mercy is even better. I only wished the best for him and his family. I never wanted to be a home wrecker. I started to distance myself a bit so Pastor Brown could focus on saving his marriage.

God must have been listening to my prayers. A few weeks later, Pastor Brown asked me to have lunch with him. He said he had something to share with me. When we met, he said he had been reassigned to another church in Florida. I was shocked and happy for him all at the same time. I knew I would miss him dearly, as he as my confidant. I had somewhat fallen in love with him but never told him. I cherished his companionship. I would miss him so much. He left shortly after, and we lost contact. Before he departed, he looked me in my eyes and told me I was very intelligent and a remarkable woman and that someday I would make my dreams come true. He said he knew I would do great things. He said I had what it takes. He said, "I can't wait to go to the bookstore and see your book on the shelf." He said he'd be looking for it. I kept his encouraging words close to my heart. Someone believed in me. This meant more to me than anything. I'd never had that before, and it felt wonderful. Good-bye, Pastor Brown.

Life continued as usual in my household. I missed my mom like crazy. I didn't realize how much not having her in my life anymore would affect me. I really needed my mom, and she was no longer with me. I wanted so much to fill the mommy void in my heart. I really needed my mommy. I felt a huge amount of guilt, and mourning the loss of her wasn't easy. I felt like I was being punished for the way I treated her, for the last words I'd said to her. I felt so guilty that it suffocated me at times. Mourning her death really put me through emotional turmoil.

One thing I wanted was for Mom to have a daughter she could be proud of. I felt like I had disappointed her. I lived in her shadow since the day she kicked me out of her house. I hadn't done anything but prove that I wasn't any better than her. I thought just how right she was and just how wrong I was for trying all those years to prove her wrong.

These thoughts took over, and I couldn't easily shake them. I kept wanting much more, and it was time to change my life. I was still working for Turner Enterprises. Mr. Turner knew a lot of people who also owned a lot of real estate. A dear friend of his, Mr. Wright, visited the office regularly. Turner Enterprises managed his property and his accounts. We processed and collected rent from his tenants. He was also a prominent black man. I was impressed to see black professionals doing big things. I lived in the hood and wasn't surrounded by these types of people. Black educated people who owned their own homes, drove expensive cars, wore nice designer labels, and owned their own businesses. I wanted to be just like them someday.

They were richer than I thought Mom and Mr. Bruce were. We were still considered poor compared to these business guys. They lived in mansions. Their homes were the kind you'd only see on the *Rich and Famous* TV show.

This made me want to be a better person more and more as I surrounded myself with people who had more than I did. I finally built enough courage to ask Mr. Wright if he had any available property that I could possibly afford to live in. To my surprise, Mr. Wright said yes. "I just had someone move out this week and was about to list it. It's located in the burbs, on the outskirts of the city, in a rural area, but the schools are great, and the apartment is nice and clean." He said it had two bedrooms. It was actually located in the same town where the truck-driving school was. I loved that area. Not many black folk lived out there, but I thought that would be even better. I was so excited at the possibility of actually moving to the suburbs, I couldn't think about anything else. Three weeks later, I had signed a lease and made it happen. I had gotten the girls and me out of the ghetto. Unfortunately, Ethan was part of the package. I mean, he was my husband. When it was convenient for him.

So many things were going on in my life. I started showing up late for work. Ethan could feel me emotionally slipping away. He could tell I was fed up with his bull crap and was picking fight after fight, night after night. I was exhausted. I started making simple mistakes and couldn't ever do anything right. Ethan accused me of sleeping with Mr.

Wright; he was convinced that was the only way we were able to move out there. I had to have slept with Mr. Wright. Why else would someone like him allow a poor, helpless black girl move into an apartment as nice as this? As usual, Ethan couldn't just be happy we got a lucky break. It always had to be a negative reason why we were blessed.

I worked too hard and had come too far to continue dealing with his mess. Life was looking up, and I was tired of feeling stuck in the same rut Ethan had become accustomed to. I wanted more and was determined to do whatever I had to in order to create a better life for the girls and me.

Unfortunately, I got fired from my job. I felt defeated. There was no reason I should have lost that job. I blew it once again. Mr. Turner had taken a chance on a poor black woman from the ghetto, and I failed him. I didn't live up to my expectations, and I am sure I didn't live up to his. I could have gone far in that company. But I was so absorbed in my messed-up life that I felt like I was back in high school, dealing with Mom's abuse. Ethan had started affecting every decision I made, and I continued to let him destroy any good thing I tried to accomplish.

One Friday evening, Ethan called on his way home from work and asked if the girls and I would like to have pizza for dinner. Of course, this was always a treat for the girls. He agreed to pick one up on his way home. It was about three when he called on his last break. He got off work at 4:30, so we were expecting the pizza to arrive shortly after. Almost three hours had passed—no Ethan, no pizza. I knew he probably stopped by one of his women's house and lost track of time. I got upset because I had told the girls we were having pizza for dinner, and they were waiting for Daddy to walk through the door any minute. I had already set the table with paper plates and glasses for their Kool-Aid, and we waited and waited and waited. The girls were hungry. I ended up feeding them boxed mac and cheese for dinner, to their disappointment after having their hearts set on pizza. At this point, I had no idea when their dad would arrive.

Another hour passed when he finally showed up with a very cold pizza in hand as if nothing was wrong. I was so upset. I said, "Are you kidding me? You just walked in here like everything was normal with a cold pizza? Seriously, Ethan?" Not seconds after I confronted him, he left-handed me so hard across my face it sent me flying across the room, right in front of the girls. The shock on my face had to be priceless, because I looked at him like he had lost his mind. Then Ethan ran over to me to teach me more lessons, to teach me to keep my mouth shut and not to ever question him again about what he did. He clearly got his point across, and I endured another beating, but this time in front of my children. When he finished, he conveniently left our apartment. His usual pattern was to go in the room and pass out. But clearly he was more sober than usual. That meant he was well aware of his actions. I should have known he had an agenda. He was trying to get back to whomever I was keeping him from. The door slammed. I picked my battered body up off the floor as my children watched, tears streaming down their little frightened faces as they shook uncontrollably. I held them in my arms, and we all cried together. I apologized for their father's behavior and told them he loved them and, that Daddy was just having a bad day.

I had flashbacks from when I was a little girl. I had witnessed my mom go through this and remembered how badly it scared me. All I could think of was how my girls would someday have the same struggles growing up and how it was up to me to change that. It was time to escape. I knew I only had a small window of time to get the girls and me out of the apartment and find somewhere safe to hide where Ethan couldn't find us. I was terrified. I started shaking with fear. I got on the phone and called, Ally. Ally and Corey had moved out of the city back to our small town to be closer to her family. They now had three children. Ally was terrified. She didn't want anything to do with my escape. She was scared Ethan would come back before she could get us out safely. She wasn't sure she was willing to take that chance, but I begged her. I begged and cried for Ally to help me. If there was ever a time I needed her to come through for me, it was at this very moment. I was determined to get out, and it had to happen now.

I wasn't quite sure of a plan just yet, however. I had to find somewhere to stay where he couldn't find us, somewhere he wouldn't think to look. I had made friends with this wonderful woman who worked at the local bus and train station. Her name was Cheryl. I'd actually met Cheryl the first time I tried to escape, after Ethan had raped me. She was the one who sold me my ticket. Cheryl was smart and beautiful. She had worked for the train station almost twenty years. She had a daughter and was a single mom. I admired her strength as a single mom. She made good money and was doing very well for herself. She loved Brooklyn. She would help me out when I had to work late and would pick Brooklyn up from preschool and watch her for me until I got off work.

Ethan didn't know where she lived, and he wasn't able to scare her off like he had done all my other friends. I called her in a panic and asked if Ally could drop the girls and me off at her house, only for a couple days until I figured out my next move. She was more than glad to help out. She was glad I'd finally gotten enough courage to leave this no-good monster. She used to tell me I could do better and that Ethan never deserved me. She shared with me that she was once a battered wife and that men like Ethan are sick and need help. She said some of them never change.

It's funny how others can see things you are too close to see when your judgment is clouded with fear of the unknown. I hurried and packed a few necessities. I was afraid I wouldn't get out in time. I heard someone coming up the stairs to the apartment and panicked. I froze and wondered what would I do if it were Ethan. I had no answers. I knew there was no way I would get out alive if it was, and that fear paralyzed me. Instead, it was Ally. She had made it across town in record time. She was more scared than I was. She kept asking me if I was sure this was what I wanted. I kept saying, "Yes, Ally, but we don't have time to discuss it right now. We need to leave now! Let's go!"

It took a couple trips up and down the stairs for me to feel I had enough for me and the girls to get by in case we needed to stay longer than a couple days. I'll never forget the anxiety and fear as we drove away from my home. I was watching every passing car, thinking this was too good to be true, that he was going to catch me before we could make it to the next stoplight. I was so terrified of getting caught. Ally was shaking; she couldn't believe it was happening. Her loyalty was with me, but I had put her in an uncomfortable position, and she could only imagine how furious Ethan was going to be when he came home to an empty house.

Ally drove us to Cheryl's house. Cheryl was waiting at the door to greet the girls and me with open, loving arms. She was so happy to see that I had the courage to flee. She embraced me with love and compassion. She knew this was very difficult for me and probably one of the hardest decisions I had ever made. She was right; it was the hardest decision I had ever made. Nevertheless, I was done with that life, and I never wanted to return. I knew I would never allow Ethan to hurt me again. I had no idea how I was going to raise my children alone, but at that moment, I didn't care. I was jobless, carless, and now homeless, but most of all I was finally free. *Thank you, God! I know I will find a way. One day at a time.*

Mr. Shultz, a powerful businessman, said, "Good for Star. My mother told me a man is weak if he has to put his hands on a woman. My mother told me to never hit a woman. If I ever felt that angry, I should be the better man and walk away." The other men in the crowd surrounding me agreed wholeheartedly, that men should keep their hands to themselves. The women in the crowd were praising Star's amazing courage for finally leaving Ethan. They named her the hero that night.

I smiled and agreed. "Star has always been my hero. She was a very special friend. I was scared to death that day she called me. I must have run every stop sign trying to get to her and the girls before Ethan returned."

Mr. Shultz raised his champagne flute and toasted. "To Star's bravery!"

Someone else echoed, "To Star's bravery!" Glasses clanked, and we drank to salute Star's bravery.

Chapter 10

I really enjoyed the reception. By the time Adam returned to drive me back to the hotel, I was exhausted. I had talked so much and smiled so hard, my voice was hoarse, and my face hurt. Marissa said she'd see me later tomorrow, right before I met the mayor and his wife for lunch. She assured me by then she would have all the information needed to cover the three-page spread in the magazine. Before I departed, Pam reminded me of tomorrow's schedule and said Adam would be back to pick me up in the morning at 9:00 a.m. sharp. First thing on the agenda was meeting up with the children on their field trip to the 9/11 memorials. I nodded in agreement that I was clear about tomorrow's schedule. Pam could tell my brain needed to rest. She smiled, gave me a hug, and said, "Have a restful evening, Ms. Knight."

Adam escorted me to the limo and opened the door for me. I was greeted with calm, smooth jazz playing in the background. It was exactly what the doctor had ordered to help me relax and wind down. I sat back and enjoyed the ride.

When I tipped Adam to thank him for everything he'd done, he said, "No, I'm sorry, Ms. Knight, but I can't accept this. You do so much for others that I can't take this from you." I told him to please take it, and if he felt compelled to pay it forward, then that would make it a double gift. I said, "There's always someone who needs it more than you."

Adam took the generous hundred-dollar tip, tilted his hat, and said, "Have a good evening, Ms. Knight."

I said, "You too, Adam. Good night."

I drew a nice bubble bath, and as I soaked in the oversized whirlpool tub, remembering the day I helped Star leave Ethan and how frightened we both were. All I could think about was how Ethan must have felt when he walked into their apartment and realized his family had left him. He was convinced Star would never leave him. Ever!

For the first time in years, I knew I would never look back, no matter how bad things got for me and the girls. I was determined not to fail. My girls were my inspiration. I was doing this not just for me but most of all for them. I wanted them to have more than I did. I wanted them to know what a better life felt like. I wanted to know what a better life felt like.

When I left Ethan, I had nothing. I didn't even have any dignity. How could I? After all, I had allowed him to strip me from anything that made me worthy of being a human being. I let him tear me down. I let him almost destroy any hope I barely held onto.

I realized my entire life was wrapped around his wants, his needs, his dreams, his failures, his identity, his depression, his alcoholism, his drug addictions, and his weaknesses. Everything for the past ten years was all about him. As that reality sank in, I got angrier, not with him but with myself, because even after all this I still loved Ethan. I wanted so much to save him and us. I wanted so much not to take the girls' daddy away from them. They needed their daddy; every little girl needs her daddy. I couldn't believe, after everything, I was still in love with my children's father. This saddened me because I really trusted and believed Ethan would be a good husband, an awesome dad, and a provider for our family. It really hurt to realize I was wrong. Ethan couldn't do it. He let us down. He let himself down. *How are they to look up to him now? What will they think years from now? What memories will they have?*

I felt sorry for him but not enough to put myself back in the prison I had just escaped. No matter how much he begged and asked for forgiveness, I would not give in, not this time. I never looked back, not once. Ethan never found us after I left, and I didn't contact him for weeks. I'm sure he was worried, but I had to be clear that I didn't want anything else to do with him. When I finally did contact him, I convinced him to leave our home so the girls and I could move back. I had no where to live and I felt I deserved to live in our apartment, because I had worked hard to get us out of the ghetto, and the girls and I deserved to at least have a decent roof over our heads, even though at the time I had no idea how I would maintain it financially.

Ethan agreed to leave, and we moved back home. I'm sure he only did this because he was sure he could convince me to take him back again. It worked for him so may times in the past. He moved in with his mother and told her it was only temporary. To his disappointment, I never took him back, and I never considered forgiving him for what he did to me all those years. All I could think about was, *How will I take care of my children?*

First thing I needed to do was find a job. I caught a taxi to the nearest temporary service, and they assigned me to a clothing factory in the next town, about fifteen miles away. I had no idea how I would get to work; it was so far away. Fortunately, it was just outside the city limit, and a bus did go out near that area. I just had to walk the rest of the way, just like I'd done in the past. This was perfect, because I needed employment, and I wasn't being picky. Second thing I needed was to find transportation, because there wasn't a grocery store nearby, and I needed to get things for the girls. When Mom died, she had an old Toyota. Dallas had it parked at his house. I called him and told him about my situation and begged him to give me Mom's car. He agreed, and I made arrangements to travel to Chicago to get the car. I had to get a sitter for the girls. It was a long weekend and meant arranging to pick up the car and drive it back to Atlanta.

Third thing I needed to do was find a lawyer and file for a divorce. I had no money, and this was all new to me. I found out quickly I was too poor to hire a lawyer and someone told me about legal aid. They had lawyers who did pro bono for low-income people and could probably appoint me a divorce lawyer. I went and filled out an application. Not long after, I was contacted by letter and told that I had been approved. They gave the name and location of my lawyer. She was a white female with a northern accent. She was awesome; she had my best interest at heart and knew I wanted full custody of my children. I'm glad she was smart because I didn't know what I wanted other than my children. As long as I had full custody of the girls, nothing else mattered. However, she insisted I ask for child support. I didn't quite understand what that meant or how it worked, but I allowed her to make the best decisions for the girls and me.

Ethan tried to play hardball when I first filed for a divorce. Ally reluctantly served him the divorce papers. I knew he wouldn't let anyone else get that close to him. He had moved out of his mother's house and gotten an apartment. He said it was to show me he was being more responsible. He was still trying to save our marriage.

I didn't believe it. Once Ethan and I separated, so many rumors about how many women he had slept with surfaced. He played me like a violin. I was the dumb, naïve wife and the biggest joke in our small town. They say the wife is always the last to know. I heard Ethan had slept with female family members and friends. He had no scruples. He was a low-down dog. He fought the divorce hard in the beginning, until one day out of nowhere he showed up at the apartment and asked if I could rush the divorce as quickly as possible. I had no idea what the sudden urgency was all about. But I contacted my lawyer before he changed his mind. I was granted full custody of the girls, and Ethan was summoned to pay child support. To my surprise, less than a week after the divorce was final, Ethan remarried.

I tried to warn his new wife about him. I tried to tell her she just got my leftovers and he wasn't the man he pretended to be. But she was in love. I couldn't blame her. I once walked in her shoes. She really thought she had something. So did I once. I laughed at how she protected his reputation and accused me of telling lies about him. She said I was just jealous because I had let a good one get away. I knew she would find out the hard way, just like I did. Time tells all.

Being single was tough. This was all new to me. I went straight from high school to being a wife, and months later becoming a mother. This was the first time I had ever really been on my own. I really didn't know what to do with all the freedom. I had no one to tell me what to do and when and how to do it—except for the girls, but that didn't count. Every decision I made from that day on, good or bad, I had no one to blame but myself.

I had never really dated and didn't know how to start. I had no plan. I learned as I went along. Dating was hard because I never saw myself as an individual. I had always belonged to someone. I was always Ethan's wife. Never just Star. Who is Star? I was about to find out. It took me a while to discover who I was and realize no one owned me. I was really free. It was hard on me financially, especially when the girls' dad quit his job. He thought I was getting over on him having to pay child support. He really had a problem with the state taking the payments directly from his check. I thought he was being selfish. Why wouldn't he want to take care of his own children? I'm not sure why his behavior surprised me, because he never wanted me to succeed without him, and not paying child support would guarantee my failure.

Ethan had visitation rights and had started not showing up on his weekends. I'll never forget how I would get the girls all dressed up and ready to spend time with their dad. They would wait by the door for him to pick them up, and he wouldn't show. They would cry, and I would have to find ways to make up for the disappointment he continued putting them through. They were young, and they didn't understand why their daddy didn't live with us anymore. They loved their daddy, and they blamed me for him not being around.

When he wouldn't come get them, his new wife, Abby started to fill in for him. She was trying to be the perfect stepmother and wanted to get to know the girls, and I had no problem with that. She never did anything to me, and I was glad she stepped up and took responsibility for her husband's shortcomings and assisted with the girls. She had a son from a previous relationship. As mothers, we wanted the kids to get to know one another. The girls started looking forward to their biweekly visits again. They had grown close to their stepmom, Abby. She really cared about the girls and grew to love them as her own. Abby's son's name was Tyson. He was much younger than the girls, and they loved having a stepbrother. She and I built a friendship over the months and interactions of exchanging the girls on Ethan's weekends. I really liked Abby. I felt sorry for her deep down inside. I dreaded the day Ethan showed her his true colors. Because a wolf is a wolf is a wolf is a wolf. He would not be able to control the urge to harm her for long. It was in his DNA to hurt women.

One morning, Abby invited me over for a cup of coffee, and I was happy to join her. Ethan came home and was shocked to see me sitting at their dining room table, laughing and talking with Abby. When he saw us together, we couldn't help but chuckle at the look on his face, his puzzled expression. He felt threatened by our relationship. It bothered him that we honestly liked each other and had developed a genuine friendship. This was not what Ethan had expected. Ethan hated when he felt out of control.

One weekend, the girls were staying with Abby and their dad. It was about two in the morning when the phone rang. It was Sophie. She was crying and saying her daddy was in the other room hitting Abby in the face, and Abby was crying, and she was afraid because Abby was pleading for him to stop, and he just kept hitting her. Sophie begged me to come get her and Brooklyn because they were frightened and didn't want to stay with their dad anymore.

I was furious! I couldn't believe my children had to witness their father hurting someone else they loved, and it frightened them so much that they had to find away to call me in the middle of the early morning for me to come rescue them. I swear I must have run every stop sign just like Ally did when she came to rescue me and the girls from the psychopath. I was in shock. All I could think of was the fear in Sophie's voice, crying for help. I felt I couldn't get to them quickly enough. When I finally arrived, their dad had left the house. Abby was severely bruised. She kept apologizing for Ethan's actions. I didn't want to hear it. I just came to get my girls. All I cared about was getting my girls home to a safer environment. The girls were not allowed to visit their dad again after that. I just wasn't taking any more chances. This really hurt Abby. She missed them so much, but she understood.

Abby called me a couple days later and apologized for not listening to my warnings about Ethan when they first married. She said she was terrified to leave him. She said she didn't know what to do. I said, "Pray and somehow try to find your inner strength. In an abusive situation, no one can save you but you. You'll know when you're ready. Until then, I will keep you in my prayers." She said thanks. We grew distant after that. Ethan refused to have her contact me. I understood her dilemma and didn't take it personally.

Things were getting harder and harder for me financially. I struggled trying to keep my mother's car running so I could get back and forth to work each day. The car broke down on my way to work one morning. It had been leaking oil something fierce, and I didn't have money to put it in the shop. I was running late for work that morning and didn't have time to poor the usual three quarts of oil it needed daily to get me back and forth to work. I was praying it would make it, and of course the engine locked up on me right on the highway. It just shut down. I was so mad at myself for not taking the time to poor the only quart of oil I had left into the car. The engine seals were broken so badly the car oil would run out as soon as I'd poor it in. You could literally see the oil puddle forming underneath the car before I could drive off. I knew it was only a matter of time before the engine would give.

I was minutes from my job and stuck on the highway. A coworker recognized my car broken down on the side of the road and stopped to pick me up. I was grateful because I needed my job. I was still a temporary employee, and clocking in late would count against me.

I knew the person who picked me up. He was a friend of the family. He lived next door to us when I lived in the ghetto. He was Cindy's boyfriend at the time. I'd never really gotten to know him because Ethan was always so jealous. He was dating my niece's mom, and they had a daughter together. Bethany was born a month after Brooklyn. They were very close cousins.

Quinton offered me a ride home after work, and I accepted. He was nice. I didn't feel nervous or uncomfortable because I felt I already knew him. He extended his offer to pick me up the next morning. I accepted without hesitation. It was one less worry I would have that evening. I had enough to worry about, like how I was going to replace the car that just died.

Quinton picked me up and dropped me off every day for a couple weeks. During this time, we talked about a lot of things. One evening when he was dropping me off, he admitted he had a crush on me for years. I was flattered. We were just friends, and I'd never thought of him any other way. We were practically family—his daughter was my daughter's cousin. I kept things between us strictly platonic. It was better this way. Although I appreciated everything he was doing for me, I knew hurting Cindy would be awful. I'd known her and her family since I was fifteen years old. I also knew how she loved Quinton. He was the only man she'd ever let live with her and her mom. He was special to her.

At work, people had noticed Quinton was giving me a little more attention than before, and rumors quickly started in the factory that we were sleeping together. This bothered me, because it was not true. I hated being the center of gossip, especially in that type of environment. Factory workers have nothing more to do than to stir up trouble, and they thrive off of someone else's misery. It was the thing that motivated the workers.

Not long after, I was able to purchase a vehicle. It wasn't anything big, just a small car. My credit had rebuilt itself over the years, and it felt good to be able to walk into a car dealership after all those years and be able to pick out a car and drive it off the lot again. But this time I was a single mom, which made me feel even better.

I felt better now that Quinton no longer had a reason to see me every day outside of work. I thought this would give us some distance because I could tell he was growing more feelings for me as the weeks went by. I was trying my hardest not to give into his kindness and modest advances. I would either laugh and joke it away or ignore him. It worked until one evening he showed up at my apartment unannounced. The girls were at their dad's, visiting for the weekend. I had caved in after Abby called one day, crying about how much she missed the girls. I wasn't sure exactly how I felt about Quinton just stopping by unannounced. He could have called first, but maybe he knew I would question his motives.

The evening started out innocently. We talked about everything. He kept bringing up his crush he had on me, and he had convinced himself I felt the same way but just didn't want to admit it. Before I knew what was happening, I woke up in my bedroom in his arms. Crap! What had I just done? I knew this wasn't a good idea. It was too late to turn back now. It all happened so fast, not at all planned. One minute we were just friends, and the next we had become lovers. Just like that. I couldn't believe I was that woman who knowingly sleeps with another woman's man. I felt ugly and ashamed. Once again, I had slept with someone else's man.

This was my first relationship after my divorce with Ethan, and it was very messy. I was confused. I thought I was head over heels in love with Quinton. I thought he was my soul mate. I thought for sure he and I would be together forever. I got his name tattooed on my shoulder, and he had mine tattooed on his. I was sure this love was real and it would never end.

Quinton received a phone call one evening when he was visiting me. It was from one of his ex-girlfriends. He had a few. This one also had a baby by him, a little boy. She told him their son had been murdered. She was crying and hysterical. He jumped up out of my bed and quickly got dressed and left. Later he told me his son, Jeremy, died. He said Julie's current boyfriend killed him. I was in shock. Quinton was angry and so sad. His pain was unbearable. I had never seen a man cry like Quinton did, losing his only son. It was a nightmare. I felt so much guilt. I felt if he hadn't been with me, maybe Jeremy would still be alive. I could never in a million years know what that pain must have felt like and prayed I'd never find out. I just wanted to be there to help Quinton through this difficult time. I thought it brought us even closer.

I was wrong. It had only complicated things even more. During Jeremy's funeral, Cindy found out about us. She noticed when I came over to give my condolences; I was wearing the same gold bracelet she was wearing. It didn't take long for her to put two and two together, and she was furious! What is it about men who cheat and buy their mistress the same gifts they buy their significant other? How tacky is that? Nevertheless, Cindy threw Quinton out immediately. Of course he had nowhere to go but to my house.

I honestly had no words, no excuse, no good reasoning to give Cindy other than I knew I made a mistake, but I was in too deep now and just went with the flow and hoped for the best. I had no idea how to stop or fix the madness.

Unfortunately, when Quinton and I were forced into a much more serious relationship than I had planned, things turned from bad to worse. We just didn't get along. I didn't really know Quinton that well. Living with someone and working with him every day, you get to know a person quickly. The things I found out about Quinton made me question if he was the right guy for the girls and me.

Two weeks after Jeremy's funeral, Quinton got fired. He was jealous of a guy that had a crush on me and was making advances toward me. Quinton had seen him flirting with me and just lost it. He threatened the guy, and they fired him on the spot. I'm sure his emotions were high, especially after losing his son. But now he was unemployed, and I couldn't take care of a grown man and two children.

Quinton started staying out all night. Some nights he wouldn't even come home. Of course I automatically assumed he was cheating on me. This led to many arguments, and once he pushed me so hard I fell into the Christmas tree the girls and I had put up earlier that day. Quinton was starting to become more violent, and his rages were out of control. It got so bad I had to put him out and quickly got a restraining order against him.

This pissed him off so bad; he said he would get revenge and was going to kill me. It got so bad that the police patrolled the outside of my apartment for days, protecting me. It was awful. I was terrified. I couldn't believe just months before I thought I was madly in love with this guy. I thought he really loved me too. We were soul mates. We had tattoos to prove it.

I was free and single once again. I found myself turning thirty and wanted to celebrate, so I traded my small economy car for a fancy sports car. She was a beauty! I had always wanted a sports car, and now I had one. Not practical with two growing girls, but I wasn't being practical right now. I was being selfish. I felt like I deserved it. The girls would have to adjust. *They're still young enough to fit in the backseat,* I thought. They wouldn't be too uncomfortable.

Things were going well for me, and I was able to provide for the girls more after I got hired on permanently at the factory. I didn't have to worry about Quinton as much since he had moved out. I was really in a good place despite the messy breakup. It was inevitable Quinton and I would break up. Mom always told me how you get together is how you stay together. And Quinton and I didn't get together in love and light; it was pure darkness. Therefore, no light could have ever shined on all that negative energy he and I represented as a couple. We hurt too many people. I hoped to learn from it and move on.

Mom's brother, my uncle Joe, his oldest daughter, Kelly, was getting married. I was excited about Kelly's wedding. The family hadn't been together since Mom's funeral. This would be a special moment for Kelly and the family to celebrate young love. Although a divorcee, I supported all marriages and hadn't grown bitter at all. I still believed in love. I couldn't wait to take that long drive back home and share this moment with cousin Kelly.

I had a new spirit when I turned thirty. I felt free and in charge of my life. I felt it was my chance to finally get it right. To finally do better for the girls and start all over and move forward toward more good than bad. I was excited about the endless possibilities that lay ahead. Unfortunately, Quinton wasn't so happy about me moving on. Our breakup devastated him. He refused to accept it. He was still stalking me, and when he found out I was leaving town to attend my cousin's wedding, he picked the night before to show up at the apartment and threaten my life with a gun. I was terrified. Quinton was hurt and angry. He put the gun to my head and said he would kill me if he had to live without me. I held my breath and just looked into his hazel eyes, hoping to find whatever love we had between us for him to see this wasn't a good idea. We stared at each other for what felt like hours but was only a few seconds. He pulled the gun away from my head and said, "I hope something bad happens to you when you take your trip back home. I hope something bad happens to you," as he ran down the stairs from my apartment, got in his car, and burned rubber, speeding away. Tears started falling from my eyes. Fear, confusion, all I know is those words resonated with me on a level like when Ethan's mom would cast spells on me. It definitely got my attention.

The wedding was awesome, and Kelly looked beautiful. It was Memorial Day weekend, so I didn't have to be back to work until Tuesday. I stayed with Dallas and his wife, Jeannie. They actually let me stay with them. It was nice. I guess some things changed a bit once Mom died. The girls and I were having a wonderful time.

Dallas was a biker and was in a biker club. The guys in his club were riding that weekend, and he asked one of them if they would ride me on that back of his bike so I could join him, Jeannie, and friends on the ride. I didn't have to worry about a sitter because we were surrounded with family, and the girls were spending time with their Great-Grandma Maria. She enjoyed seeing the girls. Grandma Maria loved all her grandchildren and really enjoyed being a great-grandma. She was youthful still and full of spunk. She was always happy when she had family around her. Grandma Maria believed family unity was the key to the strength that kept family strong. The energy was always powerful when everyone was working together for the good.

The biker guys pulled in front of Dallas's house on a sunny Sunday afternoon, the day after the wedding, ready to roll. I enjoyed motorcycles. I grew up with them my entire life. Both Uncle Danny and Uncle Joe were bikers. Mom and Dad also owned bikes. I was fascinated by them but respected them because I knew how dangerous they could be.

Dallas introduced me to the guy who agreed to ride me for the day. His name was Johnny. Our greeting was short as he extended his hand to help me onto the back of his bike. He told me to hold on tight, and he quickly sped off, following the pack of about fifteen bikes to our final destination forty-five minutes away.

The day was perfect. I felt safe. I felt free and happy. The crew stopped at the famous custard shop to get ice cream. This was the first time Johnny and I actually had time to really chat. He wasn't very handsome, but his demeanor was sweet and gentle. After the ride was over, he asked me out on a date. He said he thought I was nice and wanted to get to know me better before the girls and I headed back home to Georgia. I gladly accepted. I was single and saw nothing wrong with dating. I hadn't been single long, but who cared?

The first date with Johnny was simple and nice. We didn't do much. He showed me where he worked and what he did. He worked at the local university. He showed me around campus and he took pictures of me during our entire date. Johnny was a freelance photographer in his spare time. I thought it was cute and a nice icebreaker. When he brought me back to Dallas's house, he said he wanted to come visit me when I returned to Georgia, and I agreed to a third date. I thought, *If someone would travel all the way from Illinois to the state of Georgia, just for me, then he must really like me.* I was smitten.

The weekend was perfect! It was wonderful reuniting with family I hadn't seen since Mom's funeral, and it was good visiting with my little brother, Dallas. He was a dad and husband now, and he was doing very well. I was so proud of him. He joked about my tattoo and asked if I was going to keep it now that Quinton and I had broken up. I said, "I have no idea. I just hate that I was so stupid I actually did something like this." The golden rule about tattoos is not to get someone's name tattooed unless it's a child, relative, memorial, and so forth. Definitely not a boyfriend you might break up with. I should've known better. But at the time, love was blind.

I told Dallas what Quinton did right before I took this trip. Dallas said, "Wow, how creepy is that?"

I said, "I know, right? Keep us in your prayers, that the girls and I get home safe." He hugged me and said he would. The girls and I were ready to head home. Oddly, I couldn't find my car keys. One minute I had them, and the next minute they had disappeared. Everyone started looking for them. We looked for over an hour, and it was getting late. I had to leave or else we wouldn't get back home in time for me to go to work on Tuesday morning. It was a twelve-hour trip. We couldn't find the keys anywhere. Luckily I had brought my spare set with me. Not sure why, but it was clearly a good decision.

I was feeling really good driving home. It didn't even feel like the trip was long, as the girls were happy and laughing and playing in the backseat. They kept talking about how much fun they had with their cousins, and they just seemed happier than I had seen them in a while. I was happy with them. We were happy. They fell asleep, and I was alone with my thoughts. I was smiling while I was driving and started reminiscing about the trip and meeting Johnny. I was really excited about returning home and wondering how long it would be before I heard from Johnny again. He seemed really nice. *I guess if Dallas introduced me to him, he must be a good guy. Right?*

I was making good time and was right outside the Georgia state line when suddenly my car slipped off the right side of the road in a heavy construction site. My tire dropped about a half a foot off the highway at more than 65 mph, and it frightened me, I quickly turned the steering wheel back to the left to get back onto the highway. In a matter of seconds, I had lost control of the car.

There was a concrete bank separating the four lanes. Good thing, because my car was heading right into oncoming traffic on the other side. My car hit the concrete barrier and kept ricocheting off the bank, bashing back and forth, swerving out of control. It was all happening so fast, and for some reason, I wasn't frightened. I was calm. I knew exactly what was going on, and I knew it wasn't good, and I had no idea how the girls and I were going to get out of this alive. But for some reason I can't explain, I was completely calm and didn't panic.

I saw semis, trucks, and cars swerving and slamming on brakes to keep from hitting us or to prevent me from hitting them. I could see everything around clear as day. However, I felt like something or someone was with me. Sophie had awakened after the car slammed into the bank, and Brooklyn was still sleeping. She knew something was wrong and started to cry. I quickly looked back at her and touched her hand. I calmly told Sophie that Mommy was in a horrible car accident and to stay calm and not cry. I assured her we would be safe and somehow I was going to stop the car and get us to safety. My car had been hit a couple times by other vehicles as they were trying to avoid my out-of-control car, and I was now spinning in the middle of the highway.

At that moment, everything started moving in slow motion. I heard cars brushing by me, trying to avoid hitting me, I felt trucks swerving, trying to avoid hitting me. At one point, I felt my car slide underneath a semitruck, and I closed my eyes because I knew this was bad. Then suddenly my car stopped spinning. It was facing the opposite direction straight toward oncoming traffic. All I could think was, *I have to get this car off the highway,* and without hesitation, I pressed on the gas as hard as I could. I turned the car toward the left into whatever was waiting for us off the road.

In my head, I thought we would instantly come to a stop, but that wasn't the case. Instead, it was a very steep ravine, and my car was plowing through bushes, rocks, and debris, which covered my front windshield, I couldn't see anything. We were moving so fast; I had no idea when the car would stop or how. Slamming on the brakes frightened me, so I decided not to do that. Suddenly the car stopped. It was sitting straight up, nose down and rear up in the air. It felt like we were hanging in a harness in midair. I looked around and couldn't believe we were all okay. Brooklyn was hanging from her car seat, still securely strapped in and, believe it or not, still sleep. She had no idea what had just happened. Sophie just looked at me with disbelief and in shock in her tiny, trusting eyes. She stayed calm, as I had instructed her. She was waiting patiently for her mom to give her additional instructions.

I suddenly smelled gasoline coming from the car, and I started to panic. I knew I had to get the girls out of the car before it blew up. I was stuck in my seatbelt and couldn't get it unstrapped. Suddenly I heard voices. Someone was outside the car, trying to rescue us from the vehicle. I was being pulled out to safety, and so were both my girls. It was all happening so fast. We were all carried to the top of the highway where a couple of ambulances were already waiting, and people where everywhere. They were amazed we were alive and had no major injuries.

I was in shock as they were loading the three of us in the ambulances to take us to the nearest hospital. I kept hearing voices in the background saying it was a miracle we lived, and it was amazing no one was seriously hurt. One person said, "I don't see how they came out of that horrific accident without a scratch. I saw the whole thing, and I knew they would be dead by the time we got to them at the bottom of the ravine." They were all shocked and surprised they had just witnessed a miracle. The ride in the ambulance was frightening, as I was separated from the girls. I couldn't be there for them to make sure they weren't afraid.

Hours later, once the girls and I were evaluated for concussions, internal bleeding, broken bones, and so on, we were finally reunited and discharged. Now reality set in because we were still more than two hours away from home, with no transportation. I had to call the girls' dad to come get us. Ethan arrived with his wife, Abby. I was happy to see them. He hugged the girls, and Abby hugged me. Ethan asked where my shoes were. I said, "I don't know. I didn't have any on when I arrived at the hospital." I noticed I actually didn't have anything I needed. Personal things were in the car. Ethan spoke to an officer at the hospital and found out where they took my car and asked if they would allow us to go and grab some personal items. They said yes, that the salvage yard was open twenty-four hours. Ethan got directions, and we loaded up in his car.

When we arrived, there were so many wrecked cars that I couldn't find mine. The guy gave us an idea where to search; it hadn't been that long since it arrived. I guess I was a bit overwhelmed. Ethan spotted it. Once I saw it, I just started crying. Good thing Abby was there to stay in the car with the girls. No way I would've wanted them to see it; it looked as if it had been crushed by a bulldozer. I felt lucky to be alive and lucky my children had lived through this accident as well. I knew I had to have been protected by angels that day. It was nothing short of a miracle we survived. We walked away from that accident shielded by the angels God had assigned to wrap their holy wings around each one of us.

When I returned home, I called Quinton's mother, Ms. Diane. We had become very close when he and I were dating. I told her about the death curse he tried to put on me and how we survived the car accident. She said as much as she wanted to say it was a coincidence, we got into the accident after he wished me dead. It was a bit eerie knowing how it all played out. She promised to let Quinton know that his mean words almost manifested and not to ever say anything that evil to another human soul as long as he lived. That was just mean and uncalled for. He knew better. She said she didn't raise him to go around putting guns to women's heads and threatening their lives. She was very upset to hear he had done this.

I had to take a week off work to recover from body aches and pains. The doctors said I would have some bruising, but I didn't believe them until I could barely walk the next day. I was stiff in my neck, my back, my arms and legs. I had black and blue marks in areas I didn't remember injuring. Yeah, I needed to recover. When I was home recovering, all I could think about was why I survived. Life was different for me after the accident. Almost dying really put things into perspective. I knew my life had been spared for a purpose. I knew I was on earth for a reason. I knew right then that everything I was going through was for a purpose. I had no idea what that purpose was, but I was determined to find out. I was sure I was meant to do something remarkable. Why else would God send his angels down from heaven to protect me that day? I remembered how calm I was during the entire accident. It had to be the spirit of God that gave me that peace. It had to be his angels that comforted me. *I'm special. I'm blessed. I'm here for a purpose.*

I was tired of the factory atmosphere and had my mind set on getting some kind of office job. I didn't see myself working in a factory the rest of my life. I also started thinking about trying college again. I really wanted my degree. My doctor had a nurse I befriended during my annual visits, and she had a sister that worked for a major bank in town. One visit, I was telling her how I wanted to get a better job. She mentioned her sister was looking for a receptionist and thought I'd be perfect for the job. She told her sister about me. I interviewed for the position and got the job. I was excited. This was another a great opportunity for me to prove I could do better things with my life. Things were really starting to look better for the girls and me.

This job allowed me to dress business professional again. I missed that from when I used to work for Mr. Turner. I was right back in my element. I was feeling good, looking good, and rebuilding my self-confidence. My new boss, Rosalind, was intelligent. She had her master's degree, and I admired her. Someday I wanted to be her. She was very encouraging and mentored me. She knew I had it rough as a single mom and would always question how I was supporting the girls and myself on my low income. I'd tell her I didn't know how I was doing it. "I have no choice. Therefore, I don't think about it. I just do it."

At one point, she suggested I should quit that job and get on welfare like most other single black women did—let the state pay for my education and afterward get a better-paying job. My pride got the best of me. I looked at women on welfare in shame. It was typical for black women to be stereotyped as lazy and willing to have babies they couldn't raise, looking for a free ride. I refused to be judged as one of those women, and I just couldn't do it. I was too proud to be on welfare. At least I thought so. I'd rather work two and three jobs before I stooped to that level. I was paying for daycare before and after school until I got off work and barely making it. The girls weren't old enough to be alone at night; therefore, a second job wasn't an option.

Johnny had started visiting regularly and had sent for me by train a couple times. He was very romantic and a gentleman. I didn't know much about him other than what he told me. He owned his own home, he had a great job, made good money, and was crazy about me. He wrote me love letters almost every day. He and I became serious. One minute I was working this awesome job for Rosalind, and the next minute, I had all my belongings packed into a U-Haul on Thanksgiving eve, on my way back to Chicago to start a new life with Johnny.

When I arrived in my new home with the girls, my new life wasn't at all what I had imagined it would be. I found out Johnny had four kids instead of the two he mentioned. He had an estranged wife. He was in the middle of a messy divorce and had women calling the house day and night, disrespecting me something awful. I was confused, hurt, and felt trapped. I wanted out. I had nowhere to go. I sold everything I worked so hard for, because I didn't need any of my things. I was moving into a home that was already furnished. Therefore, I hadn't felt the need to keep anything.

When I left my perfect life for Johnny and found these things out about him, I felt betrayed. If I had known half the truth I discovered in the first thirty days living with Johnny, there was no way I would have ever given up my life for that misery. He tricked me. He lied to me. He used me. My track record once again wasn't looking good.

I was angry with Dallas. I blamed him for introducing me to this pig and not warning me of his past or his current situation and allowing me to get involved with such a creep. I asked him if the girls and I could move in with him and Jeannie, just long enough for the girls and I to get back on our feet. He said no as usual. I felt alone once again. Now I lived in the same city as Dallas, and he wouldn't help me. I hated him for that. It put an even bigger wedge between us than when Mom died, and we grew apart. We stayed in touch but kept our distance.

Rosalind helped me get a job at a sister bank downtown Chicago. I was grateful to her for using her connections. I had a phone interview and was hired on the spot. It was a teller position instead of receptionist. I was okay with that because I had done it back in high school. Hopefully it would go much better than it did back then when I could never get my drawers to balance.

A young woman named Nancy Irving would come into the bank to do her transactions, and I got to know her a little. She found out about my situation and insisted the girls and I move in with her temporarily until I got on my feet. She said ninety days should be enough time for me to save enough money. I graciously accepted. I had nowhere else to go and had to get out of Johnny's house before one of us killed the other. Our relationship had become that intense.

Johnny was my first crazy love relationship. He definitely brought out the worst in me. I faced insecurities I had never known existed before that relationship. It was horrible. I found myself feeling so isolated, being so far away from home, and I missed Momma Laverne and her family. I regretted moving back to Chicago, especially now that Johnny and I weren't getting along.

I remember literally feeling sick to my stomach when I realized the position I had put the girls and myself in once again. I felt like a failure and an idiot. I was disappointed with myself. I couldn't believe I was starting all over again, especially over a guy. I thought I had learned my lesson by then.

Things weren't working out so well between Nancy and me. She called me lazy because I slept a lot, and I had no strength after working all day and taking care of the girls all night, staying up with them to assist them with their homework and so on. I was mentally and emotionally drained all the time. My fatigue was horrible. I felt sick all the time, and I blamed it on the enormous amount of stress I was under.

About a year before, I was diagnosed with a serious medical condition. I hadn't shared it with anyone, not even the girls. The doctor recommended surgery, but I wasn't ready. It would be a life-changing major surgery, and at the time I was transitioning from leaving the factory job and working for Rosalind. So I chose to hold off on the surgery until I got settled at the new job with health insurance and such. Unfortunately, I moved again, this time out of state before that could happen, and now I was back to square one until I could find time to have the surgery. Based on my symptoms, things were getting worse.

It was the girls' first Halloween, in our new town. We were still staying with Nancy. She was out of town visiting her family back in Georgia. She was from a small town thirty minutes outside the town I lived in. That was how we started talking and became acquainted. We were both from the same area and had a lot in common. Johnny felt somewhat responsible for my situation and always kept in touch. We were still good friends in spite of everything. He wanted to do something special and asked if he could take the girls trick or treating. I agreed to let him. He picked them up on his motorcycle and said he would bring them back within a couple hours.

It was late, and they hadn't showed up yet. I got worried and called his house, but there was no answer. I waited a little longer, because I didn't want to miss him when he brought the girls home. It got later and later, and I started to worry. They should have been back by then. I decided to drive across town over to his house to see what might have happened.

As I was pulling up to Johnny's house, cop cars were everywhere. I was afraid one of the girls was hurt and Johnny hadn't had time to call and tell me. My heart was racing a mile a minute. I was afraid to find out what had happened. I got out of the car, and the cops stopped me from entering the home. They immediately started questioning me. They asked who I was and what I was doing there. This made me even more afraid of what was happening. It had a bad feeling; something was wrong. I told them I was there to get my girls, and had anyone seen them? The cop said, "Two little girls?" I said, "Yes, are they here?" He said yes and motioned for the other cops to let me pass by the roadblocks and the yellow crime scene tape they had surrounding Johnny's house. It was dark and looked like a crime scene in a movie. I even saw a crime investigation van parked in front of the house. I wasn't sure what to expect when I entered the home.

When I walked inside, I thought I was in the middle of a CSI episode. Cops were everywhere. They were tearing the house apart. Johnny was nowhere to be found. A cop was sitting with my girls, talking to them, asking them all sorts of questions and writing on his pad. They seemed to be fine, and when they saw me, they ran past the cop and gave me a big hug. I embraced them and held them so tight. I asked them if they were okay. I asked what happened. They kept saying the cops took Johnny away in handcuffs. I was like, for real? Why? They said they didn't know and they were scared. I tried to calm them down by asking them if they enjoyed their time with Johnny, and they said yes, but the cops took their candy away too. They said it was evidence. I said, "I'm sorry. Mommy will buy you more candy."

This whole thing was getting worse by the minute. One cop asked me to sit down and had another cop take the girls from me and continue asking them more questions. I told the cop that pulled me over to the side to speak with him that I wasn't going to answer any questions until someone told me what was going on. He said Johnny was booked on suspicion of first-degree murder. I was like, what? I couldn't believe what I was hearing. I could tell the cop was dead serious. He asked all the questions you see in the movies. I was in shock. I couldn't believe this was really happening. This was so unexpected. One minute my life was somewhat normal, and the next, I'm in the middle of a murder investigation on Halloween night. How spooky was that?

Story had it the woman who was murdered worked at the same university Johnny did. She left work early to pick up her daughter's costume and never made it home. Her husband was concerned and started calling around for her, but she never picked up the costume. This made him more concerned because she would never disappointment their daughter. He was certain something was wrong. So her husband drove to the university, and when he saw her car was still parked in the lot, he called the police. He reported her missing. Even though it hadn't been twenty-four hours, he knew something had gone seriously wrong.

The university police immediately started looking for her on campus and found her in the basement of the building where she worked. She had been raped and strangled. They said Johnny was the prime suspect. They found intimate pictures of her hidden in one of the drawers in her office desk and traced them back to Johnny. This was another thing I hated about him. He used photography as a hobby to lure women into feeling pretty by convincing them to let him take sexy photos of them. I think this was his way of flirting with them. All women want to feel pretty, and when a man takes pictures of you, I guess that works. It worked for me. So I can't blame her. I was pissed because I knew that his obsession with taking these types of photos of women would come back to haunt him someday. Well that day had arrived.

Johnny was later released because they had no hard evidence he had actually committed the crime. The FBI was called to take over the case because of how horrific the murder scene was. They harassed both Johnny and me for days. They followed me everywhere I went. They tapped our phones and listened in on all our conversations. Once they almost had me convinced Johnny was a cold-blooded murderer. They would make up stories and lies, saying whatever they need to say to get you to say or feel a certain way. They interrogate you to the point where you don't know what you're saying or thinking anymore. They twist your words, your thoughts, and make you start to second-guess your own truth. It was not like the movies. This was real life. It was absolutely frightening and exhausting and horrifying. It sucked the life out of me, dealing with this type of investigation. Especially when they already thought he was guilty because of his color and race. They wanted to pin this on Johnny because he was black. It would give them great pleasure to say a black man did this to this wonderful white wife of a prominent doctor. They said I was an accomplice and was covering up for Johnny. They were just waiting for me to slip up and give them some kind of evidence that Johnny really did commit this awful crime. They wanted to pin this on Johnny. To my knowledge, they weren't even looking for anyone else.

Johnny felt we were victims of racism. Johnny may have been a lot of things, but a murderer wasn't one of them. We were furious and tried to get a lawyer and found out the entire city was untouchable. The lawyer listened to our complaints and advised us to basically deal with it. He said the city was on lockdown, and they would side with the police, and no one would dare take this kind of case against the cops in this community. We were strongly advised to drop it altogether or the police would make our lives a leaving hell. He added they would for sure run us out of the city if we pursued this.

I couldn't believe this was actually happening. I was furious! "You mean to tell us we have no legal authority to protect our rights?" We tried to contact the local NAACP. No one ever answered the phone, and no one was ever in the office when I'd drive over in person. We tried contacting the national NAACP office and followed the procedures and submitted a written complaint as instructed by them. We followed up and did everything they asked us to do, and they never responded. We had nowhere else to turn. I knew Johnny was innocent, but the police and FBI were determined to prove me wrong. Almost a week had gone by, and Johnny and I were becoming hopeless. Every day we would watch the news and listen to the community talking about this. We didn't say anything to anyone other than family because we didn't want to lose our jobs. Every day was a nightmare. We wanted it all to end. We needed them to catch the real killer and stop focusing all their time and energy on an innocent man.

It was hard going to work every day, being followed by the FBI and not letting on to my coworkers that I was in the middle of one of the biggest high-profile murder cases ever in this university community. My anxiety level was over the top. Three days after the victim's funeral, I was at work and heard the university police called a press conference to report breaking news in the case. The news conference was at noon. I couldn't wait to take my lunch break. I ran downstairs to the break room. Almost everyone else was in there waiting to here the breaking news as well. The university's chief of police was there with the FBI; he announced they had found the murderer. They said it was a young white male student who attended the university. He had allegedly been stalking the victim for months. She apparently had given him the cold shoulder once or twice without realizing the severity of his attractions toward her. She has assisted him once or twice, and he had become obsessed with her. He would ask her out, and she would politely decline. However, he didn't take her rejections well.

He was so overwhelmed with guilt after he raped and killed her that he killed himself by throwing himself in front of a freight train. He approached her the evening she was leaving to pick up her daughter's costume and forced her back into the building. He lured her down to the basement area, to a small storage closet. Things got out of hand, and he raped and killed her.

The police claimed to have found lots of evidence in the guy's dorm room, even a suspicious e-mail he received the night of the murder from a friend asking if he was the one who murdered that woman. The evidence proved Johnny hadn't committed the crime. So why were they so adamant about charging an innocent man for a crime he didn't commit? I was relieved and pissed all at the same time. Seriously? Johnny never had sex with this woman, nor did he kill her. And the real murderer gets off scot-free because he takes his own life. Of course the police and the FBI never apologized for how they treated us. It was as if it never happened. I was glad they found the real murderer and closed the case. I felt sadness for the woman's husband and their little girl. But I was happy it was finally over. It was a horrific experience. When you are in a real situation like this, it is stressful and very scary. You have no idea how things will turn out. We were fortunate. It could have been much worse. We had no defense. Our truth wasn't good enough, and that was very frightening.

I was distracted with everything going on, and it was hard to concentrate at work. My drawer at the bank kept coming up short. I could never figure out why. I knew I was doing a good job, but this had become a serious issue. I was verbally warned and then written up. One week after the murder was solved, I showed up for work and was immediately summoned to the boss's office. Less than ten minutes later, I was being escorted to my workstation by security. I was instructed to gather my personal items. I had been fired.

Chapter 11

My wake-up call came a bit too fast. I slept well, and the breakfast I ordered before bed last night was right on time. Oatmeal, fresh blueberries, chopped walnuts, and earl grey tea bags with raw honey, my favorite. My cell phone was already going off. I answered; it was Beth asking if Pam had given me today's itinerary. I assured her Pam had taken care of everything. Adam would be there at nine to pick me up and drive me to the 9/11 memorials so I could give my speech to the elementary kids from Queens. Beth said the mayor and his wife really enjoyed the show the night before and couldn't wait to have brunch with me at eleven. She said his wife wanted to hear more about Star. She said she read the book and was amazed at her strength and her courage. She said she was not sure if she would've survived if her life had been like Star's. I responded, "I believe everyone has a story. We are all born here for a purpose. At least that's what Star would say. She really didn't think she was special. She felt God had a plan for her life. Her difficult times were in his plan. She knew somehow she would need to dig deep within her to find light in her life of darkness. Star never gave up. She had so many reasons to give up and quit, but she continued and always hoped for the best. In her mind, she felt that something would have to give sooner or later, because she had nothing else left but to believe in a dream that seemed so out of reach. Star believed in miracles."

Beth said, "Well, I've kept you long enough. Marissa should be stopping by to get another piece for her article. She'll meet you in the hotel bar located next to the steak restaurant for cocktails at five, after your return from receiving the key to the city. This will give you two plenty of time to wrap up the interview before the gala tonight. I apologize I have your schedule so crammed this time around. It's just that so many people wanted to meet with you this year, and you had so little time and so many special events on the agenda during this year's visit. We've waited a long time to reward Star's work on this level. Thanks so much for your patience. Hang in there, Ally. The gala will be the grand finale. It's in Star's honor, and we are happy to celebrate the success of the book making the *New York Times* best-seller list. You should be so proud."

I said, "It's like Star's dream come true. I only wish she was here. She really deserves this honor."

Beth and I hung up. I ate my breakfast and took thirty minutes to meditate. Star showed me how important it is to still your mind each day from all the business so that the inner powers of magic and love can work from the inside out. She said this was the key to allowing the universe to manifest miracles in your life. She said without stillness, you don't give your mind the treatments it needs to live in the moment. When Star first got into meditation and awareness, people thought she was weird and didn't really take her seriously, including me. However, once I started attending yoga classes with her and meditating on a regular basis, my life changed in ways I never imagined possible. Star did yoga every day and mediated twice a day for an hour each time. Her entire life evolved around these priorities. Everything else was secondary. Once I finished mediating, I got dressed, and Adam arrived to take me to the 9/11 memorials. After my talk with the children, I met with the mayor and his wife.

The mayor's wife was beautiful. She had on a white Jackie Kennedy Onassis style dress with white pearls around the neckline. It was very classy. She had simple pearl earrings to match. The mayor had on a dark gray suit, with an extra white, sleek shirt with expensive cufflinks. They looked like a gift his wife might have bought him. He had added a pop of color with his blue and silver necktie. They looked like they were out on a date. They briefed me on the key to the city ceremony and discussed how excited they were about presenting me the key in honor of Star. The mayor's wife couldn't help but bring up Star and wanted to know what she did after getting fired from her job at the bank. She said even though she read the book, she knew there are usually things that are not mentioned. I told her she was correct. "I believe Star had the most trouble when writing the book. She could never figure out what to tell and what not to tell. She had so many things happen in her lifetime, she couldn't put all of it in the book." I began to tell her more about Star's amazing journey. Sipping on our third mimosa, they both listened attentively.

I picked up a newspaper on my way home. I had to find a job fast. I had no time to waste. Nancy had given me two weeks to get out of her apartment. She said she had enough of my laziness and all the drama I brought with me. She was pissed about the murder case, as if I could've kept that from happening. I hadn't slept in weeks, and I was exhausted emotionally and physically, but I had no time to worry about these things. I had to find a place for my girls and me to live, and I needed to get another job.

I saw an ad in the paper for a position as a personal shopper at one of the major department stores at the mall. It paid more than what I was making as a teller to start, so I thought it would be good. When I turned the application in, the lady at the desk asked if I had a minute. She said the human resources manager wanted to look it over before I left. I said of course and waited on a bench on the second floor near the public bathrooms. I sat for about twenty minutes. I was asked if I had time for a quick interview, and I said of course. I was hired on the spot. I started two days later. I had been unemployed less than forty-eight hours and was now making more money. This was my lucky day. That same week, I found a small two-bedroom basement apartment and moved in that weekend. It was a nice, quiet, and safe neighborhood. I didn't enjoy living below ground, but it was better than nothing.

I loved my new job. However, things had gotten so bad financially my car was repossessed. I worked weekends, had to take the bus and the rail everyday to get to work. I hated the rain and cold weather in Chicago. I'd worked until closing many nights and would have to take the rail at dark after hours. It was scary. I would pray to God to protect me all the way home. The girls were finally old enough to become latchkey kids—kids who had to be left alone at home while their parents worked. I was still on my 90-day probation, didn't qualify for medical insurance yet, and my medical condition had worsened and I needed to have the surgery. My biggest fear was how would I provide for the girls and me during the six weeks of recovery without pay. I was in limbo, and my symptoms were getting worse.

It had only been a year since I left Georgia, and already I had gone through so much. I gained more than seventy pounds. It happened so fast. I hadn't even realized I gained so much weight. I blamed most of the weight gain on my health condition. But I had a dirty little secret. I had started binging. It was how I coped with all the stressful situations I had to deal with. Eating had become my new addiction. It made me feel better.

I had no one to turn to. I needed someone to be there with me. I called Momma Laverne. She flew from Georgia to Chicago to take care of me during the first week of my six-week recovery from surgery. Dallas didn't even come visit me while I was in the hospital. Something about Jeannie and him was weird to me. I couldn't quite figure it out, but this created distance between him and me. No worries though. Momma Laverne was there, and I enjoyed her home cooking. No one cooked like her. When she left, I really missed her. Not the girls, they said she was too strict and wouldn't let them do anything. Momma Laverne gave me a lecture that I had allowed the girls to become a bit spoiled. She said I needed to be a bit more stern with them or else they would end up walking all over me. I listened and decided to try to gain some control over the girls' behavior. I was left to complete my recovery alone and had way too much time on my hands to reflect on my life. I thought about where I was, where I wished I were, and where I wanted to be. I was disappointed with my life. I had begun to blame Ethan for the struggles I was going through. I felt if Ethan had at least been a responsible parent and paid child support, we wouldn't have been in that situation. I was mad at him and thought about how unfair this cruel world could be. I was fat and ugly. I couldn't get a date if I begged for one. I learned quickly that fat people are treated much differently than skinny people. I was ashamed and embarrassed at how I had completely let myself go. I was sloppy obese and had really given up.

I went to the doctor to complain about not being able to sleep. He told me he was concerned about my well-being after asking me a few basic questions. Next thing I knew he was on the phone, setting up an emergency appointment with a psychologist. He told me to leave his office and go straight there. I didn't think too much of it at the time. I was in total denial. I was operating in full survivor mode and followed his instructions, as I was always obedient, regardless of who was giving orders.

When I arrived at the clinic, I sat in the waiting room only a few seconds and out came a female doctor to greet me. She walked with me down the hall to her office. She was short like me with blonde, bushy hair, and she wore wire glasses. She was so kind and warm. I had no idea what to expect. I wasn't sure what my doctor had told her after I left his office. I did notice she was very careful with how she spoke to me and how she approached me. It was like I was this fragile piece of glass, and she didn't want to crack or break it. We talked for forty-five minutes before the alarm went off. She scheduled appointments for me to meet with her weekly. She contacted my primary doctor and prescribed two prescriptions, an antidepressant and anxiety medicine.

I was fortunate my insurance covered the therapy sessions. It all happened so fast. One minute I was seeing the doctor for lack of sleep, and the next thing I had been diagnosed with severe depression. Whatever that meant. All I knew was suddenly my life had taken a turn for the worse once again. I didn't quite understand what it meant to be diagnosed with severe depression. Was I really depressed? I didn't feel any different than I'd always felt. What was so different? I was confused. I didn't understand it all.

During the visits, I learned a lot about myself. I had no idea I never took the proper time to deal with all the horrible things that had happened to me in my childhood. I had no idea everything I went through in my past affected everything and every decision I made in my current life and my future. I just never thought of things that way. My new therapist, Dr. Jane Bryce, told me I'd been suffering from depression since childhood. I didn't know children could suffer from depression. This was an eye opener, and it didn't make me feel any better; it actually hurt knowing this truth. I started feeling sorry for myself, something I had never really done before. I didn't enjoy feeling this way. I was realizing so many things about who I was and how I had been victimized my entire life. It was hard to wrap my mind around this new awareness. I was having difficulty accepting it as fact. *God, help me understand*, I prayed each night.

I remembered how sorry I used to feel for other people. How I would have so much empathy for them. I never thought in a million years I was actually that person. I never took the time to feel sorry for myself. I never showed myself compassion. I had no control over the abuse my parents did to me. They were my parents. I trusted them. I never allowed myself to realize how bad they really hurt me. How they destroyed me. How it affected the way I internalized love. I had no idea what physical, mental, and emotional abuse does to a person. I was that person and had no one else to compare me to. I didn't know anyone else like me. I dealt with it the best way I knew how. I buried it. I ignored it. I convinced myself it never happened in order to survive—until now. I had to face my fears. I had to stare the truth in the face. I had to look at the only reflection in the mirror. That reflection would be me. I saw me for the first time.

I was face-to-face with who I was, with what I looked like. With the consequences a person like me faced. I suffered from posttraumatic stress disorder and severe depression. I never knew how to deal with the things I had endured until now.

I'm not the strongest survivor? I'm this weak link. How do I continue now? What will people think? How do I feel about this? Am I still living in denial like my mom did? Like my dad did? And like Dallas still does? I was paralyzed with the thought of actually finally having to face the truth of my past. *What happens to me now?*

I wasn't sure I was ready for it. I'd been running from my past my entire life. Now Dr. Jane was forcing me to wake up from my bad dream and talk about it. Weeks went by, and we talked and talked and talked. I cried and cried and cried and cried.

Depression doesn't have a look per say. You can't point it out on the streets like a red car passing by or recognize it by appearance. You can't see molestation or rape or always notice a battered wife. We don't all look or act a certain way. I hid my misery for years, and no one found me out until then, all because I couldn't sleep. I wondered what I said or did wrong to be found out. How did my doctor know?

It felt like the longest road I had ever walked. I had to go through therapy in order to be cured of a disease I didn't fully understand. This road was dark, and I longed to see light. I couldn't see my way out of this darkness. I felt ashamed and hopeless. It was lonely, and I was afraid. I had no control over my condition, and I hated being medicated. The drugs caused me to have hallucinations. I sometimes felt more depressed. It was awful.

But the hardest thing about being diagnosed with depression was going through this as a mother. I felt like I had failed my girls. I felt I wasn't strong enough for them. I felt defeated. What would they think of me now? I would tuck my precious girls into bed at night after we said our prayers and I kissed them good night. I would go to my bedroom, close the door, and weep. I loved them more than I loved myself. I wanted to make them proud to call me mom. It killed me to think I could actually lose this battle. I convinced myself I was okay and that I was doing well. I just needed to keep on pushing on. *I can do this, and every day is better than the day before. One day at a time, Star. One day at a time.*

A customer I assisted regularly at work invited me to visit her church. I always felt something was missing in my life when I didn't feel close to God. I wondered if God would forgive me for falling short of his glory. I felt like the biggest sinner in that depressive state and wondered if there was room for people like me in heaven. The girls loved our new church and made friends quickly. They were happier than I had seen them in a long time. I was a nicer person and wasn't yelling at them all the time like before. We looked forward to Sundays and Wednesdays.

We became members, and I was asked to tell my story at a family and friends day shortly after I rededicated my life to Christ and was baptized for the third time. I felt good about my life and how far I had come. I wanted to share this special moment with my family. I invited Dallas, his wife Jeannie, and their boys. I also invited my father. They all came. After I told my story of where I had come from and where I was today, I ended it with how wonderful life can be and how you can overcome anything with perseverance as long as you never stop believing. I received a standing ovation. The visitors and members were all impressed with my story and how I survived. Therapy was going very well, and I felt like a new person. It was at this moment I found my purpose. I am to tell my story to those who are willing to listen. I was born to share hope. I am here because I believe.

I started exercising every day to lose all the weight I had gained. I was determined to get my life back on track. Working at the department store was hard on my back and feet. The long hours were awful. I could never plan anything because my schedule would change weekly. I wanted to go to college. This was always my dream. I wanted to be an example for my children. I wanted them to go to college someday, and I wanted their mom to be educated as well. I wanted to become a true survivor and not a person with issues. I wanted to give other young girls and women who suffered from the hands of abuse someone to look up to. I wanted to show the world people like me could beat the odds. *I can be successful and have anything I want in life.* I wanted to do this for myself and later use my story to give others hope.

I was determined to beat the depression and become someone significant in the world. I was tired of feeling alone and lost. I had lost a little weight but still had a long way to go. I thought I was on the right track, so I stopped taking my antidepressant, without Dr. Jane's permission. I felt better and had convinced myself I was fine.

Things were looking up. I was offered a job at the local university as an entry-level secretary. I had to complete a training program before I was transferred to a permanent department. When I first started, I didn't know how to type. I learned computer programs and software. I learned how to write business letters, memos, and all the secretarial skills necessary to be an employee at the university. This made me proud.

I kept my department store job and worked part-time nights and weekends. I bought a brand-new car after bussing and taking the rail back and forth to both jobs for an entire year. It was awful during the winter months. Standing at the bus stops in Chicago winters was torture. It felt good to have transportation again.

I hadn't noticed that shortly after I stop taking my meds, I started feeling lonely again. I desperately wanted to share my life with someone. I hated making decisions. They were getting harder and harder to make, and I wanted someone to share the responsibility of raising the girls. Single parenting was very difficult.

I did manage to face my biggest fear and enrolled in community college. I'll never forget the first day of classes. I felt like I didn't belong, and I felt like everyone I walked by could tell I didn't belong there. I felt stupid, and I knew I wasn't smart like other people. I questioned many times why I was trying to be something I could never be. What was I thinking? Seriously? That's what all the voices in my head kept telling me. They tortured me and laughed at me. When I tried to fight off those awful thoughts, I would tell myself failure was not an option. *Therefore, face the fear head on.* The worst to me was not trying at all.

School was harder than I imagined it would be. When I took the placement test, I passed at an eighth-grade level. It was embarrassing. After I spoke to an advisor, they said it would take years before I could work my way up to college-level courses. This was discouraging. I was embarrassed at how dumb I really was. But I didn't quit. I started in this special program for adult students who had to basically go back to high school in order to reach college-level learning. In addition to working two jobs, now I was attending college. My plate was full.

I desperately tried dating again and had no luck. I felt my weight had a lot to do with why I wasn't getting any attention. Nothing like when I was smaller. Then one day, I went to get my income taxes done, and this guy kept staring and smiling at me. The ladies in the tax shop told me his name was Ricky Hayes and that Ricky was a good man and that I should give him a chance and let him take me out on a date. Ricky was smiling the entire time. He enjoyed the girls going to bat for him. He got bold and asked me out on a date before I left. I politely said no thanks and left. When I went back to pick up my refund check, Ricky was there again. He walked up to me and asked me why I turned down a date with him the last time I was in there, and I said, "Because I don't know you."

He said, "Well how are you going to get to know me if you don't give me a chance and let me take you out on a date?" It wasn't like I had guys beating down my door, so I accepted. We went bowling, one of my favorite things to do, and we clicked instantly. Six months later, we were engaged.

Not long after our engagement, I started to see some red flags. Some were very similar to the destructive patterns in my past relationships. The biggest weakness I had was submission. I had been taught since childhood to be totally submissive to men. I didn't know how to balance giving into Ricky's authoritative nature, and before I knew it, he was controlling everything. I even allowed him to control the girls. I wanted to be loved so badly, I was willing to compromise everything to get it. Once again, I settled. I had never been taught that love doesn't hurt. This was all I knew.

As children, our first lessons of love come from our parents. They teach us what love is. My father loved me and showed me by taking my innocence away from me. My mother loved me with her abusive behavior and hurtful words. Ethan loved me with his fist, his jealousy, and his control. I loved my children with the only heart I had, a broken heart. I loved them with the only love I knew, the love that comes from God and not man. Mine could never be as perfect as his, but I could love them, as I knew he loved me; this was all the love I had. It was all I knew to be true.

The wedding was quickly approaching. Everything about Ricky and me was wrong. I lost meaningful friendships over the decision to marry him. My dear friend Cheryl, who took the girls and I in temporarily when I left Ethan, warned me I was making the biggest mistake of my life if I married Ricky. I ignored her warnings. I convinced myself she was just jealous and she wished she was getting married instead of me. I couldn't see that she noticed something wasn't right about the relationship. Cheryl said he was controlling me just like Ethan did and I was refusing to see the signs. Cheryl said I was vulnerable because of my weight and that I was only letting this guy in because he liked big girls. I had always been stubborn and didn't always want to face the truth. I mourned losing a good friend over a man, but I knew I was in love and that was all that mattered.

Ricky and I argued all the time. The night before the wedding, after Ricky and I returned from the rehearsal dinner, we got into a huge fight. We were both so upset we called off the wedding. He called his parents, who were staying with his sister, and they rushed over to our house to talk us into going through with the wedding. They were convinced we were suffering from wedding blues and stress. We agreed to go through with it. I mean, Ricky's parents were paying for it. What other choice did we have?

It was a very large wedding. I made my dress, and Ricky's mom, Ms. Lucy, made my veil and my train. She also made the largest wedding cake I'd ever seen. Ms. Lucy did weddings as a hobby and enjoyed doing this for her only son, Ricky. She was more excited about us getting married than we were. Ricky's sister, Vivian, was our wedding coordinator.

All my friends were in my wedding. Ally and Corey came all the way from Georgia; she was my maid of honor. I had always wanted a real wedding. Dallas gave me away. Dad was there, and he was very proud. He liked Ricky, what little he knew of him. I remember walking down the aisle and wanting to turn around and run as fast as I could. Everything in my spirit felt wrong. I couldn't believe I was going through with this. The ceremony was beautiful. Pastor Ford said, "I introduce to you, Mr. and Mrs. Hayes."

Three weeks after being Mrs. Hayes, I knew I had made the biggest mistake of my life. Ricky was into church heavier than I was. I left my church home and had become a member of his. His control got worse, and my submissiveness to his control made me feel helpless. I was determined to be the best wife ever, in spite of everything, even if it meant giving Ricky complete control over me and the girls. I was willing to make that sacrifice. Deep down inside, I was hoping this would somehow turn around. Things had to change for the better, I thought.

Ricky was angry and miserable all the time. I argued more with him than I ever did with Ethan. The only good thing about the marriage was my in-laws. I was in love with them. Ricky was from a southern family. With me living in Georgia so long before moving back to Chicago, I missed that southern comfort that folks had. His parents gave me that warmth. I loved their genuine hospitality. Their family bond was everything I had dreamed a family should be. I loved being a part of that; it made me feel wanted. Ms. Lucy and I were so close that when I called her on Ricky's and my first anniversary and told her I was leaving her son, she begged me to give it one more year. For her, I would do anything, and I stuck it out one more year to the date. I left Ricky on our second anniversary. Three months later, our divorce was final.

My second marriage had taken a toll on Brooklyn. She hated me for allowing Ricky to mistreat her. Even though Ricky never put his hands on me, the verbal, and mental abuse hurt a lot worse than any physical abuse I'd experienced. I did allow him to spank the girls. I regret that decision now, but at the time, I thought I needed someone to help me discipline the girls. I was wrong. I can only hope I did the right thing by getting out of the marriage as quickly as I did.

After another failed marriage, I felt guilt like never before. I had no idea I was still suffering from depression and how the disease contributed to why I was still making such bad choices. When you're suffering from depression, you're not able to rationalize and make sound decisions. You're not in your right and sound mind. After the divorce, I found myself sitting back on Dr. Jane's couch, trying to figure out where I went wrong. Well, the first thing I had done wrong was take myself off of the antidepressant before she approved that I was healed. Listen, we can't heal ourselves. Depression is real. We need to learn how to respect the journey of recovering without trying to rush it like I did. The last two years of my life could've been avoided had I not tried to rush things.

My marriage to Ricky destroyed my credit. I was on academic probation and had to quit community college. My third car was repossessed. The girls were both in high school now, and my only focus was their future. I wanted to get back in school but wasn't quite sure how I would do it. One thing I was learning was that life stops for no one, even when we make mistakes. As long as God gives you light in the morning, what I call another chance to get it right, then that is another day you can change your life. One day at a time. I was still in the game of life, and I was still looking to find a way out of my darkness. I was convinced God loved me enough to lead me out of the tunnel of misery. I was convinced as long as I reached for it, I'd be able to grab a hold of hope sooner or later. It was what I believed.

Chapter 12

The mayor's wife was shocked. She said, "I never knew Star had married again."

I said, "I know. She didn't want anyone to know. She wanted to forget that moment in her life. She was so ashamed it didn't work. Her wedding was so big, and she felt so much guilt for ignoring all the signs God had given her to warn her not to marry Ricky. Out of fear, she went along with it anyway. After divorcing for the second time, her life changed for the worse. Star was still struggling with depression and with her spiritual life as well. She wanted to continue to believe that she was someone special, but it was hard to hold on to those thoughts. She was adamant about searching for the key to life, the key that would open the door to love, peace, and happiness. Star was a deep person. Her soul was pure, and as I watched her second marriage end, I honestly didn't know how she would survive. Her challenges were real, and her struggles were tough."

The mayor said, "Hey, it's time for us to give you the key to the city. Our driver is here. Let's go do this. I'm so excited about this ceremony, Ally. This is so deserved. I really wish Star were here to receive this."

I said, "She's here in spirit. I know deep within me, Star is closer than we think. She's always watching over us. I feel her near all the time. I'm honored to accept the key to the city on her behalf. I'll make sure her children, Sophie and Brooklyn, get this key to keep and cherish for their mother's many accomplishments. I wish they could be here, but believe it or not, Star's oldest granddaughter, Lynn, is getting married this weekend. I hated to miss it, but I had to be here for Star. Sometimes these things can't be helped. Lynn is Sophie's only daughter; she's the one who inherited Charlie horse. Oh how Momma Lilly loved that horse. The stories they've told about Charlie horse have been in the family more than two generations.

"Star had it refurbished before she gave it to Lynn. She wanted it to look brand-new like the day Momma Lilly gave it to Sophie. Everyone knew how special Charlie horse was. He was a part of the family. He will surely continue on for many generations to come, just another part of Star's legacy that will live on forever."

The drive to Time Square wasn't as bad as noon traffic has been in the past. I felt like the mayor must have had magic powers, and everyone knew he was coming, so he arranged the police escort and had them make sure his route was flawless, as if he were the president. I enjoyed sharing this power with the mayor, and to think it was all for my best friend, Star.

The weather was perfect—not too hot, just right. The sun was shining as bright as the star it is, just like Star would've liked, almost as if she was creating all that positive energy. When we arrived, and the driver let us out, the crowd was already hyped. I see pictures of Star's book and awards displayed on all the electronic billboards surrounding Time Square. *Wow!* I thought. *Wow!* I was speechless. It was a celebration of life. It was amazing. I had no idea the city of New York loved her so much. This was priceless. The mayor looked at me and nodded to ask if I was impressed and if I approved. I responded by wiping the tears from my eyes as the crowd roared with excitement. I was overwhelmed.

The mayor was introduced, and he said a few words about Star and how the city was honored to call her one of its own. They said Star had donated more than five million dollars to the Boys and Girls Club, the local libraries, and the after-school programs for the areas of the city's less fortunate. The mayor said they had since created a college scholarship working with Star's foundation, "Star Tree," and were able to send five students to college each year, full tuition paid to any college they chose. The crowd clapped and roared even louder. One young girl was introduced as the first recipient of the Star Tree scholarship and told the audience what type of life she came from. It mirrored Star's a bit, and she said how happy she was to have the opportunity to attend college. She said she wanted to be an astronomer since not many minorities study science and the stars. She said she was determined to make Star proud. The crowd cheered her on in support, and I thought the praise would never end. Everyone was so excited. I was blown away by the amount of money Star's foundation had given to the city. Star was a millionaire. *Wow, this was her ultimate dream. To have more than enough to give back.*

The mayor asked his wife to come forward to help him give me (Star) the key to the city. She asked me to come up and join them. When they handed me the key, I swear I felt Star's spirit with me. I accepted the key and gave my speech.

"Thank you, city of New York. This is the greatest city in the world. Star thanks you all as well. I promise I will never abuse this privilege, and I will honor and cherish this moment forever. This city meant a lot to Star. She loved New York. Thank you for supporting her story and loving her as much as I do. Thank you for believing in her dream. Star was an amazing person. She honestly had no idea her book would change so many lives. I'm glad to know that her life and her struggles were not in vain. Thank you all …"

Suddenly, ticker tape started coming down from all the buildings, and the city roared louder and louder. Someone started chanting. "Star, Star, Star, Star." It continued for what felt like hours but was only until the mayor silenced them to thank everyone for coming and to thank me for accepting the Key on Star's behalf. He said he had a surprise for me. I couldn't quite take much more, but suddenly everyone was silent in anticipation of what was next. The electronic billboards suddenly changed, and they all had the title of Star's book and famous actors with titles of characters from Star's book next to them. *OMG!* Her story was officially a Broadway play. I dropped to my knees in shock. The crowd roared and clapped and whistled louder than a Super Bowl crowd. It was magical. As the mayor's wife helped me up, she hugged me with tears in her eyes. I was crying like a baby. I couldn't believe my eyes. Star made it. Her story was on Broadway. She' was a real star.

The mayor and his wife ended their speech. I bowed and said thank you a hundred times over. They left, and I stayed and signed autographs for a couple hours. Beth showed up to help control the crowd flow so no one would harm me or get out of control. Once I signed what seemed like over a thousand books, and autographs, Beth had Pam take over and said she would see me later at the gala. She said Marissa was waiting for me at the hotel bar. She said after I met with her, Scotty and Jesse would be in my room to assist me with hair, makeup, and my wardrobe. She said they planned to make me look like a million bucks. She said this was the grand finale, and I had to go out with a bang! Beth said, "I have no idea how the mayor plans to top this off with next year's event." I agreed. I said, "Yeah, looks like you have your work cut out for you." We both laughed. Adam drove me back to the hotel where Marissa was waiting patiently.

Marissa said she watched the key to the city event on live television. She said, "Wow, what an amazing honor, Ally. I know the headlines tomorrow are going to be amazing. Star has a Broadway play about her life. That says a lot. That play is going to be just as successful as her book. It will reach so many people. It might even go international." I said, "Yeah, who would've thought a poor girl from Chicago would have such an impact on the world? She is truly shining."

Marissa said, "So where did we leave off?"

"I don't remember. How about I start with how important it was for Star to go to college." After seeing that young girl who was the first recipient of the Star Tree scholarship, all I could think about was when Star dreamed of getting her college degree someday.

My education was my biggest goal. If I could graduate from college, I could do anything, I thought. I wanted to accomplish something I had only dreamed about. I wasn't very smart. But I was determined to do this no matter what. I needed to do this for the girls. I couldn't expect them to do anything I wouldn't do myself, and I wanted them to go to college. I wanted them to be better than me. I wanted them to have more than I had, and I wanted them to be successful. I knew if I could convince my girls to go to college and get a degree, they would be on the right track to a better life than what I was able to provide for them. I knew college would give them a better foundation.

I continued to struggle financially. Ethan never paid child support. He had proven himself to be the deadbeat dad after all. It hurt because the girls deserved so much more. Not only did he not pay to help support them, he deserted them as a father. He wasn't there for them; he abandoned them. I'm sure this impacted their lives. What daughter wouldn't want her father's love? I always felt if Ethan couldn't contribute financially, at least he could have given them emotional support. Something was better than nothing. Girls need their father.

I still had problems with relationships. Unfortunately, it took years of therapy before Dr. Jane convinced me I was worthy of being loved. I had never felt worthy of anything, and as a result, I continued picking the wrong men.

One Wednesday night while attending Bible study, the message was about the Israelites wandering in the desert for forty years after they lost their way trying to reach the promised land. The pastor handed each member a mustard seed and spoke about our faith. When I received my mustard seed, I held it in my hand. A feeling of comfort came over me, and God spoke to me and said, "I will release you from the desert after forty years. You will be free to love and be loved. This I promise you." At that moment, I felt a sense of assurance. I had something to look forward to. I had three more years to wander in this lonely desert, and then I'd be free. *That shouldn't be too long*, I thought.

Unfortunately, I wasn't a very patient person. Three years seemed like an eternity. I trusted God and his promise to me, but I wanted it now, not three years from now. Therefore, I continued dating, hoping I would find the love of my life much sooner.

My relationship with Sophie had become challenging, especially her last couple years of high school. I learned teenage girls are not easy to communicate with; I could only imagine how difficult I must have been at her age. Things were so bad between us; I wanted to kick her out of my house. The only thing that saved her was I didn't want to repeat what happened between my mother and me. I had to make sure Sophie had a better chance than I did. Getting kicked out of my mother's house created the path of destruction. I was set up to fail. There is no way a person can be forced to become an adult in that way and have everything work out perfectly. I always felt, had my mom forgiven me that night and allowed me to stay home and graduate from high school with her support, I would've taken a different path. I wanted Sophie to have that chance. I wanted her to go to college, and failure was not an option. If I kicked her out and she failed, I would blame myself.

Therefore, I endured her disrespectful ways, with a goal in mind. I was going to get this sassy-mouth child off to college if it was the last thing I did. Believe me, she went kicking and screaming. I remember the day I dropped her off and moved her into her dorm room. We were barely speaking, but I didn't care. Sophie was going to college even if she hated me. I kept telling her one day she would thank me, regardless of how she felt about me right then.

I was no longer taking medication for depression but continued to see Dr. Jane because I felt safe there. One day I attended a session, and Dr. Jane informed me she was releasing me from her care. I was shocked. She was more than my therapist; she had become my friend, my confidante, and I wasn't ready to let that go. I was afraid and questioned her decision. I wasn't sure I wanted to be cured from my depression. It frightened me to go back into this unfair world without her protection. I wasn't sure I could do it without her. She assured me I would be fine and that she'd done all she could do for me. She said she knew I was ready to put everything I'd learned about myself to the test. She said the world was ready for the new me. I finally had an identity. *I know who I am now and what I want and how to get it.*

It had been a decade of sessions. I honestly didn't want to leave, but if Dr. Jane said I was cured of my depression, then I had to respect and accept my healing. I remember walking out of her office with my head held high. I wanted to make her even more proud of me than she said she was. I was determined not to disappoint her this time. She was an awesome doctor, and she was my mentor and friend.

I was promoted at my job at the university and was serving a six-month probationary period. Unfortunately, I was demoted on the last day of my six-month review. I remember my boss explaining to me that I did a great job, but I kept messing up on anything dealing with numbers and words. She said she hated having to tell me I didn't make my probation period and that she would have to let me go. By now, I was crying. She'd already had a box of Kleenex behind her and handed me a few. She asked if I had ever been diagnosed with dyslexia. I told her no and asked why. She strongly suggested I see a neurologist and get tested. She believed I was suffering from some kind of learning disability. The tears kept falling from my eyes as I wept silently and listened to her suggestions. She seemed really sincere, and I could tell regardless of the situation, she really did care.

After I was demoted back down to my previous level, I followed through with her advice. I made an appointment to speak with a neurologist, and he arranged for me to take several tests. I'll never forget the day he called me into his office to give me the results. He was an older man, his head covered with gray hair. He looked like he had years of experience in his field. He wasn't very nice, and his communication skills needed some work. He didn't administer any of the tests I had taken. His nurse practitioners had done most of them. I was sitting in his office with anticipation, waiting to hear if anything was wrong with me. He said I didn't have dyslexia. I sighed a sound of relief.

He said I had receptive and expressive language disorders. I had no idea what this meant exactly, but his way of explaining it to me was asking me what kind of job I currently had, and I told him. "I work two jobs," I said proudly, "one as an office support person and the other in retail." He responded, "I believe you would be more successful cleaning houses or waiting tables." He strongly suggested sticking with my department store job, saying it would probably serve me best because my mind wasn't smart enough to do anything else. I immediately started feeling sorry for myself and couldn't hold back the tears as I listened to this high and mighty, educated doctor tell me I wasn't worth much of anything because of my learning disorders. Don't get me wrong. All the occupations he listed I'd done before, and proudly. However, I had always seen myself capable of doing much more.

Receiving this new information about myself really took an emotional toll on me. As if things weren't already difficult enough. Now this? Some things started to make sense to me. I started putting pieces of the puzzle together. This new knowledge explained why I felt I had to overcompensate for everything. I never knew I actually suffered from learning disorders. I realized I struggled for years with words, numbers, comprehension, and a lot of things, but never once did I ever consider it was due to a severe medical condition, a condition I'd had most of my life. Maybe I was even born with it.

Each time, I thought I was making progress, and then something like this happens. I was moving backward once again. It took me weeks to accept this news as I researched my condition until I could gain some kind of understanding of what I was actually dealing with. It was more complicated than I thought. There were many reasons why I could be this way, but one really stuck with me, brain injury. Did I have seizures due to brain injury when I was a baby? Did I suffer these injuries from head trauma by the hands of my mother? I doubt I would ever find the answers to these questions. What matters was how I would live with the disorders. What do I do now? Once I found enough strength and picked myself up off a familiar pity potty once again, I was determined to prove that doctor wrong. *I didn't come this far to let a couple of disabilities stop me. I've come this far because I'm intelligent. He may have been right about my diagnosis, but he was dead wrong about my capabilities.*

I signed up with the state of Illinois disability program. They assigned me a caseworker, and she set me up with an organization in town that assisted people with all types of disabilities. I attended sessions twice a week for more than two years. I hated it at first. I saw no reason why I had to do this, and at the time I couldn't see any results. I thought most of the exercises were unnecessary. I had to get special permission from the disability offices at the community college to assist me with special needs and devices to help me learn better. It was a humbling experience for me.

Soon I was on my own again. I took the tools I learned from my disability sessions and applied them to my personal life and the workplace. I realized how helpful these programs were for people with disabilities and how they equipped people like me with the proper tools to succeed. There was no cure for my condition, but I was able to learn how to live with it. I learned to use my strengths to accomplish my goals and to understand my weaknesses and not allow them to defeat me. I started noticing a difference immediately. I was able to focus better. I no longer made mistakes with numbers and words like I had done in the past. I was amazed at how much better I was performing at work. I learned how to live and accept my disability.

Brooklyn was leaving for college in a few weeks. I was so proud of her. We had an awesome relationship the last two years together without her sister, Sophie; this was a special time for us. All I ever wanted for Sophie and Brooklyn was to provide them love unconditionally and a better life than I had. I believe I accomplished this on my own as an uneducated single mom. I got both my girls off to college. This was a huge accomplishment for me. I felt proud.

Now that Brooklyn was in college, I could quit one of my jobs and finally focus more on my dreams and goals.

I was turning forty in a few months and was still single. I swear I must have dated every type of guy on the planet by then—the con artist, a cop, the principal, a doctor, the criminal, a businessman, the single dad, the liar, the cheater, the user, the confused, the immature, the hood rat, the musician, the thief, the momma's boy, the alcoholic, and now Superman. At least that's who I was hoping he was. He flew into my life with a cape on his back, and I believed I was Lois Lane.

Unfortunately, it wasn't quite how I imagined. In my heart, I had always hoped for Prince Charming, but instead I always got the fake heroes who all failed at rescuing me on time.

Marissa asked if Star had given up on love. "Yes and no. Yes, in the sense that she just had no idea how she would find love so late in her life. All Star yearned for was true love. She was convinced it existed and that someday it would find her. She believed when God spoke to her, he would always keep his word. She believed in God's love most of all, and his love never failed. When her heart was lonely and sad, her faith was always strong. Star would always tell me, 'The only thing you can ever test God on is his promises, because unlike man, God never breaks a promise. We all have that grace, no matter who we are or what we've done, or where we're at in our lives. God loves each and every one of us. He doesn't keep track of our failures. He loves us and only wants the best for us, and he always keeps his promises. He promised me three years ago I would suffer until I turn forty. I believed him, even if I only have a few months left. I believe.'"

I prayed. "Dear God, I know I'm not forty yet, but I'll be forty in a few months, and that isn't a long time. I do not doubt you, God, but I will say for you to make this happen by then, it would have to be nothing short of a miracle. I'm just saying ..."

Now that the girls were gone, I really enjoyed my new independence. I loved my fancy loft apartment in downtown Chicago. Living in the city was exciting.

I was still dating a little but nothing serious. I was finding that men my age just don't know what they want anymore. It was so frustrating. Sometimes I really wondered if something was wrong with me. I told myself, "If I were a man, I would want me. I have baggage just like most people my age, but I have a good head on my shoulders in spite of the things that were completely out of my control. I'm wiser, I'm smarter, I'm beautiful, I'm working on my education, and I'm worth it. I deserve true love. I've more than paid my dues in life. It's time for the universe to turn all the negativity and suffering in my life around and reward my strength and endurance with the ultimate prize—love."

One Sunday, I got up and didn't feel like going to church. I didn't want to put on makeup or even try to get cute. I just wanted to be my natural me. So I pulled my nappy hair back into a ponytail and threw on some Victoria Secret sweats, with some Old Navy flip-flops, to run some much-needed errands. The day was going well. I never do anything without a list, and I had almost checked off everything except car freshener. I was in Walmart in the auto section looking at my choices when this tall dark-skinned man walked down the aisle and stood next to me. I almost fainted. He looked just like Denzel Washington. He had his swag and all. I was star-struck. Other than him being fine as wine, he smelled good too; all I could think about at that moment was, *Darn it, I look a hot mess.* I kept telling myself, *Don't look up. You don't want him to see you like this.* On the other hand, I chuckled to myself, thinking, *I'm sure he doesn't even notice me anyway.* All this crap was going on in my head when we suddenly reached for the exact same air freshener and our hands touched. He looked at me, and I looked at him in that moment, and we both yelled, "Ouch!"

I said, "You shocked me."

He said, "No, you shocked me." We both laughed.

He said, "I come here just to get this scent, and you must be the one buying them all up when I can't find them."

I said, "Of course it has to be me, because I stock up so I don't have to keep coming out here to get them." As we both stood there talking, I noticed his soft green eyes, and I was mesmerized. I thought I had died and gone to heaven. His smile lit up like a full moon on a calm summer night. He seemed nice and sweet, almost unreal.

He joked and said, "Well, I'll try to leave you a couple next time I come, and you'll know I was thinking of you. Will that be okay?"

I was like, *OMG! Is he flirting with me? Me? Is he really talking to me?* I responded, "Yeah, and when you come, and they're all gone, you'll know I wasn't thinking of you."

He said, "Oh it's like that, huh? Wow, you don't seem like the type that would be that mean."

I said, "How do you know what type of person I am?"

He said, "I can tell you're not a bad person." He said he could tell just by looking into my eyes. He said I was beautiful inside and out. I almost wet my pants hearing those exciting words coming from that handsome stranger. Then he said, "Well, they have four total. I'll take two, and you take two, and then we'll be even. Will that work for now?"

I said, "Yeah, that'll work—thanks."

He said, "You're welcome." He took his two car scents and politely said, "Well, have a good rest of the day, beautiful lady."

I said, "You too," and we both walked away, going in separate directions.

When I left Walmart, I thought about him and wondered why my entire stomach felt like it had a nest of butterflies inside it. I felt something I had never felt before. It was unusual. I felt an energy I never knew existed. I felt warm and safe and calm, and I thought I felt love. I really didn't quite know what love felt like, but if it felt like that, it felt good. I wanted more.

I thought of him as Mr. Green Eyes since I never got his name. I remember every time I'd go to Walmart, I hoped to run into him again but never did. Months went by, and I was convinced I would never see Mr. Green Eyes again. I continued dating, in case one of the guys might be the one God intended for me to be with. I was keeping my options open. I didn't want him to get away. I know I sound desperate, but I was helping God out. I mean, I didn't want the right guy to get away, so I was playing it safe. Right?

One guy I was dating, his name was Tyler. Tyler was an awesome friend but a horrible boyfriend. So Tyler and I agreed to be friends instead of lovers. We became very good friends after we broke up. Tyler and I had become so close that we would talk about everything, even our dates with other people. We'd become best friends, with no hard feelings between us. Some people are just better off as friends, and we had a mutual respect for each other on that level.

Tyler would always talk about one of his male friends. He talked about how he was concerned about him because he was going through a messy divorce. Tyler said he had no place to stay, and he was letting him stay at his place for a while until he could find a place to stay. Tyler said he was a nice guy. He said maybe he would ask him to come out with us one evening. Tyler and I did this regularly. Whenever we didn't have dates and got depressed, we would give each other a call and ask to meet up at a hot spot downtown. I had my loft apartment, and I loved that because I didn't have to drive home if I had too much to drink.

One evening, after being stood up for a date once again, I called Tyler and asked him to meet me at our favorite downtown bar. Tyler was always game for hanging out because we would act like boyfriend and girlfriend, so people would leave us alone, and we could people watch and talk and laugh without feeling like we were out to meet someone. It helped keep people from hitting on us. It was our thing we did, to relieve loneliness. It was fun, and he would look after me, because he didn't drink, and I could overdrink, and he would take me home to my apartment and stay with me to keep me safe. I loved him for that. We just clicked, and our friendship was priceless!

When Tyler arrived, he wasn't alone. He was with a friend. His friend was Mr. Green Eyes! *OMG! What? Mr. Smell Good is Tyler's friend who's going through the messy divorce?* When our eyes met, those darn butterflies woke up inside of me again. They were flying and fluttering all over the place with all kinds of happiness. I could barely breathe. I gasped when Tyler was introducing us, and I could hardly speak. I tried not to make it too obvious that I was overwhelmed with love at second sight. He reached out his hand and said, "Star, so that's your name?"

I said, "Yes, and I didn't get yours. I'm sorry, it is …"

He said, "Alonzo. My name is Alonzo." I noticed his hand was just as sweaty as mine, and we held on a bit longer than normal. Once we realized this, we slowly let go and just stood there looking kind of silly.

By now Tyler was like, what the hell? The look on Tyler's face was not good. He asked, "Do you two know each other?"

Alonzo and I stood in silence waiting for the other to respond. We both looked at each other, and Alonzo said, "No, this is the first time we've met." I nodded in agreement, not sure why I agreed to Alonzo lying, but I didn't correct him.

I said, "So this is the guy you've been telling me about?"

Tyler said, "Yep! He said his divorce was final this week, so I decided to bring him out to celebrate with us. He's a single man again." They bumped fists. I thought it was adorable seeing the bromance these two guys shared. They were so cute. I could tell it was going to be a fun night sharing it with now my two best male friends.

The night was perfect! I had two of the finest men in the bar. We laughed and people watched. Alonzo was funny; he had joke after joke after joke. He had Tyler and I laughing so hard I lost my voice. He had us crying and on the floor all bent over, holding our stomachs; we were laughing so hard. I thought Alonzo was so amazing; I loved his personality, and I loved his demeanor. I thought, *Why would someone let him go?* He was perfect! When the DJ played my favorite songs, either Tyler or Alonzo would ask me to dance. Sometimes they'd both ask me, and I would bump and grind on them both. I felt like the luckiest woman. I know there were some haters, wishing they were in my shoes right. I loved it! The night turned out better than I expected. It ended without me overdrinking, and I was able to walk home sober. I most likely was on my best behavior because I didn't want Alonzo to see me in a dark way. I wanted to be on my best behavior and not embarrass Tyler in front of his friend. I'm sure he appreciated that.

When I got home, the butterflies in my stomach decided to take a rest again, and I went to bed dreaming about Alonzo. I woke up thinking about Alonzo, and I went to work, to the store, and to church with Alonzo on my mind. I wondered if Alonzo was thinking about me. Then I snapped out of it. *Back to reality, Star. This is real life. I'm sure Alonzo isn't thinking about you.*

Life went on until one day out of the blue my phone rang. It was Alonzo. I didn't even know he had my number; I hadn't given it to him. Therefore, the first thing I said was, "How did you get my number?" He said Tyler gave it to him. Then he said his ex-wife and he got into it over this girl he was dating, and she wouldn't watch their son for him. He said he knew it was short notice but asked if I would mind watching him just for the night, if I didn't have anything planned. I was a bit thrown off and had to gather my thoughts a minute, as this was honestly the first I heard about Alonzo having a son. I asked how old he was and what his name was. He said his name was AJ, short for Alonzo Junior. I chuckled and said of course I'd watch him. Alonzo said he was an avid gamer and wouldn't be much trouble at all. He liked pepperoni pizza and Mountain Dew. He said he'd bring that with him when he came, and he should be no worry for me at all. He said he could pretty much take care of himself. Alonzo asked if I had a gaming system. I said no, that I never allowed my girls to play them. I thought they were distracting, and I wanted to be sure they went to college and did not waste their precious time on stupid video games. When I allowed them to play, it was a treat, not a normal everyday activity. Alonzo said, "Well, Nintendo was AJ's first word, not mommy or daddy."

I said, "That is so sad," as we both laughed. Alonzo and I finished discussing the details of me watching AJ for the night, and he dropped him off an hour later.

He didn't look anything like Alonzo to me. He was bright skinned with a high yellow complexion. He had big eyes, not green like his dad's but a little on the hazel side. He had his dad's big nose and tall build, but that was it. I didn't know what his mom looked like, but he must have looked more like her than Alonzo.

Alonzo was right; AJ was no trouble at all. He barely said two words to me the entire time. He quietly played his video games and was in his own world. It was perfect for me, as I was studying for an exam, and I enjoyed not having interruptions. Alonzo picked AJ up around one in the morning. AJ was asleep, so Alonzo scooped him up and gave me a friendly hug and said, "Thanks so much. I really appreciate you coming through for me."

I asked him how his date went, and he said it was good. I responded, "Well, I'm glad everything worked out." When Alonzo left, I thought back on his hug. There was electricity going through my body when he touched me. *I really need to get a life*, I thought, *and quit making all these things up about how I feel every time I get around Alonzo. We're just friends, nothing more.*

About a month later, I had taken my break at work, and one of my coworkers came in the break room to find me. She said I had a visitor. I was shocked someone would come to my job to see me and was a bit nervous about who it might be. When I got around the corner, back to my desk, I looked up, and who did I see but a handsome, tall, green-eyed prince. It was Alonzo. I must have had a smile so big across my face; the entire office could see it. I tried to calm myself down and said, "HI, Alonzo. What brings you here?" after giving him a friendship hug.

He said, "Oh, I was just in the neighborhood and thought I'd swing by and say hello."

I said, "I still have ten minutes of break left if you'd like to walk to the garden with me." He agreed. The building I worked in had a beautiful outdoor garden area, with concrete benches and beautiful statues and flowers. It was warm and sunny outside and would be the perfect place to talk, rather than the break room where nosy coworkers were. We sat and talked and laughed about our mutual friend Tyler. Suddenly a bee flew down my dress. I'm allergic to insect bites, and I panicked. I jumped up and started screaming and trying to get it out of my dress before it stung me, and Alonzo jumped up and without thinking put his hand down the back of my dress and swooped the bee up in his hands. He pulled his hand out and tossed it to the ground so hard he killed it. It all happened so fast. I was so ashamed that I apologized for my actions, and Alonzo calmly said, "No problem." I explained the bad experiences I had and how I was allergic to them, and he just looked at me with sweet concern in his eyes. I told him I should get back to work, and he agreed. He politely said good-bye, and I thanked him for thinking of me. I walked him toward the front of the building, and we said our good-byes.

When I got back to my desk, all I could think about was that electricity I felt when Alonzo put his hand down my dress. I swear, when he touched me, I felt electricity shooting through my body. *What is it about that man that causes my body to respond in ways it has never with any other man I've ever met?* I thought. I wondered if he felt the same thing I felt. Then again, I would quickly ignore that thought and remind myself, *We are just friends.*

It was one week before I turned forty. I was still single and had no prospects in sight. At times, when I thought about it, I would feel sadness, and at other times, I would tell myself being single at forty wasn't all that bad. I enjoyed my independence and wanted to know if I was really ready to give all that up to be with someone. I convinced myself that my independence was worth more than compromising. *Men just complicate things, and why complicate my perfect single life. Right?*

It was almost midnight. I would turn forty in just thirty minutes. *I'm alone, but I'm safe. I'm afraid but not sure of what. I'm excited about this new stage of my life. Things are going well at work. School is going well. I should be finished soon. I'm no longer struggling financially, and I bought a new car a few months ago. Sophie and Brooklyn are both doing well. Sophie's a sophomore in college, and Brooklyn's a freshman. It's taken me forty years to learn who Star is and what Star represents. It's taken me forty years to know who I really am and accept me for who I'm not. I feel like forty is the new thirty.*

At 11:55 p.m., I got out of bed and got on my hands and knees. I wanted to give God all the glory for everything he'd done for me. I started to pray, "Thank you, God, for your mercy and your grace. Thank you, God, for always taking care of me and working everything out for your good according to the plan you have for my life. Thank you, God, for giving me the strength to get this far, and I ask that you give me more strength to carry on, to continue to do your good works. I know you have a plan for my life. I know it has been spared several times for a purpose that will change and touch the hearts of people someday. I know I had dreams of becoming a motivational speaker and writing my own book. Instead, you had other plans for me. I'm not bitter, God. I know you would never put a desire so strong in my heart and not allow it to manifest. With that said, I will never stop believing in my dream. Amen."

Once I finished my prayer, the phone rang. It was now midnight. I was officially forty years old. I just knew it was one of the girls, as we'd had this family tradition for years of who would be the first person to call and wish the other a happy birthday when the clock struck twelve. I jumped back into bed where my cell phone was and answered.

"Hi, Star," the voice said on the other end of the phone.

In shock, I was not quite sure whose voice it was, yet it sounded familiar. It was a guy, and he asked how I was doing. I said, "Fine," still trying to figure out whom I was talking to. I was thinking it must be some deadbeat I dated in the past, remembering my birthday and wanting a booty call or something. I waited for him to say something again, in hopes of picking up on the voice.

He said, "This is Alonzo."

I said, "Alonzo? Is Tyler okay? Did something happen?" He assured me Tyler was fine and that they were actually together, and Tyler told him it was my birthday, so they decided to give me a call. I heard Tyler in the background, yelling, "Happy birthday, gorgeous!" Tyler always called me that. I smiled and told Alonzo to tell him I said thanks. I was excited they had thought of me. It felt nice to hear from my two best male friends. Alonzo said he was calling for more than just to say happy birthday. I paused and asked, "What's wrong?"

He said, "Nothing, but will it be okay if I come talk to you in person later today?"

I said, "Sure." He sounded so serious. I was concerned. I had no idea why Alonzo would want to talk to me in person. What could be so important? Tyler was acting a fool in the background, so Alonzo quickly asked if he could stop by around one. I said, "Sure."

He said, "I'll see you tomorrow," and hung up.

I lay there for a minute trying to gather my thoughts about what just happened. I got up from my bed and walked toward the large window in my bedroom. I moved the semi-sheer curtains and looked at how bright the stars in the sky were. I closed my eyes and wished that this would be a good year and that God would keep his promise. I said amen once again and stood there and soaked up the star lit sky a bit longer. Then I went back to bed. I noticed there was a sense of peace I had not experienced before now. My body was calm and at peace. I slept like a baby.

I got up and went to church. When I got back home, I patiently waited for Alonzo to arrive and did some reading since finals were quickly approaching and I wanted to not fall behind on my studies.

My buzzer went off right before one o'clock. It frightened me, as I had forgotten that Alonzo was stopping by. I asked through the secure speaker, "Who is it?" I heard a soft voice say, "Alonzo." I buzzed him in. When he arrived at my door, he knocked softly, and I went to the door to let him in. When I opened the door, Alonzo was handsome and smelling better than usual. He was nervous and looked uncomfortable. I'd never seen him this way. I gave him a friendly hug, because I thought he really needed one right about now. He hugged me back but held on a little too long, like when we shook hands months ago. I felt a bit uncomfortable and pulled my body away and asked him to come in and have a seat. Once he sat down on my living room couch, I asked him if he would like something to drink. He said, "Yes, I'd like a glass of water." I asked if he'd like ice. He said yes.

I handed Alonzo the glass of ice-cold water. He sat there and drank it in silence. I watched with curiosity, wondering if he would say something. I was starting to get nervous because I had never seen him nervous. He started with small talk. He asked how was church and did I sleep well. I said yes, and then he said, "Oh yeah, happy birthday." I said thanks. He talked about how Tyler asked him to drive thirty miles outside of town so he could have a love affair with this girl they just met last night at the motorcycle club. He said he'd fallen asleep waiting for him in his car outside her house. He said when he woke up, it was early morning, and he realized Tyler had left him out there all night. He said he was mad but couldn't do anything about it, because by the time he realized what happened, Tyler was coming out of the girl's house and jumped in the car like nothing was wrong. Alonzo said he was so mad he didn't talk to Tyler the entire ride home; he dropped him off at his apartment and went home to try to get some sleep before he had to come see me. Alonzo said he was tired, because he felt he hadn't really had a good night's sleep. I told him Tyler was wrong for making him sit outside a stranger's house while he got his groove on.

I said, "You are a true friend to do something like that." I told him Tyler was taking advantage of their friendship.

He said, "Exactly. That is why I'm here. That's what I wanted to talk to you about."

Alonzo said he recently found out that Tyler and I were not dating. I started laughing. I said, "You actually thought we were an item?" He said yes. I asked, "All this time?" He said yes. I said, "Tyler and I haven't dated in more than three years. We tried it once, and it lasted a couple months. We quickly realized we were better friends than lovers. I admit, at first we were friends with benefits, but that didn't last long. Once we both started dating other people, we kept it strictly platonic." He said that's what he thought when he first met me, but when he would ask Tyler questions about me, he would say he and I were still seeing each other romantically, so that meant I was off limits.

"Tyler made it clear you were off limits and you belonged to him."

I was really trying to sort out why it mattered to Alonzo that Tyler was lying to him about me, so I asked, "Where are you going with this?"

Alonzo paused, took a deep breath, and said, "Because when I first met you at Walmart, I couldn't get you out of my mind. My stomach was doing flip-flops, and I felt lightheaded, and I had these feelings I had never felt for a woman before. I knew you were a stranger, but I just couldn't stop thinking about you. I kicked myself for not getting your name or a phone number. I had to live with the fact that I would never see you again, and I had missed my opportunity to be with the woman I had always dreamed about. I remember going to Walmart almost every day, hoping to run into you again, and never did. I was so torn over how I would accept I might not ever see you again that I started praying to God to allow our paths to cross just one more time, and if he did, I promised I wouldn't let you out of my sight again. I promised I would do everything in my power to share how I felt about you even if I looked like a fool. Then God answered my prayers. Tyler talked me into going out with him that night after my divorce was final. He said he wanted me to meet his girlfriend. When I saw it was you, I was crushed. I honestly felt angry. I asked God why would he allow me to have all these strong feelings toward a girl who wasn't available. God then whispered in my ear, 'Be patient, my son.' I have to admit, I'm a lot of things, but patient is not one of them. I had no idea what God meant by that, but I stuck it out, and last night when Tyler was flirting with that girl, I questioned his motives. I asked, 'What about Star?' He said, 'What about her?' I said, 'How would she feel?' He said, 'She wouldn't feel anything. We're not dating.' I couldn't believe what I heard. I said, 'What? I thought you said she was your girlfriend.' He said, 'Yeah, she was years ago.' I was so upset, but by now this girl was in the car with us, and when he said it was your birthday, he grabbed my cell phone and dialed your number. That's when we called you last night. When I got off the phone, Tyler seemed jealous. Even though he was all up on this girl, he was upset when I asked if I could talk to you later today. I was confused. I know he knew I had feelings for you, and he was keeping me from being with you. I'm not sure how that makes me feel. He must still have feelings for you. That's the only thing I could think would justify his actions. When I found out, I knew I had to come see you."

Alonzo was sweating; he was nervous. I felt I needed to get him more water, but he grabbed me when I tried to go and refill his glass. He took the empty glass from my hand and sat it on the coffee table. He held both my hands in his. He looked straight into my eyes and said, "I'm that guy. I'm that guy, Star. The one you've been searching and waiting for. I want what you want. I'm that guy."

I was frightened hearing this. I asked, "How do you know?"

Alonzo said, "My spirit told me. I feel you all the time. I know when you're sad, I know when you're happy, I know when you're scared, I know when you're safe. I can feel you when you and I are not together. That is why I checked on you that day when I came to your job. I knew someone had broken your heart. But at the time, I thought that someone was Tyler."

"Oh my gosh! I remember that day. I had just broken up with this guy I thought was the one—only to find out he wasn't the one either. I was crushed and sad. I was tired of trying to find my Mr. Right. I had given up. I was hopeless that day, and God sent you to me to check on me. How sweet."

Alonzo squeezed my hands tighter and said, "I've never felt this way about anyone before. I can't even explain why I feel this way about you. But, I promise you if you give me a chance to love you, to show you that I'm that guy you've been praying for, I promise I will never hurt you like all those other guys did. I promise."

I was speechless. I was flattered, and at that moment I realized Alonzo felt the same magic I felt about him. He had been fighting those feelings just like I was. I realized those feelings were real, and they were alive, and our souls connected in spirit. We had never kissed until then. Alonzo reached and pulled my head toward his hypnotic green eyes and kissed me so softly. I didn't pull away. I allowed myself to surrender to that moment I would never get back and allow this to happen for whatever it was worth. Alonzo then picked me up like the officer and a gentleman and took me to my bedroom. He laid me on the bed and slowly took off my clothing, all the time assuring me that everything was going to be fine. He had this safe look in his eyes. He stared at me with certainty, and I stared back in agreement. When Alonzo had me completely vulnerable, he looked at me one more time and said, "I love you, Star." At that moment, I believed him because I needed to.

Hours passed, and it was dark outside; I must have fallen asleep. I woke up in Alonzo's arms, naked and happy. I was lying on his chest listening to his heartbeat while he slept. I remember feeling loved. *I think this is what love feels like,* I thought. *It feels safe and protected.*

When Alonzo woke up, he seemed relieved. He was different. I was sure he would leave and not ever come back. He got what he wanted. *I fell for his game, and I'm sure once he leaves, he'll pull some guy line on me and break my heart like all the rest of them.* I was wrong. Alonzo never left. We were inseparable from that day forth.

Chapter 13

A year later, I asked Alonzo to marry me. I wanted to keep him in my life forever. We eloped at the county court house and flew to Vegas for a weekend honeymoon. It was intimate and simple and just the two of us, just like we'd always imagined, minus the tropical island. It was perfect.

Everything about Alonzo and I worked. Everything. He was my best friend, my soul mate, and my husband. Alonzo kept his word, and we were happy. Everyone said I had the pregnant woman glow. I was happier than they had ever known me to be. I felt I could be my complete self with Alonzo. He was so laid back, and he never tried to change me. He loved me for the good and the bad. He loved me unconditionally. Alonzo taught me how to love back. He taught me that love is warm, safe, and not mean or evil. He taught me that love forgives all things, and it doesn't harm and isn't harmful.

Alonzo and I bought a house. We traveled, and we went to church together. We grew more in love as the years passed. Alonzo and I were one. We called ourselves Yin and Yang. Yin means female, negative and passive, the moon, and yang means male, positive and active, the sun. Yin and yang are opposites. You can't have one without the other. Alonzo and I were one. I was happy, God kept his promise.

I was nervous, excited, and happy. I wasn't sure if I wanted to cry or just soak it all in and hope the moment would last forever. Alonzo was dressed so handsome in a fitted black suit. He kissed me so softly on the forehead and told me he loved me. He seemed happier than I did. Sophie was adjusting my cap, making sure it wasn't going to fall off. I ordered the wrong size, so she clipped hairpins on it to keep it snug. She gave me a big hug and kiss and told me how proud she was.

The best feeling for me was being able to share this special moment with my family. This more than made up for my high school graduation when no one was there and I felt so alone. Not this time.

The president of the college started speaking, and I started to reflect on what it had taken for me to get there. I thought about all the things that had happened in my life since I graduated from high school. How hopeless I felt after Mom kicked me out of the house. How lonely I felt when Dallas turned his back on me. Oh, and he was there with his new wife, Michelle. She and I got a long much better than Jeannie and I did. Dallas and Michelle had a baby girl named Lacey. Lacey is so special; she's lucky to be alive. She was born with her heart in the middle of her chest. She had to have open-heart surgeries shortly after birth. She was in critical condition, and the doctor's didn't think she was going to make it, but she did. We were all convinced her Grandma Lilly, was comforting her in the hospital, and she was the angel watching over her that saved her life. She acted just like our mom. She changed Dallas more than Michelle had. Lacey softened Dallas. He was a different man. He was happier than he'd ever been. I was glad they were here to share the moment with me.

I continued listening to the president's speech with tears falling from my eyes. Life was more than I could've dreamed. I'd waited for this moment for a long time, and then I heard my name. I stood up and started walking toward the stage to receive my degree. My family was screaming and yelling so loud it felt like they were the only ones in the audience. When I shook the president's hand as he handed me my diploma, I was smiling so hard my face hurt.

I can't explain how proud I was of getting my degree. I graduated with a master's in psychology. Yes, exactly, a master's degree. I had gotten my associate's shortly after Alonzo and I got married. Then I continued on and received my bachelor's. My job was going well. I was able to land a job as a director of graduate programs in the psychology department. This was one of the best days of my life. I couldn't believe that a little messed-up girl like me could finally accomplish something as big as that. I knew now I could do anything I set my mind to. I was ready to do even more with my life.

Fifty is the new forty.

I was thinking it was finally time to write that book I'd always wanted to write. I had a lot more to share now. The desire to write my story had never left my spirit, and I'd never know if it would change lives if I never wrote it. Yeah, I was in my fifties, but it's never too late to reach your dream. Dreams don't have a deadline. The only thing that stops a dream is death. I still had time. I could do this.

Sophie had a friend who had written a book a few years before. I contacted her and asked how she did it. She gave me a lot of good information. I shared what I learned with Alonzo, and he encouraged me to start writing. Sophie and Brooklyn were very supportive. They asked me all the time how the book was coming along.

Friends would ask over the years, and I would tell everyone I was still working on it.

Writing your own story isn't easy. I honestly don't know how people before me did it. Talking about writing a book sounds good, but actually writing it is very difficult. Nevertheless, I'm not a quitter, and I'll do my best to make this last dream become a reality if it's the last thing I do. I'm determined to get this book written and published. God didn't put any of my desires in me and not have a plan to carry them out. Everything he's planned for my life has happened up until now. So why wouldn't my book be another one of those miracles? Right?

Alonzo helped me turn AJ's room into my own sacred meditation room, after AJ graduated from high school. I started meditating regularly after my third round of depression. Depression comes and goes throughout your lifetime, depending on what curve ball life decides to throw your way. Thank God, there is a cure. I've battled it more than my share, and that darkness is real. I chose after the last time to learn how to still my mind and protect it from darkness. Meditation gives me light and peace. Meditation saved my life. I can't imagine my life without it. It feeds my spirit and rescues my soul. I'm a different person now that I know exactly who I am. I know I have a higher power that has always been with me and in me. I now know how to exercise my consciousness on a higher level, and I use this gift to stay motivated in some of the most challenging moments in my life. This works for me. Meditation has been around for thousands of years. I didn't know something so simple could be so powerful. I'm glad it discovered me. Even over fifty, I feel like I can accomplish anything. I can still become a motivational speaker and travel the world and share my story when my book makes the *New York Times* best-seller list.

Marissa dropped her stylus. She had been recording and also taking notes on her iPad. When she bent down to pick it up, she noticed my tattoo on my left angle. She said, "Shooting stars, right?"

I said, "Yes. I got this tattoo in honor of my dear friend Star. It keeps me grounded and reminds me of her every day."

Marissa said, "I read in the book Star had her boyfriend Quinton's name tattooed on her right back shoulder."

"Yes, she did, but once she and Quinton broke up, she had it covered. It was such a bad cover up, because everyone who saw it after she thought his name was covered could still see it. That bothered her. Once Star married Alonzo, she decided to get a beautiful yin yang tattoo. It covered the two previous ones before very well. She was pleased. Her yin yang tattoo reminded her of the light and darkness in her life. It reminds her how in order to have true balance, one cannot exist without the other. It reminded her of her relationship with Alonzo and the facts of life in general. It was exactly who Star was and how Star lived her life. She loved that tattoo."

Marissa responded, "I bet it was as beautiful as Star."

"It was. She took me with her when she decided to get it done. After Star turned fifty, she changed. She was a different woman. She had no regrets in her life. She was happier than I had ever known her to be. It took her fifty years to get to this stage in her life. She said the older she got the more she wanted to make things happen, and she did. She was always grateful for the years God blessed her to continue reaching her dreams. I'm not sure if I could have held on to my dreams past a certain age. It just seems like after a while you should accept the life you have and let certain dreams go. Not Star. She never stopped believing."

Marissa said, "It's a good thing she didn't or else none of this would be happening right now. Her book, her foundation, and now her Broadway play. What an accomplishment."

"Yeah, this is all Star's dream. I just wish she were here to experience all of this. She would have been so humbled by the success of her book and becoming the philanthropist she always dreamed of being. Her entire life, she said if she ever became famous, she would give back to those less fortunate. She would give back to the programs that changed her life while growing up, so other young children would have hope like she did. There is a place in my heart that knows she's here with us right now. She knows this is happening, and she is very pleased."

Marissa asked, "Whatever happened to Star's dad? Is he still alive?"

"Yes, he is. Star and her father came a long way. He contacted her when she turned fifty and wished her a happy birthday. Star would always feel some kind of way when he called. She still had bad feelings toward him because of the abuse. She had never gotten over him molesting her all those years."

"Where is he now?" Marissa asked.

"He still lives in Chicago in the same town as Dallas. He actually lived less than a mile from Star for more than twenty years. Dallas and Star acted like he didn't live in the same town. Both Dallas and Star both said if anything ever happened to their father, don't call them. This was their thing they said all the time. They had no sympathy for their dad. He was a drunk and lived like a bum, and they were ashamed of him. Dallas had no respect for him, and Star hated him for ruining her life. She found it hard to forgive him for what he did to her all those years. Fourteen years he violated her. That's a long time. It almost destroyed Star. I'd say that was her hardest wound to live with. That scar never healed; it never went away."

One evening after work, I was just about to do yoga, and the phone rang. It was Dallas. He said our dad was in the hospital, and the nurse said he probably wouldn't make it through the night. I was shocked. I dropped everything, and Alonzo drove me to the hospital to see my dad. The drive was silent. I had no words. I really didn't even understand my actions. *I mean seriously? Why do I care what happens to this monster? He's an awful man. He ruined my life. I hate him.*

Just a month before, he called to wish me a happy Independence Day. He did this from time to time. I swear I thought he was drunk when he did this. I mean really? Who calls to wish someone a happy Independence Day? He never forgot my birthday, even though I wished he would. Sometimes out of the blue he'd call just to wish me happy Lord's Day on Sundays. I hated getting those calls. I hated talking to him. I was always so angry with him; I thought I was grown and would be brave enough to tell him off for like the hundredth time. He always told me how much he loved me, and I never accepted his love. He'd always go into his many God-loving stories of when he was a preacher, and all I could think was, *You stupid, sad drunk. You don't know what love is. You hurt me, and you never apologized for what you did to me.* When I would ask him why he never apologized, he'd say, "Because

I didn't do anything wrong." He said, "I loved you, and God is love. Therefore, if I loved you in that way, it wasn't wrong." I'm convinced my dad was a very sick man. I was so angry I couldn't get an apology from him that I was done speaking to him. He even had the nerve to speak ill of my dead mother, and I actually quickly came to her defense, which surprised even me. He always told the story of how she tried to kill him. I was so mean. I said, "Too bad she didn't succeed." Yeah, I was not a nice daughter. I cut our conversation short and felt satisfied in my meanness and hung up the phone. I felt like I was stronger now. I told my father he was an evil man and he didn't deserve my love.

Dad was in his late seventies and still a drunk. He lived on his own at an assisted living apartment building for low-income senior citizens. I think I may have visited him once since he moved there. I was so uncomfortable when I was around him, and if we were alone, my fear was worse. I hated how afraid I still felt around my dad. I always felt like that helpless, vulnerable little girl again, even after all these years.

When we finally arrived at the hospital and made it to the critical care unit, I saw my dad. At that moment, I immediately realized he couldn't hurt me anymore. My dad was completely helpless and fighting for his life. He looked worse than the last time I'd seen him several weeks ago, walking back to his apartment. Since we lived so close by, I'd see him walking sometimes. He looked as well as a career alcoholic can look. It was when I didn't see him from time to time I would call Dallas and ask if he'd seen his dad lately. I guess a part of me did care a little.

He looked like he had aged a hundred years. He looked afraid and lonely. His girlfriend was there in the room waiting for me to arrive. She said she had just gotten the news my dad was in the hospital as well. She had her grandson with her. Dad had known this woman since she was fourteen, and she was only a year older than me. You do the math.

She told dad I had come. He was unconsciousness and did not respond. I sat next to his bedside, not sure exactly what was going on. I tried to ask his girlfriend for answers, but because she was not family, the doctors refused to share any information with her. I could tell she was uncomfortable after I arrived and immediately looked for an excuse to leave. I was fine with that, as she looked like she had lived a worse life than I had. I kind of felt sorry for her. I thought, how sad, because she was a very beautiful woman before she allowed someone like my father to ruin her life.

He looked like he had a stroke. Both his hands were all curled up on his chest inward. He looked like Mom did after she had her stroke. His breath stunk, and his teeth looked like they hadn't been brushed in a year. His hair was thin and gray; he looked like a lost dog. He weighed about 140 pounds and was very fragile. I thought, *What happened? How could this be the same man I just saw walking home the other day?* I was still struggling and asking myself why I was there. He'd been in the hospital several times over the years, and I never bothered to see him. *Why am I here now? What's different? Could it be that Dallas said the nurse said he wouldn't make it through the night? Am I here thinking he will finally say he is sorry for the way he treated me, now that he's dying?* He had a nurse in his room that never left. She couldn't tell me much, but I did find out that dad had been there almost ten days. She said they had been trying to get a hold of next of kin since he'd arrived. She said he'd gone from bad to worse since then. She said they received a call from his girlfriend who said she hadn't heard from him in a while and wanted to know if he was in the hospital.

"We told her yes, he was a patient, because that is public information. Once she arrived and found out how bad he was, she called his son, Dallas, who contacted you."

I said, "Yeah, Dallas called me, and I came as fast as I could. Where is Dallas?" She said he had left and said I would take care of everything once I arrived. I was told I would not be able to get answers this late and Dad's doctor would be in to see him tomorrow, and if I wanted to know more, I needed to be there then. It was midnight, and I knew Alonzo was tired, as he had already fallen asleep in the chair in Dad's room. I agreed to go home, since I knew there was nothing I could do, and return early in the morning to get answers.

At eight in the morning, I was back at the hospital. Dad had another nurse watching him, and he said the doctor would be in to see him within a couple hours. I looked at my dad with all those tubes in his mouth and his nose and arms. All I could hear was his monitor beeping while the nurse continued to watch it as if it would cold blue at any minute. I kissed him on his cheek and started rubbing his forehead, and I prayed that God would help my dad. I talked to him to let him know I was with him and that he was not alone. I wondered if he could hear me and if he knew I was there. I tried again to get more answers from his nurse, but he wouldn't assist me. He apologized and said the doctor had been waiting for a family member for days to come see about my father and that she would be pleased to tell me the status of my father's health.

Finally, his doctor arrived with a team of specialists. They were taking very good care of him, and I could tell they were concerned about him. There were five doctors, and each one specialized in something different, but his main critical care unit physician was a female doctor who looked like she was from India. She introduced herself to me and shook my hand. She told me in front of my dad that he'd had all positive results since he'd arrived and how far he'd come. It was hard for me to wrap my mind around him being any worse than what I was witnessing. I sensed she wanted me to step outside so she could talk to me in private. Even though Dad was unresponsive, she felt he could probably still hear us, so I told Dad I loved him and that I would be right back. I was just stepping outside his room to talk to his doctor. I gave him another kiss, this time on his cheek, and I squeezed his hand to give him assurance. When I stepped outside his room, his doctor said my father was a very sick man. She said she didn't really know what caused all the conditions he was experiencing. She said he was lucky to be alive. She said she knew they had lost him a few times and couldn't find any reason why he was still with us. She said he had a team of doctors, each treating him for different chronic conditions. She introduced me to them as they named their specialties. She said my dad had two large blood clots in both his lungs. That was why he was on oxygen, and without it, he would most likely die. She said he was in a lot of pain. She said she was not sure if he had a stroke. Because he was so fragile, they had only been able to treat the most serious life-threatening conditions one at a time. She said his body couldn't handle them treating them all at once, so each day, they would decide which chronic condition they could treat in order to treat another and so on. She named all of his conditions and walked me through everything they'd done for him from day one of his now eleven days in the hospital. She said she honestly had no idea how he was still with us. She had given up on him because she knew they had done everything they could for him. She told me she was glad to see he did have family because she thought he was going to die alone. She said they would take things minute by minute, hour by hour, day by day, and she promised to do everything they could to save him. She told me I needed to complete DNR paperwork. She said this would be a good time to see if my father had a living will. She asked who his power of attorney was. She stressed the importance of having these documents in order before he passed. "I'll send a caseworker down to talk to you about all this and assist you with getting these documents in place." She touched my shoulder to give me comfort and said she would be back to check on him tomorrow.

When she left, my mind was racing, and I was in shock. I sat down in the chair next to my dad and looked at him so helpless and wept. Processing all this information was emotionally overwhelming.

In the days and weeks to come, I stayed by my dad's bedside. One evening I was talking to him so he could hear my voice. I heard patients could sometimes hear even when they're not responsive; therefore, I tried it each day in case my dad could hear me. I was telling him how big his beautiful great granddaughters had gotten, and he suddenly opened his eyes and smiled at me. He couldn't talk, and he couldn't move much. He was still on oxygen, but they had finally taken the tubes out of his throat. They had been feeding him through a tube, because he hadn't eaten in weeks, and they didn't want him to starve to death. Even after they removed the tubes, he didn't eat for four days. I was concerned. I ordered breakfast, lunch, and dinner each day, hoping he would get stronger and try to eat. He had to be fed like a newborn baby, because he was so weak and still couldn't move his arms. I would spoon-feed him every day as I watched over him and stayed with him for hours each day. He was so grateful I was there, I could tell, even though he couldn't tell me. I could see it in his eyes. I could tell he was frustrated because he was helpless. He tried harder and harder each day to try to do things himself, but he just couldn't do it. In his humility, he would surrender and allow me to help him. He listened to me and let me take care of him. He had to trust that I loved and cared for him enough to want him to get better. I'm sure this confused us both, because I would've have never thought in a million years I would ever have compassion for a man that had hurt me the way he had.

I met with his caseworker once a week to get his progress report. His reports weren't positive and hopeful at all. For the first time, I realized my dad's life would never be the same. Dallas was missing in action. I hadn't heard from or seen him since I first got the call Dad was in the hospital. I felt alone, and I was sad for my dad. I had suddenly become my father's caretaker. The timing couldn't have been worse. I was already in a dark place with other things going on in my life, things I had no control over. Now I had to add this to my already stressful list of challenges. I honestly thought I would lose it. I never knew how strong I was until then. This was by far my most challenging life experience. So many emotions were wrapped up in this situation. I had to face so many things, being there for my dad. I had to heal wounds I never knew existed. I was a mess. In spite of my feelings, I cared for him like he had been father of the year. I cared for him like he was my father and not the monster I'd known him to be my entire life. I showed him love and compassion I didn't know I had for him. I gave him a reason to live by giving him hope.

Over the weeks, the caseworker sensed my struggle. I never told her why, but she knew the wounds had to be deep. She could tell this situation had taken its toll on me. She asked if going through this with my dad was somehow a healing experience for me. I told her absolutely not. I was almost pissed that she would say that. I responded, "This experience just reminds me of the word irony. When I look at my dad, I see irony. Who would've thought out of all of his children—and he has four of us all together, his first two from his first marriage—that I would be the only one here taking care of him?" I felt he hurt me the worst. None of his other children had come to see about him, and he'd been there more than six weeks. I was still surprised I was there. Ask myself every day, why? I still don't know the answer.

Dad had no clean underwear, no socks, no clean clothes, no nothing. Alonzo and I had to get his personal belongings and get the keys to his house to get him some items. When Alonzo and I arrived at Dad's apartment, we were greeted with a smell that burned the hair in my nose. It was horrible. There were maggots all over the kitchen counter and stove. Maggots in a candy dish on his living room/bedroom floor that looked like it had been there for countless years. It reeked of alcohol and vomit and had piles and piles of sweepstakes/get-rich/you've-won-a-million-dollars mail that had piled up for years, with paper bugs and insects crawling all over and underneath the envelopes. It was disgusting. At that moment, I felt ashamed that my dad had been living like this for years, and no one knew or cared. What did he do to each of his kids for us to disown him to the point where we would become disconnected and allow him to live this way?

Alonzo and I, without saying a word, just started cleaning like we were on the TV show *Hoarders*. It took hours just to be able to see the floor. Alonzo and I had to leave several times to go and purchase more large garbage bags and cleaning solution. I'm terrified of maggots, so Alonzo dealt with them as I handled everything else. I loved Alonzo even more for helping me do this for my father. He knew how I felt about him all these years. He knew how awful of a father he was and how he abandoned Dallas and me when we were growing up. He never paid child support, just like the girls' dad never paid. Sadness came over me when I saw the piles of sweepstakes mail, some as high as three feet tall. This explained why Dad always mentioned he was a millionaire and how he was always very confident of his financial wealth. Of course we all knew he was delirious, but he believed it, and now I saw why. My dad had fallen victim to elderly scams. Scams that give elderly people like my dad hope. He had hundreds of these ready to mail with stamps and money orders in them. It was so sad. He'd always talked about winning the Nobel Prize and even had a certificate that came in the mail saying he had won and what his winnings were. He was so proud of this fraudulent document that he framed it and put it on his bare walls. The only décor he had in his entire apartment was his Nobel Prize certificate.

When I looked around for clothes to take back to the hospital, I found no underwear, no socks, no pants, and a couple shirts that were so dingy with only one button. At that moment, I felt more shame that my dad had lived this way. Don't get me wrong. Karma is bitch, but this was just sad. I wouldn't have wished it on my worst enemy. When Alonzo and I finished cleaning his apartment, we went to Walmart to buy my dad everything he needed to stay in the hospital as long as he needed. He needed clean underwear, T-shirts, socks, slacks, deodorant, toothpaste, razors, mouthwash, and a pair of house shoes, in case he got better and could walk. We made sure he had more than enough.

At that moment, he wasn't just my dad. He was a human being, and all I could think was, *No one deserves to be mistreated at a time like this, no matter how awful of a person they have been. He is still a human soul, a spirit that God created.*

Dad was happy to receive his items. He was grateful and couldn't wait to wear them each day. When Alonzo and I went to visit him, he had on a new outfit every day. He looked happy and jazzy. I honestly don't think my father had had underwear, socks, and T-shirts in years.

Dad was in rehab by now, and they said he still wasn't getting better. They said he would need to be put in a nursing home. My heart was heavy when I had to break the news to him. I will never forget the look on his face. He felt defeated. He did not take this news well. It was the second time since my mother's death I saw my father cry. This news hurt me more than it hurt him.

During the weeks I spent with my dad I learned a lot about him and more about myself. We spent hours and hours together, talking about so many things. I learned my father was a very intelligent man. He really loved me. He shared things about me the past twenty years that I didn't even know he knew. He kept up with the girls' and my life even when I didn't care anything about his. He told me about boyfriends I had and went into detail about how badly they treated me over the years and how I deserved better and how he'd pray that God would bring me someone like Alonzo. He and Dallas would talk about my well-being, and he would always pray that someday I would find real love. He said when Dallas told him about Alonzo, he felt peace and happiness for me. He knew his little girl would be fine.

I listened to his stories, and he had many. He wouldn't stop talking. He wanted me to know everything, as if this would be his only chance to tell me. I realized my dad cared even when I hated him.

When it was time for Dad to go to the nursing home, I left work early that day so I could be there with him and make sure he got settled. I wanted him to know I was there for him. To my surprise, I learned he was not going to the nursing home after all. His doctor said he had miraculously taken a turn for the better. She said she had no idea what happened, but he could go home. She said he would need a nurse to assist him daily for a few weeks until his strength came back, but she felt he could go home. *Wow, again I've experienced a miracle. My dad is going home.*

My dad was quite the ladies' man, even in his seventies. He had a few nurse groupies by the time he was discharged. All his favorite nurses came outside to say good-bye to him, and some of them even cried. He promised to get better, and when he did, he would show them his G-Baby. They were like, "G-Baby? What is that?" He said, "Have on your dancing shoes because I'm going to take you up on that dance you promised me when I couldn't walk."   He said to the nurse that flirted with him the most during his stay, "Remember?" She smiled and said,

"Yes, I remember. I told you if you walk and get better, I wanted the first dance." My dad looked forward to that day, and it was all he talked about when I took him home. It was good to see him in this light. I believe God had a plan. He wanted me to forgive my father. He found a way for me to forgive him in my heart, with my entire soul. I went from hating him to loving and forgiving him. He never apologized to me, and that was okay. I learned more about what love is. Love is forgiveness. When I went home that night, I added more quotes to my vision board that hangs on my wall in my meditation room.

"If we really want to love, we must learn how to forgive."—Mother Theresa

"Forgive them even if they are not sorry."—Julian Casablancas

"The weak can never forgive. Forgiveness is an attribute of the strong." - Ghandi

"Forgiveness is unlocking the door to set someone free and realizing you were the prisoner."—Max Lucado

I was no longer a prisoner. I am no longer weak. I was free now to be used as the vessel God put on this earth. I understood my life has a purpose. I had been lost in darkness, and now I finally saw the light. My life was full of darkness until I allowed love and forgiveness to light my path. I could see now and realize this light shines in all of us. Sometimes we just need to look for it deep within ourselves and trust it when it guides us. No matter how dark our lives get. We must always believe light will always outshine it someday.

That same year, I invited my dad to spend Christmas with my family for the first time ever. He was honored, and we had a wonderful time. I bought my dad one of the nicest G-note harmonicas they had at the music store. The salesman said it was the best brand they carried. When my dad opened his gift, tears filled his eyes. He was overwhelmed with joy. He immediately asked Dallas to wet the wooden keys so he could play it. When Dad blew the first note, it reminded me of how much I loved him as a little girl. I still loved the sound of its bluesy notes; I loved how happy my dad was when he played his harmonica. I remembered how when he played his harmonica, it always brought happiness to all that heard it. Everyone this Christmas day was sprinkled with the same magic I felt for years. A spiritual transformation, it's what I call the melody of love. *Harmonica Blues*.

Marissa responded, "Wow, Star finally forgave her father. I don't know that I could've forgiven someone who hurt me like he hurt her. It really speaks highly of the kind of compassion Star had for others, especially when so many people hurt her throughout her lifetime. Speaking of her life, what happened to Star? I heard so many different versions."

"It all happened so fast. One minute she was here, and the next she was gone. She was running errands on a Saturday morning like she'd done for years. She received a call from Alonzo asking her to stop by Walmart to pick up their favorite car fresheners. When she was in the aisle where she and Alonzo met twenty years earlier, she noticed a strange piece of paper taped to the fresheners she usually got. She reached for it and realized it had her name on it. She snatched the paper off the hook and unfolded the paper. When she opened it up, it read "Will you marry me again?" She thought it was strange, and no sooner than she realized what was happening, Alonzo came walking down the aisle with a ring box in his hand. He knelt down on one knee and asked, "Will you marry me again?" Star was stunned. She had no idea Alonzo had planned this. Because Star asked Alonzo to marry her, she'd always wondered if she hadn't asked him first, if he would've ever asked her at all. His answer was of course, but Star always doubted because he never got the chance. Well, this was his chance, and he did. It was so romantic. Of course she said yes, and he picked her up and spun her around in the aisle as they celebrated their upcoming vow renewal.

Alonzo planned everything perfectly. Star had always wanted to go to Fiji, and he coordinated an all-inclusive trip to Fiji that included a private wedding on the beach, just the two of them. Just like they did the first time when they eloped at the courthouse. But this time, Star wore a beautiful wedding gown, and Alonzo wore a tux. It was perfect. After they renewed their vows, Alonzo had planned for them to take a small single-engine plane to a more remote island nearby. They would have the island all to themselves just for the night. It was set up so beautifully. It was a magical paradise.

"Tropical storms can come out of nowhere in that area, and their wedding anniversary was during hurricane season. Star always hated the fact she didn't research this before she planned their first wedding, because almost every year they celebrated their anniversary, they had bad weather. It was inevitable. It never stopped them though, because they promised each other that they would celebrate their union each year by doing something special. This was both Alonzo and Star's third marriage, so they thought of each year as a huge accomplishment. Both understood how difficult marriage could be, from their previous experiences. Celebrating twenty-years of marriage was very special for them.

"They boarded the plane. The pilot said he'd flown in worse storms, and this one wasn't as bad as most. He was certain he could get them to the island safely. He knew how important it was to them, and he wanted them to have an awesome second honeymoon. Alonzo and Star felt safe, and they had weathered several of these tropical storms on many trips in the past, so they weren't afraid. Sadly, the plane went down somewhere between the two islands. They say it exploded in the ocean on impact. It was horrible. It all happened so fast. Witnesses say they saw this huge fireball in the far distance and a lot of black smoke. Hours passed before the coast guards reached the crash site. When they did, they found no survivors. They searched and searched and searched for them and found no one and not even any of their belongings. The storm had turned from bad to worse in a matter of minutes. They found themselves in the middle of a cyclone. No one really knows for sure what happened—why the weather turned from bad to worse in a matter of minutes. No one ever will. They searched more than seven days for their bodies, but they never found them. They pronounced them legally dead on the eighth day. They said there was no way anyone could survive out there in those conditions without food and water that long.

"When we all received the news, it was devastating. Sophie was the first to receive the call, and hearing that her mother was dead paralyzed her. She had to contact the entire family, and once she contacted me, I told her I would take over with contacting everyone else so she could be with her family. Star's death was honestly the saddest thing I ever experienced. When I lost Corey to cancer a few years ago, I was lost and lonely. But when Star died, a part of me died with her. Star was special. It's like she had some kind of magic about her. Anyone who's ever been around her would know exactly what I mean by that. Her spirit was alive like no other. She was a beautiful person inside and out. She was truly a shining star. Momma Lilly gave her the perfect name.

"Star was the type of person that always had everything in order. When she died, and the lawyers read her will, to everyone's surprise, we each received a key with the word *Believe* engraved on it. Each key opened a safe-deposit box, and each one of us received a special letter from Star telling us how much each of us meant to her. Only Star would do something like that in case something happened to her. When Momma Lilly died, she hated the fact she had nothing from her mom to keep with her. She wished her mom had left her one last letter. It really bothered her. She promised herself she would never leave her children or anyone she cared about wondering how she really felt about them. She took the time while she was living to leave a small piece of her so our hearts could heal a little easier without her. She wanted us all to know she would always be with us.

"When Sophie opened her box, she found more than a letter. She found a book. Star had self-published her book and it was scheduled to release on Christmas day, the same day Grandma Lilly was born. She hadn't told anyone. I believe she was planning to surprise us. Sophie was overwhelmed with finding this special gift. She had no idea her mom had finished writing her book. After she had read her mother's book a hundred times over, she realized why it took her mother so long to tell her story. Sophie believes it's because Star never wanted the story to end.

"I was fortunate to be one of many promoters of Star's book, since everyone knew I was her best friend and would be able to share moments about Star's life even her children didn't know about her. I started getting contacted to speak at events and attend book signings on her behalf. I enjoyed doing this because my life was lonely after Corey died. Our kids were grown, and I was alone. It actually gave me something to do. I enjoy watching Star's dreams come true. I enjoy being her voice. It's my way of giving back to her cause. It keeps her alive in my heart."

Marissa said, "I'm also honored to be a part of telling her story to the world. The magazine spread is going to be so good. This is some good stuff I got from you this weekend. Oh, I wanted you to know, I purchased a ticket. Or should I say, the magazine purchased me a ticket. They bought me the one-thousand-dollar plate. You know, the seats go all the way up to ten thousand a plate."

Who would've thought Star would have a fundraising gala like rich people and have guests willing to pay as much as ten thousand dollars for a fancy dinner? I was sure her Star Tree Foundation would easily raise more than a million dollars at tonight's event. What a dream come true.

"Well, that's it," said Marissa. "We can wrap this up. I think I have more than enough for your feature in the magazine. Don't forget, you're scheduled for a photo shoot tomorrow morning before you catch your flight back to Chicago. Adam will be here to pick you up at six, and the shoot starts at eight o'clock sharp. I'll be there to make sure everything goes well and they get the shots I need for the cover and the spread. Other than that, we're done. Thank you so much again, Ally, for this exclusive interview. I know you're a busy woman, and I just want you to know I appreciate all the time you took with me to get Star's story. No one knew Star like you did, and she is fortunate to have someone like you to keep her story alive."

"You're welcome, Marissa. It was a pleasure working with you as well. I can't wait to see the magazine on the shelves. I'm excited. This is the first time I've ever been on the cover of a major magazine. I'm amazed at how much my life has changed since Star's book was published. Who would've ever known it would change so many lives?"

Marissa said, "Thank goodness she had a friend like you, Ally. Someone who's willing to go the extra mile to keep Star's spirit alive. Again, thank you so much, Ally. I know you're exhausted. So I'm going to leave and see if I can't get half as pretty as I know you're going to be tonight after your glam squad is done with you. Tell Jesse and Scotty I said hey, and I'll see them later tonight. We're actually sitting at the same table. It should be fun."

When the mayor introduced me, I made my entrance by walking down these spiral stairs like Cinderella. I felt beautiful and honored to be the guest of honor. There were so many people I could hardly breathe. I was treated like a queen. The event was perfect. After dinner, a live band was playing soft jazz in the background, Star's favorite music. The food was fabulous. The spread of after-dinner treats was even better. Food, drinks, and good conversation are always a good formula. The mayor introduced me to so many people. I networked, talked, and laughed and enjoyed myself. Everyone who attended was more than happy to be there and to give to Star's foundation of helping women and children who were less fortunate. I politely excused myself from the crowd and went to the bathroom.

I was glad no one was in the bathroom. This gave me a moment to myself to exhale and soak it all in. The entire weekend had been full of surprises and exciting moments and experiences of a lifetime. I stared at myself in the mirror in silence. I enjoy praying out loud, so I started to pray. "God, thank you for everything. Thank you for your love. Thank you for your peace. Thank you for your guidance. Thank you for protecting me and watching over me. Thank you for using me according to your will and not mine. Thank you for this moment. Thank you for this miracle. Thank you for keeping your promise as always. Amen."

My gown was a form-fitting, mermaid trumpet style, so I had to unzip it to go to the bathroom. When I came out of the stall, I thought I was still alone. I hadn't heard anyone enter, and I washed my hands and was fixing my makeup and my hair. I tried to zip my dress back up but was having a hard time with it. Suddenly Marissa came out of a stall surprised to see me, but without hesitation, she ran to my rescue and said, "Oh, let me help you with that." She started zipping me up and suddenly let out a loud gasp and let go. At first I had no idea what had just happened and why she reacted that way. Then I realized what she saw—my yin-yang tattoo on my right back shoulder. *Oops*, I thought. I turned around, and saw the look of disbelief on Marissa's face and put my finger up to my lips and said, "Shh."

Edwards Brothers Malloy
Oxnard, CA USA
January 18, 2016